Moses

The Lost Book
of the Bible

𝔐𝔬𝔰𝔢𝔰

The Lost Book
of the Bible

A novel

Leslie H. Whitten, Jr.

New Millennium Press
Beverly Hills

ISBN: 1-893224-03-1

Printed in the United States of America

New Millennium Press
a division of New Millennium Entertainment
350 S. Beverly Drive
Suite 315
Beverly Hills, California 90212

10 9 8 7 6 5 4 3 2 1

I have been a stranger in a strange land....

— Moses, in the Midian Desert
Exodus 2:22

Contents

Moses
The Lost Book of the Bible

Foreword

by Virginia P. Jones-Haarwick
Collman Professor Emeritus, School of Middle Eastern Theology
Brampton University, Brampton, N.H.

NCE AGAIN, MY ASSOCIATE, DR. BERENICE GALIPULLUCI, AND I find ourselves in the dismaying arena of popular publishing. The contretemps surrounding our last and only such venture in 1989, *The Lost Disciple: The Book of Demas,* should have taught us.

So why have we taken on new controversy? Let me briefly explain. Because of our work on the *Demas* documents, we are in possession of four papyrus scrolls, these even more interesting and, if they are authentic, more important than *Demas.* It occurred this way:

In 1996, the renowned Egyptologist Dr. Ibrahim al-Hilaly of Cairo approached me at the World Conference on the Nineteenth Dynasty in Alexandria. In a low voice, he told me that a former Sudanese graduate student of his at Cairo University had called him a month ago from a secure telephone in Khartoum. The student, one James Lado, was now a major in the army of the Republic of the Sudan, a land in the midst of a devastating civil war. The major said his artillery unit had recently shelled a rebel raiding party at the ruins of a Christian monastery near Sennar, a hundred and eighty miles south of Khartoum. The rebel commandos had intended to blow up the Sennar dam, which was vital to the Khartoum government's hydroelectric and agricultural needs. Leaving their numerous dead behind, the insurgents fled with their wounded to the large helicopter that had brought them and flew back to their operations base at Kurmuk.

The next morning, Major Lado ventured with his jeep into the bombarded area, where the monastery's ancient foundations had been upturned. Amid the snarled metal of mortars and recoilless rifles and mangled bodies, he discerned the lip of a pottery vase protruding from the dirt. He dug deeply around it with his military knife and determined the urn was intact.

Major Lado had studied anthropology and archaeology under Dr. al-Hilaly and judged the vessel to be of antique design. He kicked dirt back over it, planning to come back early the next morning on the pretext of taking a last look at the remains of the rebel camp. He returned shortly after dawn and, with a spade, quickly dug up the jar. It was earthen brown pottery, weighed some twenty pounds, and was just under two feet long. Excitement growing, he used the knife to chip out the clay sealant and, with care, gouged and shook out the long-crumbled wax and the thin wooden buffer beneath it.

Wiping the nervous perspiration from his forehead, and—lest he soil the urn's contents—rubbing his fingers on his trousers to clean them, Major Lado

Instead, rather than risk arrest by airport agents, he took annual leave, purportedly to go by steamer to visit his parents and siblings at Juba, far up the White Nile. His real destination was Uganda, a country sympathetic to military deserters from the Sudan. But at Bor, the last Sudanese port before Juba, he was removed from the steamer by government security men. His wife has since learned from sources in Khartoum that he was shot and killed during an attempted escape. It is to Major Lado that we dedicate this book.

During the last two years we have been translating and preserving the scrolls at the Olivian Documents Laboratory in Boston, which had helped us with the *Demas* papers. A few months after the urns' arrival, we learned that rumors of their discovery and removal had reached the Sudan. To avert diplomatic problems, we and the State Department have assured Khartoum that as soon as the translating is completed, the vases and scrolls will be returned. Sudan's national museum will thus effortlessly acquire a priceless jewel.

As further salve, we will allow the Sudan, rather than Brampton University, to release our translations to international scholars. This will avoid the academic debacle that ensued after the discovery of the so-called Dead Sea Scrolls.

These events only await the distribution of our popular book—*too* popular for our tastes—which you hold in your hands. It is being published now to forestall any pirating of our discovery by unscrupulous publishers.

Next year, in our extensive scholarly work, we will deal with the context for the scrolls' assertions, and with our *modus operandi.* Meanwhile, for the general reader, we feel some background is critical:

The author of the manuscript calls himself Zetes, a person of Greek-Egyptian-Hebrew ancestry, who claims he was a contemporary, amanuensis, and faithful friend of Moses. We have determined, via radiometry—a method popularly known as carbon 14 dating—that the papyrus and ink on it originated between 1200 and 1300 B.C. The vessels, both from design and manufacture, are almost certainly from the same period. From the absence of minute modern pollutants in the clay, we are sure that the containers are not recent counterfeits.

But there are important caveats. Reputable historians have contended, inter alia, that the Exodus—the flight of the Hebrew slaves from Egypt—never occurred; that Moses was not a Semite but an African, an Egyptian, a leper, a priest of the god Aten; even that he is pure myth, a creation of the Israelites in search of a hero. His birth date has been estimated variously from 1420 to 1220 B.C. Another cautionary note: The miracles that supposedly shook Egypt are nowhere mentioned in the multitudinous Egyptian hieroglyphs in tombs, on stelae, in other stone cuttings, or in other contemporary records. Indeed, the first historical mention of Israel does not occur until the so-called *Israel Stele*, carved during the reign of the Pharaoh Merneptah, circa 1225 B.C., well after most historians think the Exodus had ended. Even the location of Mount Sinai has never been established.

Nota bene also that no reference to Moses occurs outside the Bible—or Torah (the five books of Moses)—until many hundreds of years after he died. And these, by such historians as the Greek Hecataeus (fl. 350 B.C.) and Egyptian priest Manetho (fl. circa 250 B.C.), both apparently based on earlier Egyptian sources, are at odds with each other and with the detailed biblical accounts. Nonetheless, we are convinced that he did exist and that many of the biblical stories at least *originated* in real events, though often blurred by the sandstorms of time.

As one intriguing example among many, Zetes expands at length on the marriage of Moses to an Ethiopian woman described briefly in Numbers 12:1. But Zetes' Moses also often differs from the Bible's. Zetes presents him more as a mix (in his early life) of Prince Hal and (as an older man) Thomas Jefferson than as the stern, consistent leader of the Hebrews.

The reader may find a few textual notes useful:

We have generally used accepted English style for antique words—for example, summer for *shemou*, castanets for *crotals*—and names—Thebes and Memphis for *Opet* and *Men-nofer;* Ramses for *RMSS;* Moses for *MSS.* Most often, we have used English equivalents for measures of distance, length, quantity, and so on. In some cases, we have defined common words, such as *cubits,* in text, then continued to use them without conversion.

We have done our best to adjust dates to our modern Gregorian calendar. Total accuracy was not possible. As examples, the periods of the Pharaohs' reigns remain in dispute, e.g., the enthronement of Ramses II—called Ramses the Great—is variously dated from 1304 to 1279 B.C.

There are a few internal inconsistencies in Zetes' account. He seems two decades off for the building of Pi-Ramessu. Equally perplexing is his dating of the Kerman kingdom in his own time, more than a hundred years after most historians believe Kerma fell to Egypt. Perhaps archaeologists simply have not discovered evidence of this successor Nile monarchy. Or perhaps, to aggrandize Moses, Zetes treats his minor victories and a petty kingdom as more important than they actually were.

In the interests of clarity (or brevity) we have inserted some anachronisms—e.g., soul, a concept expressed by the Egyptians as *ka* or, sometimes, *ba*, and reins and martingales, there being no modern equivalent for somewhat similar elements of an Egyptian horse's harness. We have used *Imenty* for the dwelling place of the gods of the dead (and the dead themselves) because the concept of hell (and Hades) is so different.

In the scrolls, sentences, paragraphs, and chapters—even words—run together. We have tried to convert them into modern usage, including quotation marks where suitable. In addition, while Zetes seeks to replicate Moses' stammer in his scrolls, we have cited it, but seldom mimicked it.

In conclusion, we leave the judgment of the scrolls' authenticity to history, hoping new discoveries will elucidate all ambiguous matters. *Habent sua fata libelli*, as the poet and grammarian Terentianus Maurus said, and as I choose to translate, "Books have within them their own destiny."

Zetes One

AM ZETES, NAMED AFTER THE SON OF BOREAS, THE NORTH WIND, and the nymph Orithyia. My father, who called me Zetes because an oracle had prophesied that his first son would be blown to all the corners of the world, is Lysymachus of Mycenae, a Greek merchant. My mother was Hannah, daughter of a Hebrew trader, also of Mycenae, and of an Egyptian woman of Shmoun, or as the Greeks call it, Hermopolis. My father is the partner of his father-in-law, and I was to have been their successor.

It was as their representative that, at the age of thirty, I encountered Moses, whose life I saved on the day we met in the wilderness of Paran near the town of Kadesh-barnea. Four weeks before, my slave and chief assistant, Tsu-ting, a small, wiry Shang from China, had received reports that an army of Hebrews was in Paran. They were preparing to invade the land of the Canaanites through the vast deserts of Negeb. These Hebrews were, apparently, seeking to reunite with other members of their small race still resident in Canaan.

Tsu-ting's information was seldom inaccurate. My grandfather had bought him at an exorbitant cost because of his intelligence, rarity, and good condition and assigned him to me as my protector when I first went into trade. Tsu-ting and I were certain there was an opportunity here for profit. At Gaza, the merchants had built up a store of Syrian coats of mail—metal disks the diameter of cow eyes thonged to ox-hide jerkins—bronze Hittite and Egyptian swords, slings a bit the worse for wear, and almost unused shields bossed with the lion symbols of the Eastern Horites. For these goods, we hurriedly exchanged quantities of Bactrian lapis lazuli, Ninevahian necklaces, Amou gold, and assorted silver plates and cups.

On our camels, Tsu-ting, my other assistants and slaves, and I set off across the Sharuhen wilderness for Kadesh-barnea. All day and much of the night ,beneath stars so low it seemed we could pluck them like figs, we drove ourselves. During most of our days, the dry air of early summer caked our nostrils with the dust of our laden mounts. Yet at times, near springs, it was surpassingly sweet with hyssop and myrtle, or tangy with the mint and fennel crushed by our camels' hooves, or rank with asphodel.

A day's distance from Kadesh-barnea, we left the desert and its nettles and thistles and passed through groves of junipers, odorous turpentine trees, and gall oaks. We arrived in the hill country near Zin, where ahead we saw the orderly tents of a large encampment. Leaving most of our men and the hoard of arms behind, Tsu-ting and I rode our camels toward the tents, followed by a camel boy leading a third mount with samples of our shields, armor, and weapons. As we drew nearer, we saw men divided into two groups. Their angered voices stilled as they noted our approach.

"Peace and the God of Abraham's blessings on you," I cried out several times to them in Hebrew, a tongue taught me by my mother, hoping they would not be offended by the Greek patina that coated all of the half-dozen tongues in which I had at least bazaar competence.

When we were seventy-five yards away, a tall man in the Hebrew red-and-blue kilt raised his arm to us, and shouted with a slight stammer, "Peace to you, kinsman or stranger. Dismount and bring only your pack camel. We will speak with you."

"No!" cried another man, even taller and as bulky as a fatted African ox. "Do not approach, visitor! You come upon men in dangerous discourse. Go back the way you came. I, not this man, have authority here."

I hesitated. Conflict was the last thing I wanted. But to return to the coastal road was to abandon hope of selling my goods. We dismounted and I nodded at Tsu-ting, who jerked twice at the halter of the pack camel. With an accommodating belch, the beast moved. The camel boy, eyes wide with fright, held our riding camels and watched us go.

As we entered the tent camp, I saw that on a gradual slope leading up to the two groups of men were thousands of people, most of the men in kilts or brightly colored tunics drawn over one shoulder. The women, farther back, wore headbands and longer tunics also colorful and fastened over one shoulder. Ominously, among the two dozen or so men around the two leaders, those in the larger group held stones, the smallest of which were the size of pomegranates.

The first man, in his mid-forties, chest bare and tanned, and long muscled at arm and leg, raised his hand in polite salute. As I walked into the crowd of contentious men, he said with embarrassment, "At another time we would be more hospitable. You come from the direction of Sharuhen. Before you state your business, tell us, have you seen Amalekite or other Canaanite armies in your passage? It bears upon the disagreement you see here. Answer honestly."

"No, sir," I replied, "a few nomads by the springs, two groups of traders, one in slaves, another in linens and other cloths, none more than twenty asses and camels in number."

On either side of the man protectively were two younger men clad in kilts, both like their leader with black triangular beards, one dark skinned and stocky.

I would learn later that he was a stonecutter whose name was Joshua. The other was Caleb, lanky for a Hebrew, with a long, colt's face. Although they were not armed, they looked as ready to spring as desert lions. To my surprise, a grizzly dwarf, old and lame looking but in full armor, stood just to the left of the rangy man.

"Moses, let us go at least to the borders of Canaan," said Joshua, a deep, pale scar over his right brow and a small down-turned mouth marring his otherwise handsome face. "It is as Caleb and I said. If the Amalekites, if *any* of them, were going to fight, they would be lying in wait for us at Sharuhen or on the road here. We can gather our strength there until we are ready to march into our Promised Land."

Tsu-ting had been unloading my samples. Diverted by my slave's clatter, the man named Caleb pointed at the arms. "Is that all you have to sell?" he asked me with a touch of scorn.

I quickly assured him and the others, "No, no, in that grove of terebinths I have enough to outfit an army: Hittite and Syrian armor, Horite shields, the sharpest swords. At prices a leper beggar can afford. Trust me."

The broad, round tree of a man whom I took to be the leader of the larger group interrupted. "This man is a spy. He speaks Hebrew like a Canaanite." Several behind him joined in. "A spy! Yes, come to judge our strength! Stone him!"

"No!" I pleaded as Tsu-ting moved up beside me, his small, strong fingers on his short sword. "A Greek. See, *light* brown eyes! A round face! Curly hair! But my mother, oh believe me, sirs, was a devout Hebrew. Her name was Hannah, 'merciful' in our beloved language, as I beg you to be to me."

"An Anak liar," said the heavy man. "Stone him!"

"No," roared Moses. "He is God-sent!" Though he was outnumbered, his voice caused the men, even then cocking to throw, to lower their forearms but not to drop their stones. "If Jehovah yet lets us move to the north, we will need this good merchant's weapons." He fixed deep brown eyes on the other big man and said more calmly, "Brave On, son of Peleth, you defy Jehovah when you ask for the stoning of this innocent trader."

The man named On summoned from behind him a man in a brown cloak, his face covered with hair, a wild, brave light in his eyes. "Spare the spy for the moment," he said. "Geuel, tell them all, now we are assembled. Tell them what *you* saw."

The man named Geuel turned to the multitude on the slope, as many as six thousand, I estimated. There was not a sound among them save for the occasional dog bark or donkey bray. "As Moses commanded us," he cried in a high voice that carried far, "we went among the Canaanites in secret, without swords, and at true risk. We journeyed from Zin to Rehob and Hebron. And see, it is true that the land is one of milk and honey."

He signaled two burly men forward bearing a long pole. From it hung bunches of grapes and bird nets containing pomegranates, figs, and other fruits. "We brought back these as proof," Geuel continued, "but, brothers, the cities are walled, the men therein are behemoths. We were like grasshoppers compared to these Anak giants. In spite of what Joshua and Caleb say, all of us but they agree we can never go into Canaan."

From the crowd came voices of men and women, "We dare not go into Canaan and die. . . . Moses has deceived us. . . . Let us make On our captain. . . . He will lead us back to Egypt. . . . Jehovah will kill us in this land, us, and our babies. . . . Better to live as slaves in Egypt, which we know." Yet, there were other voices, almost all men, saying, "On into Canaan! Even if we die, we will be done with this accursed desert. . . . Into the Promised Land!"

I had heard of the emotionalism of these tribal Israelites, but I was not prepared for what I saw. Moses, their leader, hearing the tumult, the discord within his flock, dropped to the ground and began rubbing his face in the dry dirt. Behind him a thin, pallid man, in what was obviously a priestly robe of gold, blue, purple, and scarlet threads and a sash of the same material, fell and did the same.

Moses' two young lieutenants, at this shocking sight, tore off their kilts and, standing in their loincloths, rent their outer garments with their teeth and threw them in the air.

"Never! Never return to Egypt!" cried Joshua, raising his short powerful arms to the skies. "Fools! Moses is our leader. Await his decision. The Lord loves him."

"The Lord will deliver this land to us," screamed Caleb, also thrusting up his arms. "Do not think of Egypt. When the time comes, the Anaks will be bread for us to eat. Their blood will be our honey to spread on it. Pay no heed to On!"

The dwarf limped to our weapons as Tsu-ting thrust into my hand a shield to ward off the threatening stones and held a corselet of bronze before his own face. We were bound in by the crowding men or would have retreated to our camels and fled.

While Caleb and Joshua turned their backs to harangue the crowd, I saw the giant, On, lift his missile, big and round as the balance stone of an olive press, and lunge to where Moses lay face down in the dirt, ranting in prayer to his Jehovah. Two of On's confederates, stones also raised, pushed up behind him.

I could not stand by and watch the murder of a man who, already, I favored over his adversary. Did the thought also go through my head that if Moses were dead and these people went back to Egypt there would be no sale of my goods? Whatever the case, I impulsively thrust out the shield and struck their leader's pillar of an arm, knocking the stone from his hand. It dropped with a thud a foot from Moses' head. I wheeled and protected myself from the stones of On's two aides.

Moses rose and, yelling like a bear enraged by hunters' lances, grabbed up a sword from among our samples. The priest, his brother, if I read his similar though more delicate lineaments right, scrambled up and fled back into the crowd. Tsu-ting kicked more swords to within reach of Joshua and Caleb.

The stones were flying at me now, for I had thwarted On single-handedly. Rocks struck me in the head, knee, and chest, beating me to the ground. The shield fell from my hand. My Chinese slave dropped his armor on my chest to protect me and snatched up a lance from beside the rearing yet tethered pack camel. On had recovered his stone and, his collaborators occupied with Moses, Caleb, and Joshua, made me his target.

He raised the boulder over me to crush my head. I scrambled frantically but fruitlessly to pull the corselet over my face. Believing when convenient in all gods, and thus none, I nevertheless called on the one closest to hand. "Save me, God of Abraham!" I screamed. I saw the twisted, murderous expression on my assailant's huge face.

Then, to my amazement, On's mouth suddenly sprung open, spouting blood, as if it were a fountain. Through the top of his massive hairy chest came the point of one of my best Armenian lances. The Shang had saved me even as I had saved Moses. One of On's minions was now bent over my gallant slave, striking his chest with a stone. I saw the glints of armor across my vision, the man wearing it not much bigger than a large dog. There was the flash of a sword. It severed the shin of the man battering Tsu-ting. I was dazed and in agony from head to knee to calf, and I did not see the stone that knocked me unconscious.

I wept for Tsu-ting as I came to. Silent as he was, he had been my dearest comrade, my most zealous assistant. As I looked around, I saw that Moses had been hit. He knelt on one knee, shaking his head dazedly. His two captains had been joined by a dozen swordsmen in army kilts, one of whom was standing astraddle my chest to ward off any further blows.

Joshua was shouting at the top of his voice, "Kill the lot! Every one of them that drew his sword on us." His newly arrived swordsmen needed no encouragement. The ensuing carnage, however deserved, was ghastly. Severed heads rolled down to where wives scooped them up in their skirts. The stumps of right arms squirted blood while left hands tried frantically and vainly to stanch it. Throughout the Hebrews' internecine bloodletting, I, feeling pain beyond measure in my right knee, held the hand of Tsu-ting. It gripped me back. We were both alive.

When the killing was done, I propped myself up on an elbow as Moses, his grogginess shaken off, addressed the multitude. I was dumbfounded at his recovery. His mild stutter gave his commanding voice a compelling sincerity.

"Jehovah has struck dead the spies he had me send into Canaan, all but Joshua and Caleb," he shouted. "He has slain On, who would have defied him and led many of you back to Egypt. But I have begged him to spare you. I asked Jehovah, 'What will the Egyptians think of you if you massacre your own people? They will say you were not powerful enough to care for them, not wise enough to turn them to the ways of righteousness.' I asked him to forgive you though you do not deserve forgiveness."

By now, Joshua had seen my suffering and put part of the kilt he had thrown into the air under my knee, and the accursed rock that had almost killed both Moses and me beneath my head, wrapped in Caleb's dusty kilt. Despite my pain, I listened to Moses as he continued, his voice on that summer day's light air carrying far into the huge crowd that stood at the foot of the bare mountains of Paran.

"The Lord Jehovah answered me, 'I will pardon them, although they have never ceased to defy me, but they shall remain in the wilderness ten, twenty more years, and many of the bones of those who accompanied you from Egypt will lie in the sand and never reach the land of milk and honey.'"

At this there was an enormous moan from the crowd, but Moses raised his blood-smeared arms and called out, "The Lord says further that those who choose to go away on their own, yea, though there be two thousand, shall do so, but without his blessing. He warns you not to return to Egypt, for he will surely permit the Egyptians to slay you, men, women, and children. Nor will Jehovah let you take the weapons belonging to Israel with you, for they will be needed by those who are loyal and who prepare anew to take possession of the Promised Land. You shall take your children, your flocks, your herds, and your goods, buy what arms you need with your own gold, and be gone from his sight forever.

"He knows that there are some few among you who will try to invade Canaan immediately instead of waiting in the wilderness for his order. 'This is madness,' he says. 'You who seek loot there will be looted. You who pillage will yourselves be pillaged. You have deserted me, and so I shall desert you. But because you are brave, if foolhardy, you shall keep your arms.'"

Several of Moses' followers and their wives carried me to a large goatskin tent near that of Moses. It belonged to the dwarf, a Syrian whose name I learned was Bes-Ahrin, and indeed he looked like the grotesque but powerful Egyptian dwarf god, Bes. I was installed on a raised bed, primitive but in the Egyptian style with carved wooden oxen heads at each corner. A woolen sack filled with straw was my mattress. Minutes later, Tsu-ting limped in. Obviously, he was hurt less than I. Then, Moses came to thank me for saving his life.

Afterward, the dwarf gave me a strong draught of palm wine. It must have been drugged, for I again slid from acute discomfort into slumber. That evening, Tsu-ting returned.

"When they had buried their dead," he recounted, sitting on a low chair, "I wondered what to do with our wares. I came to you, who were unconscious." Tsu-ting looked pleased with himself as he got to the point.

"I went to Moses, their leader, who said the arms of those who are abandoning him will suffice him. He said his God is permitting them to buy weapons. He required them to buy from us, and they paid in gold, silver, ivory, a few leopard skins, and some desert fox furs. We are left only with the slings, not in good condition anyway. Those we can sell to the Canaanites on our way north. They will take anything that kills. And Moses himself bought four of our camels, saying they were not used in Egypt, but that he could use them here. When the sands settle, your father and grandfather will realize a profit."

Within two days, it was evident that my knee was broken. I would not be able to travel for a long time. I rewarded Tsu-ting with a *deben*—two and a half ounces—of the Hebrew gold and, in a note to my father, explained what had happened. I begged him to give Tsu-ting his freedom and I promised to make my way back to Mycenae as soon as possible. Tearfully, Tsu-ting got our camels together and departed for the coastal road.

After my men had left, Aaron, brother to Moses and high priest of the Hebrews, who had fled the fight, came to my hut. With him was Bes-Ahrin and a tall black woman. By the oil lamp, as they applied wormwood oil to my knee and bound it between boards, I observed her. She had Grecian features like many Ethiopians–Cushites. She was dressed in a costly, tightly woven wool tunic dyed yellow, blue, and red-orange. It was adorned by a single golden necklace that threw speckles of light on the walls of the tent as she worked over my injured knee.

"I came to thank you for saving Moses," she said. "I want to make sure all is done for you that can be done." She spoke to me in precise but accented Egyptian.

"You are from Cush from the looks of your dress, but your Egyptian is far better than mine," I said, confused. "You were a slave in Goshen? You came eastward with Moses, too? You do not look like any kind of slave I ever saw."

"The answer, Zetes, is yes, I am from Cush, and no, I was never a slave in Goshen or elsewhere. I am Moses' wife; my name is Sebah. And I do not forget debts. Nor does he."

Each day, Moses, his aristocratic wife, Caleb or Joshua, sometimes Aaron, and Moses' sister, Miriam, came to see me. Bes-Ahrin, whom I found to be a witty and intelligent conversationalist, spoke at length with me about Moses, the Exodus, my travels and his.

To the Israelites, I was a wounded hero. But it was soon evident that my knee, while it might heal, would never bend again. The trader's life, with its long camel rides whether I felt up to them or not, its squatting in bazaars, its lifting of wares, and its hurried walks in rough dirt or badly cobbled streets or bazaars, was going to be beyond my ability for the rest of my years.

Another week and, with the help of a crutch, I began to stump around the camp at Kadesh-barnea. There were fewer people than I had seen on that first sanguinary day. As Moses had predicted, two thousand had deserted and gone southward to Ezion-geber. Five hundred others had invaded their Promised Land and had been butchered by an army of Canaanites and Amalekites. Only a few returned and they headed south to join the two thousand.

One day, I saw two scribes, shriveled Egyptians, sitting cross-legged outside their tents, with their papyrus, their reed brushes moistened at the ends to keep them soft, and their palettes of gum-and-lampblack ink. Bes-Ahrin told me they had been made slaves in Egypt because they adhered to the heretical monotheism of the Pharaoh Amenophis IV, later called Akhenaten. Along with motley other non-Hebrew slaves, the two scribes had fled with Moses when he led the Israelites out of Egypt four years earlier. Moses had instructed them to record the Hebrews' history from the stories that the Hebrew elders had passed down for hundreds of years about their patriarchs, Abraham, Isaac, and Jacob, and their sundry offspring.

Without ever having read the two scribes' "history" of the Hebrews, I was willing to wager that it had about as much truth to it as the Egyptian myths in which the scribes had been trained. In these stories, Pharaohs consorted, counseled, and cavorted with gods in the forms of lions, jackals, hippopotamuses, falcons, and the like.

As I came to know Moses, I was to feel that while his tribe often strayed from the God of Abraham, Moses did not. I saw in him affinities to the Egyptians of fifty years before who had worshipped and died for their eccentric Akhenaten. This Pharaoh had "killed" Osiris, Isis, Amun, and all the other gods save the sun god, Re-Horakhty, also called Aten. Subsequent Pharaohs had reversed all his acts.

One day, just as the sun went down, Moses, Joshua, and Caleb came by my tent with an atrocious wine the women of the Hebrews had churned up from grapes bought along their route. We made small talk about my injury, and Moses, always direct—when he could afford to be—looked into my eyes. "Zetes, you saved my life. Would you consider staying with us?"

"What choice do I have for the time being?" I asked. "A crippled trader is no more a possibility than a kind-hearted scorpion."

Moses smiled and went on. "I am talking about staying permanently. You have seen my scribes . . . loyal to me, yes. And they profess love of Jehovah and truth, as befits men writing our history. I have inspected their work. It is . . ." He did not want to insult them. His large forehead with its bushy eyebrows wrinkled and he pursed his wide, thin lips, ". . . as uneven as the road between Memphis and Thebes: sometimes smooth as the side of an obelisk, sometimes bumpy as a crocodile's back, sometimes true as a falcon's dive, sometimes as questionable as a barber's prophesy. There is hope. They are training two young Hebrews in their craft."

I had seen these youths in camp, proudly wearing their flat-bottomed pen sacks on shoulder thongs, hands smeared with black and red ink, the latter for chapter headings, and at their waists sheepskin bags of limestone flakes on which they practiced cursive script. I guessed now what Moses might want of me.

"I have written down many of our laws," he said, "laws about behavior, property, our religious rites, *everything* Jehovah wants our people to observe. But in time we will need—to pass on to those who come after us—a record of our Exodus to the Promised Land, with all its triumphs and disasters."

I could not help interrupting. "Moses, believe me, the record that comes down to your people will not be the fragile papyrus scrolls you prepare today. Passing time, not scribes, makes history. What you, or your two Egyptians, or the youngsters in training write today will be changed as it comes down through the centuries. It will be translated from your Egyptian or Hebrew to Greek or Hittite or who knows what language. Ten years will become twenty, twenty forty, a man who dies at sixty-five will die at a hundred and sixty-five to increase his majesty. The marsh you crossed to escape from Egypt at Lake Timsah, the Sea of Reeds"—for already I had heard of that—"will become a depthless sea, and your crossing a miracle. Believe me, I have seen it happen.

"For instance, in Babylon, where I have traded, there is a story, preserved on stone, that King Sargon, born a thousand years ago, was also the son of a king and ruled four hundred years. Yet in Sumer, it was said that Sargon was the son of a gardener whose mother, to save him from an angry king, floated him out on the Euphrates in a basket coated with pitch, from which a servant of the goddess Ishtar rescued him, and Ishtar elevated him to the palace. Both of these stories cannot be true, sirs, but surely there was a king named Sargon, and surely the stories began as one."

Joshua simply sat with mouth open, his eyes bugged out in disbelief. "What is surprising?" I asked. "I am only saying—"

"I know the story well," Moses broke in. "Joshua is surprised because he knows my mother set me afloat in a reed basket on the Nile. I was found by a princess and for twenty-six years was raised as a prince of Egypt." He said it as matter-of-factly as if he were telling me how to trim a horse hoof.

The wonder of coincidence, I marveled, and added, "And the Egyptians believed that Horus was hidden in the rushes by his mother, Isis, lest he be destroyed by his evil uncle Seth."

"Children of the bulrushes," Moses observed with a smile, but he was diverted only briefly. "Now, back to my proposal. What I wish is that you stay with us as a scribe. It is, as you know, a role honored by us only slightly less than priests. I would want you, instead of devoting yourself to the distant past, or recording the Law, to write of more recent events and of the present. In Greek, if you like. Talk with Joshua, Caleb, Aaron, Miriam, the others here. You will want to include what led me to organize the Exodus. I will speak with you sometimes in the evenings of my days in Egypt, in Cush, in other foreign wars and lands, in Midian. Sebah was my betrothed before I fled Egypt the first time. Her memory will be helpful. Speak to Bes-Ahrin. He has known me since I was a baby.

"If need be you can go back along our route in reverse. Talk to Zipporah, my former wife. She is honest . . ." he again smiled, ". . . maybe too honest for my own good. And her father. He is an admirable man. To my son, Gershom. If you can do it discreetly, without danger to yourself, go to Egypt. I can give you names and you can say you are writing a history for the Greek world of the countries of the Great Green Sea"—the Mediterranean—"and plan to mention the Hebrews. Do you see what I mean? Eventually, the two Egyptians and the two young Hebrews will reach the present in their writings. Their accounts and yours will ensure two contemporary reports on Israel in these days and will help prevent preposterousness and contradictions."

I was flattered at Moses' offer. Besides, I was developing a liking for this heroic man and his people. And what awaited me back at Mycenae? A life as a well-to-do clerk? By contrast, the interviews on Moses' behalf when I could travel would take me to new places where I would talk with interesting people, unencumbered by the demands of trade. Only my time and inclination and my half-crippled leg would determine my pace.

Furthermore, although I had been good at trade, my curiosity had never totally revolved around numbers and goods. Rather, it was the events of history, the differences in languages and religions and peoples, that intrigued me. I had preferred studying the awesome paintings in the tomb of Thutmose, third of that name, called the Great—into which I had bribed entrance—to the stacks of papyrus notes in my father's warehouse. I had found that observing the stilted movements of a desert scorpion as he copulated was more absorbing than hearing from a thieving Susa dealer in myrrh and cinnamon about the sexual habits of his competitors.

Moses offered me a new freedom, too. For within the broad latitude of this Hebrew history, it would be I who determined where I went and with whom I spoke, not my assertive Hellene trading family.

Two days later, I told Moses that before I decided, I must first read what the Egyptians had written. But the two scribes considered their scrolls sacrosanct, as if they had been inscribed on the inner walls of a tomb. Moses, however, sternly ordered them opened, and for three days I went through them. The script was beautiful, every character a work of art.

What I read confirmed my fears about its accuracy. In the remote Hebrew past, the scribes wrote, men wrestled with angels, serpents talked, fruit was magic, and a woman had a baby at the age of ninety—to mention a few excesses. The story of Moses, although the scribes were writing it even as it happened, seemed to me fantastical. His walking staff became a snake; God personally handwrote commandments on stone tablets; the entire Egyptian army drowned when a shallow lake closed in on them; the Nile turned to blood; locusts ate up everything in Egypt; and hail killed all the cattle. Only later did I realize that in much that they wrote there were, at the least, elements of truth.

"How can you record that kind of thing?" I asked the scribes one day. "You were at the Sea of Reeds. I've talked with Caleb about it. It did not happen that way."

The older man looked at me for some time. "Zetes," he said, "you are a Greek. You do not understand. But you should. Do your people believe in the stories about Zeus or Apollo? Do they think the sun is a chariot driven across heaven?"

"No, of course not," I said. "Only the common people, the simplest country people, believe these myths."

The second scribe, almost as old as the first, smiled. He was completely toothless. "Yet you do acknowledge that the sun rises, do you not? Come, come, you have answered your own question. Now leave us to our work."

I went to Moses, fuming and pugnacious, and told him what I had discovered. "Much of what they write is milkweed fluff. Not just about your patriarchs. About you. About Aaron. Bes-Ahrin told me you were educated at the palace with the most learned scholars. How can you let balderdash become history? It is cynicism, Moses. Like beating your head in the dirt the day I met you. I am not a fool. I know that peasant custom is not natural for you."

Moses looked at me, much as the old scribes had. "Zetes, how carefully did you listen to me? I want two histories. I have seen what they are writing. I know some of it is the stuff of myths. The worst of it I must amend or delete.

"But as to the miracles, you say I am cynical. First, I believe every nation needs myths. Five hundred years from now, the most extreme of these anecdotes about Aaron and me will not be believed by intelligent people any more than they are now. But they will be stories for parents to tell to their children, as you Greeks tell of heroes turned into constellations that all may see shining in the heavens, or how the father of gods became a swan to sire twins. Do you think people turn into pigs and trees? Of course not.

"And do not dismiss all that you have read in the scribes' work as fantasy. God was and is present in all the phenomena that have happened to me and this nation." He patted me on the arm. "And as to my striking the earth with my forehead, I was foreign enough when I came to these people. I have adopted their customs when I could. And wisely."

"But you want me to—"

"Yes, I want you to write the truth as *you* find it. Something that can be preserved, just as the scribes' tales, in pottery vessels fired so well they will last down the ages. I want our leaders in millenniums to come to know what we Hebrews did, acting out the wishes of our magnificent God. But I want them to see it from two points of view, as all men see life from many different windows, and on many different days."

Back in my tent, thinking about it, I asked myself: *Zetes, is not his logic as valid as yours? You do not believe in God. He does. Can you say for certain that you are wiser than he is?* Next day, I wrote my father, telling him that my leg would end my life as an active trader, that I could not bear to work in our warehouse in Mycenae for the rest of my days, that I was becoming a historian, and that I loved him. I asked him to send me the substantial sums I had put aside from my labors. I said I would return in a year or two to visit or to remain.

Chapter One
Moses: The Beginnings

Y PURPOSE IN THIS BOOK IS NOT TO TELL, WHATEVER YOU MAY think thus far, the story of Zetes, son of Lysymachus, but of Moses, son of Amram and Jochebed, the great leader of the Israelites, my complex, brilliant, and, yes, sometimes contradictory benefactor.

It is, as Moses has asked of me, based on our many conversations; on talks with his family (his father and mother long dead) and with old acquaintances among the Israelites; and on discussions with Egyptians in our multitude and in Egypt. Some had encountered and known him as a child under the Pharaoh Horemheb and at the court of the Pharaohs Sety and the first and second Ramseses.

For those who come upon this scroll, let me begin with the conventional curse: May Jehovah, God of Moses and my mother; may Apollo, the favorite of my father; may Thoth, to whom my maternal grandmother sacrificed; may all the numerous gods of Canaan and the other lands through which I have passed curse the hand that changes a word of what I write, as century upon century unrolls. Now, I commence:

Moses—of this I am sure whatever his addlebrained scribes may record— was born in 1330 B.C., in the thirtieth year of the reign of the Pharaoh Horemheb. This Pharaoh was a tall, inflexible man, childless save for adopted daughters. He was rumored to have lost his masculine parts in a battle with the warriors of Palestine.

Horemheb began his rule at Thebes in the south. But as commerce with other lands flourished, he spent more and more time at Memphis, far to the north. But more than his dread of the fanatic Libyans to the west, Horemheb feared an invasion from the northeast, and with good reason. The Hyksos, violent foreigners, had swept in and conquered Egypt three hundred years earlier, ruling with barbaric cruelty. Their capital was Tanis, in Egypt's Land of Goshen, where foreigners, including the Israelites, were concentrated.

In the Hebrews, Horemheb imagined—needlessly most thought—allies for any invading force. Still, their numbers in the northern provinces, or nomes, were growing. They were industrious, strong-willed people. Their ancestor, Joseph, had been a vizier to the Pharaoh Amenophis, first of that name, and had invited his fellow Hebrews to Egypt centuries earlier.

In any case, Horemheb, not wanting the Hebrews free, yet not wanting them to migrate back to Canaan, from whence they had come, and thus deprive him of cheap, good labor, enslaved them. He put them to work in the Land of Goshen. His taskmasters set them to making bricks for warehouses, for the dwellings of rich Egyptians, and for walls, schools, barracks, warehouses, and the like. He had others tend royal stables and priestly fields, serve as dock workers, and, indeed, labor in all jobs suitable for the uneducated.

According to a lewd Egyptian joke, the mud, sand, and chopped straw trod by Hebrew brickmakers sent vapors to their testicles and proved a powerful aphrodisiac, thus leading to the increase in their numbers. Alarmed at the rapid breeding and reports that they were restive, Horemheb issued and made public this edict: "The King of Egypt, Sun of the Nine Bows, whose name is lauded from Orontes to the Land of Cush, Majesty of Upper and Lower Egypt, gives this command to his Vizier: Make it your business to break the Hebrews, train them to the service of Amun, order the midwives to slay their newborn males. Spare the newborn females that their tears may replenish the sacred tears of our mother and consort, Isis."

For all these high-flown words, at least two Hebrew midwives, Shiphrah and Puah, secretly spared the babies and were called before the Pharaoh to be punished—all this I heard from one of the midwives' daughters. "Oh, shining face of Re"—a sun god with whom the Pharaohs identified themselves—Shiphrah said, "pardon us. The women of the Hebrews bear their babies so rapidly that our aging legs cannot carry us there in time. Through the kindness of Min, god of fertility, your women of Egypt moan and cry for many hours and can be delivered of their babies with due preparation."

The Pharaoh, perhaps because of the midwives' ingenious excuse, only had them whipped, not flayed. He issued a second edict, which, after the usual recitation of his titles, decreed: "The newborn males of the people who call themselves the children of Abraham shall be drowned in the Nile lest the God of the River, Hapi, as bull, be displeased and deny us inundation. The body or its lower part will be proof for the purposes of reward."

This injunction was enforced—if haphazardly—not by the regular army, but by the rabble militia: Amorites, Moabites, Edomites, and the like, a vicious and corrupt lot. They and the police entered the Israelites' homes at will.

Among those who hid their newborn sons were a brawny mortar foreman, Amram, and his shrewd, spare wife, Jochebed. They had named the child Moses, for "drawing out," as they intended to draw him from harm's way. Their one-room dwelling was distinguished from those of poorer neighbors by its small oblong windows, limestone chips tamped into its mud floor, and raised wooden platform on which Jochebed could weave and prepare meals. Indeed, it was the platform that saved her new baby. During the day, in a hole beneath the platform lined with flax and a blanket, she placed the child, feeding it whenever it cried.

Such deception, however, could not last. When a poorer neighbor's baby was grabbed up before its mother's eyes by a Moabite militiaman, the distraught and impoverished woman informed her baby's killer of the infantile babbling and occasional whimpers she had heard in the next dwelling. For this information, she was promised a minuscule share of the soldier's bounty from the murder of her neighbor's son.

The militiaman went to Amram's house, lifted the platform, and saw the two-month-old boy in the padded hole. He demanded the treasure of the household—a goat that provided milk for Amram's and Jochebed's two-year-old son, Aaron—to buy silence for a single day. That night, Amram sorrowfully tarred Jochebed's well-made cane basket with the pitch they had frugally saved from the fire to caulk their door. They lined the basket with the one expensive piece of cloth they had, the veil of Egyptian linen Jochebed had worn at her wedding. They did not dare use rougher Hebrew cloth lest it give away the origin of their vessel-to-be.

Next morning, the baby fed, Jochebed and her seven-year-old daughter, Miriam, began the two-mile walk to the Nile. There, in the town of Tanis, beside a summer palace, the Pharaoh had built a pavilion where his family, including his many nieces and adopted daughters, could bathe.

Just upstream from the princesses, Jochebed and Miriam tucked in their long tunics and waded into the river. They watched the pale and olive grace of the naked splashing bodies. Handmaidens stood by with towels and robes on the colorfully painted rush mats that kept their dainty feet from the shore's gravel and mud. The two Hebrew slaves noted the gleaming white tents, where, on cushions, the princesses could loll between dips. Kneeling beside the tents were naked women dancers ready to pluck up tambourines and castanets. The women were guarded by a sturdy young dwarf with a sword almost as long as he was. The entire scene was almost beyond the simple imaginings of Jochebed and Miriam.

"Do not fail me, my little Miriam," Jochebed whispered to her daughter. After a silent moment, the mother launched the basket out through the reeds, squeezed Miriam's hands, and silent as a crane, waded back to shore. The little girl squatted, clothes dragging in the water, and observed. Almost clear of the reeds, the basket snagged and Miriam waded deeper to free it. Then, like a serene regal barge on a tranquil sea, the humble shiplet floated toward the bathing women.

Miriam saw one of them, a fragile, small-breasted woman, turn and point to the craft, heard her call to one of the handmaidens on shore, and saw the maid, jangling gold forearm bracelets, robe and all, plunge instantly into the river and splash toward the slowly swiveling basket. The princess waded ashore, where another maid toweled her with a linen cloth and quickly slipped over her a robe bound by a gold brooch at the shoulder that left her right breast bare. In a moment, the soggy handmaiden arrived with the basket.

Miriam picked her way quietly out of the water and hurried down to the royal tent, where the youthful dwarf glared at her and barred her way with his sword. She gesticulated at the scene by the Nile. There, the princess and her maids were gathered around the basket and the baby, now yelping with fear. The manikin studied Miriam for a moment with penetrating eyes, then imperiously bid her to follow him to where she was pointing. He gripped her forearm firmly while he waited to be recognized.

The princess—pretty in a small-featured way—was chucking the baby under the chin, cooing variously about the whimsy of Repit, the consort of the Nile god Hapi, and whether the child might not be hungry. Miriam had no knowledge of the Egyptian gods, save for such occasional oaths as "Osiris quarter you," or "Isis curse your muddy womb." But she knew the Egyptian word for *hungry* well enough. "Princess, exalted one," she called out, "he will soon be hungry. I know a Hebrew woman who will give him suck."

The princess took the baby in her thin arms as a servant combed her hair with an ivory comb. She asked a woman in her entourage a question, and the woman translated Miriam's words. "Let her come to me, Bes-Ahrin," she said to the dwarf, who released his grip on Miriam's arm. "Is this a Hebrew baby?" the princess asked Miriam through the translator.

Miriam, wise in the ways of all oppressed children, replied, "I do not know, daughter of Re. I was seeking batensoda fish that swim upside-down in the shallows when I saw you with the baby. I hoped you might give me some tiny piece of silver for my offer to find a wet nurse."

The princess was Mutempsut, daughter of Horemheb's chief general, Ramses, first of that name, and had been formally adopted by the Pharaoh. She laughed at the doughty, bedraggled waif who had stopped crying under her soft ministrations. "I will play with this sweet creature a while," she said. "Come back after the seventh hour—no, let it be the 'straight hour'—about two o'clock. Bring this woman you mention and I will give you my answer." She signaled to the maid combing her long wet hair, who handed the comb with its design of carved lotus flowers to Miriam, a few strands of hair still in it.

Miriam ran home and breathlessly told Jochebed, "She will do it. I know she will. See what she gave me."

When Jochebed and Miriam went to the Princess Mutempsut, only she, her dwarf and maids, and the slaves folding up the tents remained. The princess held the baby in her arms. Already, he was swaddled in royal Egyptian linen.

"I have not wearied with this small charmer," said the princess through her translator. "I will name him Hapi-Set to honor the river god who gave him to me and my family god, Sutekh, namesake of my brother Sety-Seth," she said wanly. "And I want him nearby so he can visit me from time to time before I go to Punt, the Divine Land"—on the Gulf of Aden—"where I am to be married. Indeed, if Horus and his daughter goddesses agree, I may send for him and raise him as my household slave in Punt."

Jochebed paled. That would mean her son would be castrated before he reached puberty and made a court eunuch. Such acts were against both her feelings as a mother and her religion. *May she die twelve times in Punt before she sends for him,* Jochebed said to herself. "Exalted One, you are too generous. I would almost do it for Your Kindness without payment," she told the princess with a low bow.

Mutempsut smiled. "Ah no, I will give you payment, enough for good food to keep your breasts. Give me your and your husband's name, Israelite, that I might send my dwarf so you can bring this infant when I would play with him."

Jochebed did so, then said, "Exalted daughter of Re, the Pharaoh's soldiers and police may try to take him and kill him even as I nurse him."

"I have thought of that," said Mutempsut. "Take this ring." She gave Jochebed a ring on which was engraved a uraeus, the royal cobra. "Show this to him who comes and bothers you, and ask that he take you to his superior. He will bring you to me, and from that time on you will not be disturbed."

Satisfied that her baby's life had been saved, Jochebed fell to her knees and reached up and touched the princess's outer smock. But in her heart, she resolved that she would never call her son by his Egyptian name, Hapi-Set. For her, it would be Moses. For was her baby not just "drawn out" of harm's way but from the Nile itself?

Jochebed saw the princess weekly, summoned to her rooms in the palace so Mutempsut could spend the day dandling Moses. There was nothing odd about Jochebed being in the palace. Over time, Hebrew slaves had been brought there as nurses and to perform menial jobs such as cleaning and helping the cooks.

Following each visit, Mutempsut gave Jochebed a thin gold ring that Amram could barter in the market. Three months after she found Moses, she said to Jochebed, "The time has come. I go to Punt. I may send for you and the baby. Be ready." There was no mention of Amram or her other children. Jochebed asked no questions. She had decided that even if she and the family had to flee, she would not let her boy become a eunuch.

The sea voyage to Punt—called the Divine Land because it was thought most ancient gods originated there—was twenty-five hundred miles. But the exhausted Princess Mutempsut was determined to make the best of her marriage to its crown prince. It was dynastically important to maintain Egypt's wavering control over the country's ivory, aromatic gums, ebony, and gold. Her bridegroom, a man more than twice her age and effeminate, showed her only ceremonial interest. She missed Egypt, and especially wished she had spent more happy days with her little Hebrew baby. For although she did not acknowledge it, her heart had told her after the first few weeks that the baby was Jochebed's son. Already she knew she could not castrate him and was devising how to raise him in her palace in Punt, perhaps as a page or groom.

Mutempsut soon realized that her husband, who felt and looked like a sun-dried date, preferred his boy slaves to her. Nevertheless, he quickly managed to impregnate her, and a sickly dark-skinned son was born. When he was two months old, palace schemers killed both her husband and his senile father, and the princess escaped only with her baby and her dwarf, Bes-Ahrin. Her husband had providently sent her handmaidens back to Egypt when trouble was rumored.

She could not take passage from Punt without the rebels knowing it and killing her baby, the final direct heir to the throne. So, still nursing the infant, she escaped overland. The resourceful dwarf, bartering jewelry as they went, took her westward by ass, then back toward the Red Sea. Though a princess, she had to lodge in peasant homes, strange dwellings like coconuts cut in half. At the arid Red Sea port of Assab, inhabited mainly by impoverished eastern Ethiopians, they hired boatmen and two elderly sisters as nurses and swept northward, aided by strong, hot winds at their stern.

The jungle shoreline turned to desert and at Qusae, a port eighty miles east of the Nile city of Coptos, Mutempsut established her identity. The local factotum provided his hardiest donkeys for the trip through the mountain passes and across the badlands, but the colicky child grew sicklier with every mile. At Coptos, again they found a ship. Downriver at Abydos, they did not even pause to sacrifice to the formidable god Osiris despite the objections of the devout Bes-Ahrin.

Mutempsut's son died as they approached Memphis. The dwarf silently blamed the death on the sacrilege at Abydos. The two Ethiopian women who had cared for the baby when his mother was too weak to do more than feed him were desolated. They oiled and wrapped the tiny dead body in clean linen, preparatory for its mummification and funeral at Tanis.

But Bes-Ahrin, while his mistress lay feverish and frail, hatched a desperate plan. He knew that the loss of her baby, whom the princess had held as dear as her own life, had crushed her. She had loved being a mother, and the child had given her hope that she might one day be the mother of the king of Punt, or—who knew, if Ramses, second of that name, were to die—of the Pharaoh of Egypt itself. Bes-Ahrin was determined she should have a baby of her own.

The dwarf's plan called for killing the Ethiopian sisters lest they tell of the baby's death when they reached Tanis. Mutempsut, in a faint voice, directed him to let them go. "They have tended me like twin mothers. Free them, Bes-Ahrin, give them gold for their silence." Mutempsut invoked Hathor, cow goddess and patroness of the dead. "May her mercy follow my child. She would doom us forever if they died at our hands. And Bes"—the dwarf's namesake and a powerful god of children—"would abhor us both to our dying days."

The dwarf, both superstitious and obedient, weighted the little corpse with a stone wine jar. At midnight, when only the steersman was awake, he eased the bundle into the Nile at the end of a short rope. Next morning, they landed at Memphis and the Ethiopian women, one of whom had seen the body of their erstwhile charge lowered over the side, were sworn by Bes-Ahrin to secrecy. "By all the gods," he charged them, "and particularly my patron, Bes, who is as ugly as I am and can be as cruel, I will behead you if you talk. I vow it!" He sent them back to Assab via the Red Sea. Little could Mutempsut and Bes-Ahrin know that the fate of Egypt—and Israel—would be chained to the sparing of these two elderly maids.

Stricken almost to death, Mutempsut set sail toward her favorite royal residence at Tanis, tended only by her dwarf, who let no one else near her. Outside Tanis, the tiny man told Mutempsut what he planned, urged her to lock the door to her cabin, and ordered the boat to shore. There, he bought a horse from a stable, rode two hours through the dark, and rapped on Amram's door in the slave quarter of town. Amram, fearing murderers or militiamen, grabbed a heavy tool for smoothing mortar. He was startled at the sight of the dwarf, who wore a short-sleeved coat of mail and was armed with a long, curved sword. Bes-Ahrin stood dimly in the flickering light from the oil lamp that was never extinguished so that fires need not be freshly kindled each morning. Amram let him into the low-ceilinged room, but held him at bay with the tool.

"Get Jochebed," whispered Bes-Ahrin in simple Egyptian that Amram, as a foreman, understood. "Quickly, show her this!" He held out a solar disk on an amethyst necklace that the princess had worn when Jochebed had last visited her. "I speak with the Princess Mutempsut's authority."

The parents of Moses, asleep in his crib, their two older children shivering behind them, were soon before the dwarf, like prisoners awaiting their sentence. They stood on the cold mud and limestone-chip floor as Bes-Ahrin addressed Amram in his deep voice, allowing him time to translate for Jochebed: "My mistress is sailing even now from Punt. Her husband and the king are killed by their rivals. When she comes, she wishes to take your son with her. She will raise him in the palace as her own."

"No, we will keep him," said Amram in Egyptian, but his tone needed no translation and Jochebed nodded in affirmation.

"Do not even imagine it," said the dwarf. "The Pharaoh, our Mighty Bull, is hard on you Hebrews. The Princess Mutempsut will make certain your son lives as a prince, free of whips or mutilation, and will never lack for anything. Do not be fools."

"No," said Amram, stubbornly.

"Imbecile!" said the dwarf. "While the princess is too good-hearted to hurt you, I promise you that tomorrow you two will disappear, and your children will be taken away as slaves, their future to labor all the twelve hours of the day in the mud, until they drop. Do not doubt me, Amram. In any case this child will be mine, for I will not leave here without him."

"Give us until tomorrow," said Amram.

The dwarf laughed silently, showing thick-gapped teeth in an enormous mouth. "So you can flee before morning? No, the baby comes now. You know it will be loved." He looked serious. "Even I like the little fellow. Prepare him to go."

The two parents looked at each other.

"He will kill us," said Jochebed in the Hebrew tongue.

"Yes," said Amram, gripping the mortaring tool even more tightly, "unless I kill him."

The dwarf, understanding enough, drew his sword, looked around, and adroitly jabbed it through their precious water bag, made from a small goatskin and hanging from the wall. "That could be you, Amram," hissed Bes-Ahrin.

The water spewed out and Jochebed rushed over to stanch it with her fingers. "Put the tool down," she said to her husband. "Bring me pots to catch the water."

She began to weep as she let the water flow into the vessels, and Amram fell to the ground, his heavy face pressed into the limestone chips and mud as he, too, wept. When he rose, Jochebed dropped the flat goatskin and lifted the sleeping Moses from the earthenware crib Amram had fired, for wood was precious in Egypt and the poor even used earthenware for spoons.

Bes-Ahrin, gentler now, put two *qites*—a half-ounce—of gold on the worn table, enough for a dozen goatskins. The two parents dressed Moses in the blue-dyed Egyptian swaddling clothes, now too small for him, that Mutempsut had provided for his visits to her at the Pharaoh's palace.

Two hours later, Bes-Ahrin was smuggling a little bundle aboard the ship. He changed the wet, sleeping infant into colorful Puntite baby garments, also too small for him, and placed him in the excited Princess Mutempsut's arms.

The baby was still there when the princess, splintered by the death of her son and her terrible disappointments, returned to the residence at Tanis.

Moses was no darker than many Egyptians, and because the baby he replaced was of mixed parentage his color raised no questions. His supposed father had Mediterranean blood that might have offset his African stock. To cloak his age—more than a year older than the Puntite baby would have been—Mutempsut continued to dress him as a young infant. If some of the court gossips wondered at his size and meanly hinted that the princess might have been pregnant when she left for Punt, no one dared explore the issue.

Horemheb had first planned to send an expedition to Punt to avenge his son-in-law's murder. But the cost and the damage to his trade with the Divine Land convinced him otherwise. To salve his conscience, he had a hymn sung by two hundred priests on Moses' first visit to Thebes. He placed on his adopted grandson's shapely head a miniature disklike diadem sprouting two cormorant feathers, a symbol of Min, whose cult originated in Punt. After noting how healthy the child seemed, he gave a palace and pavilion in Tanis to Mutempsut.

As children do, Moses quickly adapted to the name Hapi-Set, although the new name did not sound right to him. With the word "Moses," he had associated a tall, firm woman, his mother, warm in body and manner. The word had meant cozy spaces; the smooth boards of a platform (and when he crawled or fell down two hands' breadths from it, a rough floor); and an enclosed space for sleep, where when he turned he touched hardness and heard the crush of straw beneath his blankets. Often, it had meant two comforting bodies when, frightened in the night and crying, he was lifted into a larger bed.

Even when Hapi-Set became familiar to him, he sensed the absence of that warmth, that easiness, and the certainty of his mother's voice. His new mother's clothes smelled like flowers, and in the morning when she came to him and put her face down to him, the same perfume was on her skin. His new bed was deep and silent, never crackling when he turned, and all its sides were soft. When Mutempsut came to his room and took him from his crib to her bed, he had trouble sleeping, for she held him tightly, sometimes murmuring when he wanted only sleep.

Had he been able to define it, he would have said the first mother was gentle, consistent, and sometimes staunch. And his new one was sweet-smelling, pliant, and unpredictable.

By the time he was six, Prince Hapi-Set, son of the Princess Mutempsut and the late crown prince of Punt, was already showing his precocity. Like other princes and sons of the highest officials his age, he was schooled under the royal scribes, priests, and retired military heroes.

On rush mats in a sunny, bare room of Tanis's principal palace, he sat with his writing board on crossed legs. Because the children were all sons of the elite, they scrawled in black and red ink with their brushes on torn pieces of papyrus instead of limestone slates or jagged stone chips.

Within a year, Moses was moved into a class of princes one to two years older than he was, although they thought he was even younger due to the camouflaged circumstances of his infancy. Among his new classmates was Ramses, a sturdy, audacious child, whom Moses—a year and a half his junior—had already begun to look up to.

Their genealogies were parallel. Ramses was named after his and Moses' grandfather Ramses—in Moses' case, *assumed* grandfather—the military chief of the Pharaoh Horemheb. The elder son of this Ramses was already a famed general, Sety, who also resided at Tanis. And Sety's eldest sister was Moses' new mother, Mutempsut. Thus, Moses and the child Ramses, oldest son of Sety, were first cousins.

Moses learned writing and reading more rapidly than any student the scribes had ever had and was precocious at sports and military schooling as well. Ramses, while also an excellent student, surpassed even Moses in his athletic and military courses. They fast became rivals and best friends.

Their training began after breakfast with a two-mile race in diminutive armor. After the run, an old Shardanan warrior—both his ears sheared off by some enemy—coached the boys in hand-to-hand combat. Moses, already large for his age, fought ably, beating by strength and guile all but the ferocious Ramses. When Ramses conquered him, the other princes, perhaps smarting from their defeat at a younger boy's hands, used the traditional wooden rod with a hand carved at its end to thump him all over his head or body. Moses, bruised and abraded, took it angrily, vowing he would someday vanquish his cousin.

Once, after wrestling Moses to defeat, Ramses said to him as he squinted back his tears: "You will never beat me, Hapi-Set, until you learn that in fighting there is no such thing as friendship. If you were winning, by Wadjit, the serpent goddess, I would bite your finger until you screamed and surrendered. Why don't you do the same when you fight?"

It was a lesson that Moses took to heart. A few months later, in a fight with seasoned oak rods meant to train the boys as swordsmen, Ramses, overconfident, missed Moses with a wide swing. For an instant he was off balance, and Moses caught him with a sharp blow to his wrist, sending Ramses' stick flying. Without waiting for Ramses to regain his weapon, Moses beat his arms rapidly and fiercely. Ramses gamely lunged at him, but Moses stopped him with a stunning blow to the head that sent him into the dirt.

"Do I need to bite your finger now to get you to surrender?" Moses goaded the groggy boy.

Ramses, even incapacitated, would not give up. "Never, Puntite pissdrinker!" he cried and tried to rise.

Moses pushed him back into the dirt with the end of the stick. He raised it as if to strike Ramses in the head, and looked at the gnarled old coach, watching nearby. "Let him be, Prince Hapi-Set," growled the former warrior. "You are the winner. Get up, Prince Ramses, and clutch the forearm of a worthy young fighter."

It was a measure of Ramses' character that he did not hold his defeat against Moses. In future matches, Ramses was more cautious and, therefore, victorious.

Ramses also excelled in hurling missiles at a round target of sewn ox hide made taut by soaking. On it was painted in green, yellow, and black a gaudy cartoon of the Hittite king Subbiluliumma, who had grievously defeated the Egyptians and chased them all the way across Syria a few years before. The two generals-to-be flung spears, the lighter javelins, and stones from slings at the mellifluously named king and then shot him with triangular bows. The muscular young Ramses was first with spear, javelin, and bow. Moses was first with the sling.

By the time he was ten, Ramses bested his younger cousin in most things military and athletic, but there was seldom a contest in matters of the mind. "I could throw a javelin all the way to Byblos," Ramses once confided to his comrade between classes as they drank small beer from pottery bottles and ate bread by a palace pool. He threw a bit of bread at a sunning turtle and hit it. The boys watched as it flopped from its warm stone into the water. "But I cannot match you, Hapi-Set, in geography or mathematics or the science of the climate."

"Or history, or astronomy, or foreign words," Moses chided him. "But Ramses, you do well in architecture, in knowing how many bricks it takes to build a wall, in military tactics and army rations . . ."

". . . and the study of our gods."

"Who have favored you with only half a brain."

For answer, Ramses, laughing and cursing him with other oaths he had learned from the Shardanan, wrestled him toward the poolside, determined to throw him in. Moses broke free, and with Ramses whooping in pursuit, ran back to the classroom.

Ramses' and Moses' destinies changed mightily in the year 1320 B.C. when Horemheb died suddenly—so suddenly that his expansive tomb at Thebes was largely unfinished. But he had already picked a successor, his vizier and general, Ramses, first of that name. And this Ramses, already almost as old as his patron, was certain to name as heir his illustrious son, Sety, first of that name, scarred victor of innumerable battles in Palestine, Syria, Nubia, and Libya. Sety's first son was Ramses, cousin, friend, and sometimes rival of Moses.

"You will be Pharaoh," said the eleven-year-old Moses one night as the two boys lay on a hill looking in the July sky for Sopdet—called Sirius by the Greeks—the goddess of festivals. Below them the Nile in flood stage glistened and rolled in the moonlight.

"I will start with the Libyans. I will sacrifice every other Libyan male to Seth. I will build temples and palaces as no other king has ever done," said Ramses, already imagining himself in a chariot with his lances, javelins, and arrows. "You will be my vizier and give me advice. For every mistake, I will have one of your fingers cut off."

"Then I had better be Pharaoh, for I would only have you beaten when you were wrong."

For a moment, Ramses thought his friend was being serious, then scoffed amiably. "Little Hapi-Set, you are the son of a dead prince of Punt. And your mother is no Hatshepsut," he said, referring to the powerful and conniving woman who ruled Egypt two hundred years earlier. "My father—oh Osiris's balls, if he would just leave me alone until then so I can enjoy life a little. For when I am Pharaoh I will have to wear the blue headdress and act like a Pharaoh." He picked up a stick and pretended it was the royal scepter. "You shall be rich, Hapi-Set, and have a hundred beautiful wives."

He waved the "scepter" at an imagined courtier. "You, sir, shall live," and he waved it again, "and you, sir, shall die. And you will be enriched. And you, Nunrah"—a young uncle to both Ramses and Moses through one of Sety's many sisters and half sisters—"for being an arrogant coward shall have your lands and property taken and your pizzle made into a spoon handle. Or maybe I will burn it as a sacrifice to Seth, my father's namesake. And yours, Hapi-Set."

Seth, or Sutekh, was a god of viciousness, chaos, rape, argument—and power. He chopped his brother Osiris into pieces, and Osiris's priests taught the boys a dirge that began, "Seth hid the sun in the wings of the sacred vulture, slew the noblest of the gods, Osiris, and damaged the eye of Horus. . . ."

"Seth is but one of the gods, oh divine master," Moses mocked Ramses' piety. "There are far too many. Keeping track of them makes my thoughts whirl. What they do, what they stand for. What heads they have, falcon, fox, ibis. What I think, Ramses, is that it makes more sense for there to be only one god."

"Heresy, Hapi-Set, sacrilege! Never talk of a single god to anyone but me. The gods, all of them, have made Egypt great."

"What has made us great is the men of Egypt, like your father, our grand-father, fighting for us all these years."

"Fighting for the gods, at the orders of the gods."

"Well, one god would take care of it all. One god, steady as a bright star. When I pray by myself, that is the god I pray to. Pa netcher, god without a name. If I had to I would call him Osiris. But I leave him vague on purpose. God No-Name. Oh yes, in classes—why invite trouble?—I pray to the god whose day it is and chant whatever the priests tell us to."

"You say your one god is like Osiris. Why not Bes? He's a household god of Punt—is he not? That diseased little place that killed your father. I admit he's a god I fear. With his bandy legs and toad face . . . like your mother's Syrian monster, Bes-Ahrin." Ramses pulled his mouth wide with his thumbs and pushed up his nostrils with his forefingers, a fair approximation of the dwarf's face.

Moses laughed but felt guilty, knowing that Bes-Ahrin would die for his mother. And perhaps, because of her, would die for him as well. However, the dwarf detested Ramses, who reciprocated the feeling. There was good reason on both sides, going back many years. For one thing, after Princess Mutempsut bought Bes-Ahrin, her brother, Sety, Ramses' father, took a dislike to the cantankerous deformed ten-year-old. Sety lost his temper one day and would have killed the dwarf on the spot if Mutempsut had not put herself between them.

Ramses had embraced his father's dislike of Bes-Ahrin. At the age of nine, he and a dozen other boys—Moses was not one of them—had harassed the dwarf with training lances. Bes-Ahrin had not dared fight back lest he kill one of the youngsters. They had stripped him and humiliated him, his lumpy body bleeding from a dozen light wounds.

A year later at Thebes, during a visit by Sety and Ramses, a palace dwarf was caught putting arsenic—a powder imported from India and refined as zarnig in Syria—into the young Ramses' beer. Under torture, the dwarf had blamed Bes-Ahrin. To be sure, Bes-Ahrin was Syrian, and the dwarfs, midgets, hunchbacks, and other grotesques kept in rich houses were known to maintain a loose confederation in Egypt, and indeed, throughout the region. Additionally, Ramses' death might have opened the way for Moses to become Pharaoh, once Horemheb, Ramses, first of that name, and Sety had all died.

Bes-Ahrin had vociferously denied the charges, as there was no proof, and he was five hundred miles downriver in Tanis at the time. Princess Mutempsut, appealing to her adoptive father, Horemheb, had protected Bes-Ahrin, pointing to Sety's attempt to kill her dwarf when he was ten and Ramses' own torment of him.

Moses now attempted to patch up these ill feelings. "Bes-Ahrin is good to me," he said to Ramses that night beneath the stars. "I tell you, in sword practice I cannot best him. And he has made me a bronze dagger. I will give it to you."

Ramses spurned the gift but regretted that his sally had turned into an insult of the god Bes, and had hurt Moses' feelings. "Why does he hate me so? I played only an innocent trick on him and he tried to poison me. So we are quits. To be hated by a dwarf is bad luck. Remember? Amenemope said, 'Don't tease a dwarf." Mercurial Ramses. The thought of bad luck upset him, and the idea that anyone could dislike him had taken the joy from his evening. He sighed. "Back to Sopdet. Whoever sees her first gets the choice of chariots in the race tomorrow."

"Look there," pointed Moses. "While you quoted Amenemope, I saw Sopdet."

Ramses strained his eyes. "Yes," he said, fair as he generally was in the end. "The choice is yours, old sling stone."

Chapter Two
The Young Generals

RAMSES WAS NOT ALWAYS AS PIOUS AS HIS FATHER AND GRANDFATHER. On a trip to Thebes, the two boys, now fourteen and thirteen, did what adventurous princes had done for centuries: They bribed a priest to lead them at night, when no one was near, into the tombs of the Pharaohs. They even entered the narrow passage that led into the sealed inner sanctum where the royal sarcophagi lay. There, by the wavering light of a resin torch, they read of the victories of Ahmose, of Tuthmose the Great, third of that name, and others.

Ramses was fascinated by the mummies of baboons, falcons, and other animals, and the varieties of weapons under the entrance and antechambers of the tombs. Moses, by contrast, was taken by the already archaic writings on the wall about Ahmose, who had driven the Hyksos kings of the east from Egypt. Beating the Hyksos had been a close thing. But you would not know it from the unctuous, interminable comparisons of Ahmose with the gods. Moses found the embellishments annoying.

One morning the two boys stood on a dry hilltop across from the Valley of the Kings, where the monumental temples and burial places gleamed. "While we are here," Moses said, "I want to see Akhenaten's tomb."

Ramses spat in the dirt. Successive Pharaohs had repudiated Akhenaten's monotheism and over the years his name had been expunged from stelae, monuments, and all public buildings. Even his tomb had been partially destroyed.

"Never," said Ramses. "I cannot afford to be seen anywhere near that tomb. Our grandfather would ship you off to the Libyan border if he knew you had gone in. Besides, we have not seen Gurna. The tombs of the nobles there, I am told, have the best wall paintings of horses and battles in Egypt."

Moses obligingly went to Gurna nearby, and even in the flare's wavering light, the pictures were wondrous. A giant stallion, perfectly drawn and colored, was above a sarcophagus, ready for its noble occupant to rise and ride beside Egypt's other heroes on the Fields of the Afterlife.

But the next night, Moses went on his own to the tomb of Akhenaten. It was less interesting, although the paintings of the Pharaoh, his wife, Nefertiti, and their daughters were touching. Akhenaten had loved his family and his single god, Aten, more than Egypt, its people, and the thousand gods in ten thousand forms that they had invented. In the guttering light, beside the towering sarcophagus, Moses thought, *Akhenaten was defeated, yes, but due to his fumbling, his weakness, his inability to sway the rebellious people, not because of his belief in Aten.*

"I could have done better," the thoughtful youth said quietly to the thin-chested ruler in his blue crown, his wife and children on his lap, a daughter patting him fondly under the chin.

When, the next morning, Moses revealed his secret visit, Ramses shouted, "You lunatic. You defy me this way?"

"You are not Pharaoh yet, my cousin," said Moses without rancor. "Come now, it is done. I will make amends."

"Why do you have to know about these things, Hapi-Set?"

"I want to know everything," said Moses, serious now.

"Ah, and it will get you in trouble, serious trouble someday," said Ramses, his anger fading as fast as it had fired up.

Ramses, first of that name, was dead. Sety was Pharaoh. And he was at war on two fronts, the east and the south. Young Ramses, eighteen, and Moses, almost seventeen, stood by the long quay at Sais watching the slaves and common soldiers loading war chariots on the barge for the voyage to Elephantine. The river port was four hundred and eighty miles upstream as the sacred ibis flies, but half again farther on the twisting Nile. The strategic city was threatened by the rebellious warriors of Nubia, also called Cush and Ethiopia. The black nation and its allies were on the march again after decades of subservient peace. Their goal: to take advantage of the new Pharaoh's absence on campaigns in Syria and Palestine.

The giant barges, each behind a towboat whose wide rectangular sail was dropped across the deck, also carried barley and emmer, and oxen, goats, and quail—alive and packed in loose reed baskets. Forward, under leather coverings, were lances, arrows, bows, slings, and coats of mail and helmets.

The eight barges and towboats at Sais would join others as the young Ramses, the nominal though not actual leader of the war party, progressed upstream past Memphis, Menat Khoufou, Panopolis, Abydos, and on to Opet-Thebes. There, the exalted triad of Thebes—Amun, his consort, Mut, and Khonsu, their child—would bless their campaign.

"For once, I thank my father for pushing his blue hat into my nose," said Ramses, as chanting porters carried on the last of the stores. "What better general to give us than Nebari? Father could have used him in Syria," he added.

The old warrior was to meet them in Thebes. He had won battles from the lands of the Hittites to central Libya, losing one eye and a hand, but was unmatched in Egypt for his guile and his bravery.

"I was thinking how odd it will be to fight my relatives," said Moses, for a

Puntite contingent had traveled north to fight beside the Cushites. "I talked to Mother about it. She never speaks of my father."

"Even when you told her you would be fighting Puntites?"

"She looked nervous—well, she always looks nervous. She said, 'Do not regard them as relatives. It is too painful. Let us erase Punt from our lives. You are Egyptian.'"

"And, thanks to the gods, an African ox of an Egyptian," said Ramses, for Moses measured six feet one inch, two inches more than Ramses, who was tall for an Egyptian. "Good to have enough meat beside me to stop a Nubian lance," Ramses added, playfully bumping his companion almost into the Nile.

Moses was as eager for the battle as Ramses, who had already been on two minor campaigns on the Libyan border. All their young lives they had trained for just such expeditions against the enemies of Egypt and her gods.

Like the giant Cretan sponges used by their teachers to explain hydraulics, Moses had absorbed everything his teachers had to offer and his curiosity had remained undiminished. Now he would learn about war and far places. Would they see herds of giraffes as numerous as flocks of sheep, as he had been told, lions twice the size of those he and Ramses had pursued on horseback and slain with lances near the Red Mountain? Did people in the jungles of southern Cush really live in trees and eat poisonous snakes? Honeyed scorpions that he had eaten on a wager with Ramses, Moses thought, were bad enough.

It was the tenth day of their journey, and Ramses was entertaining a dozen other princes in his quarters on his and Moses' towboat. "Who among us will be the first to have a Nubian princess?" Ramses asked, well into his cups.

The wind had died, and as was the custom on war journeys, the princes had taken turns beside the lowliest soldiers at the oars. Now the young men slouched in small chairs with falcon heads, or sat on pillows on the flawlessly woven and dyed wool rugs. Eye-catching scenes of war in blue, red, black, orange, and purple ornamented the wooden walls of Ramses' dining room.

While they drank, the royal cabin, more like a small palace, yawed as a gust of northerly wind puffed out the heavy sail. "More likely sex with a rough ape for you, Ramses," said a former schoolmate. "Look at the red hair all over you."

"Seth's favorite color. He loves red hair," said Ramses, signaling his cup-bearer to pour glasses all around, delta wine from the royal vineyards. At a single clap of his hands, dancing women they had brought aboard at Shmoun—and would put ashore at Noubit—came out with their sistrums and castanets.

"Mighty are the warriors of young Ramses," they crooned, "who go forth in the name of Seth, god of the Ramessides, to vanquish our enemies. Splendid are they in warfare and love."

The women were young, of all shades, their bodies clearly available beneath their sheer girdles. On their heads they wore white cloth cones filled with pomade, as both men and women did at formal dinners in Tanis or Thebes to impart sweet smells. Their necklaces of semiprecious stones jangled almost in time with the skilled click of their castanets.

"Nubian princesses will be no match for Egyptian girls," said Moses, into the wine himself, feeling vigorous, but nervous, for he had not yet had a woman.

Ramses never let his younger friend get away with a pretension. "How would you know, Hapi-Set? You have never slain a maidenhead, but only strangled the serpent between your legs."

The princes roared at Ramses' joke. Moses started to anger at this breach of confidence. For Ramses had begun an active sex life at the age of fourteen with just such dancing girls as these. But to be churlish at such insults, particularly justified ones, was to be childish and unbecoming of a warrior.

"There are no maidenheads here," he said, lifting his silver wine cup toward the swaying women.

"So much the better to strangle your serpent," said Nunrah, who against Ramses' wishes had been allowed on the campaign. Again, the company laughed.

Thus challenged, Moses had no recourse. He rose and staggered toward his sleeping room. At the door, he asked of the half-dozen dancing girls, "Who will be mine tonight?"

They stopped their song. Their kohl-ringed eyes opened theatrically wide, making them look like young owls, but they chirped like sparrows, for they smelled gold. "I will, Prince Hapi-Set . . ." "Try me, Prince . . ." "*I* will slay your serpent, tall Prince," said another, her arm tattooed with blue dots in the form of Bes. It was this last to whom he signaled.

He was making love to her a second time when, an hour later, Ramses staggered into the room, and fully clothed, fell to the low bed and began to rend the room with snores. At Noubit, two days later, the dancers left the boat. Moses gave his brief lover a small golden statuette of Hapi, his namesake.

After a fortnight more on the Nile and by horseback, Moses and Ramses reached the field at Semna just south of the second cataract. The very dust in the air seemed scorching. It crusted in the nostrils of man and beast and powdered their skin and the carts and chariots, working its way into food, axles, everything that was not sealed. In their chariots, side by side, the two princes listened nervously while their stallions waited calmly and the Egyptian general, Nebari, addressed the troops.

The rugged old warrior, bare-chested save for a wide ribbon covered with glistening gold bees around his neck, spoke of how wisely and kindly Egypt had treated the Cushites and the other "peoples browned by the sun, as the Greeks call them." But, he said, these supposed allies had overrun the outposts of Ikaita. The small garrisons had been slain and mutilated, their aging priests of Amun left gutted and rotting, their simple shrines defiled with human feces.

A half-mile away, Moses could see what looked like a never-ending ant-hill of soldiers, the enemy. They, too, would be hearing from their leader, he knew, a chronology of Egyptian infamy. They, too, would be eager for battle and the spoils of war, or perhaps, as he was, wondering where they would be at day's end.

"Because of the barbarity of our enemy, on this day," cawed Nebari, "if you have slain or gravely wounded an enemy, remember his face or armor. When we have won our victory, return to him. If he is alive, kill him, and in both cases shear his penis, and put it in your tunic"—a practice of some older generals. "The scribes will record the gold to be given you based on the number of these trophies. Let no man take the member of his comrade's victim."

Nebari prescribed the treatment of healthy prisoners—how they should quickly be handed over to the supporting militia for branding. He ordered his troops to leave enemy booty in the field until the victory was won so it could be fairly divided. He described the scrutiny with which the god Seth would be observing the battle and how, if the god did not punish cowards, he, Nebari, would by publicly blinding the miscreant and driving him into the desert that lay just to the east of the field of battle.

Ramses, beside Nebari in his gold-overlaid chariot, grinned fiercely beneath his visor. Moses was more reflective, and more daunted. For Ramses had no fear of falling in battle. He was convinced that a hero's death would lead him into Imenty, the domain of the gods of the dead, where all the pleasures of this life were magnified a hundredfold.

As Nebari exhorted the troops, Moses' mind wandered to this idea of the gods protecting mortals. Surely, the Nubian leader was invoking the same gods only a half-mile away for men equally confident of divine shielding.

Nor was that the only contradiction that occurred to Moses. Although it did not seem to bother his Egyptian brethren, if one worshipped Seth and his incarnation, the Pharaoh Sety, would not that infuriate Seth's blood enemies, Osiris and Horus, and Osiris's unforgiving wife, Isis? In fact, how could one invoke any of the pantheon, for all the gods were jealously and constantly squabbling over prerogatives, forever changing shape, one day a bull, the next a lion, a griffin with a man's body, a hippopotamus, a crocodile, a star?

Moses would have liked a god to pray to at this moment, one strong and noble who would join him in fighting off his fear. One merciful, just, and intelligent. What did it matter what one called him? Aten, the sun god of Akhenaten? Or, perhaps, Osiris, who, on the whole, was closest to the god Moses imagined?

Nebari ended his rallying speech. Moses, godless, pushed back his trepidation on his own. The twelve buglers blew their polished copper and silver instruments. They pealed three pure notes, two ascending, the final descending, and repeated the call over and over.

At the sound, Nebari's Shardanan guards set off at a run. Fearless brutes from the east, they had been captured, then trained—in suicidal fashion—to clear the way for the royal Egyptian charioteers. Moses, Ramses, and the other princes and generals moved out behind them at a gallop, the horses resplendent with their cockades, their ribbons lashing the wind. Behind the chariots rushed the archers. A hundred yards from the enemy, they paused to fire a volley over the heads of the Egyptian charioteers and into the ranks of the Nubians. Next came the spearmen, javelin hurlers, and slingmen, who unleashed their missiles when they were only fifty yards away.

Once the first weapons were launched, the Pharaoh's infantry ran past the other foot soldiers, screaming the names of their protective god, Sety, and his manifestations, "Son of Re! Golden Horus! Mighty Bull!" They held high their flails—free-swinging curved swords at the end of elongated handles—and ordinary swords and lances. At the rear, shouting encouragement, came the supporting militia, the provisions unloaded from their six-oxen carts and replaced with additional weapons and oversized braziers of burning wood, in which irons were heated for branding prisoners. The clatter of the charge and the rumble of the heavy wheels made a deafening din as the bitter dust enveloped both armies.

Moses did not think as his driver lashed on the twin stallions. He felt not fear, but only war. He saw Nubian arrows felling Egyptians. He saw Cushite chariots racing toward the first ranks of his countrymen. He perceived where his spears and lances or his sword could wreak the most damage. He was as excited and yet as assessing as he had been when he sought the spot behind the shoulder bone of a lion or gaunt desert wolf where a lance jab would injure or kill.

Ramses was ahead, his steeds breasting the protective guard of Nubian lancemen so that he could face head-on his royal opponents in their chariots. Through the spangling, strangling dust, Moses saw his friend's mouth open in a cry of triumph as his long lance plunged through the crossed leather chest guard of a black prince. The dying man grabbed the fatal weapon with both hands as his driver sought to keep the ornate brown-and-gold Nubian chariot from tipping.

Moses wheeled past his own guardsmen at a gallop toward his first target, a white-haired foot captain with burly arms, spear cocked. They were so close that he saw the man's face clench as he propelled his spear. Both Moses and his driver ducked. The spear's haft struck Moses a glancing blow as it passed, but his young body quickly regained balance. He leaned from his chariot and nicked the left arm of the dark warrior as the man put his shield protectively before his face.

Then they were past the enemy foot captain, but stalled by Moses' own bodyguards, who were slashing with their long-handled swords at a covey of spearmen and adversaries with throwing sticks. Again Moses crouched as the war sticks and slung stones rattled against his chariot, followed by the heavy clunk of a spear that was thrown so hard it pierced the bronzed wood near his shin. His swarthy Midianite driver lashed the horses to extract them from the melee of striving bodies.

The stallions plowed clear, but their momentum left Moses surrounded by Nubians. Seeing the princely sacred ram embossed in gold on Moses' chariot, a dozen Cushites rallied to attack. A husky soldier in a panther-skin vest grasped one of Moses' stallion's martingales, a second seized the other horse's reins. The war horses reared loyally, lashed by Moses' driver. But a gigantic soldier wielding a war mattock caved in the Midian's ribs. Moses stabbed the man in the chest with his lance, withdrew it, and set about defending himself, knowing the odds were against him, but not caring. He had become a creature of battle to the exclusion of all else.

Suddenly behind him he heard mixed cries and screams. Busy warding off attackers, he dared not look. But he knew the wild voice that soared above all others. The Nubians who had been slashing at him with swords and jabbing with lances swivelled to protect themselves.

It was Ramses with his picked Shardanans. "For Seth and Sety!" his friend and now savior howled from his chariot as his driver crashed his chestnut stallions past Moses and into the enemy warriors. The Shardanans, moving as a phalanx, mowed down the first of the Nubians. The others broke ranks and fled. Yet the two holding Moses' horses were steadfast. One had wrapped Moses' reins around his forearm, and Moses jumped the two and a half feet to the ground, and, with his sword, took the man's arm off at the elbow.

He knew he would never forget the unbelieving look on the man's face as he looked at the stump of his arm spouting blood. Then the Cushite fainted and collapsed, joining a half-dozen others around the chariot in what seemed a writhing crocodile pit of men in agony.

When Moses knew he would not die, he looked up at Ramses, whose driver held in the crown prince's horses. His friend's face was tightened in anger. "You stupid *Aamou!*"—Asian: an insult in Egyptian—he screamed, "don't ever get that far ahead of your guard again! Never!"

That night, Ramses was still furious when Moses went by his cousin's goat-hide pavilion. "Is that what you learned in the desert? To go into a lioness's den alone? Didn't you see me fight on the fringes, keeping the Shardanans near me? Moses, fool!" Seeing Moses' tears—for he was, after all, still a youth—Ramses moderated.

"Are you going to sacrifice my vizier-to-be for one miserable barefooted Ethiopian's cock that we could not even stay around to cut?" His humor made better by this sally, he added, "Here, drink some wine. Stop crying like a child." But he could not resist more words of chastisement. "If you had spent more time studying chariots and less on where the weather and waters come from, you would be a better soldier, little Hapi."

For all the carnage, the Cushite armies were largely intact. For days, their rear guard fought viciously as the bulk of the troops made an orderly retreat to the mud-brick fortress of Diffima, fifty miles to the south. The Egyptians followed, their supplies in the lighter barges they had used since they had passed the first cataract. Other support troops kicked their oxen carts down the rutted pathway beside the Nile.

Diffima was not easily assailable, with its high crenelated battlements patterned after the Syrians with whom the Nubian kings were once allied. But the Egyptians quickly cut off the supply route to the south. Then they encamped to plan. The wheeled rams and catapults, so successful in the eastern wars, were not easily transportable. Nebari had thought them unnecessary against the Nubians. His forces would have to scale the walls, occupying the defenders on the ramparts while his ax men chopped and his sappers pried at the giant carob doors. There was no other way. Two nights before their assault, knowing his men must have a hiatus before what would be a slaughter on both sides, Nebari posted pickets and turned the camp over to revelry. There would be an entire day to recover.

The Egyptians drank huge quantities of beer and vile, potent, local palm sap wine; spitted oxen over fires; and raped their women captives and, in some cases, young Nubian boys. The heavy smell of incense, burnt all night over sacrifices by the priests, seemed to bless the bestiality. A few hours before dawn, the sated soldiers slept to renew their strength.

It was at sunrise that Nebari, for all his military guile, was taken by surprise. The dark portals of Diffima swung open with a scrape. The eerie, high-pitched oryx horns, war note of the elite and fanatical southernmost Cushites, sounded along with the thud of ceremonial water buffalo skin drums. In the soft, rosy light, a gush of warriors poured into the fort and rapidly massacred the stout Egyptians that Nebari had prudently posted.

At the same time, from tangles of tall underbrush and thick stands of acacia behind Diffima, the remaining chariots of the Nubians streamed out. They had designedly retreated ten miles south of Diffima and then traveled back all night. Howling war cries to the gods, the charioteers charged through the Egyptian pickets and into the encampment. Behind them ran Ethiopian reinforcements that had stealthily marched up from Puba during the night.

The Nubians, famed for their swift bronze sabers, slashed the sleeping Egyptians where they lay. They cut the guy ropes of the princes' and other officers' tents and their lancers jabbed through the tough goatskin at the trapped men within. The screams drove the Nubian drummers, horn blowers, and war chanters to a bloodthirsty frenzy, creating a barbaric ululating cacophony.

Ramses' Shardanans, who drank no alcohol, preferring to vent their self-expression with rape, sodomy, and some few incidents of mayhem on less-valuable slaves, instantly rallied. They died almost to the man as the officers struggled from their toppled tents and roused their logy troops.

Once awake and fighting for their lives, the Egyptians were able at a terrible cost to turn the tide. Moses and his cohorts, whose swords were tangled in the collapsed tents, plucked up the fire-sharpened fir spears of fallen Egyptians to drive back a band of Cushites. It was each man for himself. Moses entered a copse and came on two opponents, a lancer and a slingman. The first was a muscular man of perhaps fifty, wearing the ostrich-feather insignia in his helmet of a royal guardsman. The slingman was no bigger than a thin boy and wore a bronze coat of mail, a visored helmet, and gold armlet—all embossed skillfully with lions rampant. He was already whipping around his egg-sized stone in the leather pouch—a weapon with which the Cushites excelled.

With his spear, Moses parried the lancer's thrust and tried to knock down the arm of the boy before it could release the stone. His spear clanged against the gold armlet, deflecting the stone and knocking the youth to the ground. He quickly turned back to fend off the lance.

Desperately, Moses smashed the man's weapon to the ground on its next thrust. As the lancer snatched it up, Moses jammed his thick leg on it and snapped the staff. With a short stab, he pierced the older man's neck to the spine.

The lad had risen and Moses swung his spear, knocking off his bronze helmet and sending him again to the ground. He brought the spear up to stab his young but dangerous adversary. Even as he lunged, he diverted the thrust rightward. For the fallen warrior was not a boy, but a girl. Her black hair, unconfined now, sprung from her head like the bushy tail of a stallion. "A girl!" he exclaimed. "You might have killed me."

"So kill me, mud-mullet"—the most stupid of the delta marsh fish. Her Egyptian was schooled, but with a Cushite accent. Her eyes were wild with terror. "Kill me!" She saw the royal uraeus—the cobra—on his helmet. Her tone softened and she pleaded, "Kill me, but do not defile me. You are a prince. I am a king's daughter."

Moses had been too astonished to think of rape. Indeed, he had thought he would simply send her back with a soldier, perhaps a lightly wounded one, to be branded as a slave. And that quickly, for he knew he must rejoin the fray. But here was bounty, a prisoner who could be exchanged for riches if she were returned unharmed to her father, assuming he was still alive.

She saw his hesitation and expected the worst. "You have slain Sekiyim. Give me his lance that I may use its point on myself. You will see how a princess dies."

"Come along, little black minnow," said Moses. "Enough theater. I am not interested in seeing how a princess dies." The stammer which was to afflict him even more in later life overcame him. "Get up," he managed with a prolonged stutter.

"My head hurts."

"Get up," he now ordered her firmly. "If I leave you here, the next soldier who finds you may give you hurt in more places than your head. Here, signal your surrender."

Reluctantly she lifted her thin arms and raised both little fingers, the universal gesture of capitulation. Two of Moses' cohorts had found him and looked curiously at the girl. To one who was bleeding from a cut in his side, he said, "Take her rearward. Protect her. She is royal and will command a ransom. You shall share when I collect."

"Where shall she be branded, Prince Hapi-Set?" the soldier asked.

"Leave her unbranded. She will be worth more." He looked at his unusual captive. Her harmonious young features might become more than merely attractive when she grew up, he thought. At his glance he saw the fear go out of her eyes and something else, perhaps curiosity, replace it. "What is your name, child?" he asked, himself only two or three years older than she.

"Sebah, daughter of Paras, ruler of Barbaht." This small southern Cushite kingdom, Moses knew, was important because it was the Nile terminal of a mountainous trade route from Punt.

With a quick look at his spunky captive, Moses and the second soldier returned to battle.

At day's end, the Nubians and their allies had retreated back inside the fortress with several captured Egyptian princes. The Egyptians were in full control of the now-ruined farmlands and orchards surrounding the fort. No one had won.

Moses had his prisoner brought to his tent that evening, lest she be damaged during the night by some wayward warrior. She looked like a skinny waif despite the gold military scales of her corselet. Ramses and three other princes dropped in to see this curiosity after their suppers.

"Nephew Hapi-Set," said Nunrah, "what baboon king can give you as much ransom as I will for this little stick? I warrant she still carries a lizard skin"—a hymen—"between her legs. Is that not so, little monkey?"

Shocked, Sebah glanced at Moses.

"I'm holding her for ransom," Moses said calmly.

"Come, come," said the older prince, querulous now, wide eyes in his anomalously small head heated from drinking, "how many *debens* of silver, Hapi-Set?"

Moses was about to give him another measured response, for his widowed mother was not so powerful in court that she could always protect him, and Nunrah was a talented intriguer. In theory, even Ramses was required to show deference to his uncles. But Ramses broke in:

"Brother to my father, keep your manly sword in your scabbard. Let us drink wine, and leave Hapi-Set to his booty."

"No, Nephew, my sword is ready to find a livelier scabbard. How much, Hapi-Set?"

Ramses looked at Nunrah, an awkward man of moderate height, tried to keep his temper, and failed. Of the dozen princes on the expedition, all younger than he, Nunrah was among the least esteemed as a warrior.

"Uncle," said Ramses, his anger showing in the iciness of his tones, "I forbid Hapi-Set to fight you for his trophy lest he shed your royal blood. Perhaps it would be a fairer match if his little black leopard fought you herself. I would bet four gold cups against two that she would send you to your tent with your nether sword bleeding in your hand."

The company laughed. The lecherous Nunrah quaffed wrathfully at his wine. And, Moses thought, Ramses, he, and Sebah, who had said nothing, had all made a dangerous enemy, one who would never forgive or forget this massive indignity.

Old Nebari invested the fortress, this time sending scouts far to the south of Diffima day and night to make sure there were no reinforcements. His choices were limited. He could starve out the Ethiopians with a long, trying siege. He could bypass Diffima and march on Kerma—the capital of Nubia—more than two hundred miles south, with the dangers of unknown diseases and the inevitable wear on his troops. Or, with fewer men available to him now, he could try as he had originally planned to win the day with a costly all-out assault.

None of these options appealed to him. Nebari considered: He had achieved the main purpose, driving the enemy back from Egypt's borders and inflicting on them terrible losses. Why not negotiate? For Egypt, diplomacy had always been a preferred and successful alternative. The princes, led by Ramses, agreed with their general. If the Nubians paid generous reparations, if they agreed to a prisoner exchange, if their king journeyed to Diffima from Kerma and swore renewed fealty to Sety, then the Egyptians would withdraw.

The Nubians, Moses knew, were honorable, if often cruel. They even had a tradition of waiting for an enemy to notify them that their full forces were assembled before attacking. Their breaking of truces with ferocious attacks was undertaken only on the commands of their gods, as interpreted to their somewhat muddleheaded kings by a theocracy of priests.

In any case, those in the fortress—the Nubian princes and lesser tributaries, such as Sebah's father—agreed to send a party to Kerma to ask the principal king of Cush to come north to Diffima to parlay with the Egyptians.

For Moses, it was a rare time of leisure. While the Nubian royal party was journeying from Kerma, he kept his young hostage in his tent, both guarded (for she was a high-spirited girl who might well try to escape) and protected by his handful of trusted retainers. He had time for crocodile harpooning in the Nile with Ramses. They were guided by Nubian princes, who, now that a treaty was to be negotiated, left their fortress and were soon on comradely terms with their erstwhile enemies.

Indeed, Moses took Sebah, on her promise that she would not flee, to visit her father, whose leg had been broken in the battle. They found King Paras in a small, regal room dominated by a rhinoceros skin, with horn intact, on the wall. The king's face was as compact as a black walnut, his diminutive body hard with ropy muscles. He lay bare-chested on an ebony bed, long white hair all but concealing his carved wooden headrest.

Moses left Sebah alone with her father and later that day returned with his hostage to the Egyptian camp. On the following morning, he brought Ramses' physician to the king. The doctor smoothed vile poultices of lizard livers and fish oil on Paras's discolored leg, then, with a warning that he was about to cause him pain, gave him a knotted leather thong to bite. He ordered Moses to pull the leg above the ankle. As Sebah wrung her hands and the king bit the leather and groaned, the doctor pulled above the knee and gingerly fitted the shin bones into place.

He braced the leg with two pieces of aromatic gum tree and gave the king an amulet of the wedjat eye to keep close to his thigh. It represented the restored eye of Horus, blinded by Seth, and thus was said to bring on wholeness and health.

"Without this painful procedure, Your Majesty, your leg would have looked like a broken arrow for the rest of your days. We should have set it three days ago," said the doctor.

"Why?" groaned the king with game humor. "Was I not spared this pain you inflicted on me for three days?"

Each day, Moses continued his walks with Sebah and each day found excuses to make them longer. He was charmed by her cheerful curiosity and her observations. She told him of the succulence of baked ostrich eggs; of how rubbing turpentine over the wild bulls that her people domesticated rid them of virulent biting flies; and of how superior Upper Nile flax was to delta reeds for making rush mats. She plied him with questions about Egypt, from the location of stars in the northern skies, to the names of its spring flowers, to the breeds of its war horses.

One afternoon, on the way back from a visit to her father, Sebah mentioned a trip to Punt that she had taken with Paras on a state visit. Moses told her of his own father's death there and his mother's flight. She listened sympathetically, and described what she remembered of Punt's capital, Zeiloh. "There is a wonderful market there, right beside the sea of Aden. All things come there from deep in Africa. Baboons, gorillas, zebra, even a rhinoceros, snakes"—she looked down at his thigh—"as big as your . . . upper leg." Moses saw her momentary embarrassment and blushed himself. She went on:

"Perfumes, and dried incense and frankincense trees in big clay pots that merchants buy for planting in their own country. And slaves," she said, "naked men and women whose children were torn from them and left behind, perhaps to die, when they were taken." She shook her head, but thought of a jest. Looking at Moses, she added, "Wretched captives of foreign tyrants like I am now—"

"Princess Sebah, please, I never required you to be naked," he interrupted.

She squinted at the thought, then said curtly. "We do not have slaves in Barbaht." As she babbled on, a child's encyclopedia of knowledge, Moses thought uncomfortably of the slaves from Punt he had seen unloaded from the long kebenit boats at Tanis, some dead from the privations of the voyage. The slaves had black torrents of filthy hair and spoke no language anyone could understand. They and their families were settled in hovels worse by far than those of the Hebrews. They did the most repugnant work in Egypt, emptying sand boxes beneath the toilet holes, removing garbage to the river, cleaning feces and discard of all kinds from the abattoirs.

"And the kings of Punt, and the people, what are they like?" Moses asked.

"I learned that the kings are sometimes pale, like you, Hapi-Set, and sometimes as black as I am. They fight, and are deposed, and return, and fight some more. In such a fight, your father and grandfather, no doubt, were killed. I am sorry."

"It was long ago, Princess Sebah," he said, feeling oddly defensive. "Are there royal tombs for those kings who fell?"

"There are temples, royal tombs, nothing so grand as at Thebes, where Father took me when I was very small, but I cannot say for whom they were built. You would like to see your father's, yes? I can ask my father about it."

"No, no," he hastened. For whatever reason, he wished their talk of his father to remain private to them.

As to the princess's own family, her mother was dead and her brothers had been killed in the little kingdom's endless skirmishes with its more powerful neighbors to the north and the south. Her father, she said, had told her he was too old now to sire any more children. Either she or a first cousin would succeed him. Paras had not yet decided, but she was unsure she wanted to be queen, even if he chose her.

When she greeted her father that day, Moses was touched, as always, by their affection for each other. The king so needed her care—and she so yearned to give it—that but for the certain objections of Nebari and his fellow princes, he would have turned her over to her father even before the treaty.

One day, as they returned to the Egyptian camp, Sebah led Moses toward a loop of the Nile that ran sluggishly between banks covered with species of broad-leafed trees he had never seen. In the shallows of the dark river, he saw the backs, large as small islands, of a half-dozen hippopotamuses and two calves. Half-in and half-out of the water, a female was snorting loudly and splashing as if in pain. Moses felt a sympathy for the heavy beast, wondering why she suffered.

"She is having a baby," said Sebah knowledgeably. "Oh, oh," she quickly added, pointing to a crocodile still as death in the grasses above the animal. The predator was waiting for the infant to be born; with the mother too exhausted to defend it, he could dash down and snatch it up.

Moses, who had bested his old rival Ramses only with slings, pulled his from his belt and picked up a stone the size of a pomegranate. In an instant he had whirled it and struck the crocodile, not on the head where he had aimed, but on the back. The reptile sidled away, even as the herd male, seeing the crocodile, roared and swam protectively toward the female.

Sebah clutched Moses' arm admiringly, then, embarrassed, said, "If you had left me my sling, I could have done as well . . . perhaps," she added when he smiled down at her. As they walked on she said, "When I am older, I will go with the men on a crocodile hunt, maybe even for rhinoceroses. My father and his hunters killed the one on the wall of my father's room when I was ten, and he promised me I could go when I am sixteen."

"How did he kill it?" Moses asked. "Pike or pit?"

She looked at Moses mockingly. "A king trap a beast in a pit?" she asked. "Is that the way Egyptians kill rhinoceroses?"

"We have no rhinoceroses, Princess Sebah," he said. "And lions? Your kings kill them with pikes, too?"

"Yes, here, then here," she pointed first to her eye, then to her stomach.

He followed her finger. He had already noted her modest breasts in the linen tunic he had loaned her for sleep before she had gotten her own clothes from the fortress. And he had begun to think of her, young as she was, in connection with his interlude on the boat with the dancing girl, for at fourteen a girl became a woman in Egypt, as a boy became a man at sixteen. "Look here, Sebah," he said, addressing her in the familiar, "I am not returning you to your father so you can get gored by a rhinoceros or trampled by an elephant."

"Would you care?" she asked, trying, but not entirely succeeding, to keep the mocking note in her voice.

Warrior though he was, Moses answered nervously, "Well, I would not want to see you get killed. No. You are . . ." He let the sentence die and looked for a less personal subject. "And the lions to the south. I am told they are as tall as elephants. How are they killed? . . ."

A week later, the treaty was solemnized with a tribute from the Nubians and their allies of exotic animals, gold, aromatic gum, ebony, and ivory; the exchange of documents written on the best leather; and the swift carving by Egyptian artisans of a limestone stele stating the terms of the treaty and showing a triad of Ramses, Nebari, and the Nubian king before the fort.

When Moses surrendered Sebah to her father—without ransom—the grateful king gave him a rhinoceros horn engraved with marching Barbahtian soldiers. Sebah left her father's bedside long enough to accompany Moses to the fortress wall.

The town had quickly recovered from the brief war. People in brightly dyed clothes chatted outside their mud-brick dwellings and in the dirt streets, and bustled in its market, where goods were spread out on palm mats: tropical vegetables, fruits, exotic meats, and Nubian copper and pottery ware.

"If you come back in peace to Nubia," said Sebah, "will you sail on to Barbaht? It is but a week to the south of Kerma. My father will be well by then and would like to see you."

"And you, little princess," asked Moses, "would you be glad to see him who all but killed you that day?"

She looked up, her eyes as black as and far deeper than her skin. "Yes," she said. "I would be glad." Impulsively, she took his hand, squeezed it, and dropped it. "In fact, Hapi-Set, I am not sure I can be happy if I do not see you again."

Moses already knew too much about the vagaries of war, and of life, to make promises. But he resolved to send her each year some small inoffensive and unprovocative gold statuette or perhaps jewelry of precious stones, carnelian, and lapis lazuli.

Chapter Three
The Builders

N THEIR RETURN, RAMSES AND MOSES FOUND THAT PHARAOH Sety's victories had been even more spectacular than theirs. Sety had restored peace—and tributary status—to Syria and Palestine and achieved a truce with the factitious Hittites.

Nebari's report to Sety on the two cousins convinced the Pharaoh that he had two young but able military resources, and he made prompt use of them. In the next seven years, Ramses and Moses carried on Sety's military campaigns. They fought against Libyans, Hittites, renegade Syrians, and the Sea Peoples—Greek islanders who had settled in Palestine and were called Philistines. They returned briefly at times to Egypt, Ramses to his family in Thebes, Moses to Heliopolis, to which his mother, now ailing, had moved with Bes-Ahrin to escape the damp, miasmal months in the delta.

Sometimes now they led Egyptian armies alone, sometimes together. Both suffered injuries and gained substantial victories. Their defeats were few. When a force from Canaan ambushed Moses' army, Ramses was quick and violent to avenge this setback. When Ramses was wounded in a skirmish with pillaging Harrians, Moses, at the head of his own Shardanans, returned the favor. He butchered the Mitanni band and raised its leaders' bodies on stakes alongside the road to Harri.

Peace at least temporarily enforced, the aging Sety could now turn to the temples and palaces that had been on his mind for years. He had picked a site for Pi-Ramessu—"the estate of the Ramessides"—two miles from Tanis. It was to be the capital of Egypt, with palaces for himself, his family, and the main officials, subordinate temples, and dwellings for the ordinary people. Although it would succeed Thebes as the seat of government, the royal tombs would remain upriver at Thebes.

Moses, albeit only twenty-three, was ready to leave the life of a military leader. His uncle Sety's demand that he help Ramses with the construction of Pi-Ramessu was therefore opportune. The palace architects and builders, recognizing the fading health of the imperious Pharaoh, had grown slack, and Sety no longer trusted them to give their best efforts to his plans.

"I want it started before I go to the Valley of the Kings," Sety told his son and nephew. "This lot of builders has no dreams. I am sending them to the Red Sea to dig minor barge ports for copper ore. Bring to Pi-Ramessu the vigor of youth as you did to my wars." Sety fancied himself a wit. "Plan for me victories over limestone instead of Libyans," he smiled.

But it did not take a palace physician to see in the Pharaoh Sety's pallor and occasional trembling that he might be wiser to speed up work on his tomb instead of his new capital.

Ramses and Moses stood on the granite base of a Pharaoh's statue that had fallen into the dirt centuries earlier. The statue lay beside it, its broken arms and trunkless legs covered with convolvulus and bougainvillea. The two young men could see before them the ruins of the older city of Avaris, whose weathered walls and roofless dwellings would have to be cleared for the new town. So far, the Israelites and other slaves had only begun building a small section by the river.

"Can we do it?" Ramses mused, even he overwhelmed with the duty his father had assigned him.

"Not in our lifetimes," said Moses. "We can come close."

Ramses unrolled the papyrus with his new architects' designs on it and turned to orient himself, using as his benchmark a pyramidal tomb surrounded by weeds. Its wall had long since been vandalized for its limestone. Moses held one side of the scroll and the two of them imagined the city-to-be.

"Coming close may be pessimistic," said Ramses. He had been as good an architectural student as Moses. "We'll need a new draft on slaves, thousands more, foremen, taskmasters. We'll need the gods only know how many regiments of militia and soldiers. They'll scream over doing common labor. Carpenters, artisans . . . and getting the limestone, bringing wood downstream, we will need much more mud-brick production. . . ."

Even brash Ramses hesitated as the full force of what was to be done struck him. "The gods . . ." he began.

"The gods? Ramses," Moses said good-humoredly, "*we*, not the gods, are going to have to do it. Do you think Auntie Isis is going to chisel a twenty-ton block for us? There are one hundred and eighty-two *major* gods in Egypt. I know, I put myself to sleep one night counting them. And minor gods? Every ox wallow village from here to Syria has a dozen or so. And not a single one is going to pick up a burin or a mallet."

The crown prince paid the soldiers, artisans, and priests—who were forever burning incense over the limestone for the temples under construction—with bonuses, sacrificial animals, and streets of clean, temporary lodgings. Toward the slaves, Ramses showed only a ruthless practicality. If they were injured, or got sick, or were too old to continue, he simply ended their pitiful wages. If they were lazy or surly, he had them whipped, no matter how many years they had worked.

One day, the sweat streaming off his bare chest and down under his leather belt, Moses organized the unloading of massive pink granite blocks from a barge in the Pelusiac branch of the Nile. The Hebrew slaves used rollers to drag them inch by inch up the grade to where the plans had designated a temple doorway.

The taskmasters applied oaths and exhortations more than whips to keep the slaves moving. Nevertheless, Moses smelled the anger among them. These vassals, he knew, were of the same stock as those who had died bravely in Palestine against Sety's forces. In fact, one of their peculiar customs was to bury their males facing eastward toward their ancient home in Canaan. If someday they focused their fury, it could rain woe on all Egypt.

Finally, he spoke of his concerns to Ramses. "If you work the old Hebrews to death, or send those who are hurt away without any compensation, do you not see that it creates more problems than it solves? They may well be the parents and brothers of your best slaves, who will hate you even if they dare not challenge you. Resentment is a poor partner to labor. The sons will work less hard. And as time goes on, it could become much worse than just resentment."

"Hapi-Set," Ramses replied, "in leading men, whether they are slaves building palaces or soldiers building ramparts, you will just have to let me make the decisions. You know when slaves work hard, I reward them, just as I give extra grain to a young ox pulling our supplies. Old slaves get sent home, old oxen to the meat cutters."

But Moses could not let this be the last word. "You talk about the gods, Ramses. These are children of the gods, too. It makes me uneasy to see them treated as less than human."

Ramses grunted and returned his attention to a revised drawing of the sewers that would lie beneath the palaces.

Just to the south of Pi-Ramessu was a marshy branch of the Nile shaded with scrubby oaks, terebinths, and wild mustard bushes, one of the last hippopotamus wallows in the north. Although it was the reserve of the Pharaohs, it was infrequently visited by them.

At dawn on the workers' free day—Ramses, though not from love, gave even the slaves a day of rest—he and Moses and their hunting party journeyed toward this bit of northern tropics. Neither had ever hunted hippopotamus before, but Ramses had beside him in his chariot a wizened countryman who had led Horemheb on his fabled pursuits of the beasts. Behind them were two carts bearing papyrus skiffs laid athwart. Above the clatter of wheels on the rocky path, Ramses called to Moses:

"Hapi-Set, a wager on who gets the first one?"

"The first 'he,'" said Moses. "If we kill 'she's' there will be no 'he's' for our children."

Moses thought of that day when he and Sebah had seen the bull hippopotamus, gigantic tusks bared, rushing to protect his mate from the crocodile. Could it have been over seven years ago? Yes. He had kept his promise to send her gifts, and each year she had responded. There had come from Barbaht, among other things, carved miniature beasts in ebony and ivory, and a small packet of aromatics to be burned in order to repel the Nile's pervasive insects and to perfume the room.

"Children?" roared Ramses, breaking into Moses' reveries. "The gods may give us no children, Hapi-Set. When Sety dies, it will be Pharaoh this and vizier that and no time for making love or for hunting either. So let it be him or her. We kill what we find."

Their guide ignored the bravado of his masters. When they neared the place of trees and marshes, he pointed to a shady spot where they could leave the horses and chariots. Single file, the hunters entered a world seemingly replicated from the foliage and sluggish water of the jungles far to the south. Papyrus reeds twice the height of men blotted the sun. Ibises flew up with slow grace, henbirds smacked the reed thickets with their frantic wings, and swifts darted and twittered at their approach. Deeper in, Moses heard the snarl of wildcats interrupted in their assaults on birds' nests.

The leathery guide was first, then Ramses, Moses, and the other hunters dragging the skiffs. Their spears and the thick barbed harpoons were tipped with rare Anatolian iron, for bronze would pierce the behemoths' thick skins only with difficulty. The upper harpoon shafts were wrapped with the ends of woven wild bull hide ropes that were tied to floats.

"Through here, son of Seth, gift of Amun," whispered the guide. "But speak no loud words. They will not flee us, but will swim slowly away, except a cow who has a child. The males are the Pharaohs of this swamp. They snap the crocodile's back like it was a carob pod." Ramses clapped his hand on his mouth as a signal to those back in line.

The muddy bank before them was marked by the indentations of crocodile tails. The boat draggers eased their crafts' bows into the shallow water, and the pole men climbed aboard and steadied the skiffs from the sterns. The two spearmen, one of them the guide, boarded and sat amidships. Last came Moses and Ramses with their harpoons.

In the lead boat, Ramses, powerful and at rest, clad only in a loincloth, waited with his hand on his needle-sharp harpoon. The leather ropes around its notched shaft near the head, once wet, would tighten when pressure was put on them. The old hunter, in Ramses' boat, directed the poleman to glide them around a log protruding from the smooth water. The stagnant smell of shore pools and of rotting vegetation and animal matter blended with a strange musky scent. The boats wafted on the opaque water as if they were ghostly scenes from a tomb.

Moses heard a snort, then a second snort. Around the bend lay their quarry. Ramses saw the hippopotamuses first and glanced back at Moses with the same feral gleam in his eyes that Moses had seen when they went into battle together. When Moses' boat passed the tree, he saw the two magnificent beasts. The male was larger even than those he had observed near Diffima. He and the female were in the middle of the slow stream, eyes and ears above water, watching the skiffs without a semblance of concern. Again Moses thought of Sebah.

Ramses, silent as an adder, raised the cumbersome harpoon with its collar of hide rope. Across the twenty-five feet of water, Moses heard the wooden floats clack in the bottom of the boat. The noise made the male snort. The female dove, and with a splash, the male began his dive, too. But the poleman shoved the skiff directly at the monster, and Ramses, bracing against the pole stroke with perfect balance, plunged the harpoon's head into its disappearing back.

Everything happened at once. The enormous power of Ramses' thrust carried him into the water. Foolishly hoping to slow the hippopotamus's dive, Ramses grabbed a float as it shot from the boat and he went planing across the water. But as the beast went deeper and turned underwater, the ropes and floats entangled Ramses. Suddenly, with a splash, he also disappeared beneath the turbid waters.

Both boats set off in pursuit, the lead poleman stabbing the river as if they were being attacked by it. The hippopotamus sought broader water around a second bend. It was at least two minutes before the boats came around it and saw Ramses again skimming on the surface in the broad wake of the animal.

"Let go, Ramses! Idiot, let go!" Moses screamed.

The hippopotamus made a wide circle, smooth as a boomerang's flight, giving Moses time enough for his spearman to grab a float. Now, at least, the creature had to drag a skiff as well as Ramses. In a moment, the old hunter grappled a float against his skiff. But the wounded hippopotamus still towed his tormentor and the two boats as if they were straws.

His angry circular path was making a small whirlpool in the river, smashing the boats together, spinning them as the hide ropes tangled in the poles. Determinedly, the hunters and Ramses, he sometimes above, sometimes below water, hung to the floats. Moses, furious at his comrade for not letting go, thought of jumping in and wresting the float from his hand. But he knew if he succeeded and Ramses lived, the future Pharaoh would never forgive him.

While Moses thought frenetically of alternatives, the monster surfaced and charged Moses' skiff. He could see the madness in the animal's huge dark eyes as his mouth gaped, the tusks big as throwing sticks and more lethal. With a lunge that lifted his colossal shoulders from the water, the animal clamped his mouth on the side of the skiff, and dissatisfied with his first bite, opened it, chomped on it again, and submerged.

Moses' spearman amidships screamed. For an instant, before the boat disintegrated, Moses saw the float snatched from his hand and the man's lower body fly into the air, his leg snatched off by the tusks and a cascade of blood in its place. Even as Moses was hurled into the water, he knew that the enraged hippopotamus would destroy the other boat and Ramses would be doomed as well unless Moses could stab the beast in the eye, mouth, or throat and thus kill or disable him. The poleman paddled wildly for shore, while Moses swam toward the other skiff, which was making wild paths around the broad river.

The old hunter snatched the pole from his poleman and thrust it out to Moses, who reached up once, missed, and grasped it on the second try. Then, as the wiry guide shifted from side to side to keep the boat from tipping over, Moses clambered aboard and grabbed up the spear that lay in the bottom.

"Get me closer!" he screamed at the poleman, who still pluckily held the float. The man dragged at the hide rope and the skiff rushed across the roiled water to just above where the hippopotamus had dived. "In the mouth! The mouth!" yelled the old guide, still shifting his weight this way and that to keep the boat from overturning.

At that moment, Ramses bobbed to the surface, disentangled from the float ropes. His face was pale, whether from some underwater blow or too much water in his lungs, Moses did not know. Ordinarily a strong swimmer, Ramses semiconsciously patted the water as if it were a greyhound puppy, barely managing to stay afloat.

Moses was close enough now to reach for his cousin's left hand, but suddenly the water exploded as if a millstone had been dropped into a palace pond. The huge head and back of the hippopotamus surfaced, the harpoon shaft broken. But the ropes, all near the implanted head, were still intact, taut against the ropes held by the skiff man. The blood pumped from the animal's back wound like a gruesomely flowering hibiscus.

As if the water creature knew that the first savage thrust had come from Ramses, he wheeled with a rush of waters toward the half-floating man. Moses almost caught his comrade's hand again, but his fingers were slippery from the water and he could not grip it. There was no time to try again. He cocked the iron-headed spear of Syrian fir.

The tomb-door mouth gaped again as the beast propelled himself toward Ramses' head. Moses' stalwart body tensed in the bow. The poleman, following the action minutely, jammed his pole into the river bottom to give Moses the best possible earnest. The waves of the animal's charge turned Ramses' inert body, belly forward, toward the monster's mouth. Clear as a classroom drawing of a cut of veal, Moses saw the wet, pale mouth and throat, fronted by the two deadly tusks, white and unchallengeable as columns. He took a breath and sprung with every measure of power in his thighs and calves.

His spear plunged into the beast's mouth, so close to him that he could smell the steamy rottenness of the animal's diet of weeds. The hippopotamus roared in pain and slammed shut his immense jaws on the spear shaft, even as the iron sunk deep into his throat. With a crash of waves, the hippopotamus submerged, ripping Moses from the boat. Then a second massive bite underwater snapped the fir shaft, and Moses felt the rough-skinned body slam him.

When Moses came to, he was lying beside his chariot and Ramses was squatting over him. Dazed as he was, Moses saw the wide smile amidst the crisscross of abrasions on Ramses' face.

"Thank Hapi, thank Repit, thank every river god there is," said Ramses with genuine relief. "I thought you would never come around. He got away, you know. A prodigious bull."

"Oh, Ramses, spare me that insanity."

"Someday we will go back for him."

The old peasant guide was standing beside Ramses with a tiny clay jug in his hand. "The animal's spirit is halfway to the land of the dead. He will die before three days are out. His wounds will not leave him. You need not hunt him, mighty sons of Horus and Osiris, for the crocodiles, minions of Sobek, will kill him and eat him when he weakens."

He offered Moses a sip from the jug. It smelled vile and tasted bitter. But it cleared his head.

"What is it?" he said, coughing.

"It is resin, Great Prince," said the countryman, "mixed with wormwood. And the grindings of a hippopotamus tusk."

"I thank you for the draught, good guide. Tusk grindings are as close as I ever want to be to a hippopotamus again."

That night, Ramses came to the house of Moses, who was wincing as his servant rubbed him with turpentine to heal his scratches and the sprain in his right arm from where the hippopotamus had snapped the spear. In his hands, Ramses held a piece of gold sculpture the size of a child's head. It was the goddess Tawaret with the body of a hippopotamus, the legs of a lion, and a crocodile's tail. It would buy a whole lagoon full of hippopotamuses. Ramses put it beside Moses.

"They told me how you saved me," Ramses said. He was almost too embarrassed to speak further, but he went on. "I was a fool, Hapi-Set. I risked my life as well as yours, for I knew if I were in trouble, you might have to pay the full price to save me. I am in your debt for all time."

Now Moses felt his throat tighten. "You saved me outside Diffima. Had you not, I would not have been able to help you today. So, in effect, by saving me you saved yourself."

"Don't be clever, comrade vizier," Ramses replied, as gentle and yet as serious as Moses had ever heard him. "In saving me, you also saved Egypt. For I risked its life, too, in the Nile today, along with yours and mine."

On another free day, Ramses arrived at Moses' quarters in mid-afternoon with unadorned tunics and sandals in his arms. They were the garments of artisans. "Clothes for us, Hapi-Set. With them, we are master carpenters, newly paid. The sundial's shadow is lengthening. We ride to Avaris-outside-the-Walls."

Moses was almost always amenable to Ramses' spirited ideas for adventure. During the last week, he had argued with quarrymen and stonecutters who had never worked with the white limestone of Roiaou before. And they had complained about alternating it with dark red quartzite from east of Pi-Ramessu for Sety's palace. "It has never been our way, oh Prince," they kept muttering. Moses was ready for a diversion, and the two young men quickly donned the tunics.

"I would rather dress like a quarryman," said Moses, studying himself in the wall mirror. "I have become one."

Ramses laughed mightily. "Oh, we will find quarry for you, little Hapi-Set."

The two counterfeit artisans jogged along in good humor on their donkeys to Avaris-outside-the-Walls, the site of the delta's most notorious pleasure houses. There, skilled workers, superintendents, and the occasional priest in disguise could forget their labors at Pi-Ramessu for a while.

Moses had no doubt about Ramses' intentions. Since Ramses had joshed him into his first sexual encounter at age sixteen, Moses had been as active as any of his fellow princes. Sexual virility was expected, even required. The people of his time thought homosexuality went against *Ma'at*, the natural order. "I will father a hundred children by twenty wives to make sure one is like me," Ramses had once bragged to Moses, who already knew enough about the intrigues of the harems to reject the idea of more than one or, at most, two wives.

Moses, instead of dallying promiscuously with dancing girls; unstable, often treacherous temple prostitutes; and other lower-class women, preferred more sensible companions. At his most high-minded, he thought only of Sebah. But gradually fidelity gave way to ordinary young lust. He had installed one at least reasonable lutist, singer, or acrobat after another in his tent when at war, and continued to do so in his well-furnished house in Tanis. After a few months to a year he had become bored, given them gifts of silver and gold, and as kindly as he could, sent them away.

Judiciously, he had required his ladies to insert a ball of lint soaked in honey and laced with ground-up acacia, carob, and dates in their gateway of generation to make sure his seeds fell on temporarily barren ground—more gentle for all concerned than the onions used as pessaries by the poor.

What was jocularly called The Temple of the Working Man at Avaris-outside-the-Walls was, in fact, a former temple to the cat goddess Bastet. Its priests had moved to a new shrine in Itjawy, leaving behind its singers and musicians. These had been joined by local dancing girls and servers of drink and fruit. At the sight of Ramses and Moses, the brothel's proprietor rushed unctuously to them. Ramses put in his hand a piece of gold. "You remember me?"

The gold brought instant recall, a smile with two missing front teeth, and a knowing look. "Oh, son of Horus, master carpenter, how could I forget?" He looked at Moses, smiled fawningly, and continued to Ramses. "All is as you wished, immortal constructor."

The two princes in disguise sat on low chairs with backs, their legs outstretched onto rush mats. Other men of all ages sat on similar chairs or stools, or lounged on dirty cushions, drinking from goblets of beer or wine. On the walls were well-executed colored pictures of men with enormous, elongated organs beside naked girls or intently watching couples, or three and sometimes four women and men engaged in expressionless coition. Besides normal positions, there were embraces surely beyond physical possibility, even for the professional contortionists who were features of such bawdy places as this.

In front of a wall covered with a scrim of linen, four singers and four dancing girls—all wearing polished bronze necklaces, armlets, and bracelets—performed to castanets, tambourines, and a hand-held harp. The musicians were distinctly less attractive than the singers and dancers.

Moses was struck most by one of the singers. She was dressed only in a short tunic. She was strong-bodied and exceedingly pale, with malachite green circling her dark, unreadable eyes. In a contralto voice, she sang with her soprano companions the old Egyptian songs of lotuses, water lilies, lost loves, falling stars, and the passions of the gods and goddesses.

"You like her, my Hapi-Set," Ramses said when she had made her third performance and night had fallen. The servers had lit more oil lamps, and heavy wine from pottery jars had slurred his speech. "What treasures she must carry beneath that tunic. Look at those thighs. Imagine their confluence. I will buy her for you. It will cost me a donkey's worth of gold *qites*."

After more wine, and her fourth appearance, Moses was sure she was singing to him, and at Ramses' urging, he went outside—where he urinated—and then up an outside stairway to the roof. There were small partitioned rooms, open to the aureoled stars. A soft breeze from the Nile fluttered lamps of perfumed oil on the floor.

When the pale woman came to him, Moses quickly removed his garments. He undid her braided belt, passion and the wine making him fumble. She slipped her tunic over her head. Her full breasts were tipped with red nipples the size of armor scales. He started to take off her flimsy loincloth, but she whispered urgently, "Not yet, oh mighty organ of Min. First kiss my nipples so I may overflow you like the oils of Byblos when you enter me." Moses obliged, more and more driven.

At last, he could wait no more, and she was breathing and moaning as he shifted his mouth from her nipples to her lips and back again. He dropped her loincloth as they stood, and prepared to open her lower lips, to enter her. But when he did, he was revolted at what he felt. There, amid a strange, wet confusion of male and female parts, was a tiny penis, firm as a straightened little finger. "Murderous Seth!" he croaked, feeling his gorge with all its wine and fruit rise.

At that instant, he heard a roar of familiar laughter and a flaming torch was thrust through the door, illuminating the hermaphrodite's grotesque organs and her hands, hiding her face in the shame of her betrayal. Moses vomited until he was weak, as the woman-man ran down the stairs, and Ramses howled again.

They rode back to Tanis in darkness. Moses, sick and sobering, would not speak. It was not just from anger at Ramses. It was also from anger at the hermaphrodite. But his ire toward him-her gradually lifted. *Tawaret's tits!* he thought, *how terrible to go through life like that, always an object of disgust.* Before they reached home, Ramses, feeling guilty, although he seldom apologized for anything, said, in substitute, "Well, Hapi-Set, you once said you wanted to know everything."

Even though Moses often yielded to Ramses' thirst for diversion, he continued to spend long evenings on his studies. But now his goals were not just to sate a ravenous curiosity. For example, ever since he had journeyed above the first cataract, he had been assembling records of when the Nile had flooded most and least. He planned to combine his findings with the records of hot and cold years, rainy and dry years, windy and calm years, and the weather that had preceded them. By such means, he hoped to predict what the Nile's flow would be. The temple records were well kept and his old priest-teachers would help locate them.

It would be a work that could immeasurably benefit the agriculture and economy of Egypt. Estimates could be made for the week when flooding would begin (when the lands became unusable), and for when the Nile would recede (when seeds could be sown so goats and sheep could be sent out to press them into the earth). These dates, in turn, would help determine marketing and shipping schedules for grain, for river fishing, and for the other myriad activities connected with the annual inundations. Millions of *debens* were made or lost on the timing of the stages of the Nile.

Moses was certain he could do better than the court magicians. He had seen them parading around with a wooden god Anubis in a three-foot-long boat model. When a petitioner asked the god a question about the Nile, for instance, the boat would "magically" dip forward for yes, and shake violently for no—manipulated, of course, by the priests.

Yet, even the wizards sometimes had valuable lessons to teach. They used flights of herons, Nile geese, and orioles for their prophesies, along with the number of days in a year of rain and sunshine, of wind and calm. And often they produced accurate results amidst much waving of wands and recitations of spells.

The ground was not even cleared for the new capital when Moses was called one day to Sety in his summer palace in Tanis. Under Egypt's concord with Nubia, the Pharaoh needed a replacement for his ambassador to Nubia. That envoy administered the trade in ivory, aromatic gums, animal hides, and ebony between the second and sixth cataracts. His nephew, although only twenty-five, was a natural choice, thought Sety. He had, among other virtues, been in the battles that led to the accord. There was also his friendship with the king of Barbaht, Sebah's father, and his genius in disciplines from mathematics to foreign languages, which even Sety regarded with a certain awe. Thinking again of the skimpy girl who had so fascinated him, Moses was more than willing. She would be twenty-two now, of marriageable age and then some.

Ramses was unhappy with the removal of his friend and chief assistant. But he saw the benefits of it for Egypt. And he was an obedient son. At the quay to bid Moses farewell, he said, trying to be lighthearted, "Why no dancing girls?"

"Too long a trip to put up with their squabbling," Moses replied in kind.

"Do not trifle with me, old friend," said Ramses, giving him a powerful but friendly rap on the skull. "I know the reason you are leaving the girls behind. And she has a black face. Her name is . . ." Ramses searched his memory.

"Sebah," Moses helped him.

"She is the daughter of a minor king, Hapi-Set," said Ramses, turning serious. "If I were you, I would make my first wife a princess of the first rank. The king at Kerma has daughters, and there are others in Syria . . . everywhere."

"Dear Ramses," said Moses amiably, "after your choice for me in Avaris-outside-the-Walls, I am not sure I want you to pick my mates for me."

Ramses was briefly nonplussed. He turned to less serious matters. "You have the wine I gave you?"

"In my locker. I will savor every drop." It would be the best, sweet, he knew, like all wine, but not cloying.

"Are you going to grow a beard, Lord Ambassador? You still look as young as you did that day at Semna."

"A beard? Never," said Moses.

"Me neither, nor wear one if I can avoid it." Yet, as Ramses knew, Pharaohs for a thousand years all wore false beards.

The two friends seemed reluctant to part. And suddenly, both young men grew solemn. It was almost as if the comradeship they had shared for so long, and on which they had both so depended, was, in some measure, ending.

This time, Moses traveled on a royal barge, a hundred-and-sixty-foot-long sea palace, its bow and stern curved upward, with a giant sail rigged to a sturdy mast. Six courtiers and a magician, the latter to make sure the winds blew steadily, accompanied him in smaller cabins forward and aft. His four horses were stabled near his own cabin amidships. Various other retainers and staff followed on a more modest craft.

The barge called at Heliopolis on the way upriver. The Princess Mutempsut seldom left there now. She was cared for by the dwarf, Bes-Ahrin. What had seemed only an aversion to humidity had proved to be a gradually wasting disease. Her body, as well as her will, had always been frail. She had rallied only in desperation, as when she saved Bes-Ahrin from Sety, and when she fled Punt and substituted Moses for her dead child.

Moses had made it a point to visit her at least once in each of the three seasons. But, in spite of her adoration of him, it was more as a dutiful than a loving son that he came. He could not have imagined that what caused his detachment was the year and a half he had spent at the breast and in the firm, warm arms of his true mother, the Hebrew slave Jochebed.

The princess met him on the roof of her small palace, its parapet lined with ultramarine faience inlaid with designs of water lilies, papyrus shoots, and irises. The tiles of the floor depicted a lagoon with ducks, fish, turtles, and young crocodiles. Mutempsut's arms were a melancholy contrast to these bright scenes. They were no bigger around than a tent peg. A servant protected her colorless face from the summer sun with a pale blue linen shade. "My prince, my Hapi-Set," she said, valiantly rising from her armchair. "My son."

Moses held her to his chest, feeling with alarm her tininess beneath the robe of linen so fine only royalty and the very rich could afford it. Her emotional sentimentalism made him cringe and his inability to return her love made him feel guilty. "Your son, the Pharaoh's ambassador to Nubia," he said lightly, glad to be able to use his title for the pleasure it gave her.

"I wish I were well enough to visit you there, Hapi-Set," she said when he was seated beside her. Her servant brought them figs, grapes, honey cakes, and rare coconut flesh. "I have heard such wonders about Nubia but have never been there. Only to Punt." She paused, and mused, "Can it really be so many years ago that I brought you back?"

Moses, whose brain worked with such mathematical precision, had never been clear on when she did come back, and she had always avoided details about Punt or his father.

"Can you remember exactly how many years ago it was, Mother?" he asked.

She smiled uncertainly, looked nervous and said, "Twenty-three? Twenty-four? My beautiful prince, the years have flown so fast I cannot remember."

He was unsatisfied, and the subject now raised, he went on, "And my father, the son of the king. During our battles with Nubia, they had Puntite allies, but I did not concern myself with it. We were at war. Now, I will be asked about my father. What shall I say? For even though his direct line was deposed, I must have kinfolk among the Puntite officers whom I shall meet. What was he like? What details can you tell me?"

"Your father was a renowned prince, a manly warrior, and wise," his mother lied. "The family had Mediterranean blood. That is why you are not dark."

"But was he tall or short? Are there stelae to him that I could see if I journey to Punt?" Moses persisted.

She was too ill to withstand him. "I have no doubt that there are stelae. For those enemies who killed him have now been succeeded by a cousin. I have heard that there is a tomb and a stele built to him and his father by this cousin, for his body was preserved and hidden until his murderers had themselves been overthrown." She wanted to say no more about it. "Come, Moses, your visits are so short. No more talk that brings me sorrow. Tell me how the new capital goes? Will young Ramses be successful in building it? How can he spare you?"

And they were again in familiar modes, conversing about safe things. When Moses parted that day, he felt as distant from her as Nineveh, and she, doomed soon to join Thoth, forever victim of her lie, remained hopelessly hungry for his love.

Moses was glad that he had to arrive in Nubia in time for its national day celebrations and thus could truncate his visit to his mother. After a second day, he touched her nose with his, the customary Egyptian kiss. A few minutes later, Mutempsut summoned Bes-Ahrin, who entered with a short stride as precise as a hard-running pony's to take Moses to his barge.

Chapter Four
The Ambassador

T O THE SOUTH, EACH TIME THE NILE NARROWED BETWEEN CLIFFS instead of banks, the water grew roily and Moses and his staff pitched in on the ten oars. At the cataracts, porters on the land unloaded the goods, carried them around the rapids, and stowed them on another ship. The last portage was at the third cataract and then the Nile began to run between, near tropical trees raucous with the harsh calls of seldom seen birds.

At last, around a curve of the river, Moses saw the quays of Kerma, massed with people, for smaller fleet boats had earlier arrived with the news of the Egyptian delegation's approach. When Moses stepped ashore, the king's vizier greeted him in a gold-laced tunic, in his hand an ebony wand surmounted by an Eye of Horus, a powerful amulet. Beside him was the high priest of Sobek, the crocodile god, his fat chest bare and hairy, wearing a loincloth of many folds of thin brown-dyed wool and a panther skin on his back, the tail looping down to his ankles.

The priest unrolled a scroll, bowed, and handed it to the vizier. That worthy read from it a welcome to the exalted ambassador from Egypt, and, in the name of the king, invited him to honor Nubia with a visit in his palace throne room. Moses, in turn, thanked the assembly, then praised the king and Nubia in formal and extravagant terms—the language of diplomacy, stelae, royal documents, and the walls of tombs.

Lesser kings were at the quay, and nothing pleased Moses more than the sight of Paras in a leopard skin with a rhinoceros-horn headdress and a gleaming smile of welcome. His presence led Moses to hope that Sebah would also be in Kerma for the festivals attending the arrival of an ambassador from Egypt, and that she would still be unwed. Moses broke with ritual and embraced the white-haired Paras instead of formally taking his forearm.

Before the king of Nubia, a somber, crafty old man, Moses stood with large hands outstretched, palms open to show absence of malice. The monarch looked uncomfortably at this ambassador who—just as Egypt rose above Nubia—towered over him despite his soaring blue ceremonial crown. He adjusted the crown, less ornate than a Pharaoh's but, nevertheless, decorated with two stylized cobras, two young oryx horns, and a cluster of green-dyed ostrich plumes. Then he bowed slightly and that done, with a sigh, let his attendants remove the crown and replace it with a simpler and lighter helmet of lion skin, the ruff intact.

That was the signal for the festival to begin. In the adjoining lengthy hall, a dozen temple singers chanted in rhythms foreign to Moses, and dancers, fully clothed and more chaste-looking than in Egypt, pranced in rapid, high-stepping patterns.

Moses made a point of meeting and saying a few words to each Nubian official, and only his discipline kept him from beginning and ending with King Paras, for beside him now stood his daughter, the Princess Sebah, a half-head taller than her father, and without a husband.

When decorum permitted, Moses walked toward them, nervous and wishing he had something potent and calming in his goblet, even the notoriously bitter Nubian beer. Instead, he sipped the overly sweet mix of fermented date and carob-seed juice that the king had ordered his kitchen to prepare for the occasion.

Sebah was now a woman. His prediction that she would one day be attractive had proved a prodigious underestimation. The thin ben-nut tree had become a tall black pomegranate. Her white linen shift, unlike those of Egyptian ladies of the court, covered not one but both her breasts. Still, he saw their fullness through the semitransparent silk outer robe.

She extended her hand to his forearm, a greeting only the daughter of a king would accord a man, and it lingered there. Then, with a jangle of the bracelets on her bare forearm, she withdrew it, never taking her black eyes from his brown ones.

"The eminent Prince Hapi-Set honors his former captive and her noble father," she said, her deep-toned voice no longer the chattery reed pipes of a child.

Overwhelmed, Moses wanted to say simply, "Sebah, you are beautiful, more even than I dreamed you would be." But a number of other guests were around them. Never taking his eyes from hers, he murmured, "Gracious Princess of Barbaht, it is you and your warrior father, the incarnation of Min, as leopard, who do me honor." Aware his sense of protocol was failing in face of Sebah's startling allure, he bowed to her father. "Your cloak is of a leopard you killed yourself, mighty King?"

Paras smirked with amusement at Moses' maladroitness before his daughter. "Actually, Prince Hapi-Set, it is a small tiger skin. And yes, thanks to your and your physician's good offices all those years ago, I was able to dispatch her with my lance, although not without some help."

Moses blushed at his mistake, then looked with surprise at Sebah, recalling her father's promise to take her on a rhinoceros hunt. "Help? From her?"

"No," the king reassured him, "I have let her accompany me on my hunts, but only as unstoppable giver of well-meant advice, not as lanceman or archer. For I confess to you, my days of killing tigers without bowmen are over."

Paras, after asking Moses about how his life had been in the north, tactfully drew the few guests around them into conversation to allow the two young friends a few moments of quiet talk. Unable to resist any longer, Moses whispered: "Princess Sebah . . . Sebah . . . you reminded me that you were my captive. But when I saw you, so . . . beautiful, why not say it . . . you became my captor, and I became your captive."

"Fool prince," she replied in a low, passionate voice that none but he could hear, "for eight years I have dreamed of hearing you say I am beautiful. But if, as you say, I am now your captor, I will not free you as you once freed me."

"I knew you would wait," he said.

"I knew you would come," she smiled.

"If the Pharaoh had not appointed me, I would have visited you on my next voyage south to see my mother."

"A long way," she said.

"To match my long thoughts."

Next morning, Moses paid a courtesy call to Paras at the comfortable palace provided them by the king of Nubia. It gave the young ambassador a legitimate excuse to talk with them informally, as the three had at Diffima. In the course of their chat, Moses mentioned that his mother had said a tomb had been built for his grandfather and father in Punt.

"I know nothing of it," said the king. "I do recall the palace revolt twenty-five or so years ago. It is a changeable land and the tombs of their kings are piffling compared even to those of magistrates in Thebes. Still, a tomb to your father is not impossible. The king is now your cousin, son of one of your father's brothers. I go to Punt every few years and am scheduled to pay him a visit . . ."

Moses and Sebah looked at each other, and her father did not miss the glances. He smiled at them, and went on with hardly a pause, ". . . and it would do me honor if the ambassador of mighty Sety to Ethiopia could find a way to accompany me and my daughter when we go there. If I am not mistaken, Egypt does not have an ambassador to Punt. Your cousin would surely welcome a visit . . ." he smiled again, ". . . so long as you do not assert your right to his throne."

Moses spent the next morning at the celebration of Nubia's national day.

He sat in a pavilion and sweated despite retainers gently waving ostrich-plume parasols over him, the rulers, their children, and their priests, as the Nubian royal boat floated past. Its decks were crowded with men tootling flutes and women rattling sistrums. That afternoon, he stood beside the high priest of the Amun-Cush cult as the temple doors were opened, revealing the gilded god himself. Sacred lettuce heads were heaped around his feet, and Moses watched as two dozen lesser priests hoisted the statue on a litter.

Moses and the other royalty were in the forefront of the procession that made its way from the temple near the Nile to higher ground, through throngs carrying flowers and still more priests holding up smaller statues of the falcons, ibises, serpents, and vultures that represented major gods. Tens of thousands of Nubians had come from hundreds of miles away to chatter, perspire, and eat the sweets, fruits, and fermented juices sold by hawkers. The highlight of the national day was when a black Min was placed on a pedestal beside Amun and the king released the pigeons and trilling canaries that were all supposed to fly north toward Thebes. About half did as they were trained to do.

Late that night, weary as they all were, Moses visited Paras and Sebah again. They sat on the roof of the unpretentious palace, listening to the southern sounds of night-birds cawing and, far off, cries of deadly predatory cats. Incense, scented with cloves, burned to keep away the insects. "King Paras, this is not my style," Moses said. "I would be insane to say I prefer the moans of dying men to the chants of priests. But compared to what I have learned about diplomacy in these few days, there is a kind of welcome simplicity to war."

"And in hunting . . ." said Paras. "I feel as you do."

"And in taking walks beside the Nile," said Sebah.

"You cannot do that here," said Paras.

"Unless there was some understanding between you and Sebah and me," said Moses. "Can she and I spend some time talking to each other, to see whether such an understanding might exist? Tell me frankly, King Paras, do you find unworthiness in me? I beg you to be honest."

Clearly, the king had thought the matter out.

"She has been my friend and my daughter," he said. "You returned her to me untouched. She has told me how you and Ramses protected her. You gave me a leg on which to walk, and though I hobble a bit, I do not even need a stick. I wish to ask you, Prince Hapi-Set: do you find unworthiness in yourself?"

Moses thought of the hermaphrodite at Avaris-outside-the-Walls. He thought of the other women whom he had, in effect, simply used and dismissed. Cruel, yes. It was, in a way, worse than merely trafficking with whorish dancing girls, for in that no feelings were at risk on either side. He considered the pillaging and rape and looting his men had done after their victories, a commonplace of war. He thought of his impaling the Harrian marauders.

"Yes, some," said Moses.

"Enough to corrupt you, to make me hate you?" Sebah broke in, upsetting her father. "I cannot believe it."

"Sebah, quiet," Paras said to her, the first harshness Moses had ever heard in him toward her. "But answer her."

"No, not enough to corrupt me," Moses replied. "I have killed; I have been merciless; I have used people to my own purposes. But when I know I have done wrong, I have regretted it. I try to learn from it."

Paras relaxed, but continued, no less seriously, "You Egyptians take gifts to the temple of Hathor, or Ptah, or Mut, who knows? You ask them to give you a dozen wives, fifty children so you can be happy. I am dubious of too many gods, as I am of too many wives. When the mother of Sebah died, I did not want to remarry. I was no eunuch. I did what I did. But I did not bind myself in another marriage."

Moses looked at this good old man. "If we should decide we want to marry, I will vow that my heart will be only Princess Sebah's."

"Father," Sebah said, lifting her arms in exasperation, setting the golden bangles to clicking like castanets, "I waited for this Egyptian all these years. You have brought forward princes of Punt, of Upper and Lower Ethiopia, even that crown prince of Ophir. But I knew in my heart they were merely tests you were putting me to. Do you think I do not know your heart?"

Moses saved Paras the embarrassment of exposure.

"King," he said, "we will talk, come to a decision for marriage, or against it. A-A-And . . ." he began to stammer.

"And," said Sebah, laughing at the two posturing men, "he is saying that if we decide 'no,' which is hard for me to imagine, he will, with due regrets on both our parts, return me to you as he finds me now, pure as . . ."

"As a yearling wild cow," said Paras with a laugh.

Moses saw Sebah each evening of the three days before Paras and his entourage returned to Barbaht. Two aunts who had accompanied her to Kerma walked discreetly behind them as they strolled on the pathways that led through the capital's Egyptianate gardens, past the royal ponds, and down to the Nile.

At times, Sebah enjoined them to stay back when she and Moses wandered into dark copses of palm and carob. They clucked and obeyed, more fearful of Sebah's wrath than her father's. Once out of their sight, the two lovers pressed their noses against each other's, then, in defiance of Egyptian customs, their lips as Moses knew the Greeks did. He lusted for her so powerfully that it made him dizzy. She, aware of it, breathed heavily and pressed against him until he found a jolting, trembling relief. "Someday, it will be so for me," she said, half holding up his large sagging body.

"Would it were now," he shuddered.

Moses saw the Barbaht party off at the quay for their voyage up beyond the sixth cataract and into the Blue Nile. He promised Paras that as soon as he could negotiate the trade agreements, the accords for river transports, the contracts for Egyptian builders and other artisans to raise warehouses, palaces, and other structures in Nubia, he would send word of when he could come to Barbaht for the trip to Punt.

"If all is as it is now with Sebah and me, when we come back from Punt I would like to talk with you about a wedding," he told the older man. He and Sebah had already spoken of it, and Moses now wanted to make this formal declaration.

Paras answered with equal seriousness. "If I am to lose her, you would be my preference. I know you would want to take her to Egypt . . ."

"Unless I stayed on here as ambassador. The Pharaoh Sety is—"

Paras interrupted him, ". . . slowly dying. We all know that. Is there any hope for a miracle?"

Moses shook his head.

"It would be an extraordinary honor to have the vizier of all Egypt as my son-in-law," said Paras. "But a sad one, as well. If Sebah stayed with me, with you as her husband, she would succeed me and be queen of Barbaht, and a worthier one than Queen Hatshepsut"—who had reigned over Egypt for thirty-six years. "I have trained her well for that role. Without such a husband, or if she is absent, I would choose my nephew, a just, kind man."

"We would visit often. Or you could come to Pi-Ramessu."

"And leave my beautiful land, my brave, quarrelsome, and endlessly engrossing people?"

"For a man who spears rhinoceroses and tigers, all things are possible," said Moses, trying to make their talk less painful. "Could Sebah not reign from Egypt?"

"No, only from Barbaht." He sighed. "She has decided that reigning a good man's heart is better than reigning a country, Hapi-Set. That is the way of life."

Moses took his friend, the king, by his forearm, then embraced him again, risking a second embarrassment for them before the Nubians and Paras's courtiers.

For Moses, the four months in Kerma dragged on. He thought of Sebah's eyes, darker than the Nile on a moonless night, and of the orange southern moon, big as a cartwheel, gilding her black upper arms when they emerged from the shadows of trees. When she did not dominate his mind, he thought of solving the mystery of his father in Punt. More mundanely, he delved into the studies that had always diverted him: the climate, the river, the flights of birds and insects, and the manufacture of all things—from tiny ebony carvings to tapestries to mysterious sculptures of obsidian to the habits of people. For love did not stale his curiosity.

At last, he was ready for a long report to Sety. He had written frequent shorter dispatches to him and informal notes to Ramses, and had received news of Pi-Ramessu from his friend in return. But as plenipotentiary for his uncle, he had waited to write a detailed message. Now he could attest to substantial progress in trade and diplomacy.

There were, he wrote the Pharaoh, a few concerns: Ethiopia was building and buying war chariots that might, under some future king, be used against Egypt; some merchants were transhipping ivory from the south to Murzak in Libya, ivory that Moses had contracted for Egypt (he was seeking to have the king of Nubia hang the merchants as a warning to any other corrupt traders). And certain warehouses in ports on the South Red Sea were withholding large quantities of aromatic gums from trade in hopes of driving up prices. It gave Moses a legitimate reason to go to Punt to clear up the matter, and Barbaht was on the way.

After a week's sojourn in Barbaht, Moses and two of his three chief Egyptian aides joined Paras, Sebah, and ten of the king's retainers for the six-day donkey trip across the desert, then through passes between the dry coastal plateaus to the Red Sea. The two young people made no pretense of distance on the way. When the path was wide enough, they rode abreast, talking of the leather-clad people of the land and their herds of strange, long-horned cattle. Among the juniper groves, they saw ancient conelike burial mounds surrounded by low walls. In a parched market town, Paras called a halt to inspect ivory-handled swords of copper and exquisite red pottery jars with black tops. Moses bought swords for Bes-Ahrin and Ramses, and a quartz figure of Amun in his incarnation as a ram for Mutempsut.

"What will your mother think of my ways?" asked Sebah. "She sounds so. . . . reserved, and I am so outspoken."

"I am not sure she will think of your ways," said Moses. "She will think about whether it will mean she will see me less, or whether you will find her still pretty, or how the court gossips will assess our marriage."

"Hapi-Set, why do you speak of her so coldly, you who are so fair with all people, to a fault even? When we have been together a long time, will you be the same toward me?"

Moses looked at her, straight, swathed in gauzy white against the heat, her strong black arms glistening with light sweat. "If I show coldness toward you, Sebah, then the Nile will overflow in November and the sun will rise in the west."

"Mighty words, Prince," she said, then with a catch in her voice, added fervently, "I wish we were married this night."

At the beginnings of the highlands, they encountered a Puntite donkey caravan, a line of men and beasts a hundred yards long, bound for Barbaht and Nubia. The leader, who spoke a strange dialect of Egyptian, told Paras he carried leopard, lion, and kudu skins, civet musk, feathers of sunbirds, parrot, and the like. "Be cautious, King of Barbaht, son and brother to Re," said the Puntite, nervously stroking his bald head and braided beard. "We came on bandits. There may be more."

"And those who approached you?"

"The gods favored us." He gave his slave who walked behind him leading a loaded donkey a sharp order in the guttural Puntite tongue. The slave grinned and brought forth a severed head, the neck salted with natron to dry up the blood. "Here is their leader, almighty Paras," said the caravan leader. "We take this head to your vizier in Barbaht in hopes of bounty, unless you wish to redeem him here."

Paras nodded at his chief retainer, who dug into his purse for pieces of gold and silver. The Puntite went on. "Be cautious, also, Good Monarch, at the palace. Those whom the present king deposed ten years ago are dead, of course. But not their followers. He who rules Punt today may not rule tomorrow."

Paras looked concerned. "Is there active fighting in the capital?"

"No, not yet. And even if you find a new king, he will be eager to curry favor with, not kill, the renowned Paras who rules the land to which so many Puntite goods go overland."

Paras had his courtier fling the bandit's head into the thickets. Two miles along the route they found the beheaded bandit suspended shoulders down from a juniper tree, and on the limbs of its neighbors, four other men, hanged by the neck. "It is not a good omen," said one of the Egyptians to Moses.

"Dead bandits are always a good omen," answered Paras.

Moses looked to Sebah for her reaction. She was as hard-eyed, as accepting of the laws of punishment and reward as her father and Moses were. He thought again of the skinny warrior in a small man's armor who had confronted him, sling in hand, on the field of battle outside Diffima. Had she really changed so much?

At Sukit on the Red Sea, Paras's party, donkeys and all, found a Byblos-style sailing boat with a ram prow bound for the Puntite capital of Zeiloh, with woven goods, mirrors, lances, spears, bows, and armor from the Egyptian delta. The captain was happy enough to make room for royalty with its guaranteed gold.

They passed the narrow straits of Mandeb, then sailed under good winds down the Gulf of Aden toward Zeiloh. To their right, a thread of smoke rose, then swirled up in a dark cloud. Moses knew it was a signal to the Puntites that he and Paras had arrived. Soon they rounded a headland and saw a few temples and palaces of sandstone on high ground, then a lagoon packed with reed huts on wooden stilts. As they approached, they saw people crowded out on the tiny porches of the huts, waving and chanting in a tongue Moses did not recognize.

He turned to Sebah for translation.

"They are hailing you as the *ka* and the *ba*"—two kinds of souls—"of the Pharaoh. They call you 'Jabiru Bird,' a creature with a human head who represents the *ba*. My father, they are shouting, is the incarnation of Min and Re. It gets complicated. Just watch him and do what he does."

Paras, seated in a chair brought to the deck, raised his scepter left and right. Moses, in a chair set for him a pace to the rear of the Barbahtian ruler, raised his decorative Egyptian flail of office, signifying the trade of grain and, by extension, other goods.

The ship channel ran in a broad path past the lagoon's huts to the quay. As they began to dock, there was a rush of minor officials from within the town of disarrayed mud-brick dwellings. In moments, townspeople and shipping workers surrounded the narrow gangplank to see visiting royalty, a rare occurrence in the remote Divine Land.

Minutes later, almost at a run, came Moses' cousin and his wife, both of them in leopard skins and as roly-poly as young hippopotamuses. Nevertheless,

King Maliak knew the protocols of power, first greeting his fellow sovereign, then Moses, with a firm grip on the forearm.

That evening, the pudgy ruler had a feast, with delta wine and such Puntite specialties as raw gulf shellfish, whole spitted shrews, and bustard eggs served on pickled water-lily leaves. Moses diplomatically praised the shrews, but decided they would never grace his table in Kerma.

Inevitably, when the carved stone wine cups were passed, the conversation turned to Moses' father. Maliak spoke circumspectly. "I will tell you, honored grandson of Ramses, first of that name, your father was noble in every way, and suffered greatly in this life and on his way to the next. In this last matter, I hope my father and I, in building him a tomb, were able to afford him tranquility with the gods."

Moses replied with equal propriety. "Esteemed cousin, benefactor and master of the Divine Land, for that I thank you." But after the servants had poured a few more cups of wine all around, Moses fixed the Puntite king with his eyes and said, "Now, dear cousin, speak to me frankly. We are blood relatives from whom no secrets should ever be hidden." Moses saw Sebah's ironic glance, a look missed by their hosts. "And King Paras is like a father to me, soon, I pray, he will be in fact. You may speak before him as before me. Tell me of my father, I beg you."

The ruler of Punt, in spite of a look from his wife, clearly wanted to ingratiate himself, particularly now, with the commanding young Egyptian emissary to Nubia. He could not have known that Moses would, on the death of Sety, become vizier to Ramses and therefore the second most powerful man in Egypt.

He lowered his voice, lest spies among the servants hear. "This must remain among us as if in a sarcophagus," said Maliak. Seeing objections only on the face of his wife, he began. "Though Anodheb, the murderer of your father and grandfather, stole their powers, he did not dare despoil their bodies. The followers of my grandfather, your granduncle, had fled across the gulf to Arabia, but loyal friends here secured the bodies at night and performed the rituals prescribed by the gods.

"Bad luck of all kinds hounded Anodheb and the other malefactors, and from Arabia my grandfather and father were able to convince them that the gods disapproved their treatment of our relatives and that a temple to the late king and his crown prince would dispel the curse. So they built one, prevailing on my family to send funds for the construction, but without allowing us to return under a truce to honor our dead.

"My father crossed the straits in force ten years ago and eviscerated Anodheb and his evil officials in the market square, but he could not do away with all of their supporters. My father is dead now, properly honored with his own temple here in Zeiloh, and we maintain an uneasy armistice with our enemies. But they now control the marsh land where the temple to your grandfather and father is, although it is but twelve miles from where we sit at this moment. In past years, we paid it an annual visit, although the cult of Douamoutef, as dog, which attends it, quite properly prevented anyone from entering its burial chamber."

"Is there not some way I may visit it?" asked Moses.

The king now looked uncomfortable. "Noble cousin, when I heard of your visit, I sent intermediaries to my enemies so that the little temple might be prepared and you might honor your father and grandfather. I wanted to clean its sandstone, remove the vines from its stelae, destroy the rank weeds that climb its walls. But they refused, saying I must first build a temple to *their* dead leader, Anodheb. Until then, no one may work on the temple to your grandfather and your father, nor enter it on pain of renewed violence, nor even visit it."

For Moses to pursue his request would be undiplomatic. And why should his cousin risk arousing the supporters of the men his family had killed ten years ago? Even if Maliak forced the issue with arms, some fanatic group of rebels might kill Moses or any other visitor, provoking unpredictable retribution from Egypt, indeed, destabilizing the entire horn of Africa.

And how could Moses complain about the neglect of a temple to a forgotten monarchy? He knew well how tombs of past Pharaohs of Egypt were ignored after a generation or two. With all appearances of sincerity, he said, "Steadfast cousin, I understand, and I yield. I am grateful that my father is now in the realm of Osiris and Anubis, and, thanks to your fidelity to our line, feasting, no doubt, with the gods in Imenty."

"It is the least I could do, son of Egypt," said the king, glad to be reprieved, the flush fading slightly from his face. He signaled his steward to pour more wine.

Late that night, on the roof of the palace, out of the sweltering heat, Moses and Sebah looked at the motionless gulf where the moonlight lay like a long silver scar across its dark face. "I am going, Sebah. I will enter the tomb," he said.

She did not answer at first. She knew him too well to argue when he had reflected and made up his mind. But, a king's daughter, she could see the danger: to him, to his role as Egypt's ambassador, to her father as Moses' sponsor in Punt. And she knew he was just as aware of the hazards as she was. "At least, visit it under cover of night. And do not enter."

"Not enter? Not pay my respects to my father's body? Not read on the walls the history of my grandfather? My father?"

"You defy the gods, Hapi-Set," she said lamely, for she did not believe in them any more than Moses. She turned on him, pressed her head to his cheek and took him in her arms. "And you risk everything that we now can hope for."

That gave him pause. He considered it and then said softly, "But I will do it. I defied Ramses when I went into Akhenaten's tomb in Thebes, just a boy then. Sebah, I am driven to do it. The walls will tell me from what sort of man I am sprung. Who I am. I must know. I will go alone."

She turned away from him and looked again at the sea, the farthest southern reaches of the Great Green to the north, celebrated in Egyptian song and story. For long moments, neither of them spoke. "No, Hapi-Set," she said at last, quietly and firmly, "you will not do it alone."

At midnight, Moses and Sebah—he disguised in a Syrian robe with a round Alalakh neck medallion Sebah had bought in the bazaar, and she veiled and in the coarse, full tunic of an Ethiopian spouse—passed through the last dwellings of the capital. The two donkeys they rode and the one they led were from Moses' party and found sure footing on the path, despite the dark. The tiny glow of oil lights shone in the wattled huts. No one came to the door to investigate the rapidly passing hoofbeats. And the two riders were even more silent than the night with its scrapings of insect wings, its distant and occasional hyena cries, and the far, sharp yap of foxes.

Sebah was dismayed that she was doing what her father would surely have prevented. Yet she knew that her husband-to-be, for all his intelligence and will, would not be able to enter the tomb alone. She had made the arrangements using her rough knowledge of the confusing Puntite tongue. In the disguise she now wore, she had bribed a seller of stolen statuettes in the market to lead her to a tomb robber, who had recently had his right hand severed for thievery.

Sebah told the robber that her husband believed a precious faience and gold statue of Stanqah, as dik-dik, was inside the murdered king's sarcophagus. She agreed to pay three debens of gold, more than the man had ever imagined having, if he would lead them to the temple and help them with the theft, a third to be paid when they started, the rest when they returned.

The tomb robber, a stringy, unkempt man, was on time at the rendezvous, beside a fallen lichen-covered statue of a king who had reigned centuries ago.

Moses dismounted and paid him ten *qites* of gold, then drew his sword and pointed it at their guide's throat. The man recoiled.

"Tell him," Moses said to Sebah.

Using rudimentary Puntite phrases, she told him, as Moses and she had arranged, that if he tried to betray them, Moses would slice off his male member and force him to eat it before he gutted him slowly. And Moses would want his knife. The robber nervously put the gold in the leather purse at his girdle, not taking his eyes from the giant man in Syrian dress. Then he withdrew a long dagger from inside his tunic and gave it hilt first to Moses.

The path ran straight but narrow through broom and galol trees, whose roots were cut and used as mat frames and whose bark was woven into the coarse ropes Moses had seen at the quays. The dry, sweet smell of sun-scorched acacias still hung on the night. At times, they heard, to their alarm, the crashing in the brush of large animals, hartebeest or giraffe, frightened by the sound of the asses' hooves. At one point, they heard an angry snort and the robber reined in his donkey.

"Rhinoceros," he whispered. "We must stop."

Moses recognized the first word and needed no translation of the rest. Breathlessly, they waited, then, with relief, heard the slow thump of heavy feet and the brush of the gigantic beast's graceful body against the weeds as it sauntered away—for it feared nothing in the Divine Land, not even the elephant.

Two hours into their trek, the tomb thief stopped his hard-driven donkey and dismounted. Moses and Sebah did likewise. The asses breathed stertorously. The land smelled dank. Flights of mosquitoes buzzed around them, unable to pierce the foul seepweed oil they had rubbed on their skin to stave them off. Their guide led them through a curtain of shrubby euphorbia and frankincense trees, the latter's scent mixing in Moses' nostrils with the seepweed and his and his donkey's sweat.

In the moonlight, he saw what they had come for. It was a simple blockhouse of sandstone. At its double doors, a single stele tilted in the spongy ground. Moses gave Sebah his sword and after several tries with his iron and flint sent a spark into his flax tender, blew on it, and kindled a tiny flame. He lit the smallest of the torches they had brought and gave it to the one-handed man to hold up by the stele.

"You can read it, Sebah?" Moses asked, as he looked at the hieroglyphs and script on the inferior limestone, so like Egyptian writing at first look, so incomprehensible at second.

She nodded, her face mysterious in the flickering light. "It is about your grandfather. The usual godhood things . . . son of all-powerful Amun . . . suckled at the breasts of Hathor. You know . . . then, victor against the bedouins at Aden, across the straits . . . victorious over the Ethiopians at the Juba River, turned red with their blood, etcetera, lists of the enemy dead . . . built a bridge near the bay of Hafun . . . Ah, here it is . . . had a son, the noble Dudak."

Moses started. That was his father.

Sebah was going on. "Nothing about him . . . It is getting to the lesser things . . . oh, here's some more. Crossed the river . . . they mean 'died' . . . . in the eighth year of his reign . . . nothing about how . . . that's about it. A hero obviously. You come from good vines."

Moses, disappointed there was nothing about his father, motioned the tomb robber to lead them to the entrance. It was a double portal embossed with a bronze jackal-headed Anubis, the protector of the dead, a noble god despite the jackal's reputation among herdsmen. The juniper door was sealed with four bronze bars forced through bronze brackets, then bent to clinch them. Moses, with effort, pried them loose with his sword hilt.

Inside the large antechamber, the robber held a new torch under his arm and lit it from the first one, now guttering. On the walls, hastily done hieroglyphs were already fading from the damp. Sebah scanned them. "Just more details of the exploits on the stele," she murmured.

There was an air of cheapness about the tomb, angering Moses. "Maybe in the burial room . . ." he said.

The thief dared to speak. "Syrian son of kings, your lady said we came only to seek a golden dik-dik. Surely we need not read these wall babblings. If we are found, all the muscles of your mighty arm cannot save us. Let us hurry." Moses let himself be led by the thief from the walls to a small portal, closed up with mud and sandstone rubble.

Sebah had the man put the torch in a ceramic vase that had once held the ritual grain seeds that, in sprouting, would provide the dead with food on the way to their new home. The three of them, she with the guide's dagger, Moses with his sword, and the guide with his good hand, moved the rubble and mud away. Moses and the man—Moses could not have done it alone—put their shoulders to the door and it dropped into the burial room with a weighty thud.

Two steps led down to the inner tomb. Water had seeped in ankle deep. In the room there were two sarcophagi, one larger than the other, a half-dozen poorly crafted juniper coffins, already warping, for mummified animals. The four Canopic jars for the dead's inner organs were roughly worked limestone instead of the usual gold or calcite. The furniture appeared to be worn-out temple chairs, stools, a table. There was no bed.

Moses was stricken. "May the bitch-fiend Amait curse them," he growled, the direst oath an Egyptian could utter. "And their children and their children's children." The insult to his father and grandfather! Ah, if the perpetrators lived, how he would love to kill them slowly, to mince their bodies along with the preserved remains of those that his cousin's father had already killed. To throw them in a swamp for the scavengers.

But he had to steady himself. Time was running out.

The robber said, "They buried them like paupers. There will be no gold, no faience here." His face twisted with disappointment. "Sire, you will pay me anyway. Surely—"

"Yes. Silence!" Moses snarled, still furious. He had the robber thrust the torch at the walls, which were densely covered with Puntite hieroglyphs in an uneven script. "Read it, Sebah. They will all be insults! Insults! They dared!"

She had never seen him so distressed, and hurriedly began her translations, starting with the longer text on the left wall, about his grandfather. But Moses stopped her. "No, these," he said, for he made out the hieroglyph of his father, a small aristocratic figure sitting on a king's lap, a crown prince.

"Yes," she said, beginning again. "Your father. It begins like the stele, like your grandfather's, only less praiseful . . . regal offspring of the sun . . . then . . . then . . . Hapi-Set, a story . . . more like what they do for commoners, you know . . . tells about his marriage to your mother. . . . See, he is here," she pointed to a two-dimensional prince in a kilt beside a princess with an Egyptian-style cobra in her headband.

"He is quite black," said Moses, surprised.

"In the hieroglyphs, all the Puntites are," she said. "It is a convention. They do not like to admit even a fallen king and his line might be of the Mediterranean strain. It is like showing all Philistines with beards."

"Perhaps," he said, still uneasy. She was going on.

"It says you were born, your name . . . your Puntite name, Sen-Dudak, after your father. Your mother must have changed it when she got back to Egypt . . . distinguished of heritage, though small of body . . . who would have thought you were a small baby . . . and here, nothing about the death of your father, but you and the celestial Mutempsut, princess of Egypt, leaving . . . They use the symbol of Nepthys for her, obviously not wanting to get Egyptians any angrier than they would be anyway . . . in case they ever read any of this . . . and here she and her warlike dwarf, Bes-Ahrin, escape on the fleet falcon wings of Re-Horakhty . . ."

"Go on . . ." Moses urged her, excited by this strange reclaiming of his past, feeling a sudden admiration for his mother's surprising audacity, yet stirred by a growing uneasiness. The torch began to sputter, and Moses handed the robber another.

"Hapi-Set, here is something!" Sebah exclaimed. "The new king Anodheb sent armed men, six, after you. See this hieroglyph with daggers . . . to dispatch the son of your father, that's you. To kill you . . ."

"Oh, Guzzlers of the Gods' Blood!" Moses interjected, a blasphemous oath. Enflamed, he again longed for revenge.

She ignored his outburst. ". . . lest you succeed to your grandfather's blue headdress of Punt and harm the . . . here is how they style him, 'majestic Anodheb, son of Isis and Osiris. . . . The six men were ordered not to hurt your mother or the dwarf, for they were Egyptians. . . . The assassins had thought your mother would go across the gulf of Tadjura, but discovered too late you had gone inland on donkeys, then north to Assab.

"There, see, this dwarf, whom they seemed to fear, for he looked so like the god Bes . . . the dwarf bought, no, hired, two women, sisters, of Danakil . . . that is a mountainous region of Ethiopia just west of Assab."

"But these assassins?"

"Do not interrupt, my love. It makes translating difficult. I lose the thread of it . . . and your group sailed northward. The assassins were two days behind you and found a small boat at Assab and pursued you. . . ." She pointed to the small sailing vessel with the six men in it. And ahead, between the boat's two solar disks, Moses could see the slightly larger craft with a princess in her headdress, a small, ugly god, the two forlorn-looking black women, and a frail, dark-skinned child.

"The child," Moses broke in, "me. But I was a strong baby. My mother said so, and this poor little thing . . ."

She was concentrating on the reliefs and Puntite script, which was already fading in places. "The assassins stopped at each port until they found you had landed at Qusae and gone overland toward Coptos on the Nile. Two of the men returned to Punt . . . it does not say what happened to them . . . killed I am sure." Her translations, as the writing grew more familiar, were going faster. "The other four went across the desert to Coptos and arrived there at night after your mother.

"She, you, and the others had just left aboard a fast boat, a *kebenit* . . . here, see, they are hiring a boat to give chase. . . . The winds favored them. . . . At Memphis, they docked near you and in the morning, the four men saw the two Ethiopian women leave the ship. Three of the Puntites kept them under secret scrutiny. The fourth managed to hire aboard your boat as an oarsman. He was unable to see inside the Princess Mutempsut's quarters until the dwarf left them briefly on the first day out of Memphis to give orders to the captain. At that time the Puntite went in, planning to kill the baby and then jump overboard and—I don't believe this, Hapi-Set," she interrupted herself in a shaken voice, turning to look at him, dumbfounded.

"What, Sebah? What?" he said, pushing the hand of the robber, bringing the torch so close to the wall that it almost burned her hair—as if he, Hapi-Set, would parse the strange hieroglyph script himself. "Don't believe what?" He, usually so measured, was shouting. "My mother told me nothing of this! Read on! Read on!"

Her eyes were like those of an antelope he had once surprised in a thicket while hunting, carrying death within them. The robber's hand trembled, for he, too, sensed some horror, although he did not understand a word they said.

At first when Sebah tried to continue, her lips moved but no words came. Then, alarmed by his bugging eyes that in the flare light made him look like a malevolent god, she turned back. She perused the script, her tone wooden as if she were reading her own *lettre de cachet* to her executioner. ". . . The man discovered there was no baby with the princess . . ."

Moses' mouth dropped. Now it was he who could not speak. Finally, he asked in a wondering voice, "No baby?"

All three were silent, no sound in the tomb but the popping of the burning pitch. At last, Moses said, his voice hoarse and without his usual certainty. "The spy told Anodheb that so that he would be forgiven for not being able to kill me."

She looked at him desperately. "But why, then, would he even return? He had gold. He could have gone anywhere. It says he slipped over the side of the boat immediately and swam to shore, lest the dwarf discover he had been in the cabin and kill him. And that he returned to Punt."

Moses was dizzy with disbelief and confusion.

"I do not, I do not . . ." his stammer became so pronounced he could not continue.

Sebah took his hand in her strong fingers. "There is more, Hapi-Set. I do not know what to believe, but there is more. I can stop if you wish. I can."

The one-handed man interrupted her. "Master, Mistress, we must go. Now!"

Moses grabbed him by the neck. "A word more, tomb robber, and you are in the jaws of the dog-fiend Amait!"—the most dire deity of the dead. "Do you hear? Go on," he said to Sebah.

She pointed to the spy plunging over the side of the boat, with the moon sign above him. And immediately the same man was rewarded in the royal palace of Punt, where only the night before he, Moses, had dined and drunk as a prince of Egypt.

". . . the three remaining assassins," Sebah went on, still gripping his hand, "followed the two nurses of Danakil, who were newly rich, and saw them buying donkeys at Memphis to take them overland to the Red Sea, fifty miles away. The men, too, bought donkeys and with seeming innocence joined the two old women and their guide after they had gone a few miles. There, they sent the guide across to the other bank—that means 'killed' in the Puntite language, just as in Egyptian.

"Then, oh, the gods! See, the nurses are being beaten. They tell their tormentors that you died aboard the ship and that they oiled your body and wrapped it in linen and gave it to Bes-Ahrin. One of the women watched the dwarf weight your body with a large pottery jar and lower it by a string into the Nile. . . . Oh, Hapi-Set, this cannot be true. It cannot."

"The women lied to protect me!" Moses burst out. "All of this is the work of men trying to cover up for their failure."

Sebah, as overwrought as he, said, "They were tortured, Hapi-Set, you saw the picture. And it says, 'Tests of their devotion to the goddess Maat were administered.' It was only then that they talked. They were both brought back to Anodheb and questioned here. . . . Oh, Hapi-Set, I cannot go on."

"All of it. All of it," he insisted, his voice wild.

"They told the same story when they were again tested before the goddess Maat . . . tortured . . . the poor old women. The people of the Danakil mountains believe that to lie is to be consigned forever to fire. It is well known. They did die and the story ends. . . . 'This wall is testimony to their truth.'"

Stricken as Moses was, a part of his jumbled mind remained clear, sought logic. Getting, at least briefly, control over his sea-storm emotions, he murmured between clenched teeth, "If Anodheb did not think this wall was proof that I was no heir to the Puntite throne, he would have had me assassinated even as far away as Tanis. Believing me an impostor meant he did not have to kill me. He felt he had the proof that the man Egypt thought was a prince was not. He could use it when he would."

"Hapi-Set," she said, the import of his speculation on her, on them, striking her, "do not even think the word 'impostor.' You are my prince and you are my love."

"I am not what I thought I was. . . ." he whispered, more to himself than to her. He thought of those vague intimations of an earlier warmth from someone other than his mother Mutempsut. "Oh, my prophetic *ka*. I must find out. My mother, Bes-Ahrin. I will not let them lie." The thought of his entire life as a fraud overwhelmed him and he shouted, "In the sarcophagi. The true story. They do that at Thebes. The things they want read on the walls. The truth inside on papyrus. They do not dare mock Anubis and Thoth with this dung on the wall without telling the truth, all of it, next to the mummy."

He rushed at his father's sarcophagus and tried to wrest off the lid, but even his might was not enough. "Help me!" he ordered Sebah and the man with the torch. The robber jammed it into the mouth of a Canopic jar and the three of them lifted and pushed. At last it began to slide, but it was too heavy to hold and splashed down into the water at their feet. Moses quickly prized off the coffin lid.

There lay the crown prince. No beaten gold mask, as was traditional for royalty, covered his face, only cloth and stucco, signs of a low-level official. No Book of the Dead lay between his legs, that necessary guide for those seeking their way through the labyrinths of the Underworld. Instead, there were a dozen crudely made statuettes. Moses grabbed up one, then several more. All were of men, their small penises erect, black paint like kohl rimming their eyes. Catamites!

"Oh, Aten-Osiris!" he cried, the vague god in which he had been willing to think existed in some unknowable form. He howled, all reason gone, one lewdly painted statuette in each of his hands. None of the three misunderstood the meaning of the small fired clay objects, although such insults to a buried monarch were unknown in Egypt or Nubia. All buried dignitaries were sent to the Underworld with statuettes of their wife or wives and concubines. These male figures were meant to signify that Moses' father was a lover of catamites.

Distraught, he splashed his hand in the water, found the knife, and used it to rip the plastered cloth from the mummy and the underlying wrappings of gluey linen treated with gum, resin, and natron. The features, though shriveled, were substantially intact. The corpse was clearly negroid, the features intelligent, almost feminine in their delicacy, the eyes covered with crumbling beeswax.

"Hapi-Set, he is not your father," Sebah murmured.

Moses stared intently at the revealed face. His breathing slowed. He was regaining control. At last, he looked at Sebah, touched lingeringly his nose to hers, in the Egyptian manner now. When he broke, he said, "And I am not Hapi-Set."

They tried, but could not lift the lid from the stagnant water. Moses gathered up the spent torch ends, and as they left, he kicked and strewed the stones and rubble back into the door leading to the burial chamber.

Outside Zeiloh, Moses gave the robber the remaining wages owed him. "I should kill you," he said, waiting for Sebah to translate. "Leave Zeiloh tonight and then Punt forever. Never go to Egypt. Take this secret to your grave. If you speak and are executed for tomb robbing, you will still have no rest. I will come to the Underworld and kill you a second time, and with less mercy than he who kills you the first."

Moses returned the donkeys to his sleepy servant, who saw his master's look of dismay and asked no questions. There was already the first gray light over the Red Sea.

"I am no prince of Egypt, Sebah, no, nor one of Punt, either. I am No-man," he lamented as they hurried to her father's residence.

"We do not know, Hapi-Set. Maybe your mother, the dwarf, will tell you a truer story. Maybe all this written in the tomb is false, done for some reason we cannot guess."

"Maybe," he said. But his heart and intellect told him otherwise. He could not marry her until he discovered who he was. But he wanted to hear what she would say before he told her his own decision.

"Hapi-Set, or even if you are not Hapi-Set . . . whoever you are, I will go with you. I will leave my father."

"He would kill himself," Moses said, "and if he did not, he would die of grief at your betrayal, at my betrayal, for he has been to me like the father I never had."

"I would leave him," she said firmly.

"Your love is that great?" he marveled.

"Yes. Since I was fourteen, I knew there would never be anyone else. You spared my life, and guarded . . . my person. Both belong to you more than they belong to me." Her voice was level, without any of the emotion they had both felt in the tomb.

"I love you more than life, Sebah," he said, "never more than now when I must leave you. If my mother, if Bes-Ahrin, can convince me all this is a fraud, then we . . ." Even here, he saw the ghastly humor of what he was about to say and smiled grimly, ". . . then we are guilty only of tomb breaking, sacrilege, and treason toward the Pharaoh Sety. But the words you translated, the nurses, that poor mummy's face . . ." *The statuettes,* he thought, but did not say.

"He is not your father, Moses. But you, you are the son of a king, of kings. How else could you be as you are?" She began to cry at last. "I will go with you. Anywhere."

"We cannot elope. How could we do it to your father? He would seem to his people a fool, a duped old man, for trusting us—you, the heir to his throne. How would he feel about you, about me? And how long before this, yes, dishonorable act would draw us apart, not with hatred, but simply without love?"

She sobbed noiselessly. At last the tears stopped.

"You will go to your mother? You will find a way to tell me what she and the dwarf say?"

"Yes," he said. "Now we must go to your father."

The shock of his discoveries left Moses both reeling and empty. His knowledge of animals, of people, of trees, grains, flowers, mathematics, his military honors, builder's skills—all of it seemed merely a panoply without a live body inside. And since Hapi-Set, prince of Egypt, son of the Princess Mutempsut, grandson of the dead Pharaoh Ramses, did not exist anymore, who was this person who did?

Moses did not change from his Syrian disguise, nor Sebah from her coarse tunic, before they went to Paras's chambers. Sebah always breakfasted with her father, unlike in Egypt, where the head of the household ate alone. The three of them sat in separate ebony chairs, the armrests carved with badger and fox heads, symbols of intelligence, or guile. They ignored the bitter beer of Punt usually drunk at breakfast, the joints of gazelle, the fresh bread, and ripe galol fruit.

As Moses talked, he laid down his sword. Sebah, as if to make a statement without words, poured water from the king's ewer on a towel and gave it to Moses to wipe his face and hands.

Moses first told Paras that once he knew there was a tomb for his father, he felt driven to visit it. He explained how, as a boy, he and Ramses had read the inscriptions of past Pharaohs in the forbidden burial chambers. He knew his act as an envoy of Egypt was madness, but he had done it anyway. "I had to know what the walls would tell me, Paras. I should never have taken the princess with me. But, without her, I could not have deciphered the hieroglyphs."

"If you had been caught," said the king, "Egypt would have dealt harshly with you. And I know you thought what it would have done to me. To Sebah. But I must understand your motives. In your place, I might have risked all, too. Strong men are often reckless men. And now what you found . . . I can see it has caused you grievous pain."

Moses told him everything, watching the expressions of fascination, then disbelief, then raw shock play across the classic obsidian features. When he was done, Paras put his hands over his eyes and muttered, "Let me think a moment, Hapi-Set, whether anything can be saved from this."

Sebah and Moses stared unhappily at each other while the king hid his eyes as if in prayer. For five minutes, they sat nervously, neither daring to breach the quiet. At last, Paras looked up. "Could you go with him, Sebah?"

She looked first at her father, then Moses.

"Yes," she said, "terrible as that would be. But he refused, and now that I face you, I could not."

Paras smiled, but without joy. "In those little minutes, I thought, well, I can make him a general, but my people would not honor an Egyptian commander. Or we could conceal all this, but that, I know, is not the way of Hapi-Set. Or," and he had to compose his features before he said it, "I could kill myself, let you become queen and marry a commoner. For Hapi-Set seems a king even if his blood may not be royal. But again, my people are fixed in their ways, as they have been for all time."

"It does not matter, Paras," said Moses. "Until I discover who I am, I cannot have a life with Sebah—no, nor with myself. The truth awaits me at Heliopolis with my mother and her dwarf. I must find an excuse to go there. If I am a prince, I will come down and beg your daughter's hands. If I am the son of some minor functionary—may Osiris protect my mother from such a scandal—then I will have to think what I can do."

Paras nodded. "There are celebrated warriors who sprung from the people, whose children became viziers, even kings. Your first Pharaoh, the famous Menes, was a simple soldier."

"And was killed by a hippopotamus," said Moses with sad pedantry. "Would that I had been."

The three decided to say nothing until Moses spoke with his mother and Bes-Ahrin. But already, between Sebah and Moses, there was an abeyance in their love. Both knew they had loved more powerfully than most, but not wholly. Both saw that love could lead them to disaster for Paras, for themselves, even to the destruction of love. And yet, they were guilty toward each other for not abandoning everything for their love.

In Kerma, Moses, obsessed now with finding out who he was, worked all day and late into the night to accomplish what he had set out to do when he left Tanis a year earlier. He had a ready excuse for taking a leave, promising ingenuously to return when he had visited his mother, now seriously ailing.

The Nubians saw him off with ceremony. At quayside, Moses sat beside the king and watched an entire day of festivals. Tumblers from deep Africa, some seven feet tall, did somersaults and made pyramids four bodies high. Dwarfs in high cylindrical hats rode pygmy elephants. Pennants dyed red and black waved from long poles that lined the way to the boat that would bear Moses north. Hawkers sold fat flavored with radish oil, spitted quail, slices of watermelon, and bits of bread coated with carob. A sextet of priests chanted the wonders of Hapi-Set's envoyship, invoking the names of twenty different gods, and a group of women of the temple chanted for Mutempsut's speedy recovery. The king stood and presented to Moses a turquoise-and-gold pectoral.

Moses smiled and bowed and thought cynically what the Kerman dignitaries would do if they knew he was not Hapi-Set at all but Hapi-No-Name. And yet, he had been a good envoy.

Chapter Five
The Royal Impostor

T HELIOPOLIS, THE SAILORS DROPPED THE VAST SAIL, AND THE oarsmen with a few sweeps curved the boat into the quay. Moses, heart and mind in turmoil, moved through the crowd of merchants, longshoremen, and loafers and looked up the sunlit hill at his mother's graceful palace. There, the answers to his past and his future lay. He walked rather than ride the donkey kept in a dockside stable for just such arrivals as his.

Obviously, a servant had seen him through one of the deep windows in the limestone dwelling, for Bes-Ahrin firmly marched out to greet him. Moses' chest constricted unnaturally. Moses loved the dwarf, but knew how sly he was. His only true loyalty was to Mutempsut. He would do and say only what was beneficial to her. But Moses, too, had learned much along the byways of trickery and manipulation. "Good Bes-Ahrin, how fares my mother?" he said, bending to take the man's forearm.

"Prince Hapi-Set," said the manikin, "it is a gift of Hapi, Min, and Bes in all their forms that you are here. I had sent for you not two days ago. She is fading." The look of anguish on the dwarf's face was so pitiable that Moses lost all caution. "I must talk with her," he said, "about . . . me."

"She lives only to hear your voice, Prince," Bes-Ahrin murmured subserviently, but Moses knew he had given away his own malaise. Besides, he now wondered whether he dared question her.

"How weak is she?"

"Weak, weak. She takes no wine, no real nourishment, only a little oxen broth and tea to flush out the poisons, and I prepare lotus flowers soaked in beer to ease her pain. You have nothing to distress her, I am sure. She is so weak, Prince Hapi-Set, so weak."

Moses was tormented. He decided to risk all with the prescient dwarf rather than bring alarm, or even a fatal trauma, to his mother.

"Bes-Ahrin, most loyal confidant of the Princess Mutempsut"—he hated the formality of his speech with this old friend, but only in this way could he create distance—"I am at this moment as if in the halls of Imenty, reserved for the eternally damned. Yet I realize I cannot bring my troubles to my mother. To you alone can I speak. I journeyed to Punt. I visited the tomb there of my father. I know my story from the walls of his burial chamber. I opened his sarcophagus, even his coffin. I cut the wrapping on his face and saw what was there."

Bes-Ahrin, his swarthy face paling beneath the burst of combed whiskers, said in a quiet, low voice, "Everything, Prince Hapi-Set? What can you mean, grandson of Ramses?"

"I am no grandson of Ramses. And my name is not Hapi-Set. I am, until you help me, the son . . . of the winds."

The dwarf staggered back. In a matter of seconds, his face, like a breaking sea wave, took a half-dozen different forms: surprise, fear, murderousness, cunning, disbelief, and again, fear, but not for himself this time. When he had steadied, he said in the same low voice, "Prince Hapi-Set, for that is what you must be known as, if you ask her questions about this, believe me, you will be her murderer as surely as evil Seth killed his brother, and she, unlike Osiris, will not return."

"Then it is true," gasped Moses, seeing, from the dwarf's portentous words, his last hope disappear of a life with Sebah, of continuing his own exciting and meaningful existence.

"You do not yet know what is true and what is false," said the dwarf. "You have only the words of Puntite wall scribblers." He spat in the road. "Of Puntite murderers. I repeat. If you ask your mother, it will kill her. And while she lives, I will never tell you what, I admit, you have every right to know. Even if I need to kill myself to remain silent."

Moses had already been thinking of how, by what torture, he could extract the information from Bes-Ahrin, but he knew that the dwarf's warning was absolutely valid. "Bes-Ahrin, I must know! But I swear to you I will not disturb my mother."

"Prince, mindful son of this noble princess, I long to unlock your life, although what you find inside the door would destroy less of a man than you. We are agreed then that you will spare your mother? Swear it!"

Moses looked at the wrecked face of the little man. "We are agreed, gnome. I could not do it. I swear it."

Bes-Ahrin scrutinized Moses, divined he could trust him, and went on. "Believe me, you cannot imagine her courage. And when you know all, you will see she gave you life, saved you from death, as surely as if . . . as if you were the child of her womb."

"Then it is so. I am not her son."

"Wait. Wait. I must first be assured that when she is questioned by Thoth and Anubis, she may be able to walk untroubled on the path to the Douat. For to the world beneath the world she soon must go."

"I swear again to you, I will live always as No-Name before I let my words kill her. But I must know."

"Young, mad prince," said Bes-Ahrin, losing patience with Moses, "don't you hear what I am saying? You *shall* know. Do this: Stay with us a while. Be kind to her. Tell her what things you can about her goodness to you when you were a child, for she was like Isis in her love for you. Then go on to your friend"—his face darkened at thought of Ramses—"and your work on Pi-Ramessu. When it is time, if I can judge within days instead of weeks, I will send for you. When she is safely on the other bank, I will confide in you. Everything."

"No, Bes-Ahrin," said Moses passionately, "I must know before she dies. For if she dies first, I will have no way to be sure that you will not, out of concern for her reputation, deny me the truth. Here is my order: Tell me now, everything, or rather confirm it, for I think I know it all. I will speak no word of it to her. Not one. Nor signify I have some terrible knowledge by nods or long faces. I swear this by Bes, whose incarnation you believe you are, although I do not believe in any Egyptian gods, but only in one god, whose name I do not know."

Bes-Ahrin smiled grimly. "Yes, better not to swear it by our gods, Prince, not even by Maat. For I know you do not believe. Thank Bes your mother does not know you do not."

Moses looked at the dwarf. It was all so droll, this argument over the gods when his being lay in the balance. "I would throw the whole lot of them into the Nile," he agreed. "I swear it not by any god then, but by my honor."

The little man looked at him shrewdly again for a full minute. "We will go to her. I will see by your behavior whether you can keep your end of that kind of bargain."

Moses' body and spirit emptied of joy, of peace, even as he won his victory over Bes-Ahrin. "You have already told me the worst. You know that, do you not?"

"Yes. And now, Prince No-Name, go to your mother."

The Princess Mutempsut's face was as fragile as the mummified face he had seen so recently in the tomb at Zeiloh. Her arms lay on the linen coverlet that was placed over her despite the heat. "Mother," Moses said to her, genuinely gripped by love—perhaps for the first time—and pity.

"Hapi-Set, son," she murmured, slowly raising a hand for him to take. He did so, seeing the blue veins so close to the surface of her wrist that he felt he could pluck them off, as one would lift a blue blossom petal from an alabaster table.

"Your mission to Kerma . . . you were successful?"

Moses was sure the dwarf waited just outside the door. He would be monitoring every word. "I think so. When I left for my visit to you, they had a festive celebration. Men tall as giants making pyramids of each other, dyed pennants in the river breeze. They even had a chant, 'Blessed Hapi-Set, take health to the Princess-goddess Mutempsut, in the name of Nepthys.' And they invoked the names of many gods in my favor."

"Ah, Hapi-Set, you say that to raise my spirits."

"I swear it, Mother. In my baggage, even now on the way from the quay, I brought you a gift. I will surprise you. It is of ebony, carved in Barbaht, inlaid with lapis lazuli."

"Oh, I will love it, Hapi-Set. My friends in Thebes tell me they hear from the south that the king of Barbaht has a beautiful, tall daughter." She gave his hand the slightest squeeze, and he looked into her eyes, their dullness lighting.

"Then you know," he said. It almost broke his heart to lie. But now he did, not to coerce Bes-Ahrin, but to conspire with him to make her passing easier. "She is beautiful. She longs to meet you. I have told her there are no mothers like you. And how I hate myself for not showing it before now. On my next trip north, I will bring her, perhaps as a wife."

Oh you gods, devourers of men's soft parts, he cursed them silently, having no reason not to, since he both hated and did not believe in them. But he did not take his kind gaze away from his mother. "She will love you," he said, "as I love her. And you." He was exaggerating his love for Mutempsut, deluding her. Perhaps in some deeper place she knew it, too.

"I had hoped you would wed some niece of my brother, Sety," she said, "and return to rule Punt, the Divine Land. But still, to be someday a king, the father of a line of kings . . . for though small, Barbaht is highly regarded."

"She is beautiful, not so beautiful as you were, Princess-Mother, but with laughing black eyes and kind ways." Imagining her, he dared be happy for a moment. "She plans to teach me how to hunt rhinoceros," he said, smiling at her.

"Oh, no, son, you must get her rapidly in a condition where she hunts only for a nurse. No rhinoceroses. Promise me, Hapi-Set, no, no more hippopotamuses. I know that story from my correspondents in Tanis. Does this mean you will not be vizier to Ramses? Sety is sick." Even as she died, her life was wrapped up in the intrigues and the gossip of the royal court.

"In Barbaht, perhaps I shall be both king and vizier," Moses continued his lies, sickened by them, sickened by his discovery. "There have been such things . . . in the reign of Apophis. . . . The scribes taught us . . ."

His mother moved her head from side to side dismissively. She knew the stories of past royalty better than the temple historians. "A Hyksos, dear son, a Hyksos." But she could not bear to lecture him. "Oh, Hapi-Set, I am so glad you came to me. I so love to see you happy, to feel . . . your love."

"Mother," he said, "I do love you."

And, for this brief time, he did.

That evening he ate in her room, she in bed, Bes-Ahrin at his own small table near the door, his polished sword—even in her bedroom—in his thick leather belt. Moses was too riven to enjoy the feast that the dwarf had ordered for him-slices of ox liver, giant perch, and pigeon breast. He picked at it, drank some wine, and munched a few honey-barley cakes.

At the end of the meal, Moses gave Mutempsut the statuette of Hathor in her incarnation as a cow, beloved of mothers, and she wept. Bes-Ahrin and Moses exchanged glances, tears in all six eyes. At that moment, Moses knew that he and the dwarf were eternally bound together. She caught the glance, but could not have fathomed its import, although she made a surmise about their tears.

"I will soon have need of this, Hapi-Set," she said with quiet dignity. She meant it would accompany her to her tomb.

Moses had passed the test. That evening, after they left the princess to her shallow breathing, the two men walked to the small pavilion at the far end of Mutempsut's garden. Moses stooped slightly to enter it. The dusky air was quiet, except for the small chirps of tame night-birds and the occasional rasp of crickets. Clusters of balanos trees perfumed the air, and to the west, landscaped willows and venerable sycamores were silhouetted against the last light of the day. It was unbearably beautiful, made so by the riches of the Pharaohs.

"It is a long story, my prince, for prince you must remain for a while, whether you like it or not." He paused. "Your name is Moses." He said it so softly that Moses could imagine he had been called that name before in some life long forgotten. In quiet bass tones, the dwarf recounted what he knew: from the day Horemheb ordered that the first-born sons of the Hebrews be killed, to when the princess found the basket in the Nile and the little Hebrew girl approached with the offer of a wet nurse, to the substitution of Moses for the dead Sen-Dudak.

Moses listened, absorbed, interrupting infrequently, for the dwarf's memory was good. It was, however, as if he were hearing a tale about someone else, fascinating but, not for these minutes, impinging on his own life. That would come later.

"... and so, when I recognized signs that the princess would soon be in the hands of the gods of the Underworld, I sent for you. I could not know you brought with you cruel whips of knowledge that would compel me to tell you this story."

"And my parents' names?"

"Jochebed and Amram, alive in Tanis, as they were, Hebrew slaves. He is a foreman at Pi-Ramessu, almost as broad as you, she aging but straight, healthy. Your brother, Aaron, is too clumsy for real work, but has a good mind. He translates Hebrew into Egyptian at the warehouse, where the Hebrew artisans keep their tools and some of their goods. Under no circumstances must you see them yet. It could be your and their deaths. I will arrange a visit when the time is opportune. I promise you that."

"My sister?"

"Miriam. A widow with two daughters. Wordy as she is, it is still no miracle that she has not exposed you. She knows I would kill her and her children if she did."

Moses shook his head. Now that he had it all, he could begin to think how it might affect him. "Better this Amram as a father than the sad, effeminate prince of Punt," he mused. Yet it was all so depressing. So final, for Sebah was lost.

"Better, yes," said Bes-Ahrin, his voice rising with heat. "Imagine him, preferring these painted boys to your mother. The gods know I wanted to kill him. I am glad, Hapi-Set, that they defamed him with the statuettes you found. Glad."

"My visit to his tomb destroyed me, Bes-Ahrin."

"The princess you intended to marry? Is that your meaning? Loss of a woman is not the same as destruction."

Instantly angered, Moses said, "Listen to him who speaks of the loss of a woman. You—"

"Loss of a woman is not the same as her death, Prince Hapi-Set," Bes-Ahrin said firmly, and Moses accepted it.

"I cannot argue that. I will be true to my promise. I will go downriver in a few days," he said. "I will ask Sety if I can help Ramses with Pi-Ramessu again. I will tell him that Kerma is tranquil and that anyone can be our envoy there. My uncle will let me stay in the delta, knowing my mother will not be long on this side of the Nile. I will act as if I know nothing until you summon me."

"Then?"

"I will come to see her a last time. And I will come again—in what? three months?—to join you in Thebes when the royal embalmer and his servants have fully prepared her for the ceremony at her tomb. I will accompany her to her temple. Then, I must see my parents and, after that, with or without them, farewell to Egypt." He looked at the dwarf seriously. "Unless you decide to kill me."

"Do not think I have not thought of it." He shrugged. "But to kill the person she loved best in all the world?"

For a sudden moment, he wondered whether his mother and this brave deformed man had been lovers. Stranger things had happened. He did not ask. "Her tomb is ready?"

"Yes. Every detail. It has engaged me for months."

He could not resist one question. "Didn't you ever want any other life, Bes-Ahrin?"

The little man shook his head negatively. "I was a difficult son to my parents, Prince, and they sold me to Egyptian traders. When the princess saw me on sale at the market in Pelusium, the scars on my back looked like a reed mat. She pitied me, bought me, gave me a life as her protector—"

"—who saved her and wound up saving my life as well," Moses said. "For if you had not brought me out of hiding with my parents, I might have died under the decree of Horemheb."

Once more Bes-Ahrin grinned, illuminating his ugly features. "Perhaps. You are as willful as I was, Prince. If you had remained with your parents, one Egyptian or another would have killed you, with or without a decree. I would have done it myself if you had been my slave."

Again, Moses lingered. For when he parted, he parted also with the world in which he had existed all his witting life. "I cannot work as a slave," he said. "When I leave Egypt, I will take nothing from Sety or Ramses. Nor will I say anything about my story. Although I think now it is impossible, I may yet devise some way to bring the princess of Barbaht to me, wherever I am, even if I must wait until her father is dead."

"I would not write your future on a stele if I were you," said Bes-Ahrin.

Well before Moses' boat reached Tanis and Pi-Ramessu, he had decided he could entrust no word of his extraordinary story in a letter for Sebah, although it lay as heavy on his heart as a sarcophagus lid of Aswan granite. Only when he left Egypt could he write, and then it could be delivered by no one but Bes-

Ahrin, and he only after Mutempsut was dead. Moses moiled and moiled over what he would say, but reached no conclusions.

When the boat docked at Pi-Ramessu, he saw the stacks of limestone slabs, quartzite, sandstone, timbers from Lebanon and Syria, and tools made in the factories of Bubastis. The ground, which had been largely covered with under-brush when he left, save for a few ancient buildings, now was cleared and stakes marked where first floors of temples and palaces would soon begin to rise. As full of trepidations as he had been at Heliopolis, he stepped onto the quay, and, leaving his baggage with porters, walked alone to find Ramses.

Inside the new city a-borning, Ramses looked up from where he was ordering a stonecutter to number blocks of Roiaou limestone so that they might be placed accurately on the foundations of a small temple to the sacred bull of Ptah.

"Comrade Hapi-Set," the crown prince said with pleasure, embracing him, his sweat slick against Moses' own perspiring chest. "Back to the building of royal cities, hunh?"

"At last," said Moses, feigning a happiness he could not feel while the lie of his birth lay between them.

"And your mother. You found her better?"

Moses recalled how Ramses always preferred to drink the honey wine of hope, while he, Moses, preferred to sip life as it came, whether sweet or as bit-ter as bad beer. "She is dying, Ramses, I await a call to go to her."

"I am sorry, Hapi-Set. But you will soon have the consolation of your cap-tive, little Princess Sebah, yes? Word reached me about the betrothal from Kerma. And I have news for you. In a short time I will marry Nofretari, do you recall her, my second cousin, one of them, from Thebes?"

Moses tried to brighten, to resume the old jesting mode, "There were so many, Ramses . . ."

"But this one I will love alone."

"No more dancing girls?" Moses asked dubiously. "You will live with her alone?"

"Don't be ridiculous, Hapi-Set. First, why should I go to my bedroom with dancing girls, when I can have Nofretari? Second, why should I favor only Nofretari when I can have as many wives of the second order as I want? I will love her alone, but not live with her alone."

"May you have a hundred sons," said Moses, pleased to hear again Ramses' buoyant rationalizations, envying his ease with the sensual part of his life.

"And you, will you prefer to be king of Barbaht when the old king dies, or vizier of all Egypt?" Ramses tried to sound merely rhetorical, as if there could be only one answer. His piercing look said he was genuinely worried.

Moses, again sick at heart, nevertheless gamely—and deceitfully—gave him that one answer. "Vizier, of course. If I stayed, the king would make her queen. But there is a nephew of Min-Paras as worthy as I am to succeed him."

"She will give up being queen someday for a sot and a ravisher of hermaphrodites?" said Ramses, relieved enough now to josh. "She must love you, old river god."

Moses could carry on the pleasantries no longer. The pain was too extreme. He changed the subject. "You can use me, hippopotamus wrestler?"

"Of course. What do you think of Pi-Ramessu?" He gestured at the stakes that marked the beginnings of buildings.

"Prodigious," Moses answered. "Where do I start?"

"With the Hebrews," said Ramses, turning his eyes from his accomplishments. "Problems. You said there would be. They work like oxen, but have the temperament of wild bulls. One of my supervisors, able but hot-tempered, buried one alive for insubordination two weeks ago. A little extreme perhaps, but I supported him. Anyway, the Hebrews are surly about it. You were always the diplomat, and now have credentials to prove it. Talk to their leaders, Hapi-Set. Calm them. I need them. One of them can do the work of two Amorite slaves. If necessary, increase their bread and beer a bit. Not too much. But why dwell on it? Do it. And tonight, we feast, drink. I have a harem of my own here. It is yours."

Moses was shaken by his assignment. But he was so deep in the quagmire of his dissembling, he could not wade out. *Suppose,* he thought, *I encounter my father, my brother?* Could I give the order to have them whipped? Hating himself, he put on his best old half-mocking manner. "The Hebrews will be easy . . . I will summon their leaders from work. I will talk to them this very day . . . like brother to brother," he jested, only he knowing how bleakly. "But no harem, Pharaoh-to-be. Your best wine though, yes. I need it more than you know."

As he walked across the limestone chips in the blazing sun, he thought of the Hebrews—his fellow Israelites. What did he know of them? Mainly that they were forever praying to their God of Abraham, a concoction, as Moses recalled, of the strict sole god of the fallen Akhenaten and a benevolent version of Osiris. *At least,* he thought, *Abraham's God is not a mishmash of every deity from every land for the last two thousand years. But the God of a desert bandit?* He smiled humorlessly. *I had better get used to him.*

Not two weeks later, word came from Bes-Ahrin that the Princess

Mutempsut had faded from wakefulness and that Moses must hurry if he would see her alive. Ramses provided him with his fastest *kebenit* for the hundred-mile river trip. It was newly fitted with a hogging cable, a giant racing sail, and his best oarsmen—all free men—to give it maximum speed.

"Can you hear me, Mother?" Moses whispered to the skeletal form whose head was as pale and smooth as an egg, her hair gone from the potions with which the doctor-priests had treated her. The lips trembled, but perhaps mindlessly. Moses held the thin fingers in his for hours at a time, as Bes-Ahrin, too inconsolable to speak, sat at his palm-fibered chair in the corner of the room, immobile as a toy king.

Two days later, after Bes-Ahrin administered a dose of willow extract to try to stop her shaking, Moses was sure she had heard him, for she responded to his questions with faint pressure on his fingers. The flickering light from the oil, perfumed with storax, touched and softened her translucent face.

"Mother, I am grateful to you. Can you hear me?" he said, meaning it, for as he had painfully considered his story over the past weeks, he saw that since the very day she had saved his life from the Pharaoh and the Nile, she had been all to him that she was able to be. Next morning, he felt her hand first twitch and then relax lifelessly.

"She is gone, Bes-Ahrin," Moses said quietly.

The dwarf moaned pitiably, his grief compressed all these months, and hurried out of the room and down the hall, groaning wordlessly. Moses heard him outside, a few anguished shouts of "No!" until his bass agony passed out of earshot.

Moses knew the mechanics of burial, nor would his scientific mind let him blot out his knowledge. He imagined Mutempsut's nearly fleshless body on the ceremonial embalming bed with its jackal gods on the four posts. The embalmer would take out the brain and all the organs but the heart, discard the brain and dry the rest in natron. Washed in palm wine, the organs would be put in four Canopic jars ornamented with reliefs of Hapi—*how ironic,* Moses thought—and Horus's other three sons, who would protect the jars and their contents.

The princess's corpse would also be dried with natron and anointed with palm oil. After two months, each limb, each finger would be bandaged separately by priests reciting prayers and spells. The mummy would be adorned in Mutempsut's royal robes, armlets, bracelets, amulets, rings, pectorals, and gold-braided sandals. Then she would be wrapped in more bandages, and a gold mask, crafted by a master sculptor, would cover her face. The body, its coffin, and sarcophagus would then be transferred to Thebes for burial across the Nile in the Valley of the Queens.

Never this for me, Moses said to himself. He thought of the Hebrew burial ground at Pi-Ramessu that Ramses had ordered dug up to make room for overseers' houses. The skeletons had a few pottery bowls and earthenware utensils around them. *Good enough for me,* thought Moses. *Good enough even when I was a prince.*

Moses stayed in Heliopolis a week for mourning. He, Bes-Ahrin, and Mutempsut's household smeared their faces with mud. The women bared their breasts, and visiting priests chanted each morning and evening, praising Mutempsut in ritualistic terms: "Oh, Princess, earthly incarnation of Hathor, why have you left us forlorn? Unspeakable is our yearning for your step in the halls of your palace . . ." and so on.

By the dispensation and order of Sety, so sick himself that he often spent entire days in bed, Moses ended his period of formal mourning early to get back to work at Pi-Ramessu.

Increasingly, he was arguing with Ramses about the treatment of the thousands of Hebrew and other slaves. It was not merely from sympathy for a people whom he now knew were his own, but from a conviction that Ramses' harsh treatment was interfering with construction of the new city. The work was slowing, and Moses was convinced that it was on purpose. And no amount of whipping, as Ramses ordered, was increasing efficiency.

Two months after Mutempsut's death, a message came from Bes-Ahrin saying that the mummification rituals for the princess were well under way and that by the time Moses arrived, she could begin her final journey upriver to Thebes. For Moses, Thebes was almost a five-hundred-mile trip. But it could not be avoided. Sety could not come and, in his stead, Ramses made the journey with Moses.

The ceremonies were becoming of an esteemed princess, adopted daughter of Horemheb, daughter of Ramses, first of that name, eldest sister of Sety, aunt of the putative Pharaoh, Ramses, and mother of the vizier-to-be, Hapi-Set. Ramses, his face daubed with mud, his bejeweled tunic torn in strips, his sword dragging in the dirt, led the funeral procession to the Nile. Moses, similarly mourning, walked two steps behind. Ramses, always splendid on ceremonial occasions, chanted the praise of his aunt in a loud voice, repeating the sentiments sung by the priests at her death, and adding many of his own: "Oh daughter of Re and Isis, linger a while yet, do not hurry so to find your home in eternal life. Can you not hear our grieving? Your brother, the god Horus, begs you to look back and comfort your own son and the multitudes of Egypt, from the Blue and White Nile, yea, even above the sixth cataract . . ."

Chanting temple women, breasts bared and faces streaked with mud, lined the path of the procession and picked up the crown prince's words, elaborating on them with even more radical encomiums. Moses ritually cried out his woe and struck his head with his fists in the ordained manner.

Behind Ramses and Moses came Mutempsut's servants with barley cakes, wine, convolvulus, red anemone, and jasmine blooms, sprouting cereal seeds, figurines—all for the burial chamber. Hired carriers labored down the hill from the Nile with chairs, a bed, even cupboards to be entombed with her. Then came young priests carrying sunshades, semiprecious jewels, sculpted wooden animal heads, and wide-winged falcons on the ends of poles for the tomb. Finally, an ornate cart bumped along, drawn by cows and bearing the sarcophagus with Mutempsut and her coffin inside.

At the Nile, the principals embarked on the one-hundred-and-forty-foot-long royal funeral boat that carried the catafalque. The other mourners, in more modest craft, crossed to the land of tombs, with its solemn mausoleums of the mighty.

With the dead princess, Moses was burying his whole past life as prince and grandson of a Pharaoh. Troubled as he was by regret and his present deceit, he nevertheless felt a certain relief. Now, at last, he could tell what he had discovered to Sebah and Paras. "I am, as we feared, no prince of Egypt," he began both letters in his quiet quarters back across the river in Thebes. "Instead, I am the son of slaves, my father a Hebrew construction foreman and my brother a warehouse clerk." He detailed the circumstances. Separately to Sebah, he passionately affirmed his love and said how he longed to see her.

To Paras he wrote, "The crown prince Ramses, when his father dies, cannot appoint a man as vizier from a race he enslaves. But, I believe, he can explain that I did not know I was an Israelite and withheld telling of it lest I disturb my presumed mother's death and burial. He could cite my service to Egypt and, I believe, would have no objection to my serving you in your army. Is that possible? If I bring some honor to Barbaht, might I not then become a suitor again for your daughter's hand? Could not a king whose daughter and whose leg have been saved by a soldier so that he can still fight rhinoceroses fight off the prejudices of a proud people?"

He entrusted the letters to Bes-Ahrin to take to Barbaht, over six hundred more miles by river to the south. The dwarf, still in pain from his mistress's death, could only nod acceptance. What withal, Moses believed that a new mission was better for the little man than returning to Heliopolis and brooding. And Bes-Ahrin, at this time, did not want to come to Tanis and daily face Ramses' enmity.

"Do you have sufficient gold?" Moses asked.

"She has left me wealthy beyond my dreams," the dwarf said, and his wrinkled face contorted even further in tears, then sobs as, for the only time in his life, he flung himself into Moses' arms as a child might.

Moses made the trip back to Tanis with Ramses, and it was on the boat that he fully realized how their friendship was changing. The Pharaoh-to-be was full of plans—for the new city; for temples and palaces all over Egypt, particularly at Karnak, where his father had already started the most majestic hall of pillars the world had ever seen; for military campaigns in Libya, Syria, and against the Hittites along the Orontes; for copper mines and canals; for expanding trade. In each case, he astutely laid out Moses' role in them. Moses tried to respond with eagerness, but he had no heart for his own lies.

"It is your mother's death," said Ramses sympathetically.

Moses felt almost resentful at his friend for making him lie. And yet Moses realized how unfair that was. For Ramses even saw Moses as his successor should anything happen to him before a legitimate son was born. True, Ramses had brothers and Sety had other nephews, as well as an ambitious younger brother, Nunrah, the prince who had wanted to rape Sebah. Nunrah had been busy since those days and even had a following of royal discontents. Ramses and Moses had once talked of how he could be sent off to fight—and die?—in Mitanni.

But Moses might have been more acceptable than any of these. He was, after all, the supposed son of the Pharaoh's eldest sister, and only Ramses was a more respected general and builder. *Son of a slave,* thought Moses with gloomy irony, *wearing the blue headdress and the royal uraeus of a Pharaoh.*

For four months, Moses hungered for the return of Bes-Ahrin from Barbaht, and at last the dwarf came, arriving by night, as he always seemed to do on portentous occasions. He handed Moses an ebony box a cubit—eighteen inches—in length. Then, he staggered off to sleep in a bed in Moses' ample quarters. Moses cut the rawhide bindings coated with beeswax on the box and withdrew two scrolls. He opened Paras's first—its wax seal bearing the ring—imprint of the crown of Barbaht—for it, not Sebah's, would dictate his fate.

"Prince of Egypt, Hapi-Set," it began. "I would agree, if you wish, to your plan, but your wait for the Princess Sebah's hand might be long, for many military victories and long thoughts by my people would necessarily precede the acceptance of a slave's son as a general. Yet, stranger things have happened. But let me propose a swifter, if more devious, answer. Could you not continue as Prince Hapi-Set? If evildoers in Punt sought to destroy you, we could recite the history of their murder of your father, and then call them not just murderers, but liars. I know how this goes against your open nature, but my dear young Hapi-Set, I am an old man, and I have made many compromises in my life, some that served me well . . ."

Well, thought Moses, *that would let me be close to Sebah and in the service of this good man. But could I bear the subterfuge? Can I?* He quickly ran his fingernail along the seal of Sebah's letter. She made no effort at discretion.

"Beloved Hapi-Set," she wrote, "I need not repeat to you how much I love you. If you do not know it now, then there is no hearing in your ears, nor any sight in your eyes, nor any feeling in your flesh. I beg of you to accept my father's desire that you remain as a prince of Egypt. Leave the delta, give up all thought of being vizier. Come here where the hyena slanderers of Punt could no longer feed on you. Here, the word of a Puntite, as you well know, is as weightless as barley chaff. We would simply deny the words and reliefs and objects in your grandfather's temple. After all, the whole building was the work of his blood enemies. Come to us in any case, as slaves' son and warrior, or as prince, and we will make you welcome and soothe the cares that began for you that night outside Zeiloh . . ."

Moses read the letters over and over and fell asleep without knowing what he would do, other than that as either an honest man or a liar, he would appeal to Ramses to release him from his duties at Pi-Ramessu. Then he would go to Sebah as soon as the winds and oars could carry him south.

Next day, again, the heavens with all their stars and gods fell on his head. Of all the Hebrew slaves, the most restive were the mud treaders. Each day, in the hot sun they trod the mix of Nile mud, sand, and chopped straw that made the bricks for walls, foundations, the better homes, and warehouses. The river flies bit them; the mud, with its sewerage, caused boils and fissures on their feet and ankles; and, always, the Egyptian taskmasters were ready with their whips whenever there was any slacking off.

Moses had increased the workers' pittance of bread, had urged the taskmasters to be less harsh, and had instituted other measures for making more bearable the slaves' work in hopes of increasing production. He was aware that his knowledge of his heritage played a part in his decisions, and was ambivalent about the ethics of that aspect. But whatever his reasons, the numbers of bricks were slowly growing.

At the end of a long day, his mind tormented by his uncertainty about telling Ramses of his ancestry, his judgment dulled by weariness, he nevertheless went down to the mud sloughs to make a sample count on his own of fresh bricks. The sun was red-orange and so low that it made the piles of mattocks handles—used to stir the brick-mud—look like polished bones smeared with blood. No one had lingered from the eleven-hour workday. Moses' estimate completed, and encouraging, he walked toward a river pond to see whether its shallows would produce another day's supply of mud.

As he approached, he heard screams, a man cursing, the erratic smacks of what could only be a whip. The cries were hysterical, and he increased his pace to a jog. Just beyond a poolside tangle of dried rushes, thorn weed, and vile-smelling asphodel, he saw a hard-bodied man beating a skinny slave who thrashed in the muddy water. "Hold, man," ordered Moses, but the Egyptian with the whip looked up furiously and went back to his merciless labor. "I said hold," Moses cried again.

"Who bids me hold?" demanded the man, pausing for a moment, obviously failing to discern the small royal cobra emblazoned on the breast of Moses' tunic. Seeing his life spared for this instant, the slave, a Hebrew from the looks of his soggy loincloth and headband, rose and tried to run from the water. But he was like a cormorant trying to take flight from a pond after an arrow has broken its wing. The man with the whip threw it ashore, drew a dagger from a cheap scabbard at his belt, and splashed after him.

Moses acted instinctively, not thinking whether the victim was Hebrew or African or Libyan, seeing only that the long-legged Egyptian would soon catch up with him and kill him. True, summary execution was the right of a taskmaster to prevent the escape of a slave, but there was no justice in a man being slain because he was trying to avoid a fatal lashing.

Moses ran into the pool to cut off the armed man, who was wildly cursing the faltering Hebrew. He overtook the pair and threw his shoulders against the whipper, toppling him into the muck and falling himself. The taskmaster was up first and, dagger cocked at his hip, redirected his fury against Moses, whose regal identification was now blotted with muddy water.

"Who are you to interfere with the punishment of a malingerer?" the man screamed, coming now at Moses with his knife, screeching obscenities, awaiting no answers. The man slashed at Moses, missed, and fell with a splash. It gave Moses time to draw his short sword just as the man came up.

The taskmaster swiped clumsily at Moses, who, not wanting to kill him, smacked at his dagger arm with the flat of his sword. The man yelped in pain and outrage, but switched the knife to his left hand and lunged at Moses' throat. Moses, so skilled in this kind of battle, could have dispatched him with a single thrust. But instead, he deflected the blow and, quick as a Greek boxer, slammed the hilt into the man's temple.

The taskmaster fell like a tree into the water, showing the whites of his eyes even in the dusky light. Moses grabbed him by his tunic belt and dragged him out. He splashed pond water into his face, slapped his cheeks, fixing his gaze on the staring eyes of his erstwhile adversary. But there was no reviving him. The hilt blow, intended to stun, had killed.

Moses looked around him. The slave was gone. The quiet night was on this place of violence. Moses looked down at the dead Egyptian. Could the slave have seen the cobra on his chest, and might he talk about how a prince had come and saved him? If that happened, informers among the Hebrews would soon pick up the story, and Ramses would know Moses had slain a taskmaster in order to protect a slave. For the taskmasters—so vital to the building of Pi-Ramessu—that would be intolerable.

Indeed, it would be to every Egyptian, including Ramses. Nor would it stop with Ramses. Why would the spies not pass the story up to Sety, whose dislike of the stubborn Hebrews was even more unrelenting than Ramses'? So, thought Moses, calmly but with a dark presentiment, should he confess, or hope the Israelite had brains enough to fear trouble all around and be quiet? If Moses made the death public, it would mean official disgrace and possibly exile. And he could not go to Barbaht after either decree.

Making up his mind, Moses, the man's whip in his own belt, shouldered the body, and staggered toward the Nile. He dropped the corpse in the shallows, found the heaviest boulder he could lift, and tied the whip to it. Dragging the body behind him, the boulder under his arm, he waded out until he was waist deep. There, he tightly tied the whip to the man's waist so the current would not float him downstream. On the shore, he found more heavy stones, carried them into the river, and made a partial underwater cairn over the taskmaster.

Even if the body were discovered before the carrion eaters—crocodile, turtle, catfish—plucked off his flesh, Moses still might escape blame. It was not unheard of for a slave to turn on a taskmaster, or even for two taskmasters, picked for their violent ways in any case, to kill each other.

At home, he whispered what had happened to Bes-Ahrin, who was staying with him. The dwarf went out infrequently because of Ramses, and then only to visit his little coterie of dwarfs, midgets, and hunchbacks, whose abnormalities bound them together. Bes-Ahrin thought soberly of the matter, shook his head, and said, "You are caught between the wild ox and the oryx. Well, better the oryx. He cannot trample you to death as well as gore you. Let us think what we can do if he gores you."

Next day, even heavier in mood from his new secret, Moses went again to where the brickmakers worked. He watched them, putting the mud in the molds, scraping off the excess with a board, and lifting the mold. He did not venture to the pond, but walked to a mud flat, where he saw the slaves—his people—carrying water jars on their shoulders to moisten the dirt, sand, and straw. In a week, the new bricks would be ready. Would he escape discovery that long?

As he reviewed his predicament, he saw at the back of the line of water carriers a burly man shove an elderly one. The graybeard's jar tumbled to the ground, spilling his water, and he fell to one knee. Moses hurried to see what the squabble was about. Almost with panic, he thought, *Dark Gods, this man could be not just a countryman, but a relative, even my father.*

"Why did you shove him?" demanded Moses.

The aggressor, hearing the Egyptian voice behind him, cast down his eyes and answered with hostile subservience, "He sloshed water on me. Look at my tunic, wet to the skin." Then he turned and saw Moses and his eyes became cunning. "Oh, it is you, worthy Prince Hapi-Set. Surely you do not mean to kill me as you killed the Egyptian yesterday . . ." Seeing the shock in Moses' face, the man went on impudently, ". . . for who has made *you* a judge and a prince over my miserable people?"

Moses' temper burst. His hand went to his sword. But he must control himself. The man he had saved had talked, and probably widely. It would be only a day, if that, before word reached Sety, who was in residence at Tanis. And Ramses. With no further word, he turned and walked to the spreading goatskin tent from which Ramses supervised the building of Pi-Ramessu.

"You killed an Egyptian because he was punishing a Hebrew slacker?" Ramses raged when Moses told him the story of the killing. "Fool! Fool! Do you see where you have put me? You must go to the family of this stupid taskmaster, make reparations, get down on the floor, and beat your witless head on it. You, a prince. Seth and all the gods! Who will respect you among our overseers, the taskmasters? Oh, the gods, you killed one of them! And for no reason . . ."

Moses, in better times, would have lashed out at Ramses at this point, or before. He had done right, not wrong. But thinking of Sebah, of his already tottering future, he dared do no more than listen, nod, look ashamed.

Ramses raved on: ". . . Can you imagine what my father will say of this? Hapi-Set, he has been a father to you as well. All your life. You know his temper. And him ailing. If he were not such a tough old hawk, this would kill him. Anyone else, even another prince, he would exile. Even execute." Ramses was calming, if only slightly. "Amait and all her ghouls! I do not need problems like this, Hapi-Set. We must go to him, before he sends for us. Let me talk. Just let me talk."

Ramses peremptorily summoned his chariot and driver and the three of them skidded off toward the palace at Tanis. Sety received Ramses and Moses immediately. His aging vizier, who loved Ramses next only to his master, whispered to them, "He knows. In the name of the gods, Ramses, tell him first that you came as soon as you knew, and did not wait for his messenger."

Sety's creased skin was white as a swan, his hostile eyes glowered from deep cavities, and his hands trembled as the end of bony arms that had once wielded the mightiest sword in Egypt. He wore a bowl-shaped wig with a diadem of braided gold whose tails hung down the back of his neck. A golden cobra with jeweled eyes intertwined the diadem. His false beard—worn by every Pharaoh—drooped to his bare chest. A servant with a shaved skull buffed his toenails. The Pharaoh's voice shouted feebly:

"Ramses, son of Re, I am too angered at the Prince Hapi-Set to hear him, but if you speak for him, I will listen. Speak only the truth, as you have always done, noble son, and eloquently, if you wish to save the friend of your youth."

In diffident but clear tones, Ramses, hand on his bare chest, formally addressed his father by his ceremonial names. "Menmaatre Sety-Merenptah, your bounty endless from your labors on behalf of the Gods, Mountain of Retenou, only companion of the deities of the White Wall"—that was Memphis. Sety made no effort to shorten the ritual, thus signifying his distress at his son for having a friend like Moses. For if Sety were not dismayed, the three would have talked in their usual manner, a bit stiff, to be sure, but still as members of the same family.

After a full two minutes of titles, Ramses told how Moses had been slashed at by the taskmaster, who had apparently gone mad. "Hapi-Set struck at him with his sword hilt in order to stun, but not kill him. But Renenutet, and Meskhenet, and Sokar of the falcon head, deemed the man should die for the indignity of an assault upon royalty. Hapi-Set has regretted a thousand times hiding the body in the Nile, instead of allowing this taskmaster's family the ceremonies of death.

"A thousand times more he has regretted not instantly coming to your majesty to confess his imprudence. I beg you, Elevated Father and God, let him make abject repentance to the family of this taskmaster, the most generous reparations, but let me keep him at Pi-Ramessu, where I truly need him to work for the gods of Egypt, first and foremost, yourself, Living Horus."

Sety listened without a change of expression. Moses began to wonder whether Sety did not want him dead, lest at some future time he challenge Ramses. Or had he, all along, wanted one of his own sons to be vizier to Ramses, however unworthy they were by comparison? Or had some other prince taken advantage of Sety's sickness to undermine Moses? Moses pondered all this, hating and resenting the intrigues of the court, the insane worship of this fickle multitude of gods, wanting only to join Sebah and her father, the sage and unpretentious king of faraway Barbaht. Moses was wise enough not to say a word during the half-hour interview. Time came, at last, for his sentence.

Sety first took a deep draught from a gold cup that Moses knew contained milk, honey, and ground ivy, a restorative. He reached toward the courtier who held the mace, rather than the one holding the royal flail, to indicate that his dissatisfaction continued. When he spoke, his wavering voice was harsh.

"Prince Hapi-Set, you are unworthy to serve our gods, in great ways or small. I spare you because my son and heir, the divine Ramses, second of that name, needs you; and because of your mother, the Princess Mutempsut, daughter by adoption of the regal Horemheb, daughter of Ramses, first of that name, and my eldest sister, now beloved of the Faithful Gods of the Underworld. This taskmaster was but doing his duty in chastising a recalcitrant slave. Can you blame him for using his dagger to assert his right on one he could not have recognized as royalty?

"What discipline can we impose on these slaves if a prince murders their supervisors? And if his body is not found, you have interfered with the right of his parents to see it taken in peace to the tomb of his fathers. For this you deserve harsh punishments. But that is not the worst."

Say what you intend to say! Moses wanted to shout at the old man, watching the flaccid skin crinkle on his chest as he drew breaths to maintain his tirade. But only through craven silence could Moses hope for a sentence that would not deny him any chance at all of ever seeing Sebah again.

At last, Sety finished. ". . . But your greater iniquity is that you kept this secret until you learned it was known. For that, you should die. But I forbear. I forbid to you the post of vizier when I go to the realm of the gods. I require my son, Ramses, to vow it shall not happen. I would banish you, except for his need of you in the building of the temples of the Estate of the Ramessides. And when he is done with you, you will serve Egypt in its farthest fields of war, and fight in the first ranks, where your death may purify you in the nostrils of the gods."

With that, he raised the mace and Moses backed from his presence, leaving Ramses to work out what announcements should be made to the court, and thus Egypt, and more particularly to the officials at Tanis and Pi-Ramessu, where Moses, on sufferance, would have to serve until he could scheme to go south in peace.

Moses' hiding of the killing built a wall of mistrust between him and Ramses. Yet, in spite of this, he labored long days, finding solutions for engineering problems, such as how to get water uphill to palace ponds. He used open-ended pottery vases snugly fitted together to make pipes that ran on a downward grade from a slow stream that he dammed on the other side of the valley. The water entered the innovative pipes at a level slightly higher than the ponds, ran down into the valley and up the hillside into the pool—a hydraulic miracle to Ramses.

And he designed different-sized pulleys so that two men could lift limestone blocks formerly raised by six. Ramses, always practical and never able to stay angry with him, praised his work and would have found some way back to their old relationship. The fact that Moses would never be his vizier left him more sorry for Moses than for himself, for there was no stricture against him using his friend as a personal advisor and aide. Let some foppish prince bear the title so long as he had Moses to help him in remaking Egypt.

But Moses, absorbed in the complexities of his life, found it hard to respond to Ramses. He hated himself because he dared not confide about his origins to this lifelong friend who had saved him from the Pharaoh's wrath. What made it worse was that if Sety discovered he was a Hebrew, Ramses would be judged by his father either a traitor or a fool. Moses was also becoming obsessed with meeting his parents, affirming to them, at least, that he acknowledged them and his sister and brother. And, perhaps most important,

Moses could find no peace with himself or anyone because of his fixation about going to Sebah.

In this last regard, he wrote to Paras and Sebah about his killing the taskmaster, his failure to tell Ramses and Sety, his reparations to the dead man's family, and his public shame. He told of Sety's decree that he must stay at Pi-Ramessu to help with the construction. He promised to find some way to return to Barbaht if they could bear with him for a while longer. Because the facts were public, he did not have to send Bes-Ahrin on the twenty-five-hundred-mile round trip. Instead, he sent the letter with a longtime servant whom both he and the dwarf trusted.

Moses' letter crossed one from Barbaht. Two weeks after he had dispatched it, Bes-Ahrin, riding posthaste on a sturdy donkey, and leading a second one, arrived at the site of a new temple to the Great Ennead—the nine most prominent gods—whose gallery of columns Moses was laying out. In the dwarf's belt was an ebony box, the twin of the earlier dispatch case from Barbaht. Between breaths, he told Moses it had been delivered by two armed warriors from Barbaht who said they had been on the trip with Moses to Punt and were the emissaries of the king.

Moses broke the seal and again read the king's letter first. "I write in haste," it said, after the salutations. "Your cousin, the king of Punt, has been vanquished in a battle with the rebels. They keep him as ceremonial king, for though he is ineffectual, he is loved by the people. However, the rebels dictate his actions under threat of his and his family's torture and death. To be concise, my representative in Punt has informed me by the most speedy means that your cousin has been forced to send two princes of the house of Anodheb that deposed your grandfather and killed your father—or those you thought to be such—with letters to the Pharaoh Sety.

"In them, your cousin says you or someone in your employ (for your guide apparently has fled forever) broke into the tomb of your supposed grandfather. They recite the story on the tomb walls and now, beside the testimony of the two Danakil women, they have located three old peasants in whose hovels the princess stayed during her escape. I fear their tale of a black baby cannot be dismissed even given the Puntite renown for lying. They heap abuse on you as an impostor who breaks into sacred tombs, disturbs the dead in their sarcophagi, exploits the hospitality of a king—your cousin—and all as an envoy of the god Sety and Egypt, a friendly power.

"It is obvious they want you dead, lest you come south with an army, claim to be the son of the dead crown prince, and wrest the throne from them. As if it would not be the best thing in the world for Punt. They defame me, saying I was tricked by you, thus making me out to be a fool, and the Pharaohs, as well. For they allege, falsely, as I know, that you have always known you were not the son of a Puntite prince, but a nameless waif the Princess Mutempsut substituted for her dead baby.

"Dear Hapi-Set, or Moses, if you must have it so, Sety will surely have to redeem himself and Egypt with Punt, one of the most treasured independent trading empires of Egypt. Nor will Nubia, though more a vassal, be comfortable, I am afraid, with having dealt with an unknown imposter whom they thought a high prince. In short, trust my knowledge of the ways of kings: Sety will have to execute you, perhaps in some dreadful way that will in part purge him of his shame in Egypt and abroad.

"Prince, for by whatever name you will be royal to me and to Sebah, my first thought was to accept you as the son of a slave, let you become a leader of my country as your great *Ra* would enable you to do, and then accept you as my son. But I cannot oppose the anger of a Pharaoh when it would risk the deaths of so many of my people in a war I could not win. Sebah is all but destroyed by these events. But she is strong, and will not abandon me or Barbaht, although her heart tells her to.

"I pray to the gods that this letter reaches you before it is too late. I have told my two loyal officers to spend whatever is necessary to reach you before the abominable Puntite couriers get to Sety. I beg you to flee immediately to some land where Egypt cannot touch you. Should you ever need gold, if Bes-Ahrin, who I am sure is also at risk, can come to me, I will have it for you with my blessing."

Almost in a trance, Moses opened the letter from Sebah. *Ah*, he thought, *my beautiful, my good.* In the letter, there were only words of sympathy, of eternal love for him, only encouragement in the most noble terms for him to be brave and to believe that he was a god among men. Only the promise that someday, somehow, somewhere, she would find a way to join him.

Moses, his pulse in his temple throbbing so fast that he was dizzy, turned to the waiting Bes-Ahrin. "We must flee for our lives, good dwarf, this very night."

The two of them galloped down the rutty work road toward their house as the sun began to dip toward the desert shrubs. Moses stuffed his necessities into two goatskin saddlebags and called into the adjoining room, where Bes-Ahrin huffed and talked to himself over his own packing.

"Tonight," said Moses, "I will visit my family. And I cannot leave without telling the truth to Ramses. If you wish to go on without me, do so. Who could blame you? Look at the trouble I have brought on you, more even than fate already has!"

Bes-Ahrin allowed himself the rudeness of a grunt. Moses smiled glumly at the gruff little man's transferred loyalty, even as tears welled in his eyes over its magnitude.

Chapter Six
The Exile

HE QUIET OF THE GLOAMING HAD SETTLED OVER THE SLAVE VILLAGE. Moses and Bes-Ahrin, in simple linen traveling tunics, walked unobtrusively down the deserted dirt alleys, none more than eight feet wide. Oil lamps glowed faintly in those few houses with windows. The fumy smell blended with the odors of waste and dry nettles, but also with the herby scent of marjoram, cumin, mustard, and bitter rue from tiny houseside gardens.

At a one-story home, more prosperous than others—as evidenced by the tiles with fig-leaf designs on its door frame—Bes-Ahrin gave a coded knock: two, then a pause, then three. At his orders, Moses waited around the corner of the dwelling.

He heard the door open, the dwarf's mutter, a gasp, excited whispers. Then Bes-Ahrin summoned Moses with a snap of his fingers. Keeping his large body as pinched in as possible, he rounded the corner, stooped through the doorway, and felt around him the arms of a warm, wiry woman with gray hair.

"Moses," she said. "God has sent you at last."

Simultaneously, he felt his father's strong grip on his shoulder, and his brother's on his arm. His sister, Miriam, spare and gray-haired as Jochebed, sniffled excitedly as she sought to find a place to embrace the visitor. "Moses, brother," she said. "God has saved you for us."

For long minutes the welcoming family cried silently, although Moses' eyes were dry. He was unaccustomed to this kind of tactile family emotionalism, and at last, Bes-Ahrin broke in.

"He comes but to tell you he is your son, your brother, but, believe me, his life, mine also, are at hazard. We flee the Pharaoh and his wrath. . . ."

"I knew when they said an Egyptian prince had killed Souhep, the taskmaster, to save the worthless Yabob that it was our son," said Amram. "We knew," seconded Jochebed.

"It is more than that," said Moses. "Somehow I will find a way to send for you. And I will tell you everything." He could not yet call them "mother," "father," "sister," "brother," though he had often done it in thought since Bes-Ahrin told him of them. He was no longer Hapi-Set. Or No-Name. But he was not yet Moses, son of the Land of Goshen.

"One glass of wine," said Aaron, his eyes alight in his intelligent, longish face, looking up at his younger brother, who was a full head taller than he was. "Father has saved it, knowing that you would come back to us. We learned all we could of you, but we kept your secret, Moses. Even Miriam," he said, not meaning to sound either humorous or critical.

"I? I?" she protested.

In a moment, Amram had an old wine jug, its mouth filled with wax. "I bought it with your first gift to us, Bes-Ahrin," he said, more comfortable with the familiar dwarf than his new son. "Now you must share it with us."

"Gladly," said the dwarf, with rare grace, "but I beg of you, Amram, pour fast and no more speeches."

"Only this," said Amram as he tipped wine into the crude pottery cups. "The God of Abraham, Isaac, Jacob, and Joseph has brought Moses home. Now, oh merciful God, protect him and us."

The simple prayer moved Moses. No flowery talk of deities with bull or vulture faces. No invocations of mere men who call themselves by the names of a dozen divinities, each pronounced as part of every prayer.

"Say 'amen,'" said Jochebed quietly to her son. "Say it. It will please our God to hear you."

"Amen, if it pleases you . . . Mother." And with hurried farewells, the large and small man faded into the night.

Every hoofbeat of the donkeys as they picked their way out of the slave village made Moses nervous. They reached the spacious dwellings of the princes and the other wealthy of Tanis and Moses stopped at a corner near the walled palace of Ramses. He dismounted and handed his donkey's reins to Bes-Ahrin.

"If I am not out in a half-hour, flee to the east, brave dwarf. You have your band of those like you to help, I know."

The watchdog geese squawked until a servant came out and recognized Moses. Ramses, sipping wine and dipping his finger into a bowl of mullet roe, was at work on the architectural drawings of two long-tiered warehouses near the Nile. He looked up at Moses without surprise. "Welcome, good Hapi-Set. Just in time to make sure I have not forgotten anything in the placement of these warehouses." Then he noticed Moses' simple traveling garments. "What is this?" he asked.

Moses was well prepared in his mind for this interview. "I come to make your life less complicated, oldest friend," he said, honest, yet tendentious. "My heart has never been more torn than at this moment. For you have saved me several times, most recently through your eloquence with your father."

Ramses, used to a more straightforward Moses, said, "Enough temple talk,

Hapi-Set. Out with, it"—he smiled with humor, but also a touch of cruelty—"my vizier-to-have-been." He put the scroll down and it rolled up of itself with a soft rustle. "No stammering. Say it."

Moses' throat was almost too dry to speak. "I am leaving Egypt tonight, Ramses. Forever. I have discovered something about myself that you will find hard to believe. But I must tell you, for it is about to be uncovered."

"Hapi-Set, Hapi-Set." There was genuine alarm, then he tried, if gauchely, to lighten it. "You sound like that crazy Libyan prince who committed suicide before we could capture him. Remember? First he peed himself, then he slit his throat."

Moses was able to summon a smile. "Ramses, that is just what I am going to do."

Ramses leaped up from his chair.

"No, no, not with a knife," he hurried on, as his friend stood poised to disarm him if need be. "Ramses, I am not my mother's son, nor the son of a crown prince of Punt. After my mother—Princess Mutempsut," he corrected himself, "fled Zeiloh, her real son, Sen-Dudak, died on the way here, in a boat outside Memphis. He was a sickly, dark baby, the journey from Punt too much for him. He was dropped overboard. . . ."

Ramses' mouth opened slackly, then he recovered enough to gasp, "Hapi-Set, I do not believe it. This is the stuff of old fables, old shadowy tales told by ancient gods."

"Oh, Ramses, would it were so. But do not stop me," he smiled cheerlessly. "Lest I begin to stammer. My mother, who will always in some way seem so, substituted for this dead child a slightly older foundling. That is why I always appeared so big for my age."

Ramses shook his head in disbelief. But the remembrance of their youthful contests temporarily diverted him. "We were almost the same age is what you are saying. No wonder you sometimes came out the winner."

It was this childlike approach to any competition, so attractive in the grown Ramses, that almost broke Moses down. "Yes," he said, "but you were the better athlete and would have won most of the time even if I had been a year older."

"Can this be true?" said Ramses, his shock returning.

"Every word of it."

"How can you be sure?"

"I broke into my father's tomb in Punt. It is all on the walls there, in the coffin. The names of my nurses who saw me die. Everything. My father's corpse was black. In the coffin were figurines . . . of catamites. My father was—" Moses turned back to the pertinent facts. "There were other witnesses. I have spoken with one." He did not want to name Bes-Ahrin. "And others"—the women in the hovels—"came forward."

"Your mother told you?"

"No. She was dying. I wanted her to be at peace."

"That sounds like you, anyway. The disgusting dwarf. He had a hand in this."

"I had not wanted to say. It was he who lowered the black baby over the side. My real mother had floated me in a basket to where Mutempsut bathed in the Nile before she went to Punt . . . to save me during the time Horemheb wanted every son born of Hebrews killed. Ramses, my mother and father are Hebrews. Do not ask me their names, for I will not tell you. But, in any case, I must flee. Even now, the new powers in Punt are sending your father a letter."

Ramses instantly erupted. "You have known this for a long time, and yet you never told me? . . ."

"I had planned to tell you this week, to ask you to try to get Sety to let me leave to go to Barbaht, to Sebah. Her father would let me serve in his army. He would give me a chance to prove that the son of a slave can be a good soldier." Moses looked at Ramses' reddening face. "As this son of a slave did for you, Ramses. As I did for Egypt."

Ramses was disarmed, remembering Moses in battle. "As you did for me, for Egypt," he repeated tensely. "But you are mistaken about my father if we had told him. If he knew you were a Hebrew he would have had you killed. He *will* have you killed. An Egyptian hero really a Hebrew slave? Oh, Hapi-Set, how could you have kept this from me? How can I find some way to spare you?"

Pain gripped Moses' heart again at his friend's fairness. "Ramses, I love you," he said, tears in his eyes. "All the sounds of battle, the peal of bugles, the laughter of wine and women, all the thrill of hoping to see magnificent buildings rise under our hands, all of this is dying in me. And I can scarcely bear it."

"I never saw you cry," said Ramses, discomposed. "Well, that one time when you were sixteen, in Nubia. Do not do it now. You already sound like an old Hebrew blubbering over short rations."

"I *am* an old Hebrew. I debated whether to tell you. I decided I could not let you learn it from Sety. I could not run away with you judging me a liar."

Ramses, for all his devotion to the gods, had a streak of cynicism that had served him well in maintaining his place as successor, and would, Moses knew, serve him well during his reign. He fixed Moses with cold eyes. "Hapi-Set—what name will you call yourself?—it is not a question of my thinking you a liar. You are a liar or you would have told me the moment you returned from seeing the writings in the tomb, and certainly after you confirmed it with Bes-Vermin. It is only a matter of degree. You are less of a liar than you might have been."

Moses could not argue the point. "Yes. I lied. Because I thought I might keep up the pretense, go to Sebah as a prince in the eyes of the world, for she and Paras know everything."

"Well," said Ramses, selling his emotional wheat at less than he had paid for it, but for the best price he could get—honesty with Moses and himself. "You have lost her. And me, too."

"Yes, lost both of you." Moses felt defeated, and even wondered if death in the manner of the Libyan prince was not the best answer. But suicide was not his way. He added quietly, "Do you have any questions? What would you have me do?" The full anguish of his deception of Ramses, of what it could do to Ramses when Sety realized it, had erased his remaining sangfroid. He drew his sword and Ramses, ever alert, dodged back. But Moses only dropped it to clatter in the silence on the blue-and-rose tiles. "You have saved me more times than I have saved you, Ramses. I betrayed you. I owe you the debt of a life. Take it if you want to, old comrade."

Ramses looked assessingly at the sword, then kicked it back toward Moses. "Go, Hebrew. I will lie to Sety. He will die without knowing you came here. I will say you fled like a coward in the night. He will not have to live long with my lie." He paused and sighed. "I will have to live with it." But with a second sigh, he added, "But I make a point of not dwelling on sorrows. I have a city to build."

They parted coldly, without a farewell embrace or even a farewell. *It is as good an ending as I could have hoped,* Moses thought. *I betrayed him. He did not betray me.*

All night long, the towering man and the dwarf rode eastward. At dawn they paused, drank some water from their leather bags, ate some bread, and moved on. Sety, sick as he was, *especially* sick as he was, would want revenge. Moses had partially purged himself of his own monumental lie, and now, as he rode, he hoped he had not weighed down Ramses with a second one too burdensome to maintain.

As penance, Moses had taken with him none of the jewels and gold he had earned as an Egyptian or inherited from his mother. So he had nothing. But

Bes-Ahrin, out of his own legacy from Mutempsut, had filled a saddlebag with gold. No doubt, Moses thought, he had buried much more at Heliopolis, where he could depend on some confederate among the legion of the deformed to dig it up as need be and get it to him.

The two fugitives slept fitfully the next night just off the road. At the copper mines of Punon, a hundred and twenty miles due east of Tanis, they slowed. Their shoulder and back muscles had stiffened; their inner thighs were chafing; their beasts were almost as weary. "Why not pause here, Prince Hapi-Set?" said Bes-Ahrin, for he could not bring himself to relinquish the name his beloved mistress had used.

Moses looked at the homely, grizzled face and smiled. "How long would it take for word to reach Sety that a dwarf who looks like the god Bes is in Punon? Ramses would take profound pleasure in having various parts of your body sent back to him, chopped up by bronze blades from the royal smelters."

Bes-Ahrin laughed in spite of himself. "Then let us leave. Might it not be wise to ride due north toward the Great Green, then bear eastward toward Canaan, or even Syria, where we can lose ourselves?"

But, of course, there was no land of dwarfs where Bes-Ahrin could lose himself. Even if there were, Canaan was under Egyptian rule and Syria, though the homeland of Bes-Ahrin, was presently at peace with Egypt. "No, Bes-Ahrin," Moses said, "there is a Bedouin people, riders of camels, that roam in the peninsula of Sinai. I had a battalion of them under me in Palestine. Good fighters. And honest. No one has tamed these people, the Midianites. Their land is owned by no one, for it is desert save for a few oases. We will go among them, both of us safer there than where Egypt has ears and arms."

"Yes, I know it," Bes-Ahrin said with a sly smile, "a land near the Red Sea, and thus closer to Barbaht than Syria."

Moses smiled, then tightened his lips. "And yet as far away from Barbaht as the moon. If like a fool I went to Sebah, and she fled with me, Sety would order some murderous retaliation against Paras. Sety will always hate me. I insulted him, made a fool of him, of his gods, of Egypt. A Hebrew prince of Egypt, a royal nephew for twenty-six years? The Hittite Kingdom will burst with laughter when they find it out."

Bes-Ahrin knew it was true. They filled their water and fodder bags at a smelly livery stable, paid the one-eyed owner his exorbitant price, and struck out into the night across the wilderness of gorse, thistles, snakes, and hungry wild beasts.

A few days later, they reached and risked riding on the Turquoise Route, a road used by caravans for centuries. By day, Moses, but not Bes-Ahrin, entered towns such as Marah and Elim, where a few markets broiled near dried palm trees, their rotten-toothed merchants sheltered under tattered tents of uncured goatskin. Moses seemed no different from any other itinerant buying food, for by now he was unshaven and dusty, his muscular beast as scraggly as he.

The dwarf met him on the other side of town and they picked up the Turquoise Route toward Dophkah, in the Wilderness of Zin, a town where, again, only Moses ventured. It was the last outpost of Egypt, its black and Arab slaves living in low, uneven baked-mud huts that made those of Goshen look like the dwellings of princes.

Moses learned from the Edomite who ran a sparsely stocked commissary and rundown inn, now empty of guests, that a large Midianite encampment lay to the west in the desolate mountains east of Rephidim. The hosteler had never ventured there, for, he told Moses, the area teemed with leopards with necks like giraffes, lions with human heads, and tigers with wide orange-and-black wings. But, added the Edomite, it also was rumored to have wells that were dug even before the time of the Pharaohs.

The two tired journeyers found no such wondrous animals, but they did find a well not far from a large encampment of tents. Bes-Ahrin sat on a rock some forty feet from the well, watching young women, all clad in coarse, long tunics despite the heat, raising water with the well's *shaduf*—a pole in a creaking wooden fork counterweighted with a heavy stone so that water could be more easily lifted.

Two of the young women efficiently lowered the bucket end of the pole into the well, then two others at the stone end raised it and pivoted the pole so that the water could empty into a trough. Another three smacked the heads of their sheep to prevent them from rushing the troughs before they were full.

The women had courteously offered Moses first use of the well, as was the Bedouin custom toward strangers, and he had refused, as he believed was required by the same custom. One of the women had brought them cups of water and they sipped it while they waited to fill their water bags.

"Well, we have left Egypt at last," Moses said.

"May Bes grant that *it* has left *us*." said the dwarf.

As they rested, swords and belts at their feet, they saw dust on the road they had just traveled and soon heard raucous laughter and the baas of more sheep. Two shepherds, broad-shouldered men in baggy loincloths and carrying heavy crooks, approached, leading some three dozen sheep. Behind them were two more husky shepherds.

Moses rose to let the shepherds know they were third in line. Their leader, a man of about forty and clean shaven, looked at the two Egyptians and said in the Bedouin tongue—an Arabic dialect that Moses understood slightly—"Look, a bearded dwarf! Shall we shear him? There's a *deben*'s worth of dwarf hair on that face!"

Moses did not want to cause trouble among people whom, for a while, he might want to join. Bes-Ahrin, from his childhood in Syria, understood enough to know he had been insulted. He glared, but also remained silent.

"First the water, then the shave," said the second man.

"Away, women," the leader said. "Stand back. Let men in a hurry have your water."

"Let the dwarf make water for your sheep while you wait," said the second man, guffawing. The leader addressed the women again, "Do we have to shove you? I say, 'Away!'"

The two other men came forward, and seeing what was going on, waved their crooks at the women, moving up as if to push them. One of the women, short and lithe, her intense, tanned face and bright almond eyes outraged, cried, "Strangers, we will not go! My father will punish you for this. You shall see."

The leader said to the other three, "Water the sheep. I'll take care of this one."

The six other women, all younger than the defiant one, began to cry "Shame! Shame!" at the shepherds, who ignored them and busily herded their sheep forward. The bleating almost drowned out the argument of the leader with the woman. Moses saw him push her with his crook, although with no particular force.

"The swords," said Moses quietly to Bes-Ahrin.

They drew their blades from their scabbards and walked quickly toward the shepherd's leader. The plucky woman was trying to wrench the crook from him. He pushed her down, and she came to her feet and struck at him with small fists.

"Your pleasure, Bes-Ahrin," Moses said, not raising his voice, "but draw no blood, hardy warrior."

The dwarf, as if he had already planned it in detail, moved forward brusquely and slashed his sword down on the crook near the shepherd's hand, dashing it to the ground. The man turned on the dwarf, not half his height, but

Bes-Ahrin raised the blade to the man's naked belly. "Shall I butcher this ram, Hapi-Set? There's a deben's worth of mutton on his withers, I will warrant you."

"Begone, offal," Moses shouted in broken Arabic at the suddenly frightened man. The other three shepherds stood by dumbfounded, until Moses and Bes-Ahrin ran at them, weapons flashing in the sunshine, with hostile cries of "Yaa! Yaa!"

The leader propelled himself backward, away from the blades, and fell over a sheep. The others tried to shoo their sheep away from the well. The animals baaed wildly. The two swordsmen slapped the men with the flats of their blades, sending all four back down the road, their sheep following in disarray. The compact young woman who had defied the bullies came to Moses, looked at his Egyptian tunic, and said, "Let us draw more water for you, Egyptians, and for your beasts. Sisters," she called.

"No," said Moses. "We wait as before."

Still fired by her brush with the shepherds, she was in no mood for deference. "Come, come, sir, enough of this. Accept the water so we can all be about our business."

So resolute was her manner that Moses complied, amused. When their water bags were filled, he and Bes-Ahrin helped water the women's sheep. That done, they bowed to them and left for the encampment to seek at least a night's lodging and perhaps some sense of whether this might be a temporary home for them. The women began to gather together their flock.

When the woman and her sisters returned to the home of their father, by far the most luxurious of the city of tents, her face, even beneath the tan, was flushed.

"How are you back so soon, Zipporah?" he asked.

"It is well I am not back later," she said. She told him of the unusual Egyptians who had put the four brazen shepherds to flight and then helped water their sheep. As she spoke, her mother and, a moment later, the second wife of her father, parted the linen curtains of the entranceway and came in to listen.

"And where is this Egyptian and his dwarf? Why did you let them leave without inviting them to come to me?"

Embarrassed at her breach of courtesy, Zipporah said that while she and her sisters collected the flock, the two strangers had ridden their donkeys toward the encampment.

"Well, then they are here somewhere. Go find them," he ordered, but indulgently. "A dwarf and a tall Egyptian are not likely to go unnoticed even among our multitude. Run, Zipporah. And you others, too," he said signaling to her younger sisters.

Moses and Bes-Ahrin had found lodging in the large tent of an old woman whose husband had recently died and who was thus happy to have paying guests. "Sirs," she held forth with some exaggeration, "you have come to the finest tent of our tribe, second only to that of our priest and king, Jethro." She pointed to the copper bowls in which she promised to stew lamb, corn, and cumin; to a glowing gob of terebinth gum in a small dish, which would keep away scorpions and sand fleas; and to the cleanliness of her rug, woven of heavy dyed wool. "I beg you stay for the first night without payment," she said. "See, I will portion off a section of the tent for you."

Moses, falling in with what he perceived was customary, argued with her until she agreed with a show of reluctance that they could pay for the first night. He and Bes-Ahrin helped hang a wool tapestry across the rear of the tent. They had just washed their bodies from their water bags and pulled close-tined ivory combs through their beards and hair when they heard a young woman's voice and the excited answering tones of the old woman.

"Sir," their landlady called through the hanging cloth, "and you also, esteemed dwarf, Jethro, our priest and king, awaits you in his tent. Hurry, and I will conduct you there."

Hearing his guests' approach, the priest-king rose from his cushion to greet them. He was stooped, but powerfully built, and ruddy-faced. His eyes squinted from exposure to sunlight, but the wrinkles in their corners turned upward, a sure sign of cheerfulness. He wore a red-and-black cloak of the most costly wool over a flaxen tunic so white it seemed to glow in the oil light. "Kind strangers," he said, "I apologize for the failure of my daughters to invite you to my tent to share my bread. Zipporah, my eldest, is generally wise beyond her years. . . ." He clucked with his inner mouth as if he could not believe it, but Moses could hear his love even as he scolded her.

She and the others, clad now also in white linen, sat on the women's side of the tent with two older women, their mothers. A frail hunchback in a lower priest's embroidered garb plucked a repetitive theme on the zither. The musician, introduced to them as Praroth, exchanged guarded looks of kinship with Bes-Ahrin. The smell of lamb from a brazier just outside wafted in. A basket tray as big as a chariot wheel of sheep's, goats', and camels' milk cheeses, surrounded by dates and small loaves of flat fresh bread, lay on a very low table in the center of the rug with its intricate palm, gazelle, and sun motifs.

The warmth and order of the tent palace enveloped Moses. And something else. What was it? He smiled. There was not a hieroglyph, a statuette, or a painting of a god in sight.

"Let us eat, Egyptians," said their host, pointing them with open hands to cushions, "for although we have often found you targets of our spears and throwing sticks and we of your bows and lances, we know there are good men among you."

No invocation of Hathor or Horus or any other gods, Moses noted. Just a welcome that transcended race and boundary. "We are not Egyptians, noble Jethro," said Moses, "although Egypt was our home. I am, in fact, the son of Hebrews, and my companion is a Syrian, sold by his family as a child."

Jethro was taken aback, but only for a moment. Moses glanced at Zipporah and saw a moment of consternation, but the priest-king nodded as if nothing was less of a surprise. "The Hebrews are even worse enemies of us Midianites than the Egyptians," he said, then laughed, showing big white teeth. "We fight all races when we are not trading with them, or protecting their caravans. The Egyptians at least have money to pay us to protect them from other Arab marauders in this part of the desert. The Hebrews in Canaan fight us on sight, and those in Egypt have no money even to buy themselves out of slavery."

Moses laughed with him. For the first time since his catastrophe in the tomb at Zeiloh, he felt a sense of contentment, of muscles easing, of acceptance. "My mother and father are just such slaves," he said.

"Their son," replied Jethro, "seems a prince who protects the daughters of a humble priest. And his friend, the mighty dwarf, drives Midianite scoundrels to fall over the backs of their sheep. Tell me your names."

They did so, and as they ate, Moses recited at least part of his and Bes-Ahrin's histories, as strangers must do when visiting far from home. He said he had been allowed to work and learn in a palace and that Bes-Ahrin had befriended him. Both had wanted their freedom and had fled, knowing full well that if they were captured they would be put to death. "We had heard of the independence of the Midianites and so are here," he ended.

The two travelers enjoyed every aspect of the meal except for the fermented camels' milk, which was served with wild honey cakes for dessert. Amid all the pleasure of the evening, Moses could feel Jethro weighing him, and, although they said little, his daughters assessing him, too.

When the Midianites parted with their guests, Jethro bid both to come again in the morning. "God, yours and mine, be with you," he said. Moses must have looked confused, for the priest-king explained, "We believe in one god as you Hebrews do. For though we fight, we are closer brothers than any other peoples near Egypt. Our god, like yours, is the God of Abraham, although many Midianites to the east have fallen away to the worship of Baal. Your people descend from Abraham's wife, Sarah; we from his true love, our Egyptian mother, Hagar."

Moses had not been a diplomat for nothing. "Our God be with you, king. Would that I dared call you cousin through our common father." Their host smiled and Moses' heart had seldom felt more pure, for he had told the truth about being a Hebrew, and no harm had come to him.

In the morning, Jethro asked Moses whether he and Bes-Ahrin would go with his daughters to the well again, in case the shepherds dared return. "If they come, do not fight. Send for me. Then, they will not come again. Not to any wells, ever."

It was, Moses realized, a Bedouin invitation to stay awhile in the encampment. And he and Bes-Ahrin were pleased to have a place to bide awhile. For example, the dwarf discovered that Jethro did no bronze making, yet the area abounded in copper, and tin could be had in trade. The priest-king already had shipping channels for malachite and turquoise to Egypt and even through the Wilderness of Paran to Canaan, Syria, and beyond. Bes-Ahrin, very much a craftsman, set up a simple forge to purify the copper ore and to make knives, bowls, even turquoise-studded jewelry that could be marketed via the same trade routes.

And in Moses Jethro saw a man ever willing to use his ingenuity and labor on the Bedouins' behalf. He began with guarding the flocks. Soon he was intrigued with the breeding of sheep, goats, and camels, known only as oddities in Egypt. For Jethro's wells, he asked a stonemason to cut round holes in flat limestone so that the forks of the *shadufs* could pivot smoothly instead of turning inefficiently in a hole in the packed dirt. Jethro, learning of Moses' days as an Egyptian soldier, invited him to train his tribesmen in spear thrusting and in the use of triangular Syrian bows, which were bought in small quantities from traders, for the desert wood was unsuitable.

To supplement the fermented camels' milk, which Moses found distasteful, he located a slightly moist area near the foothills. He bought—thanks to Bes-

Ahrin—a few handfuls of barley, smelt, and millet seed. He sowed test plots to see whether cereals would grow from which beer could be made.

Often, in the evenings, drinking hot tea made from anise, Moses, the hunchback priest Praroth—whose curiosity about the world almost matched Moses'—and Bes-Ahrin sat around a fire outside Praroth's tent. The priest, whose family had numerous flocks, was unfit for hard physical work, but his quickness of mind had been evident. His father had sent him for schooling at the Gulf of Aqabah's port and cultural city, Ezion-geber.

Moses talked of Egypt's history, so connected to its theology, and Praroth spoke of Abraham, Hagar, her encounter by the spring with the God of Abraham, and their son, Ishmael, who had founded the twelve tribes of the Midianites.

"The tribes are always fighting each other, but we agree on one thing," said Praroth, his dark eyes glowing, "We, like Ishmael, have a single god, unlike the Egyptians. And our god is involved, if with anything, with life, not death."

Moses laughed. "The gods of Egypt honor its victories, control the Nile, govern daily life. But always, always, the gods are thinking about death, how and where people are to be buried. The Egyptians, although far from morose, live every day as if they fear, even when they are happy, that they will be judged harshly by Thoth, Osiris, Anubis, and the rest of them when they go to the Underworld. I get no feeling of that here in the wilderness."

"Nor is there any," replied the priest. "Our God of Abraham, and therefore yours, rules to some extent our behavior, our lives. But largely we are left on our own to act, for good or for ill. Our community, not our god, punishes evildoers."

"Maybe," said Moses, "that is why the Egyptians are a commanding nation and the sons of Abraham are not. I do not even know what the Hebrew underworld is supposed to be like."

"I can tell you. It is like our place of the dead. The Hebrews call it Sheol, a vague, grayish land. We Bedouins, like you Hebrews, are too busy with this stern life to think in any detail of what comes next. In my opinion, nothing comes."

Jethro watched Moses as a valued addition to his tribe, and, as the months passed, also as a suitor for his daughter Zipporah. She found Moses friendly, helpful in every way, but he did not treat her with the conventional diffidence of the other prospects her father had brought to her attention since she was fourteen. They had regarded her, along with their ritual politeness, mainly as a young woman to be desired and a potential mother. If Moses imagined either, she thought, he surely kept his intentions hidden.

For his part, Moses clung to his dream of Sebah, of those long-ago nights walking by the Nile, of her courage when they had sought out his putative father's tomb, of her devotion even when she discovered his identity. When he thought of wife, of family, he thought only of her. His encounter with his true parents and siblings in Goshen had been so brief as to leave them mere symbols of family. If he had any family, it was Bes-Ahrin.

In spite of his innovative work in the encampment, Moses spent much of his time in the hills. He took his turn with the flocks, the dry air clean in his nostrils. He studied the peaks of the southern Sinai rising higher and higher until, sharp against the sky, they culminated in Mount Sinai itself. It was called Horeb, or the Mountain of God, by the indigenous desert people who had preceded the Bedouin Midianites. He learned all there was to know about the desert plants, and how a cool wind from the mountains meant rain. And often, on the nights when a breeze kept the insects at bay, he went outside his tent and looked at the heavens.

Sometimes, he lay beside the door, but at times, to be away even from the lamplight, he went to the foothills. There, a staff beside him to drive away any animals that might venture near, Prince Hapi-Set, who was to have been vizier of all Egypt, gradually became Moses, son and brother of hardworking slaves, friend of a Bedouin priest-king and his family. By all appearances, he was a still youngish man with a Bedouin's freedom and a Bedouin's simple needs. He even cultivated a beard as all men in Jethro's tribe did once they had become members of some substance (and he would wear it all his life).

But there was a difference. Before he went to sleep, he often talked in a low voice to the sky, resolving in this way the problems of his day. Yet his ruminations were not exactly soliloquies. For as time passed, amid the stars, he seemed to feel there was a listening presence.

Generally, as he talked to the stars, his eyes picked out the constellations, outlines of Egyptian gods that he and Ramses had pointed to when they were boys on a Nile hillside. He thought often of his old friend, even sometimes found himself talking to him, too.

When he mused on the Egyptian gods, he felt a serene freedom from them. He could say now what he had not dared say openly as a prince: "You are but poor things with no power over me—or over anything. Not only that, you never had any. Your only challenge is in where we locate you in the night sky."

The desert wind on his face, snug in his goatskin cloak, the hyenas howling to each other far away, he faded toward sleep even as the constellations blurred and became dreams.

Six months after he settled in with the Midianites, Moses decided to try to bring his parents and siblings to the desert. Jethro asked a trusted trader—for a fee Moses insisted on paying from his wages as a tribal worker—to inquire clandestinely of Amram whether the family would come, assuming Moses and Bes-Ahrin could smuggle them out.

Amram sent back the message that he and Jochebed feared the risk and that, besides, he was ill at present and dared not travel. Moses was concerned about the illness, but not surprised that Jochebed and Amram, and even more his brother and sister and their families, would not want to leave their known, bearable, if cruel, captivity for an unknown life in the desert. He resolved to try again and did so at least once each year, but never was encouraged to think that they would join him.

A year after Moses left Egypt, as he and Bes-Ahrin ate, the hunchback priest Praroth came to Moses' tent and stuck in his head. "There is news for you two," he said excitedly. "A comrade passing through Dophkah brings information from the delta. The old Pharaoh Sety is dead. Ramses, second of that name, is Pharaoh."

"Is there more, priest?" Moses urged. "Tell us!" Then, remembering his manners, he added, "But come in first. Share our supper with us."

Praroth entered and sat on a cushion by the low table. "Yes, generous Moses, there is more. Sad events for your Hebrews. As one of his first orders, Ramses hanged four Israelites for speaking secretly of the death of his father with pleasure. His informers are everywhere among them."

Praroth promised to ask in letters to his friends in Ezion-geber and elsewhere for more on events in the Land of Goshen. When the priest was gone and Moses' excitement had died down, he ruminated. If he had not killed the taskmaster, if his heritage had remained a mystery, he would now be vizier. Marrying Sebah would have been a certainty. Could he now beg a pardon from Ramses so that he could go to Sebah? Would Ramses free his family if they wanted to come to the desert? Moses reflected on his last interview with Ramses. No, he had wronged Ramses, and there was no forgiving. Moses was severed from him and—so he thought—from Egypt, forever.

Even in Egypt, Moses had always been alone, confiding only in Ramses. Here, there was no such confidant, both equal and entirely compatible—not the dwarf, or Jethro, or Praroth. Now, he found he no longer simply talked to the heavens, he asked questions. On a night when the scent of myrrh shrubs was on the breeze, he asked aloud, "Is there some task for me? In the fullness of time, will the presence who seems to be in the sky reveal itself to me? What about my family in Egypt? And Sebah? My love for her is like a deep but healing scar on my thigh. I see it, and I will always see it. It will never stop hurting. But I cannot make the flesh grow back, cannot rid myself of the disfigurement. It is, simply, there.

"I cannot live all my days in stasis. I must find a course, as I did in Egypt. There it was so easy: to serve Ramses, to serve the nation, to lead armies and build cities, to marry Sebah and have children, to enjoy the richness of life."

As still more time passed, he said, "I need a sign, presence in the stars. Is there a god to give me a sign, a single, strong god? Or are you—the far, vague heavens—all I can ever call on for guidance, solace, completion?"

One such night, his spoken words had drowned out the approach of steps. Desert wise, he knew it was the animal, man. The footfalls halted behind a bush not six cubits away. His hand went for the fir staff, whose point he and Bes-Ahrin had fire-hardened until it was like bronze. He rolled quickly and silently into a crouch. "Who is it? Speak! Not another step!"

"I, Zipporah," she answered hurriedly. She came from behind the bush and stood before him and he saw her shape against the stars. His threat had frightened her. "May I sit with you, Moses?" she said when her composure returned.

He started to spread his cloak for her, shivering as he bent in only his loincloth. "No," she said. "I brought a heavy shawl. Put on your cloak. You will be cold."

"What brings you here, Zipporah?" he asked, curious but not unfriendly. Even more than in Egypt, the Midianite women were under the control of their parents until they married.

"I told my mother it was time for me to talk with you, and she knew it was and bid me go."

"Your father? . . ."

". . . does not know. He would have felt it was he who should talk with you, and I did not want that until I knew how you felt about what I have to say."

Moses knew what that would be, felt a warmth toward her for her frankness, but was unsure what his answer would be. "And that is, Zipporah?" he said softly.

"I am twenty-two. It is time for me to have a husband. Until I do, my sisters cannot be wed. Since I was fourteen, my father has brought men to his tent. They have talked with me, and I with them. Several were good men, and my father was disappointed that I did not choose them. But he has never tried to force me. Then you came." She paused, but only for a moment. Her voice was clear as a well-played reed flute. "I knew from that day that you drove off the shepherds, though it was not because of that."

"Not for that?"

"Not for driving them off. Any brave man with a sword would do that. No, for letting your dwarf drive them off. And for helping us water the sheep when they were gone."

"And I liked you, Zipporah," he said, "because if we had not helped you drive them off, you would have gotten up and driven them off yourself. You allowed us to be heroes."

"Yes, Moses, but how *much* did you like me? How much do you now? Does it matter that I like you enough for both of us?"

He scratched in his goatskin bag for his flint and tinder. "Gather some dry twigs. Let me build a small fire for us against the breeze from the mountains. Then, I will tell you my story, as much as I can. And you will tell me yours. Be careful you do not prick your hands on thistles."

"Moses, do not tell a Midianite girl how to gather firewood. Even if it is night," she reproved him.

The firelight flickered on her mobile face as he talked. He saw the aquiline nose; the full lips, pursing, then smiling; the heavy brows. He could see her eyes opening and narrowing in the darkness, knowing their color was light brown, no doubt from some distant northern ancestor.

About his time in the palace, he told her no more than he had told her father. But he described his military travels on behalf of Egypt, and how he had met an aristocratic Cushite woman. They had loved each other, almost as much as life, but still not enough, he said. For when the rulers of Egypt discovered he was a Hebrew, lest it compromise her father's high position, they had forsaken each other.

"And she was, of course, beautiful," said Zipporah.

"Yes," and feeling a moment of despair in her, he quickly said, "as you are, Zipporah, just in a different way."

"She was a princess, was she not?" she surmised. "If she had not been, she would never have let you go. She protected not just some aristocrat, but her father, the king of Nubia. And you were no commoner, but perhaps a prince."

"Yes, a prince. And she a princess, but of the small kingdom of Barbaht, not Nubia." He was surprised, as he often was, by her insights and her willingness to speak them out, no matter what the consequences. And what reason was there not to be honest with her? "Yes, I was a prince until the Pharaoh found out I had been substituted as a baby for his sister's dead son. But, believe me, that must be our secret. It could endanger the princess in Barbaht, and me, and Bes-Ahrin, and your tribe, all of us, if my location were discovered."

"I understand the hazard to you and the dwarf and our tribe, but to her?" Then she understood that, too, and said, "Because she might yet change her mind and seek you?"

"It is possible. You see now that you would have a somewhat uncertain suitor."

She thought, throwing one twig after another in the fire, watching its tiny blaze and the blaze's subsiding. "You still love her so much?"

"Yes. My heart cannot abandon hope. Even though my mind knows better. And I have become a man who is different from the one who fled the delta that night. She might not want me."

"How different, Moses? Don't look at the fire that way, look at me. Answer this question while you look into my eyes." Her voice was less harsh than her words.

"Uncertain of what I want to do, more humble, more cautious, yet more certain that the world can turn upside down in a second and sling me, or anyone, or everyone, into what the Egyptians call *isfet,* and the Greeks call *chaos.*" Did that answer her? She was a woman who did not play with words. "I seem to pick women of strong wills."

"Then you have picked me? Before I spoke tonight?"

Had he? "I have thought about you," he said.

"Ah, and have you thought about other women besides this Cushite princess and this princess of Midian?"

"Not seriously."

"But there have been others."

"Yes. It is the way of men."

"I don't mean that. With me, it would not be the way of my husband."

"I can believe that," said Moses, somewhat intimidated in spite of himself.

"There would be no need for him to be," she said, her voice not so much seductive as honest, determined, and womanly.

Neither of them spoke. It was she who broke the silence. "I do not know how to be flirtatious as some royal princess would."

"Neither did she," Moses said. "I met her when she was fourteen, in man's armor, when I waged war against her father's allies. She tried to kill me. She is like you in her strength."

Again she thought, this time for a full three minutes. "Could you love me, Moses, if I accepted that you might keep the love of her in your heart? My father has two wives. In his way, he loves them both."

Moses looked at her in her woolen shawl, the cloth as impeccable as any princess's tunic. And the body it covered would be regal as well. So why should he forever spend his nights in a tent with Bes-Ahrin when he might be making lawful love to this woman, holding her warmly in his arms as he slept? Why not the exquisite explosions of love that he had had as he pressed against Sebah, but this time inside a loving body?

Why should he not sit with Zipporah cross-legged on their rug in the morning, dipping their barley bread into their milk or anise tea, sharing pomegranates, dates, olives—for they would have money enough to buy the best products of the seminomads of the oases? Why not plan together days of good labor on behalf of the encampment? Help her pack up and move on as they would soon be doing? Why should he not see a child at her small breast, see a son grow into a man as he aged?

And why should he not have someone to talk with, to reason with, to discuss his quirky knowledge and discoveries with besides Bes-Ahrin and the presence—whatever it was—whom he addressed in the stars? Would she understand his need to be in touch with this celestial confidant who had evolved in him, and perhaps outside him, from those days when he and Ramses had looked for Sopdet? *Yes,* he thought, *she would. All of these things.*

She was tense, awaiting his answer. "I could love you, Zipporah," he answered her. "I could be happy with you in our own tent, living our own life." Could he say more? Why? Was that not sufficient? But he must ask her. "Is that enough?"

She rose, walked around the fire, and knelt beside him. "Yes," she said, taking his hand and holding it to her breast.

He rose and held her in his arms. "Let us talk together with your father. He will tell us, as is right, for us to meet often, to make sure that we know each other well enough to wed."

As impulsively as she had sprung at the invading shepherd—but this time with joy and with love—she broke from him, looked in the darkness at his eyes, and embraced him again, no longer soberly, but with happiness and hope. At the same time, he, as she gripped his body, so long away from women, felt lust's hot breath in his lungs. She knew this, too. "Moses, I do not know how long I can wait," she said.

The two betrothed young people labored side by side, loading camels, oxen carts, donkeys, and the few horses with the rugs, tents, pans, grates, even Bes-Ahrin's small copper smeltery. Zipporah worked hard and with good humor, occasionally losing her temper when a rope broke or water spilled, but quickly recovering. Then, for two months, the Midianite band moved slowly through the badlands and wadis to an area of oases and old wells at the foothills of Mount Sinai.

When the tents were spread out beneath the lofty unclimbed peak, and after talking at length with Zipporah and Moses, Jethro and his wives prepared the wedding. Moses, thanks to Bes-Ahrin, was able to pay a dowry in gold and copper plates to Jethro, as was the tribal custom. The priest-king compensated for the dowry many times by paying the expenses of the wedding and with costly gifts to the young couple.

Zipporah arrived at the ceremony on a litter carried by her cousins and uncles. She was dressed in Egyptian linen, her face covered by a veil of Byblos silk. Moses wore a robe of shining linen and a thin headband of gold and turquoise. His sandals had heel straps of braided gold. Bes-Ahrin, warrior-dwarf, had bought a child's coat of mail from a Syrian trader and was the ceremonial guard of honor. The couple crushed pomegranates—that their marriage might be fruitful—and Moses, with the hilt of a ceremonial dagger, broke a vial of nard to ensure that they would forever find sweetness in one another.

"Moses, are we not the same flesh and blood?" asked Zipporah, the Bedouin bride's ritual question. And Moses answered, "Zipporah, we are the same flesh and blood." Jethro, who as the tribe's king-priest performed the ceremony, asked Moses, "Are we not brethren?" Moses answered, "So I am, Father, with you and all your people."

Jethro, abstemious himself except for the camels'-milk brew, had ordered four large amphorae of wine and other delicacies from Ezion-geber, a hundred mountainous miles to the northeast. Zipporah's sisters danced, clad in diaphanous veils, the opportunity for young males to see what lovely wares awaited them if they, also, successfully wooed. Four zither players led by Praroth, a flutist, and two matrons snapping castanets filled the priest-king's capacious tent with energetic music.

At the height of the ceremony, Bes-Ahrin and the hunchback did a joyful jig for the couple, singing an ode they had composed to Zipporah's lips (the color of anemones), her eyes (like those of a young doe), her hair (glossy as that of a newborn kid), and her skin (as it was—except for her tanned arms and face—the color of polished oryx ivory). A half-dozen of Jethro's lambs, wheat bread—a luxury—and choice fruits from the oases left the hundreds of guests sated, if not sick.

That night, Moses and Zipporah fell on their bed with a passion so heated that her moments of pain and bleeding went ignored and they slept the sleep of the fulfilled. In the morning, their heads a bit woozy and their stomachs unsettled, they remained beneath the bedclothes awhile within each other's comforting arms, sure of the rightness of life.

Two years later, their first child was born. They named him Gershom, from the Hebrew *ger,* "protected guest," with its implication of a welcome stranger. Moses and Zipporah doted on the child. He was large, likely, they thought, to grow as tall as his father, and he quickly showed signs of Moses' curiosity. A year and a half later, another son, Eliezer, was born. He was reticent, even as a baby. Thus Moses, hunter of hippopotamus, slayer of Egypt's enemies, designer of palaces and temples, lover of a Cushite princess, had, under the starry Sinai skies, become a Bedouin husband, father, a herder of sheep and goats.

The hunchback-priest kept Moses informed, at least by rumor from Ezion-geber and Dophkah, of events in Egypt. Ramses, in the fifth year of his reign, had fought a disastrous battle with the Hittites at the Orontes. His bravery was undisputed. But the fight had cost him many of his troops and supporters. Since then, there had been unrest in his kingdom.

"The former retainers of Sety led by one Nunrah," said the priest as they sat over roasted lamb gobbets one night, "are bedeviling him and he can find no way to rid himself of them. The Libyans overrun his border posts. He cannot put an army into the field against them, for he fears more incursions from the Hittites. The slaves, and not just the Hebrews, mumble against their torment—"

"Nunrah, a wicked man," interrupted Moses as he chewed. He longed, in spite of everything, to be beside Ramses in the field of battle and in the palace to counsel him on how to destroy his enemies.

"Finally," the hunchback continued, still full of news, "there are also signs the Nile flood is getting punier, and other ills of nature seem ready to plague Egypt in coming years."

Moses nodded and looked at Bes-Ahrin for comment, but there was none. He thought again of Nunrah, of Sebah, and, guiltily, of his family in the slave quarter of Tanis.

Chapter Seven
The God-Seeker

ONG FREE FROM THE COMPLEXITIES AND HYPOCRISIES OF THE LAND of the Pharaohs, Moses continued to find in the desert stars a spiritual presence and the simplicity and communication he had always yearned for. Under his breath now—for he spent his nights warm and loved beside Zipporah, except on rare occasions when he attended the wandering flocks—Moses carried on his dialogues with the heavens.

They were dialogues because he found it comfortable to believe that he was getting answers, and not just from within his mind. Surrounded by convinced believers in the God of Abraham, always thinking that some single god existed—whom he had once vaguely tried to identify with Osiris or Aten—the sense of someone outside himself came gradually and naturally.

"I choose to call you God," he confided silently, "because you give me someone to thank for my blessings, for Zipporah and our sons, for my many deliverances from the hand of death, for my contentment instead of my endless flight."

Over the months and years, Moses came to feel, without pridefulness, that he was unique as a result of his exchanges with his God. Others, such as Jethro, Praroth, even Zipporah, were god-fearing, but when he spoke to them about his God, he did not believe that they felt the same sense of intimacy with theirs. To his, he would pray one night, "You are the Great Someone, not just whom I can bless, but from whom I can ask for strength and guidance."

"How can I not bless you?" this Someone from behind the stars seemed to answer. "For you heed my words. And why should you not ask me for what you want and need, even if I do not always grant it?"

More and more, Moses, from this singular closeness, wondered whether he should not be doing something of greater purpose than he was. From God, he received no clear answer.

"Moses," said Zipporah one evening as they watched Eliezer toss a noisy dried gourd to his big brother, Gershom, "some of the time lately you are far from the encampment in your mind. Where are you today?"

"In the middle of a dust whirl," he answered. "I ask God to tell me what to do. He does not reply. I *must* do something. I know I must. But I cannot settle on what it is."

"Your parents. They trouble you the most?"

"They trouble me. But not just them. Sometimes I think of all my people in Goshen. I think of Ramses' cruelty. Of all the Pharaohs' wickedness against them. I had the power to do things for Egypt, even when I was young. It was given to me. Perhaps I could now do things for the Hebrews?"

"How could you, one man, here, do anything for them?"

"Well, in my fantasies, I have planned campaigns for leading them out, as I planned strategies against the Hittites, the Libyans, all the mighty enemies of Egypt. But I do nothing. And the years, oh good years, Zipporah, pass."

Zipporah mentioned Moses' restlessness to Jethro, for she remained closest to her father of all his daughters. A day later, when Jethro and Moses had finished the plans for a sheep drive to the north, the older man said, "Moses, I value your help more than I can say. And I love you as I would a son of my blood. But I feel a kind of second life growing in you. Is it that you think of leaving our land? Tell me, will you stay with us? Or do you know? For I have observed, and wise it is, how gradually you come to decisions?"

"You honor me, Jethro," Moses said, "accepting a wandering slave as a son, giving to me your favorite—"

Jethro interrupted with good humor. "Moses, stop sounding like an Egyptian courtier with these preambles."

Moses looked up at the sage, sun-browned face of his father-in-law and smiled. "The God of Abraham, our God in common, for so I call him now, has shaped me for something, Jethro. You may be sure I will speak first with Zipporah, then with you, when I divine what he wants."

Jethro, who had noticed that Moses, of late, spoke more piously than he himself did, said, "We humans have a way of making up our minds to do things, and then assuming it is the will of a god. Could that be happening with you?"

Moses frowned. "I hope not. I want to know the line between what I want and what I think God wants. It is as hard to be sure about as a knife mark in the water. I thank you for reminding me of that."

"When I was young," Jethro said, "I sometimes went to the high mountains for a day or two to let the sand in my mind settle and become firmer. It was there I decided to wed my second wife, the mother of four of my girls." He smiled again at Moses and Moses smiled back. They both were aware it had not been a perfect marriage. What Jethro was saying was that lonely contemplation might help lead to a decision. But it did not, invariably, insure it would be the right one.

Moses pondered Jethro's advice and, a few days later, taking only water with him for nourishment, he picked his way through the foothills of craggy Mount Sinai. Hard and muscular as a goat of the mountains, he was high above the desert plain by evening. He made no fire, but drank deeply of the water, wrapped himself in his cloak, and looked at the stars, the brightest of them as familiar to him as the lines of his palm.

He prayed, but fell asleep without answers. The next day he fasted, and that night, a little giddy from lack of food, he tried again. "God of Abraham," he said, "my mind is a plaster wall. I am ready for you to paint on it a mighty hieroglyph of where I must go and what I must do. And please, God," he added with some amusement, "give me better wisdom than you gave Jethro when he came here seeking a decision on his second wife."

Moses waited and in his mind he seemed to hear an answer forming. "Moses," the thought became word, "you alone do I allow to jest with me. With Jethro, I left the choice to him. He so lusted after that woman that he believed I suggested he marry her. Better he would have been to take her as a concubine as his ancestor Abraham did Hagar."

"And I? What shall I do?" asked Moses.

"Do not climb farther on this face of the mountain. Tomorrow," God seemed to say, "circle the mountain, fasting again as you go, the better to reach me with your words, and in the afternoon, perhaps, I will counsel you."

Next day, his stomach growling with hunger, Moses rounded the mountain and looked up at a rough trail, one used most likely by mountain lions and wild goats. The wind had begun to blow across the stony ground. Before him, glowing from the setting sun, was the largest blackberry bush Moses had ever seen, its limbs gnarled and twisted by the wind.

Moses decided he would go no farther up the mountain this day, but would sleep beside the bush as some protection from wild animals. He laid down his fir staff and again drank deeply from his goatskin bag. He was woozy with hunger and, despite his strength, utterly exhausted. The water in his empty stomach, far from relaxing him, made him giddier. He sat on the ground before the berryless bush. The wind whistled through its sparse leaves. The sun's slanting light made the trembling bush flicker with silver and touches of gold. It seemed afire.

"You said you would come to me this afternoon, Lord. I am here," Moses said, staring into the bush. He swayed, listening hard for an answer, but at first all he heard was the strong, uneven breath of the wind through the twigs and thorns. Then, as he strained, he heard a voice saying to him faintly, "I said *perhaps* I would speak to you."

"Oh, God," said Moses, overwrought by a beginning of certainty of God's presence, "do not say *perhaps*. I have followed your directions. I am ready to be your servant. Give me guidance. Use me to your purposes so I might feel whole."

"Moses, sit down and take off your sandals. Rest your feet as I talk with you." Moses did so, and the voice, reasonably if quietly, spoke like wind out of the bush:

"I have a great duty to ask of you. Sety is no longer in Egypt to kill you. If you return, Ramses will spare you even though he has many troubles. In fact, he will spare you *because* he has so many troubles. It is not for your family that I ask you to return. Your parents have died. I have taken them up to me. You will not see them until I do the same for you."

Moses was stricken. He had feared just such a thing. Was this true? Had they died before he could know them? Was this the message he had come to hear? "I will go to see if that is true," he said, "though it be in disguise and in the blackest hours of night. I will go! Jethro will help me," he said.

"No, Moses, stop the cataract of your mouth and listen," God's voice replied. "If it had been my will, they would have come out when you asked them to. But it was not my plan, nor would the life here have been good for them. You cannot save your parents, Moses." There was a pause and Moses was about to speak, when he heard God's words again, more authoritatively than ever. "What I am asking you to do is to save Israel. Before you knew me, you led many thousands of men against far lands. Now I am going to ask you to lead the army of my people, the children of Israel. Do you deny that this idea ever entered your mind?"

"No, Lord. I do not deny it. But it was as a dream, without substantiality. Not something I thought of that had any chance of success. Besides, I am not ready to do it. I have too many things here that make me content."

"Then why are you talking with me at the foot of this sacred mountain? How dare you toy with me, Moses! . . ."

Moses felt faint and leaned back on his hands.

The voice from the prickly bush went on. "The taskmasters, worse now by far than the one you killed, afflict the Hebrews. Go to Pharaoh. The time will never be better. Get him to let you lead them out of Egypt. Trust me, I will find them a land in Canaan where thousands of them still live. It will be flowing with milk and honey. That is my promise."

Moses began to doubt his perception of the voice. Could this whole conversation be a result of his fatigue and lightheadedness? But, no, it had to be real. "Canaan is swarming with powerful armies, Lord," he said. He held out his right arm, where a white scar indented the brown skin. "See what a Canaanite javelin did to me? When they combine, as they would, they are fierce. Who am I to lead the Hebrews out of Egypt?"

"Moses, think about it. If not you, who? Does Israel have dozens of generals who have led armies against tenacious adversaries? No. You alone have. I will be with you. I will be your right arm," came the word of God from the bush.

Moses still protested. "If I go to the Hebrews—you know how contentious they are—and tell them the God of their fathers has sent me to liberate them, they will say, 'You never believed in him, for you were Prince Hapi-Set, worshipper of the gods of Egypt. Tell us the name of this God of our fathers, if you know it.'"

"Gather their elders together," God seemed to reply. "Tell them you are sent by the God of Abraham, Isaac, and Jacob. Tell them you will go to Ramses, whose vizier you were to have been, and that you will convince him to free my people, your people, to sacrifice to me for three days in the wilderness."

"Ramses will never believe it, even if he does talk with me," said Moses. Now the last rays of the sun were hitting the bush, turning its silver all to burnished golden flames.

"Tell him if he does not let them go, I will smite Egypt with many afflictions. Tell him the Egyptian people will force him to give up the Israelites. Indeed, the Egyptians will be so glad to be rid of you Hebrews that they will pay you to leave with jewels and flocks."

Moses, weary, his mind unsettled, still objected. "I speak Hebrew only poorly. Besides, there is my stammer. God, be logical. Can I speak to them in Egyptian, the language of their oppressor?"

But Moses already knew the tenor of God's answer. "Moses, you are behaving like a house pet, a castrated monkey. Your speeches will be made to Ramses. And as for the Hebrews, so long as they know your mother was one, they will abide with your Bedouin tongue and understand most of it, and tolerate your stammer. Did you move your troops when, even as a young man, you spoke to them before the battles? Your stammer then was a gift. It made you economical of words and they felt your power streaming through your impediment. Did I make you a fool? How long will it take you to learn Hebrew? Meanwhile, Aaron, your brother, can sometimes speak for you. He has dealt with both them and the Egyptians all his life."

"It is not fear for my life. You know that," said Moses.

"No, it is far worse. It is fear of failure. Think, Moses. Must I recite your triumphs in the field? Must I flatter you by reminding you of your genius in all the things of the mind? Why do you seek to evade what you know to be right? Has peace left you a eunuch? I call you to liberate the oppressed people from whom you sprung, who endured while you led the life of a prince. Will you tell me no?"

Moses, at last, felt his surprise and resistance giving way to courage. *What kind of man have I become that I so defied what I know to be right?* he asked himself. "No, Lord," he said, "I will not tell you no if you give me a sign."

"Then, pick up your staff. Fix on it a head of Syrian iron, such as you used against the hippopotamus, and which the Midianites use against desert lions. It will be your staff of authority. Tell the Hebrews my name. It is *'Ehyeh,'*—I am. You shall translate it as 'Jehovah.' Now, finally, I see you will do my bidding."

Moses saw before him in his mind a gigantic crowd of people, soundlessly opening their mouths in pain. He summoned to his brain the logistics of war: weapons, armor, training camps for new soldiers, provision carts, military tents, the minutiae that he had organized so brilliantly in order to win, again and again. "I will do your bidding," he said, struggling to his feet. The bush was now dark, just a silhouette in the night.

All the next day, Moses sat at the foot of the mountain, more hungry than he had ever been, drinking the last of his water. Could he be mistaken, only imagining he had heard the bush speak? When it seemed to turn to fire, could it have been mere resin ignited by the heat of the day?

"No," he said aloud, "I heard him. He, not I, was father to those words. And why talk of resinous fire? Do I not know a blackberry bush from a pine shrub?"

He was unwilling to return to the encampment until he had begun a plan for his return to Egypt. That evening, as he entered his tent, he saw the concerned look on Zipporah's face. Before he could speak, she said, "You are going back."

"Yes."

"For your family," she said, staring into his tormented but determined eyes. When he did not immediately respond, she caught her breath and whispered almost unbelievingly, "No, it is not just that."

"No," he said. "I think my parents have died."

"If it is true, I mourn them. But you can't know."

"I go to free the Hebrews," he said, almost doubting that he had dared to put it into words.

"Moses, that is madness."

"It can be done."

"You think your God is telling you to do this, Moses? I believe it is you, talking to yourself in the desert. As I heard you talking that night when I came to you."

Surprised at her vehemence, he said, "Zipporah, it took me a long while, all my life, to arrive at a sense of this God of Abraham. I *feel* I am talking to him, and that he answers me. You say it is an inner voice, two parts of myself talking to each other. I know how complex is the mind and the soul of man, and so it is possible you are right. But I was sure when I heard him that his words came from outside me. However it may seem to others, I am strengthened and I am guided."

She looked at him, wondering if she dared go on. But she was ever impulsive, and her impulse was to speak. "I love you, Moses. I admire you. I will live with the you that is, so long as you do not ask me also to believe in this God of yours."

Did he ask her to? he thought. "No," he said, "I do not ask that of you, Little Bird"—for that was what the word *Zipporah* meant—"but remember, neither your God of Abraham nor mine promises us milk and honey without work. And if we did find it so easily, then the milk would be sour, the honey full of bear hairs. Can you go that far with me?"

She would have preferred if he had been able to concede that his God might originate in his own mind and heart, as she sometimes thought hers did. But she knew she must live with Moses' God, as he saw him, or otherwise give him up. "My God of Abraham does not require such insanity from his believers," she answered, having the last word.

Jethro made it simpler for Moses than Zipporah had. "Restless man, I have given you everything," he said. "And you have given me everything in return. I knew I could not hold you, even if I prepared my people to accept the son of a Hebrew slave as their priest and king. Zipporah has already told me her doubts. I have thought all of a day and night about it. I, too, think it is a mad scheme. But I know also that you are an uncommon kind of man, not like anyone I have ever known. I assent. Zipporah will go with you. You will have my gifts for the road. Three camels, two donkeys, stallions for you and Bes-Ahrin, and six of my best mounted warriors to get you to the borders of the delta."

Overcome by his father-in-law's generosity, Moses embraced him. "You are the father I never had, Jethro. If you had asked me to stay, I would like to think I would have done so, at least until you willingly freed me."

"I know that, Moses. So, go in peace and love. Send word to us when you can through the caravans coming to Dophkah. And take care of Zipporah and my grandsons."

At the second hour after sundown, Bes-Ahrin left Moses at an abandoned mud-brick house near Pi-Ramessu on the road to Pelusium. He entered the slave town, now relocated at Pi-Ramessu, and went to the home of Amram and Jochebed. Although Moses had said his God had told him they were dead, the dwarf was surprised and a little fearful when he found that it was true. They had died within the last three months, both from violent fevers. Amram apparently had brought the fevers from the mosquito-plagued marshes to which he had been recently demoted in favor of a younger man.

Aaron was so frightened for himself and his family by the arrival of Bes-Ahrin that it took the dwarf a full half-hour to convince him to meet Moses just outside town. Miriam had to help push him into it.

An hour later, Moses heard hoofbeats stop outside the doorway and peeked out. He emerged and embraced his brother with joy. Aaron, his courage quickening, also hugged Moses' handsome wife and two young children. Quickly, he told Moses of the death of their parents. Moses shut his eyes, waiting for the emptiness in him to fill. "I knew it. Jehovah told me. I should have come sooner. I tried to get them, you, Miriam, to join me."

"I know," said Aaron woefully. "He was once so strong. But he was already ailing from the disease of the lungs. The swamp fever had his bleeding lungs as its ally."

"I waited too long to open my soul to a return," Moses said. He would never get over not knowing and loving the mother who had suckled him as a baby. Nor the father who had given him life. He knew if his father had not been sent away like a worn-out draft animal he might not have succumbed so quickly. Though burdened by this new bitterness, Moses told Aaron briefly of his life among the Midianites and his meeting with God. All pleasure and excitement had gone out of their meeting, but he persevered, laying out his plans for freeing the Israelites.

Aaron, both a priest and an elder of the Hebrews, summoned the Council of Elders. Some sixty men—a few only in their late twenties, two over eighty—met Moses two nights later. They gathered in the abandoned field of a Hebrew landowner who had bought his freedom, and then, ever more repulsed by the treatment of his countrymen, had recently fled to Canaan.

Always imposing, by torchlight that night Moses was an almost godlike figure. The flames, wavering in the night air, reflected on the scales of the lustrous Egyptian armor he had bought at Zilu. On his wide chest he wore the bronze Midianite pectoral of Jethro's officer corps, embossed with a sun rising behind the peak of Mount Sinai.

"Brothers, you knew and perhaps feared me once as Prince Hapi-Set," he began, aware that many would only partially understand his accent, aware of his stutter. He told of the reasons for his flight, of his twelve years with the Midianites. "During those years, before my tent and in the hills, I began to hear the voice of our God, the God of Abraham, speaking to me from the stars. He told me to journey here and to tell the Pharaoh, whom I once thought to be my cousin, to free you for three days so you may go into the wilderness and worship him."

The elders had been alerted to just such a plan by Aaron, and their views of it ranged from cowardice to a desire to forget about the three-day subterfuge and, instead, instantly flee. At Moses' words, some raised their voices, saying any appeal to the Pharaoh would lead him to hang the petitioners. But these men were shouted down. "Did God give you a sign for us?" inquired an aging voice hopefully. It was that of Hur, the gaunt leader of the Council of Elders.

Moses lifted the hardened staff with its ugly iron head, the sharpened point flashing back the torchlight like a surly glint in a dangerous man's eye. "This is the staff of authority blessed by the God of Abraham. He has told me his name is 'I am,' 'Ehyeh,' but he bids us translate it as 'Jehovah' from this time forward to all the generations of man." When Moses ended, he looked to the white-haired Hur to comment for the group.

The old man, his eyes fitful with courage, said, "I have lived almost my whole life as a slave. I say, blessed is Jehovah and blessed is Moses who comes in his name." There were cheers from the majority—and silence from some twenty of the sixty.

"Speak among yourselves," Moses said. "Decide." Directing his next words to Hur, he asked, "Can you determine the views of the elders and let me know them in three days? We must not give Ramses time to plot against us if we are to act."

Moses knew that informers among the elders would swiftly get news to Ramses that he had returned. But he was not without his own spies. When he woke, Bes-Ahrin came in, eyes red with sleeplessness. "I have talked with my friends"—his network of grotesques. "The disgusting Ramses is upset, has talked of having you killed, or executing some of the elders. But old friends of yours in court have calmed him. Now he is curious. But we have an unexpected

their bricks. Now they would have to go into the fields, cut the stubble, and crush it, a job generally done by the lowest of the Libyan slaves. The decree, recited by every Egyptian overseer, called the Hebrews lazy liars.

The Hebrew brickmaker foremen, in their best tunics, went to the palace under an appeal process allowed slaves since the time of Joseph. There, at the foot of the steps, they lay on their bellies—save for their leader, a cousin of Moses named Korah. He presented a papyrus addressed to Ramses to a minor functionary. With fulsome praise, it politely protested the increased workload and implored its recession.

Korah was taken inside the palace by the lackey. When he came out two hours later, his solid, squat body was bruised and slumping between two burly guards with whips. The guards dropped Korah and beat the group of supine men who sprung up and ran pell-mell to the slave quarter, carrying Korah as they went.

Moses, Zipporah, their sons, and Bes-Ahrin were lodged at the house of Amram—now that of Aaron. That afternoon, as Moses and Aaron met with visiting elders, they heard a commotion in the street. It was Korah, his tunic bloody, and a number of the Hebrew foremen. His florid face was even redder than usual. He stood squarely on thick, bowed legs, and harangued a circle of sympathizers, pointing to cuts and dark purple marks on his simian arms.

When Korah saw Moses and Aaron, he shook his fist at them and shouted hysterically, "The Lord of Abraham judge you both! We stink in the nostrils of the Pharaoh and the taskmasters. And all because of you. You have put a sword in their hands to kill us. And for what? For three days in the wilderness?"

Moses tried to calm the man, sure that the message of the general was a sign that things would improve.

That night, as he lay in the dull light of the small oil lamp, he spoke to God. "Ramses has some sort of plan that will help him and us as well. I know it. But, clearly as the rumors from the hunchback had it and as I saw, he has been weakened."

"Trust me," Moses heard the answer. "Do not lose hope. Go back to him again. Try to see him alone."

Moses had seldom doubted his abilities as he did now. "Even the Hebrews, whom I am trying to save, do not believe in me," he said under his breath. "And who can blame them?"

Jehovah replied, speaking to that indomitable spirit of Moses that was his nature even before he knew God, "Go back. Brace up, Moses. Tomorrow. Tell him to let my people go."

This time, when Moses and Aaron entered the reception room, they found Ramses dressed casually in a lightly jeweled loincloth, his big chest crossed by leather bands. He still wore his wig. Beneath it, Moses knew, his head was shaved to accommodate the crowns of the north and of the south—elaborate headdresses worn during the most important formal religious and government interviews. Ramses was flanked only by his magicians, all dressed in fine linen robes much like ordinary nobles. But they wore sashes of leopard, tiger, and black panther skins and carried scrolls picturing animal incarnations, suns, moons, and stars. Three of them had thick wooden staffs in their hands, the tops of which were enclosed in hammered copper.

"Can we three talk alone?" asked Moses of Ramses, remembering the mysterious words of the general. To begin with, he wanted to fathom the reasons why Ramses ordered the Hebrews to chop their own stubble.

But Ramses ignored the request. "My advisors insist that the magicians show you the foolishness of your wishes," he said to Moses, ignoring Aaron, who stood awkwardly with Moses' staff.

Moses only nodded. He was convinced more than ever that Ramses was largely in the control of others. His heart, despite all the years and events that lay between them, went out to his comrade, who had hated any kind of restrictions on him.

"Show them," Ramses snapped scornfully at his magicians.

The portliest and oldest of the magi said to Aaron in a finicky, high voice, "Throw down your staff, Hebrew." Aaron stooped and put the staff on the bare tiled floor. "Can you or this God of Abraham make it into a serpent? If so, do so."

"We cannot," Moses said firmly. "It is not God's work."

The magician began an incantation, invoking at least twelve of the gods of Egypt in the flowery terms that Moses had long despised. Then, with his ringed left hand, he signaled to the other priests. With various twirlings and grippings, they dropped their staffs on the ground. The four magicians surrounded the staffs, and puffs of scented powder rose from the copper pike heads as they popped off. When the wizards broke the circle, there were three large cobras wriggling on the floor.

"Beware, Aaron," Moses said involuntarily, then he realized that the snakes, while coiling as if to strike, did so sluggishly. They were drugged. He snatched up his pole, and with slashes of the iron head smashed the cobras into a gooey mess. Then, still hot over this cheap trick, he pounded the hollowed staffs until they looked like the debris from a hard-fought battle, breaking floor tiles as he struck.

The three subordinate magicians looked with dismay at their efforts for a moment, then their faces closed. The fat sorcerer, who was more resourceful, announced as if he had somehow prevailed. "Splendid Ramses, these were royal snakes, incarnations of your own uraeus. These Hebrews have committed gross sacrilege. Let us immediately put them to death."

Ramses spoke loudly, sounding like his old self, "Miserable necromancers! You have shamed me before insignificant Hebrews." He struck his mace on the floor and from different corners of the room ran four guards armed with spears. "Take these frauds to the priests of Amun," he ordered the guards. "Tell the priests how they failed. Tell them of Ramses' anger. Let the temple do with them as they will."

Moses assumed that at least in the powerful cult of Amun, Ramses had more proponents than Nunrah. As the guards and sorcerers left in confusion, Ramses said in a low voice to Moses, "In two days, at the second hour, as I go for my walk, meet me by the river pavilion nearest the palace."

That night, Moses and Aaron spoke with the inner circle of the Council of Elders, telling them over the lamplight at Aaron's house how they had foiled the magicians. "And they will not move against us? There will be no more restrictions? We can bear no more," said Hur.

The youngest of the elders, a muscular man named Joshua, spoke out. His angry, dark face was accented by an unstitched scar over one eye—from a taskmaster's copper whip handle. "I am sick of talk about 'bearing,'" he said in a piercing voice.

Moses was wary of the man. He felt in him a murderous rage. But his fearlessness could be useful.

Joshua went on, "We who are young have our mattocks, our work knives. Let us kill Egyptians, any who cross our paths. What does Ramses have? A disloyal army. Yes, some of us would die. But in the confusion, Nunrah and his gang would be so occupied in murdering Ramses that we could escape, not for three days, but forever. And only mad dogs would follow men reckless enough to leave everything for freedom."

This man, in his late twenties, must be remarkable, Moses thought, *to be accepted as an equal among these wise older men.* Moses spoke cautiously. "Brave young man, we need Hebrews like you. But believe me. If we begin the killing, the army will butcher us like mutton sheep, and only then turn on each other. Jehovah requires that we protect our children and old people. I am a soldier. I, too, prefer direct action, but first let us try to find a way to leave, for three days—then, who knows?—without shedding the blood of our people. Will you bend your bravery yet awhile? If I fail you, do what you want."

Moses looked in the man's eyes, saw the anger, but also the depth of an intelligence that could be reached. "Give me your forearm," Moses said, "as Hebrew to Hebrew, warrior to warrior. I swear your courage will not be wasted."

Moses' task was to play tunes on several reeds at the same time. For one thing, he must forge solidarity among the Hebrews. They were divided among twelve tribes, named after the sons of their forefather Jacob, also called Israel, a name the Hebrews gave themselves as a whole. One of these tribes was the Levites—Amram's tribe—from whom a loose priesthood had developed that had a tendency to feel superior. Small wonder that there were internal rivalries for Moses to try to heal.

Second, he must bring matters to the point where the Egyptians emphatically wanted the Hebrews to leave Egypt. Finally, he must find means of siding with Ramses in a way that would neutralize the oppressive power of Nunrah and his supporters in the court, the army, and the temples.

That night he talked long and hard first with Bes-Ahrin and then with Jehovah, drawing on all he had learned about Egypt—as a student, soldier, and ambassador—about its weather and climate, its animal life, its vegetation, and, above all, the Nile. Before dawn, he sent for the men he had met with the night before, and they arrived sleepily. As they drank hot goats' milk and ate fig cakes that Miriam and Zipporah served, Moses addressed them:

"Today, we must go to the docks, I as an Egyptian and you others as slaves among the dock workers. I must know what they hear from our brothers at the oars and from the free sailors who fare far upstream. Is there abnormal heat far to the south melting the snows in the peaks more than usual? Are there rumors of coming downpours in the red mountains of Ethiopia that might send the Nile rushing into the delta? Has the water upstream a rotten taste, and is it reddish from algae? What was its highest level this year at Aswan, at Thebes, here at Pi-Ramessu? The boatmen will know.

"How is the drainage this year in the fields? If the Nile runs high and the harvest is late, there will be infestations of insects and blights from the extra days of dampness. The rotting seed stores will feed and multiply the insects. Has shemou"—the summer—"been unusually hot? For that will also tell me how the insects are breeding and whether frogs are lively or lazy."

"Have the northerly winds been steady? Have the sails slackened when boats traveled upstream? Are the wells full or dry, and have the slaves been ordered to deepen them? Are the seagulls, cuckoos, and other eaters of insects as plentiful as usual? Have people taken more or fewer birds in their nets? Do not doubt that the information you bring me is as valuable as a troop of valiant bows. For from all these facts, I will sew complicated nets. Jehovah will draw in the nets and snare the Egyptians so they can no longer cause us harm."

Moses was excited, but nervous from sleeplessness, when he and Aaron walked by the Nile as ordered by Ramses. To Moses' dismay, Nunrah, smirking, was with him, and also the magicians, saved by Nunrah, Moses assumed, from the priests of Amun. This was not the time when Ramses would dare to speak frankly with him, and he saw the masked disappointment in Ramses' eyes.

"My good vizier, and the leaders of the temples," said Ramses, "all of whom I revere, and the gods of Egypt, Nun, God of Moisture, Osiris, whose celestial corpse fertilizes our fields, and . . ." Ramses paused, then continued, "Hapi, who wears the very colors of the Nile, wish to give these worthy magicians another test, but one that you shall propose. If the royal thaumaturges fail, they will be dismissed. If you fail, you will be killed."

"And if we and our God succeed?" asked Moses.

"Then, you will not be killed. That is all."

Moses was angered—at Ramses, for being able to appear only with his guards; at Nunrah, a coward who would have bought and raped Sebah; and at the fraudulent magicians and the priests, all of them puppets to the vizier. He seethed over the thought that no matter what his knowledge and cunning achieved, it would not be enough to free the Hebrews. *Maybe,* he thought fiercely, *the way lay in the kind of terror proposed by young Joshua.* Outwardly, he was calm.

"Pharaoh Ramses, second of that name," he said, taking his staff from Aaron, "life, health, and strength be yours. Jehovah, the God of Abraham, speaks thusly through me: free his children for this religious observance in the desert. Your own festivals last two weeks in some years. My people"—Ramses smiled with grim sarcasm at these two words—"have never asked for, nor been given even three days off to worship their God. If you do not heed Jehovah, he will punish all Egypt.

"He will make the Nile and its pools run red with blood. Frogs and water snakes will swarm the land. They will enter your houses, die in your kneading bowls and in your bread ovens. Your infants will crush their bodies underfoot and whimper, and the heaps of slimy, rotting flesh will stink in the nostrils of your people. It will pollute and poison your wells. Flies, fleas, mosquitoes, gnats, and lice will infest your fruits and vegetables and enter your palaces and those of your officials; they will fly into the mouths, eyes, and ears of your children, coat the brick of your walks, and defile your good earth."

Moses knew that for all his science, for all his guile, this combination of calamities would not come about through himself alone. In his heart he felt a surging. He knew it was the tidal wave of his God, assuring him that the plagues would indeed occur very much as he, Moses, had described them.

Ramses looked at Moses. He had always admired the power of his mind, indeed, had envied it. It had not taken much, Ramses realized, to thwart a cheap magic trick by breaking hollow staffs. But he did not believe even Moses could make good on these extraordinary threats. Or could he? Ramses wondered. The Nilometer slabs in the river at Aswan were showing that the river was running only slightly above average. But the Nile was fickle. Even as mediocre a student of the weather as Ramses knew that melting snow and rains could wreck the best predictions.

"Hebrew," he said, "the gods of Egypt, for whom I am incarnate, laugh at your threats. My magicians and priests scorn them and will thwart them. If your curses prove true, and I will announce this to all Egypt"—and Moses saw a flicker of confusion on the thin face of Nunrah—"then there shall be new magicians in this land. If your boast is mere chaff, then you and your brother will be buried alive up to the neck on this spot for all of Egypt—slaves and free men—to spit on."

Moses seized the moment. "So be it, Pharaoh." He turned to Aaron, who had gone pale at Ramses' words but feared to shame himself by trembling before his younger brother. "Brother Aaron," said Moses, "hold this staff with me and we will strike the Nile with it and invoke the anger of Jehovah against this land that refuses to let our people go." As the two brothers sharply splashed the water, Moses said, "Pharaoh, vizier, magicians, if these things I prophesy do not happen in three weeks, then may all Egypt spit on our faces. May our eyes be hollowed by greedy vermin. May our skulls rot as Egypt thrives."

Nunrah suspected some unimaginable plot. "Too long, oh Ramses," he said. "Three weeks is too long. The Great Snake of the Nile has already left his cavern beneath Elephantine Island and is on its way to us. Let us set a shorter time, on the morrow, surely, is time enough."

"Nunrah," Ramses said, and all his hatred for the man was in that single word, "the Pharaoh does not go back on his pledge. I let him set the terms, as was right. For the magicians set the first contest. And lost. The Hebrew is a mountebank. You will have the pleasure of burying him when he fails.

Magicians," Ramses ordered—and now, he sounded like the Pharaoh that Moses had always expected he would be—"touch your staffs to the Nile. Defy and ridicule the Israelite madman's threats." He looked intently at Moses. "As sure as Sopdet looks down tonight on this spot as she did in my childhood and has done in all the days of time, you will lose this contest, and die."

Moses instantly saw himself and Ramses on that long-ago hillside in July above the flooding Nile when they had vied to see who would first descry Sirius-Sopdet. With an imperious wave, Ramses dismissed the brothers and turned to his advisors.

Chapter Eight
Pharaoh's Choice

HAT NIGHT, ALL ALONE AND WITHOUT INFORMING ANYONE BUT BES-Ahrin and Zipporah, Moses walked quietly through the slave quarter, close by the sides of the mud-brick dwellings so that he would not be observed.

Once at the Nile, he crouched in the reeds, only a few miles away from where his infant basket had been launched by his mother forty-one years earlier and only a few yards from where he had talked with Ramses and his advisors a few hours ago. Sirius would not be fully visible for three weeks, but no matter. He saw the silhouette of Ramses and rose from the reeds like some mythical Nile water monster. "Ramses," he whispered. There was no need tonight for titles. "Hapi-Set," came the low answer.

They did not embrace. Nor did they grip forearms. Too much lay between them. "Into the shadows," said the Pharaoh. "Those hyenas watch me whenever they can." He gave a bitter chuckle. "I told the palace guards to say I had to go out and commune alone with the god Seth, if anyone should ask."

In the gloom of the reeds, only the riverside night noises sounded, splash of frog and turtle, sawing of locusts. "Too cloudy for Sopdet," Moses said with friendly warmth. Then he asked, "What is happening, Ramses? How has it come to this?"

"I must be brief. The supposed victory against the Hittites on the Orontes ten years ago was no victory. . . ."

"Ah, I heard rumors of a disaster. . . ."

"I had never planned more carefully. Maybe if you had been there, Hapi-Set . . ." He said it without recrimination. "I was ambushed. They almost got me. I could have been in chains, led to Matulla. I lost both the regiments of Re and Amun, and if the Ptah regiment had not forded the Orontes, I would have been taken by a troop of Kashkashites. Kashkashites, Hapi-Set! I wish I had time to detail the whole battle. Of course, I had a few stelae built. The usual claims.

"But here at home, Nunrah was digging like a corpse worm in the home guard. He led the Sutekh regiment on the Libyan front and luck gave him a victory at Shweh. And most of the priests . . . they have never trusted me. I cannot understand it. I know you are wondering about why I ordered the Israelites to cut their own stubble. Nunrah forced my hand on it. But that was the last straw, if you will pardon my stupid play on words."

Moses, now that they were talking as of old, sympathized with his friend, even felt a whiff of guilt at not having been with him at the Orontes. But more importantly, he saw how much it was to both of their advantages to destroy Nunrah. Ramses was now turning to what could be done.

". . . to the present. Let us suppose I let you, a despised Hebrew, son of slaves, shame these royal charlatans again. I can dismiss them, maybe put them to death. Look, I know what you are doing. The river is already reddening at Aswan from those little strings of muck, that thickening—"

"Algae," said Moses, "but also from the rains in the red mountains of Ethiopia—"

"So if I can say to the people, behold, a Hebrew has changed the color of the Nile, and my magicians, my advisors cannot stop it, then the people will understand I mean by implication my uncle, for I dare not attack him directly. Don't forget, he does have some claim to the throne through our grandfather, rather my grandfather. Anyway, I can then announce that I, Ramses, incarnate of the gods, will cause the Nile to flow in its accustomed brown again. And, it will—"

"Ramses, let me stop you. It has got to be Jehovah, not you, who makes the Nile run brown again, who drives off the fleas, snakes, the frogs, all that. Wait, do not interrupt. There is a compromise. Suppose you were to get out rumors—particularly to the armies, whose families will be affected—that you wanted to let the Hebrews sacrifice to their God for three days after I killed those opiated cobras? But let it be known that Nunrah and his relatives, loyal to old gods and priests, advised you not to follow what you saw as the will of the true gods. And that opposition, do you see, has now led to the pestilence.

"Believe me, Ramses, this is going to be a year like we have never seen. I know you doubt that my calculations could be precise. And they will not be perfect. But, I tell you, as sure as you are beside me instead of in a hippopotamus's belly, there is a god at work here more powerful than all the gods of Egypt. When this blight begins, and it will, you can tell your people that all you need to do is let the Hebrews go and it will be all over. Time it for a week, two weeks, after the river withdraws. You can let us go and say, 'Now look, the plague brought on by Nunrah and his friends has gone.'

"Set Egypt to digging fresh wells and cleaning up the mess . . . call in your loyal generals. Tell the people and the army that the vizier and his allies must be punished. It will be a difficult time, yes. But in the end you will be able to exile these people—even kill them—and be fully Pharaoh again. And my people will be on the way to Canaan, which the Lord of Abraham has promised them, whether you believe it or not."

Ramses had listened carefully, looking nervously out over the reeds toward the palace. "All of that makes a certain sense, Hapi-Set. But you said three days. Now you talk of Canaan. I can never get by with liberating the Hebrews forever. They have been slaves since Horemheb decreed it."

"Ramses, I lied to you once, and I still feel guilty about it. I will not lie to you on this. The three days is so you can have some excuse for freeing us. When we are gone, believe me, we are gone permanently. But by that time, with these plagues, Egypt will be glad to get rid of us. You know I am no king over these people and often they cannot even hear the voice of our own God. Only half of them trust me, and they only half-trust me. I have got to produce some results, or we are all under the grinding stone."

Ramses was looking for a path without hazards. "Why should I not just let these plagues run their course, blaming them on the Hebrews, saying Nunrah and his followers refused to lift them by giving the Hebrews three days in the wilderness, and when the plagues lift, taking the credit for myself? Then I could give the Hebrews three days in the desert, kill them if they do not return—there are only about six thousand of you—and rid myself of them and Nunrah at the same time."

"If you did not let them go, Ramses, there will be a worse plague to come. There is a murderous anger among them." He started to say, "One I could not control and Jehovah would not choose to." But he did not, merely letting the words stand alone.

"You lied before. I do not trust you any more than your Hebrews do. Suppose this final threat is a bluff?"

"Suppose it is not?"

Ramses said nothing. Moses looked out across the dusky Nile, so much more narrow than it would be in a few weeks, its inexorable flow discernible by the light of a few stars.

At last, Ramses spoke. "When I have destroyed Nunrah and deposed his followers, I will tell Egypt that your people will go into the wilderness for three days of prayer—"

"No, Ramses." Moses knew that he could not return to his God and his people with this crumb.

Ramses rode over him. "Hear me out. My army will not follow you when you leave. I will assure Egypt that we are well rid of you. That it is the will of all our gods. I am giving you everything you asked, except that I want Nunrah out of the way before you leave. I can compromise no further."

Could he trust Ramses, who no longer trusted him? He was not certain. And there, alone with his old comrade beside the river, his new God gave him no advice. This compromise, in which so many things could go wrong, was the best one he could manage.

The two former friends, now allies and deadly enemies simultaneously, ended their conversation without civilities. Moses' head was full of plans as he hurried homeward.

Ramses walked through the heavy air toward his palace, unaware that a mosquito was digging into his neck until it bit. He slapped it and felt the slight wetness of blood on his skin. *A plague of insects,* he thought. *Oh, it will come. This new Moses-Hapi-Set will contrive it somehow.* Ramses thought of the night when they were boys in Thebes, when Moses went to the tomb of Akhenaten, the monotheist Pharaoh. *How he has changed. It is because he has found his one God at last, this Jehovah. And I am caught between his God and my enemies. I cannot judge his God's strength. But I must believe he is powerful and that he has imparted his powers to Hapi-Set.*

The thought quickened his steps. *Can the two of them overwhelm the will of all the gods of Egypt? And me along with them? No,* he told himself, *I am Ramses, incarnation of Seth and Re. I will not bow to Hapi-Set and this God who has taken over his body and his spirit.* He shivered in the warm night and vigorously scratched the mosquito bite. *A plague of insects,* he thought.

The plagues came, if not exactly as Moses had threatened. First, ten days after his meeting with Ramses, the Nile—just when it appeared it had reached its full level—got redder and began to rise. It was enough for Ramses to take a first step. He discharged the four magicians, sending them to the Temple of Amun to be held in separate cells.

Next, the waters spread in noisome sheets across the fields and stagnated for ten days to two weeks beyond when they should have withdrawn—not everywhere, but at Tentyris, Menat Khoufou, Nekhen, and most importantly, just north of Pi-Ramessu itself. The shallow pools ruined seed stocks, delayed sowing, and bred mosquitoes, flies, and other pernicious insects. Frogs and snakes hatched in the pools in unseasonable numbers. Then a hot sun that should have been warming moist land rapidly dried up the pools, sending frogs, snakes, and insects everywhere. They drowned in cisterns and wells, contaminating the drinking water, and were squashed underfoot. Moses thanked Jehovah each night.

Those afflicted cursed Moses and Ramses' advisors equally, for the Pharaoh had successfully blamed Nunrah, his priests, and magicians, exculpating himself. Even the untouched towns and rural areas—where Moses had miscalculated the flooding—were terrified. There, inhabitants met outside their temples to implore the gods to continue withholding the blight.

As nature returned to normal, the plagues diminished. Moses, in order not to compromise Ramses with public utterances, secretly sent word via the general that it was time for the Pharaoh to deliver on his promise, to begin to move against Nunrah. But Ramses hesitated. He did not feel he had sufficient support to destroy Nunrah. He needed more time. He replied through his trusted general that Moses could "sacrifice to your God for three days, but in Goshen, not the wilderness."

Moses had hoped the agreement would hold and was furious, feeling let down not just by Ramses, but by Jehovah. "Why are you doing this, Lord? Are you still testing me?" he complained on the night he received Ramses' message.

As in his military campaigns against Egypt's enemies, Moses, during the plagues, had been preparing contingencies. From enslaved Hebrew stevedores at Zilu he got reports of a hot prevailing wind from the east, and of locusts and fields denuded of green in Ube and the Land of the Horites. From towns throughout the delta, he heard how the miasmic excess flooding and the mosquitoes and flies that had proliferated had caused infectious boils and fevers that could only spread. He elicited information of natural conditions with all the zeal he had shown as a student, and with more rapidity.

Moses himself visited his old astronomy teacher at Tanis one night. The man, alone except for one servant in a small house beside the Temple of Amun, recognized him with a start. "Prince Hapi-Set—oh, I dare not call you that," the bent man trembled, rising abruptly from his low-cushioned chair and knocking over a silver statuette of Amun in the form of a goose.

Moses tried to calm him. "Master, I do not come to alarm you, but only to ask you a single question. In the way I asked and you wisely answered when I was a youth and you my teacher."

"Oh, Hapi-Set, the divine Sety, may he have life, health, and strength in the Underworld, ordered your name never to be mentioned after you . . . betrayed Egypt. Although, Hapi-Set, good Hapi-Set, we were so proud of you. For you were the pearl of all the students I ever taught and I saw only that you brought honor to Egypt in her wars and as her ambassador."

Moses tried again. "I did not betray her, kind Master. I believed myself a prince. But unknown to me I was a foundling. And I was banished, perhaps justly. But do not scorn me. For as you can see, I have never forgotten you, nor my other teachers, but you above all."

The aging heart of the pedagogue melted. Within minutes, he had lit more oil lamps and he and Moses were poring over charts of the heavens, notes on papyrus, and small models of the sun—in a boat—and the moon. It was midnight before Moses mounted his donkey for the long ride back to Aaron's home.

The next morning, Moses and Aaron walked to the palace. This time, the new magicians, the priests, and the aging courtiers were outnumbered by generals, men Moses recalled from his days on the military campaigns. The vizier Nunrah was not present, an absence Ramses cautiously observed was "due to an indisposition, the seriousness of which we do not yet know." After the formalities of title recitations and wishes of life, health, and strength, Moses said, "Mighty Bull, I sought this audience because my God has lifted from you the worst of the plagues he put upon you. And yet you still do not release his people to sacrifice to him in the wilderness."

"Cunning Hebrew," said Ramses, "my people appreciate the power of your God Jehovah, and some even urge that I release the Hebrews not just for three days, but forever. But others wish their slavery to be even more severe, and some even wish them killed. Indeed, I have had to intervene to prevent a group called Suitors of the Short Knives from falling on you.

"However, I knew that your death would occasion a murderous rage among your followers, who would kill many Egyptians before we could exterminate them, yes, to the youngest infant. Prospects change at the whims of the gods from day to day and are not propitious for your sacrifices in the wilderness, which is why I proposed you make them in Goshen."

Moses did not forget that he had lied to Ramses all those years ago, but Ramses had now responded with even greater treachery. "Ramses," Moses said tensely, "incarnation of warlike Seth, you were ever one who controlled events, not one to whom events were dictated. Hear what my Lord Jehovah requires:

"If you do not let his people go to the wilderness for three days of sacrifice, he will punish all Egypt. He will bring locusts to despoil your fields or a hailstorm to batter down the young shoots; or he will darken the sun to show you his power; or he will cause boils and sores to break out among your people and your animals; or he will order irresistible armies of lice or dust storms to sicken both man and beast. Even now, he ponders which of these afflictions to visit on Egypt. He will decide in the next three weeks if you still refuse to let his people go."

Ramses paled. His coterie first looked at each other, then began to whisper, generals to generals, priests to priests. Ever since that night by the Nile,

Ramses had genuinely feared that Moses, just as he said, was getting frightening help from this foreign God. In any case, Moses had used his prodigious mind to put him ever more tightly between the chisel and the rock. Suddenly angry at being trapped, the Pharaoh spoke out:

"I know what you are doing, Hap . . . wicked Hebrew. I know that your people go everywhere with questions, that you are missing at night, gathering information the gods only know where. Do you think I have no memory of your brain and how it never stops working once it has determined a course?"

"Then free them!" Moses demanded. He understood Ramses' predicament. But did Ramses understand his? Joshua's daring, suicidal influence was growing among the Hebrews. Many were willing to risk a battle to the death for freedom, although it would mean the murder of children, of elderly parents, and only a few Hebrews would escape. It was from fear of this rampage of events that Moses cried, "Ramses, you and I are like men chained at the bottom of a waterfall, waiting for the waters from the mountains to sweep over us. Break my chains and yours at the same time. Free us both, and my people, and yours, too. My God will not permit me to abide your slavery, even if I wanted to."

But Ramses had hardened. With the iron smile that had so often preceded his order to his chariot driver to whip the horses into battle, he said, "No, Hapi-Set, we must see who can hold his breath longest and who will drown beneath your waterfall."

As Moses walked bitterly toward his house, he said between clenched teeth, "Make it happen, God, make it happen."

And he heard Jehovah reply, "Do your part, son of Amram."

The Lord of Abraham, Isaac, and Jacob once again made good on his threats. But selectively. In Sais, only fifty miles west of Pi-Ramessu and one of the last places from which the inundation withdrew, there were eruptions of maladies caused by the swarms of pests. The people suffered sudden boils, fiery mosquito bites, fevers, and a score of deadly scorpion assaults on incautious children.

At Buto, in the west delta, a *khamsin*—similar to the blistering winds of a simoom—blew dust in from the Libyan deserts, and with it hatches of lice that infested humans and animals. Locusts rode a hot wind into Athribis and devoured its fragile plants. A disastrous hailstorm battered Edfou, far upstream, killing the first crop shoots and domestic fowl.

The truth is that isolated disasters hit Egypt every year. But no one could remember when one had come atop another in this way. The populace was all too ready to let the magpie goddess of rumor fly over all Egypt. The curses of Moses and his mysterious lord, Jehovah, were seen as more potent than the revered gods and goddesses of the Pharaohs.

Soon Egypt believed that tribulation was ravaging the land from Nubia to the Great Green. Ramses received reports that towns all the way to the second cataract were desolated by hailstones as big as ibis eggs. In fact, there had been only heavy thunderstorms in that area. With so many of Moses' predictions seeming to come true, few noticed that the eclipse of the sun—foretold by Moses as a harbinger of disaster—had not occurred. Moses and his old professor had misread the records or had guessed wrong, and Jehovah had decided not to remedy their miscalculations.

This time, Pi-Ramessu was spared all but the incursions of frantic Egyptians with petitions to free or kill the Hebrews. Towns annually burdened with insects—due to their own filth—or storms and arid winds joined in the general panic. Ramses' new magicians, their predecessors badly discredited, refused to cast spells to halt the pestilences. Nunrah, still vizier in name, retired with his followers to Memphis, his stronghold, to regroup and plot a new course of action. Ramses, unsure of his new allies, did not yet dare to dismiss him.

At last, Ramses summoned Moses and Aaron to the palace. He looked worn from the pressures on him. This time, he was flanked only by his own generals and a few loyal priests.

"I would rather be at war with the Hittites again," he observed to Moses, his informality an evidence to Moses that he had at least winnowed his advisors to those he could trust.

"I, too," said Moses. "It was so much simpler then."

Ramses sighed and looked at his generals, whose expressions gave away nothing. "Your God, or your ingenuity—it does not matter—has brought the majestic wheel of Egypt to a standstill. I must find a way to govern. I have cities to build. I have borders to secure, campaigns to undertake. I have accomplished that which stood in the way of an agreement before now. I have discharged Nunrah. Now I offer you your freedom."

Aaron and Moses simultaneously gasped. But both were quickly suspicious. They feared a caveat.

Ramses continued: "You may take your children, although some of my advisors urge me to keep them here to grow into slaves. You may take your goods, your gold, your jewelry, although my priests would have preferred it all go to our temples. I have only one condition. My generals, my loyal priests, all my officials insist on it. You may not take your sheep, your goats, your herds of any kinds, your pack and riding animals with you. Egypt must have this token payment for the ills you have visited upon us."

Moses, staring at Aaron, held back his own rejection, seeking an answer first from his generally passive brother. "We cannot," said Aaron firmly.

"Ramses," said Moses, "think of what you do. Without animals, we cannot sacrifice to our God. We would have no milk for our children and elderly, no cheese, no meat from our sheep and goats, no transport for our weary. We would be six thousand corpses marching toward Canaan, in doubt only where we would be buried and who would bury us. You and your advisors know this."

"Hebrew, do not be hasty. It is the best I can offer you. Buy some animals."

"You also know slaves do not have that kind of money!" Moses burst in angrily.

But Ramses went on, desperation in his voice. "I tell you, I can do no better," he repeated. "Nunrah is gashed but not gored. Let those Hebrews go who will and those who want can stay behind. And those who leave and change their minds can return. All without punishment."

Moses, barely containing himself, made a final plea. He saw, as if it were happening before his eyes, the bloodshed, the horror, that Ramses was bringing on both Egypt and Israel with this unacceptable proposal. He looked at his old friend with anguish. "Do not make me do this, Ramses," he said imploringly.

But the Pharaoh was equally trapped. "You say your God has spoken through you, Hebrew. Take our offer to him and to your people. Try to convince them. Be reasonable."

"This is madness!" Moses exploded. "Have you learned nothing?" He appealed to Ramses' generals and priests. "Do you truly advise him to do this?" Only the old general, the most faithful of Ramses' advisors, looked dismayed.

"Then it is over," Moses said, grabbing the staff from Aaron, banging its haft so hard on the floor that a tile depicting a leaping gazelle cracked through its middle. "Ramses," he roared, dropping all pretense at respect, "hear the word of the God Jehovah. Every family in the delta will feel his wrath upon their children. You will pay in blood for what you have done to us. Your choice animals will perish because you deny our animals to us. The wails of humans and the cries of beasts will shake even your palace walls. And when it is done, not even the dogs will dare move their tongues against us."

Moses could hear himself raving. But he felt in his chest, in his limbs, the power of an angry God speaking through him. Breathing as if he were wrestling, he glared at the faces of his adversaries. The priests looked at each other, and the eldest spoke out almost hysterically.

"Noble Ramses, true body of all our gods, heed what this lunatic says. We have seen his evil toward Egypt and the evil of his God. Send them away. What does it matter if they survive, for clearly they will not go without their animals? Even if we gave them grain in plenty to take, would they? Could we do without our meat sacrifices? Be done with them. Return to your heroic works and our wars—"

"Silence!" Ramses howled, himself out of control. "Do you want to die on the spot?" He gripped the hilt of his ceremonial short sword at his waist. So wrathful was he that his high blue crown tilted askew. "You, Hapi-Set, I curse the day your scum flesh was plucked from the Nile by my aunt. Go! Go! I spare you at this instant only to shelter the Egyptians whose lives your rabble would take before I executed them, man, woman, and child. Nevertheless, if I ever see you again, you die! Most horribly! At my own hands!"

Moses, striking the floor with his staff again as if he were smiting all Egypt, all Egyptians, stalked from the throne room followed by Aaron, almost running to keep up with him.

As they walked toward Aaron's house, Moses began to calm. His anger turned to woe for, persistently, he saw in his mind the kind of uncontrolled carnage he had witnessed in wars. Through Aaron, he called a meeting that evening of the Council of Elders and the main priests. Then he bade his brother and sister go with him to where their parents were buried in a common grave just outside of town. Moses had been to it several times before. This visit, he knew, might be the last.

The bodies of all Egyptians save for beggars were shown respect. Even the working poor were preserved for a while with the oily sap of a juniper tree or turpentine injected into their anuses to preserve the internal parts. Then they were desiccated for a week in a trough filled with mineral natron. If they had a few qites of gold left over, a small stele might be erected with a hieroglyph or two about their lives. Their bodies were wrapped in coarse cloth before being stacked in caves, holes in the ground, or empty tombs, a few household effects put in for use in the afterlife.

When the Hebrews were free, there had been simple graves for them, too. But now that they were slaves, there was only a pit in a weedy field, each body covered with a few inches of dirt, and although Amram and Jochebed were well-to-do slaves, they were part of this ossuary. The brothers stood before the mound, now partly grown over with nettles.

Moses knelt in the heat of day, shut his eyes, and tried to talk with his God. At first, he saw only the tiny spots and spirals in his eyes brought on by the bright sun. Then, deeper, from his brain, he asked, "God, has the time come? Must we do deadly things? Must we risk all?"

"We have done all we can, Moses," he heard the Lord's answer. "The powers of Egypt will not listen, even though their own people cry out to them to liberate Israel."

"Should we not try one more time before we bring down a rain of blood upon them? And us? I am not without new ideas."

"It is too late, Moses. Joshua and the other young men will not wait any longer. Even the older men, and some of the women, are ready to die. We have held out promises to our people, given them hope. We cannot deny them now. You know that as well as I do. As you said to Ramses, it is a time of madness. And to preserve our sanity we must act as madmen."

Moses breathed in the dry air, the arid smell of the nettles, and, faintly, the smell of desiccating flesh from the pit. "When one takes the leash off the lion, it may kill indiscriminately, Lord."

"Even so, we act in justice. All Egypt remembers—and who knows better than you?—that Horemheb, cursed is his name, ordered the death of newly born Hebrews more than forty-one years ago. Now let it be Egypt's turn. Let those who are willing slaughter the first-born of Egypt's leaders at Pi-Ramessu, for we do not have time to do this elsewhere in the land. Let those who work as palace servants help. If the first-born sons cannot be killed, let it be the first-born of their animals. Let it be done uniformly, with knives, not poison or clubs. You will find my own hand among those raised against Egypt, Moses.

"And the next day, let Israel demand jewelry, gold, silver, silks, and other valuables from their neighbors, for riches will be needed for trading as you cross the desert. The Egyptians will give all they can to see our people leave." The voice of God paused, then resumed. "You falter, Moses. Can I trust you? Did you falter when you killed in wars for Sety?"

The perspiration was pouring from beneath Moses' headband, running down his cheeks and into his beard, and from under his arms and chest, soaking even his loincloth. "Is there no other way, Lord?" he whispered, aloud now, begging.

"Can you think of one? No. There is no other way."

Moses gave a sob of despair, then set his teeth. "Jehovah, verily I faltered, I weakened. Restore my strength."

All that afternoon, as he held preliminary talks with Aaron, Joshua, and the most staunch of the elders, Moses dismally but vividly imagined the death of the Egyptian children. Several times, he thought of fleeing with Zipporah, their sons, and Bes-Ahrin. They could return to their peaceful life near Sinai. But Moses had flung his javelin. He could not make it turn and come back into his hand like a harmless boomerang.

Heavy in his heart, he spoke bluntly to the men gathered together in Aaron's front room. "Joshua, and you others, the Lord Jehovah has ordered us to act. Egypt has gone back on its promises to us, as you know. We cannot trust them, no matter what new miracles the Lord works. Therefore, Jehovah says they must be punished so profoundly that they will have to let us go. His own hand will be raised against them. On the fourteenth day of this month, two days from now—even as had been done to us in the past by the Pharaohs—the first-born sons of Egypt's leaders, priests, officials, as many as can be, must be sacrificed to show that they can no longer defy Jehovah.

"Those of you who cannot bring yourselves to carry out these acts must help clear the way for those among us who have been wronged so grievously that they can. If you cannot help in that either, then insofar as you are able, you must kill the first-born of these officials' animals. Egypt must know the power of the Lord. The death of all of these must be clean and quick, with knives or swords, not poison or clubs or other means.

"All of us must have our traveling clothes and walking staffs ready. Each family will kill a yearling sheep or goat. If a family is too poor, his neighbors must share. Roast it with herbs and eat it with unleavened bread, and for all the days of our people, this shall be called our Feast of the Passover. As a symbol of the purity of our acts, twigs of hyssop must be struck against the door lintels. Then, so we can know that no Egyptians have sought sanctuary among us, the twigs must be dipped in the blood of our yearling sheep and goats and brushed against the lintels. These are the words of the Lord."

Among these men, there was no dissent. Moses had finally caught up with the people he had been sent to lead.

When the group broke up, Bes-Ahrin went outside with Moses and said to him quietly, "Hapi-Set, there are the dwarfs of the households, and my other friends who wish to leave with you. They have their own money. They can buy donkeys from your people or the Egyptians as we flee. Can they come?"

"Of course," said Moses.

"Most are ready to heed the word of your God, Hapi-Set. The gods of the Egyptians have scorned them, made household pets of them no better than monkeys or dogs."

Moses did not ask Bes-Ahrin what he meant by their being ready to heed the word of God. He could imagine the hatred many of these deformed and undersized people must have felt through the ages. But there was something ominous in his voice. "Do not seek the life of any of the sons of Ramses," warned Moses.

"It shall be as you and your Jehovah decree," said the dwarf.

The night of the Passover, temples, palaces of the mighty, vacation homes, and farms ran with royal and aristocratic blood. Mothers and fathers screamed to their powerless gods for restoration of young lives and for the deaths of their rulers and the Hebrews. Newly born cattle lay dead in stalls, throats slit. Colts flopped their last in the royal stables. On nearby farms, the blood of livestock seeped into the soil.

Only a handful of Hebrews were caught at their gory work. They were slain by guards. A dwarf, two midgets, and a hunchback were also cut down, their bloody oversized daggers in their hands. One of the midgets, an aging, perfectly formed man the size of a large doll, was decapitated by Ramses himself after he had slain Pharaoh's eight-year-old son. Although half out of his mind with grief and fury, Ramses was unable to take revenge on Moses and the Hebrew slaves.

For all Egypt believed the Hebrew leader was the only one who could dam the torrent of horror drowning the land. Nor was that the only reason. Despite his and his wife's, Nofretari's, appalling loss, Ramses dared not decree the death of all the Hebrews, for they would fight back with the bloodthirstiness of the doomed. With their intimate knowledge of every alley and home in Pi-Ramessu where they had worked as maids, stablemen, and gardeners, they would kill thousands of soldiers and civilians even as the army obliterated them.

He was besieged by officials who had lost sons—and had other children to lose—and by others who feared their sons would be next. With one voice, they insisted he instantly rid the country of the Hebrews.

Moses, on hearing the news of Ramses' son, rushed into the quarters of Bes-Ahrin. "You defied me," Moses shouted. "Your midget killed Ramses' son."

Bes-Ahrin's face, what could be seen of it beneath the hair, flushed angrily. "No, I told him not to." The dwarf calmed. "We small people hate the Ramessides, yes. They enslaved us as no other Pharaohs ever did, for all that we lived in luxury with them. But, no, I asked him to spare the child.

"Do not forget, however, it was you and your Jehovah who ordered the deaths of the first-born. The midget obeyed you, not me. And do not think that all these deaths occurred because of us or the Hebrews who were willing to kill children. You said Jehovah would lift his own hand. Hapi-Set, I still do not believe in your God. But many more died than there were dwarfs or Hebrews to kill them. I know the gods of the Egyptians did not shed these children's blood. For me, a mystery remains, yet even I must suspect that some god was abroad in the night."

Moses bit off his anger. For as Bes-Ahrin had said, he and his fierce God were to blame for the lad's death, and that of so many others. "There was a justice in all this, Bes-Ahrin," he said mournfully. "It was a terrible justice."

Ramses sent word to Moses to come to the palace, bringing with him, if he were afraid, his own armed protectors. "You killed my son!" he screamed when Moses, with only Aaron beside him, arrived. "I would kill you. It kills me that I cannot."

"Your grief is matched only by mine. The blood of all those children will be always on me. Yet, it was at the order of my God and with my help. You must believe one thing: I ordered your son to be spared, Ramses. Surely such a little man had immense anger that he would kill your child."

"Your hideous dwarf put him up to it," said Ramses. "Bes-Ahrin will not leave Egypt alive, that I guarantee you."

"Bes-Ahrin obeyed my order and told the midget to spare your son. Ramses, think of what was put upon my God, who is a God of mercy, that he would have commanded so many deaths. Let us reason, in the name of all that still remains decent in us."

The honest, sane words forced Ramses to grip his head and shut his eyes in an effort at control. When he opened them, he looked at his generals. "You, too, lost sons. This morning when we spoke, beneath our rage we knew we must drive this evil people away to save our families and Egypt from even greater atrocities at the hands of their demon God. Tell me, for at this moment I am cursed by the gods and account you not subjects, but comrades. Is it still your wish that we free them without punishment? Or shall we kill them all, beginning with these monsters before us?"

The generals, mostly older than Ramses, by nods quickly polled themselves. The general who had stood by Ramses all through his troubles with Nunrah put his hand on his chest with dignity and said, "Golden Horus, we all say, let them go."

Chapter Nine
The Exodus

HAT EVENING, A VARIEGATED HORDE LEFT GOSHEN AND SLOWLY headed southeast: six thousand Hebrews with their hastily baked unleavened bread; dwarfs, midgets, and the deformed rallied by Bes-Ahrin, all doomed if they stayed; two dozen persecuted followers of the discredited Pharaoh Akhenaten, almost all that remained in Egypt; a hundred Egyptian soldiers and four officers who had fought under Moses; two hundred other Egyptians, who for various reasons wanted to leave; and a hundred slaves of diverse races, who simply saw a chance to free themselves.

After Moses had first proposed three months earlier that the Israelites follow him to a Promised Land, some of Joshua's friends had broken into the tomb of Joseph at Thebes. They had stolen his mummy and secreted it in a cellar from which they had removed it the night before. In a donkey cart of its own, it was now making the trip to Canaan, the land of Joseph's birth.

The line of Moses' followers stretched for three miles. Wagons stacked with possessions were pulled by adults, children sitting high on the family goods. Carts were drawn by lowing oxen; sheep and goats baaed, donkeys brayed, the few horses neighed. The Hebrews had solicited jewelry and other valuables from Egyptians near their quarter. Some were glad to buy off further bad luck, some were grateful because their sons and animals were spared, some gave simply out of fear.

Aaron, who was now regarded by the Israelites as their high priest, and the other elders led the throng. Moses, Joshua, and Bes-Ahrin, all on horseback, waited for the last family to leave the slave quarter before falling in behind them. Zipporah was among the multitude with her two sons. Watching silently and on foot were a few dozen Egyptian soldiers and their captains. When the Hebrews were gone, the soldiers, too, would go, turning over the vacant Hebrew quarter for scanty looting to those foreign slaves left behind and the poorest of the Egyptians.

All night long the Hebrews trekked. By the next afternoon, they had reached the coastal highway of leveled dirt that ran from the Nile to Canaan and the nations to the north and east. It was the shortest route for them to take. Canaan, inviting for its bounty, formidable for its armies, was only two hundred miles away. At the highway, Moses, Aaron, Joshua, Bes-Ahrin, Hur, and three of the most dauntless of the elders sat in the shade of a cart to plan. They now constituted a war cabinet that made the decisions but sought ratification—always given thus far—by the much larger Council of Elders.

"We must go far to the south," Moses said. "It will be like swallowing a stone for our people."

"Then why?" Joshua asked brusquely. Though still rash, he was becoming less so as, increasingly, he saw Moses' wisdom—and success. "I have studied your own maps and we could travel east and pass just beneath Lake Sirbonis, buy provisions and weapons in Raphia, and be marching on Gaza in two or three months."

"Correct," said Bes-Ahrin, who, as he had been for Mutempsut, was now, to some extent, an alter ego for Moses. "Your geography is perfect. And who will march on Gaza? A mob of unskilled, untrained men, women, and children? We cannot summon up two hundred soldiers, Joshua. In Canaan, we will not be fighting first-born children. I am a Syrian. I know these people, as does Moses from the wars. If we try to take their land, they will very speedily fertilize it with our bodies. And your children's and aging parents'."

Moses turned to the young firebrand. "Bes-Ahrin is right. True, there are Hebrews in Canaan who might welcome us. But they are not unified. The majority are Philistines and their allies, Hittites, Amorites, Horites, Jebusites." He held up his scarred right arm as once he had held it up to his God in seeking to avoid the very responsibility he had now undertaken. "Only skilled shields deflect the javelins of Canaan, and even then they sometimes find their mark. We could not even overcome the Egyptian frontier garrison at Zilu if they sought to oppose us, as they might, if only to take our goods."

"Then what are we doing here?" said one of the elders.

Moses was irritated at opposition, for in the Egyptian army, his orders had been followed without question. He knew he must not expect obedience from this multitude of proud former slaves. Still, it was hard for him to brook disagreements. "We are following the orders of our God . . ." he said, ". . . and the dictates of common sense. On the coastal road, there could be marauders of all kinds who have heard rumors of our riches and flocks. By comparison, the southern road toward Mount Sinai, where I first encountered Jehovah, is long. But I have traveled it. There are springs, oases. There are small towns where we can find provisions. And all the time, we will train to take over the land of milk and honey that Jehovah has promised us."

"How long?" asked Joshua and the elder simultaneously.

"Until we are ready for a war," Moses smiled. "And you, Joshua, will undergo the most vigorous training of all from me. For you will be the chief general of Jehovah, in spite of your youth."

Joshua, at first surprised, smiled, then bowed. "I am honored," was as much as he could muster.

The straggling band, already tiring, passed through Succoth and camped at Etham, then continued the next day to Lake Timsah—called the Sea of Reeds- with its marshes and springs. Moses and Joshua scouted the area, seeking dry or fordable paths through the reeds and the best places for fortifications should the need arise.

That night, the Israelites camped on the west side of the Sea of Reeds. Moses posted twenty pickets around the perimeter, two hundred yards apart, each with a ram's horn. He required three men to spend the night in the reeds, however unlikely an attack was from the east. One note on the horn would sig- nify a small force, up to four for an army. Before the war cabinet ended their day, they worked out detailed plans for an orderly departure, a retreat, or, as a last resort, a stand to the death. They would rest a day, then leave on the fol- lowing morning.

Once the shock of the murder of the first-borns had dulled to anguish, the upper-class Egyptians, fueled by justified hatred, pressed Ramses for an expedi- tion of revenge. They were joined by cries from Nunrah and his supporters, who, seeing an opportunity to regain their strength, had ventured back to Pi- Ramessu. Temperamentally, Ramses was in favor. He could wipe out the killers of his and Egypt's children in the desert, where they could not endanger the citizenry of Pi-Ramessu.

But he saw no military benefit, for he would still lose many loyal troops. And, far more importantly, the majority of Egyptians would be terrified by a slaughter of the Hebrews, fearing further curses on them by the dire Moses and his Jehovah. Nevertheless, Ramses agreed to march, but for reasons he at first confided to no one. His plan, he thought with sardonic self-congratulation, was as devious and lethal as those once provided him by his former tactician, Hapi-Set.

From scouts at Zilu, he quickly learned of the Hebrews' campsite by Lake Timsah, forty miles southeast of Pi-Ramessu. He invited his uncle Nunrah for a unity conference, and the former vizier arrived with a full complement of bodyguards.

"Uncle, I welcome you," Ramses said when Nunrah arrived in the throne room. "I greet you in sorrow and in the full knowledge that we have a common enemy. The former Hapi-Set is encamped with his riffraff at Lake Timsah. I will lead the force to destroy them, but I need a valiant leader to conduct the charge and to eradicate them, man, woman, and child. There is not a soldier among them but Hapi-Set. I will want his head, and whatever other parts you choose to bring me."

Nunrah would rather have stayed in Pi-Ramessu to pull strings among allies. But to turn down the mission was to label himself a coward in the eyes of the Egyptians, many of whom blamed his recalcitrance for the evils that had befallen Egypt. Yet, to accept was to put himself physically at risk, a danger he had successfully avoided for most of his life. He had hoped his stroke of fortune on the Libyan frontier was all the real fighting he would ever have to do.

"This honor," said Nunrah, "more becomes a Pharaoh than a mere former vizier. Do you not wish to be in the vanguard when our troops avenge our gods, Egypt, and your throne?"

"This Pharaoh has no need to prove his bravery," Ramses reminded him. "My stelae throughout the land proclaim it. I wish to restore your standing, brother to my father, and perhaps call you again my vizier. You shall yourself pick those most loyal to you: officers, drivers of chariots, archers, spearmen, lancers. They shall share your honor. I will set up a tall stele of red quartzite to you right here in Pi-Ramessu when you butcher the slave who has so insulted our gods, Egypt, and you."

The morning sun poured down on the jumbled tents of the Hebrews. House dwellers for centuries, they would need months of fumbling with instructions from Moses, Bes-Ahrin, and Zipporah before they could sew proper Bedouin tents. Still groggy from sleeping on the thin straw mats they had brought, they grumbled as they broke camp. But by noon, they were packed and were threading their way down the path sixteen cubits—eight yards—wide that led through the marshes. Suddenly, from the north, they heard four brays of a ram's horn. In minutes, a picket arrived on horseback. An army was only a little more than two miles away.

"Hurry!" Moses shouted to the people weaving through the marshes. "Hurry! If the ox carts bog down, push them aside so those behind you can pass. In the rear, leave them in the path as barricades." The tribal leaders took up the cry. Moses and Joshua organized their pathetic forces on the northern side of Lake Timsah. The defected Egyptian soldiers were armed with spears, bows, and lances, some of the Israelites with swords. A few boys had slings made of leather and cords. But most of the Hebrews bore only mattocks, adzes, oxen goads, and staves.

Another picket, this one afoot, ran in and fell exhausted at Moses' feet. He had seen the dust of many chariots moving toward them. It was a half-hour from the first horn blast when Moses saw the line of chariots on a small ridge looking down on the flat, steamy lake.

They were still three hundred yards away, but Moses could see in the center the bright red, blue, and white chariot of the Pharaoh. Its streamers rippled amid the dazzling reflections of its gold plaques. Beside it, almost equally resplendent, was the kind of chariot that Moses himself once drove. Ramses, even now, would be choosing his tactics.

Moses knew exactly what he would do, as they had done it together against enemy encampments on the move. Ramses would drive the chariots to the beginnings of the marsh and rain arrows and javelins from them on the fleeing Hebrews. Running at top speed behind them would be his slingers, archers, and javelin men on foot, and finally spearmen, lancers, and swordsmen. These last would dispatch what was left of the Hebrew defenders as they fought from behind the barricade of the final carts that stuck in the muck. Then the Egyptians could pursue and slaughter the unprotected families at leisure and begin their looting.

Moses had only a single question: why was Ramses defying the majority will of Egypt—that the Hebrews be simply avoided as one would a porcupine fish on the shores of the Great Green? *Why, Jehovah, why?* he sought an answer to his question. But the Lord did not choose to reply.

Moses heard the familiar peals of the Egyptian bugles. The doomed Israelite defenders were tense, quiet, fearful, and determined. As Moses knew they would, the chariots in all their glorious colors raced down the hill. Moses shouted to his troops to stay low behind their barricade until the first spears and arrows were launched. Amazingly, he saw the Pharaoh's chariot still poised atop the hill. What ruse did Ramses have in mind? What departure from their standard military tactics?

The Egyptian charioteers launched their arrows and spears, striking down several defenders. The few Hebrew archers shot their arrows, the slingers hurled their stones. And, as the fierce horses approached, the Israelite spearmen threw their spears. It was brave but inadequate. Only a single horse fell, the charioteer escaping from the rear.

Moses and his troops continued to hunch with their swords and work

speak, no matter what his relief over Nunrah. But with a firm grip, he took the head and the pectoral from Moses' hand, pivoted his horse, and, holding the relics aloft, rode back to his army.

There were twenty Hebrews slain and twenty more were bleeding, like Moses, from painful wounds. Some two hundred and fifty Egyptian soldiers lay butchered by Ramses' men behind the chariots, the picked troops of Nunrah.

Moses grunted uncomfortably as Zipporah dressed the gash with resin, bitter herbs, and oil, stitched it closed with clean flax threads, and bound it with linen strips. As she worked, Moses gave orders for pitching camp. Some would sleep in makeshift tents near the field of the dead, some in their wagons.

It was midnight before he, Zipporah, and the children were in a tent that Bes-Ahrin, still coated with drying mud, had helped put up. Zipporah and Moses were too agitated to sleep, despite their weariness and his pain. It gave them time to talk, which had been denied them for weeks now. Zipporah spoke quietly so as not to wake the children.

"Moses, if I thought your pain was too great for me to speak out, I would bite my tongue. Tell me not to speak, and I will wait."

Moses had known, even as far back as his decision to go to Egypt, that all was not well between them. They had taken less pleasure in their lovemaking. To her, he seemed hurried as he had not been in Midian when, the stars filling the doorway of their tent, they had loved at leisure.

"No, I can't sleep either. I have neglected you, Zipporah," he said. "I know what you are going to say will hurt, but perhaps not so much as my shoulder."

She gave a humorous *hunff* at his soldier's jest. "I have thought a long time of what I am going to say. When you married me, you knew I was not a wife who could be no more to her husband than a server of meals or a purse or a friendly body in the bed. And you knew I would speak without guile."

"Speak, Zipporah," he said. "Let it be said."

She drew a long breath and began. "Moses, I want to return to the home of my father for a while, taking the children with me. This fighting today, when you—when they—could so easily have been killed, makes it less difficult for me. I will precede you and await you near Mount Sinai, where my father will be encamped. While we are separated, weigh what part of your life our marriage is, and we can then decide what we want to do."

Moses groaned. He could not blame her, for he knew he had chosen his responsibility to Jehovah and the Hebrews over his family. He had not thought she would overcome her independent ways, but when the possibility that she might leave him had entered his mind, he had pushed it out and replaced it with the most convenient of his multitude of concerns.

Of one thing he was sure: he could not turn back from what he knew to be God's special purpose for this sometimes cowardly, sometimes audacious, always quarrelsome people. How would his followers regard her departure? Perhaps not badly. They also were focused on this adventure in the desert and, besides, would have preferred that he had married a Hebrew instead of a Midianite. But the loss to him!

"I beg you to stay. I need you," he said. "I would have been wiser, many times, to ask your counsel. But it was as if I were a slung stone, once hurled unable to change course."

"I know, Moses." Tears came to her eyes. "The very things I love you for— your bravery, your honest ways, your wisdom and quick knowledge—are now leading me to leave you."

"Then stay," he said again.

"No. I cannot. Another thing I loved you for was that you loved me as much in return. But when you found your God, he proved to be a jealous God, Moses. And I am a jealous wife. He has won the contest for your affection, dear love."

"You are determined? Can you not think some more?"

"I have only sought the opportunity to tell you."

Was it really going to end this way, with neither anger nor passion? With only a small joke about his wound and honest declarations of abiding affection?

"There are other things between us," she said, wanting to say all that was pressing on her heart. "I fear constantly for you. It is making me old. The Egyptians, the enemies you will face on the way to Canaan. And when you get there, the Canaanites. I know from my father their renown as fighters. And who knows but what some maniac or group among the Hebrews will kill you in the night. And perhaps me and the boys, too. I cannot bear it any longer."

She was so reasonable about it. But there was yet one thing. It must be said. "You are not comfortable with my God now. But can you not imagine that in the future, if I could make much more time for you and the boys. If I could go that far?"

She paused, not tearful now, simply wondering whether she wanted to cross this bridge, or rather to burn the bridge she was already crossing. "No," she said softly and finally. "I told you before we left for Egypt—do you remember?—that I thought your conversations with this Jehovah were all in your mind. I concede that I no longer believe that. I see these things that have happened—the plagues on Egypt; the deaths on the night of your Passover; your victory today, brought about by Ramses, whose son was murdered; and seemingly lesser things like finding the path through the Sea of Reeds. Even your great intellect and strength, your morals as hard as flint, cannot account for them. I think there is a god for you, Moses, and for Israel. He is always beside you. So in that sense I believe in him. But I worship mine. He does not devour my life. He is my father's god, who sets rules but is tranquil, like a starry night, and distant."

At last, Moses thought with bitter humor, *she believes in the complex, powerful, yet intimate God that lies outside me, as I first dreamed of him in the desert at Jethro's encampment, beyond the stars. Believes in my God. But worships hers.*

"Zipporah," he said, "before this battle I asked God why I was here. His answer lay in the outcome. You admit he was the creator of our victory. Why cannot you accept him as I do? You even say you believe in him, but—"

"Believe in him for *you,* Moses," she stopped him, paused, and went on. "Let us not argue about God. It will make adversaries of us, and I do not want that." She gazed thoughtfully at him. "I love you."

"But cannot stay with me."

"But cannot stay with you . . . as things are now. We will talk together when you arrive at Mount Sinai."

He sensed that talking together would not lessen their apartness. "I cannot bear to give up the children, too. Even if we must be apart, surely Gershom—"

"All things are possible, Moses," she said.

That evening, the Hebrews celebrated. They and their God had prevailed against all odds. They knew, at last, that they had made their Exodus. They were safe from Ramses. Their dead enemies and their enemies' dead warhorses were now carrion for crocodiles, swamp rodents, and vultures. Their enemies' fine arms and armor would equip the beginnings of the Hebrew army.

Miriam led the women in their dances and songs. They wore their most colorful tunics, woven in fishtail, crenulated with geometrical designs and dyed red, orange, and blue. To the tambourines' tinny beat, they whirled before the campfire. Their necklaces of semiprecious stones, their gold and bronze anklets, rings, and bracelets—some given by their former Egyptian neighbors—glinted into the night. Miriam sang:

Let us sing to Jehovah. Glory streams from him.

He has buried both horse and rider in the mud.
You blew one breath. Their chariots fell.
All Canaan shivers at your approach.

The men, passing around their goatskin wine flasks, picked up the last two vers-
es, and as Miriam composed stanza after stanza, the roar of the confident and
courageous Hebrews filled the ether between earth and heaven.

Next day, Moses sent Zipporah and their sons on camels, with Bes-Ahrin
and a half-dozen other men as escorts as far as the small port of Akwi. From
there it would be an unarduous Red Sea voyage down the Arabian littoral to
the land of her father.

That same day, Moses and his ponderous multitude trudged southward
past the Bitter Lakes. There, beneath the stars, with gloom and remorse, he
thought of Zipporah when they had been young. But that night, he dreamed of
Sebah, far across the gulf, married perhaps by now.

In the morning, he turned his thoughts back to his wards. All day, despite
his shoulder pain, he rode up and down the line to keep order. He assessed the
men to get a preliminary sense of who would make good soldiers, and the
women to judge who might be their leaders, for he was already finding that
Miriam, though intelligent, was as erratic as the desert winds.

Beside the northern extension of the Red Sea, the company marched three
days without wells, streams, or springs. Discord erupted, its locus three trou-
blemakers. One was Moses' first cousin Korah, who was his own age, a Levite
elder. He was the foreman beaten and whipped when he carried the brickmakers' petition into the palace. The others were Dathan and Abiram, slightly
younger, both from the tribe of Reuben.

Korah was clever, brave in combat, a good speaker, warm with his friends,
and devout. He generally referred to God as the God of Abraham—as Moses
also often did—but seldom as Jehovah, the name Moses had brought to the
Hebrews. More dangerously, he was a conniver and, Moses was sure, if put to
it, would be a brutal and compunctionless rival.

Korah and the two Reubenites—both also related to the tribe of Zebulun—
had strong allegiances among those who hated the Akhenaten Egyptians and
other foreigners among them. Their enmity washed onto Bes-Ahrin's followers,
who were not just mostly non-Hebrew, but whose deformities they found
repugnant.

As Moses rode by on one of these three parched days, Korah called from his cart, "Did you bring us to the desert because there is not enough land for graves in Egypt? Better slaves in Egypt than corpses in this desert. Didn't we tell you when you walked in from the east to leave us alone?"

Moses passed these remarks off with a mild, "Things are certain to get better, cousin. Bear with us."

However, the backbiting continued, and was not just limited to the clique of three. At Marah, the water was bitter but potable. "Must we drink this or die of thirst?" was the complaint up and down the line. And though they were now on the Turquoise Route and could easily move faster, there was no end to the whines about the pace.

"Jehovah will take care of us," Moses kept telling them, and Joshua, Aaron, and most of the other leaders loyally echoed the assurances. But the constant moaning of his flock sometimes tested his faith. Even as he tried to quell it, Moses began the rudimentary training of all men who were able to bear arms. These would be the militia, and from them he had begun to winnow out those who would be Israel's elite troops.

Joshua and the more military-minded Hebrews had seen how effective Ramses' foot soldiers, called running spears, could be when they had slaughtered Nunrah's men. It had been an awesome sight to see these Egyptian, Nubian, Libyan, and other regular troops at a quick run and in perfect step streaming down the hill, their spears, javelins, lances, and flails at the ready on their shoulders, or their swords raised, poised to strike.

At the rear of the dusty column, Moses' recruits, even as they walked, were already practicing the same military order, responding to the same commands—though in Hebrew—and shouting the same war cries that in Moses' youth had led to the defeat of the Philistines, Moabites, Anatolians, and other less-disciplined troops. Each morning and evening, these same men, from sixteen to fifty, rehearsed swordplay, lance thrusts, spearsmanship, and sling twirling. The four Egyptian officers who had joined Moses served as instructors. They also advised the Hebrew carpenters how to make triangular bows, hardwood spears for throwing, and lances for hand-to-hand fighting.

Joshua was ever at Moses' side, learning tactics, strategy, leadership, and especially logistics. Indeed, Moses planned to tax his followers for funds to buy arms and armor in the towns they passed on their journey. The captured arms were nowhere near enough. And, although the women were already stitching bronze scales on the leather jerkins of their husbands and sons, professionally made armor would soon be necessary.

At Elim, ten miles down the coast from Marah, just as Moses' patience was threatening to shred, the Hebrews found a dozen springs, palm trees, even a small open-air market with fresh fruit. As Moses and Bes-Ahrin strolled among the wares spread before them on worn-out rugs, they talked of that earlier comparatively carefree trip out of Egypt.

"There was freedom in no longer being at court," Moses observed, "even if it meant we both faced the puzzle of building new lives—mine on a foundation of twenty-five years of fraud."

"But you built it. Now your only problem is living it."

"Built it with God's help. And yours. I am grateful, my friend."

Bes-Ahrin found giving thanks easier than being thanked. "No, Hapi-Set, it is I who am grateful. You let me become a man. Your mother, whom I loved, treated me with kindnesses beyond gratitude. But she did not like to think of me as a man."

Moses noted these somewhat cryptic words, but did not explore them. They were before a Bedouin merchant and his wife who were selling sweet-smelling cakes.

"Baked from manna, illustrious sirs," said the woman, proffering a cake for them to taste. "Buy a dozen. They make honey seem as bitter as natron, do they not?"

"As many as this will buy," said Moses, handing the man a *qite*—a quarter-ounce—of copper.

"That, kind sir, will buy two," he said, showing a smile from which the two front teeth were gone.

The cakes, though less sweet than honey, were tasty.

"What is manna?" Moses asked.

"It comes from trees, and blows from the mountains to the northeast, making windrows," said the man. "At drought times, we find all we need north of the turnoff to Dophkah, in the Wilderness of Zin. We mix a third of meal with it and bake it."

"Windrows?" asked Moses.

"Yes, noble Hebrew, it falls as flakes that attach to lichens or form little balls. We gather it fast, for the next winds blow in quails which gorge on it."

"And you found it how far north of the turnoff?" asked Moses and Bes-Ahrin at the same time.

"Two miles, then another mile to the east, in wadis."

The Hebrews had stored water in Elim against the drought ahead, but on the road to Dophkah, Moses, with no new springs in prospect, ordered them to ration it. The measure brought outcries from Korah and his friends. "Would we had died in Egypt," they said. "At least we had plenty to drink. . . . In this wilderness, we die of thirst and hunger."

Three days later, and five miles north of the turnoff to Dophkah, Moses sent Bes-Ahrin ahead by horseback. The congregation saw the dust of his return a mile away. When he rode in, those in the forefront gathered around him. "What news, doughty dwarf?" they called as he dismounted with a thud.

"No water, good people. But also no encampments of bandits. We can but go on and hope."

Moses came up and Bes-Ahrin rode a short distance with him to give his report. "The wind blows in thick as wings with this manna. From the mountains to the north, just as the Bedouins told us. It tastes good, even uncooked."

Moses nodded. Soon, the carpers began again to deplore the lack of fresh food. But this time, Moses had an answer. "In two days, Jehovah will provide us a new kind of bread. We will camp at a place that he readies for us. There you will take out your kneading bowls and light your baking fires. If we obey him, he will provide us with the soft meat of birds to eat. Make sure as we go that your nets are mended so we may take them."

And so it was. Two days later, a mile off the road, in a series of wadis, the Hebrews found strange flakes that stuck to lichens or formed windrows of soft white balls. "God's miracle . . . we eat like the kings of Egypt . . . Jehovah provides, as Moses said . . ." the women exclaimed to each other as they ground the manna, about the size of coriander seeds, and mixed it with meal they had bought at Elim. They kneaded it, put it in clay molds, and baked it over the fire. The poorest simply shaped it in flat loaves, buried it in the sand, and built their fire atop it.

Next morning, the winds blew and the quails came and were netted. The women roasted the plucked birds—organs, head, and all—on spits. They cooked enough to provide them with cold or reheated cakes and quail all the way to Rephidim.

The drought had struck Rephidim. The cisterns were dry, the wells low, and streams were wadis even before spring was over. The townspeople hoarded water in jugs, doling it out sparingly and only to family members. The

Hebrews plodded past dead beggars covered with flies, tongues swollen from their dried-out mouths like the rotten bladders of gutted fish, stringy arms outstretched as if imploring water.

When Moses sent his chieftains among the people of Rephidim to find water, they were told to see a certain Abutief, a well-to-do date merchant. The man, richly robed, perfumed, and sleek and cunning as a civet, told Joshua he could lead them to all the water they wanted, but he set his fee at three pounds of gold. Moses resolved to push on, hoping for a spring or other source between Rephidim and Mount Sinai.

Halfway to the mountain, Moses put himself and everyone but the children on half-rations of water. The grumbling recommenced. In the evening, Moses' cousin Korah and his two main followers, Dathan and Abiram—now joined by On, a captain of the tribe of Reuben—came to Moses' tent accompanied by some three hundred of their supporters. When Moses emerged, Korah berated him: "Why did you take us out of Egypt? So that our cattle and children might die of thirst?"

The Egyptian Prince Hapi-Set might, in fury, have summoned his officers and slain the ringleaders. Instead, Moses said with forced calm, "Jehovah will provide what he sees fit." Moses was drained. His left shoulder hurt and he was sleeping poorly. His mind was not just preoccupied with his flock, but with thoughts of Zipporah and his sons. He missed them, and had begun to think he must find a way to get them back. "Tomorrow we break camp and go toward Mount Sinai," he said querulously.

"It is not walking we want, but water," said Korah with fearless disdain. His three lieutenants echoed him and were joined by cries from the crowd.

"I will pray to Jehovah and will meet with you in the morning," Moses said, already devising a plan. He called on God to give him the help he needed to carry it out.

First, he woke Bes-Ahrin and sent him to Joshua's tent. The three of them armed themselves. On horseback, with an extra horse lightly reined behind Joshua's mare, they rode at a canter back along the parched road to Rephidim and toward the walled mansion of Abutief. The bouncing gait of his horse made Moses' healing wound throb with pain, as it still often did.

The house was on the town's edge, and with its two stories and parapeted roof porch it was the tallest building in Rephidim. Three hundred yards away, they dismounted and walked their horses; fifty yards from the house, they tied their mounts to a dead olive tree.

The low, heavy door in the wall around the house would be bolted from the inside and perhaps guarded. At a corner of the wall, Moses bent, bracing himself against the mud bricks. Like a human tower, he swayed as Joshua clamored up him, chary of Moses' shoulder, and onto the wall. Then Moses lifted Bes-Ahrin and handed him up. Joshua, gripping the dwarf, slid down inside the compound.

The little warrior, with his razor-sharp sword, slit the throat of the single sentinel inside the wall door. The man slumped with a gurgle and a gentle thump. Joshua swung the door inward, and Moses passed the crumpled form on the bare, packed earth with a pitying look. Complacently, Abutief had not bothered to lock the door to a lower inside wall. Why should he? Who in craven Rephidim would dare think of doing him ill? Besides, he had bought the town's loyalty by dispensing a dribble of water.

The handsome square building was luxurious by the standards of villages in the hill country of south Sinai. There was an outer staircase to the roof, as with all the better houses of the region. The family would be sleeping there to get what small breeze there was. Moses led the three invaders up. The forms on the low beds were protected from insects by gauzy linen tents over their faces, and lumps of terebinth resin flickered in cups on bronze stands.

The nearest sleeper, a woman, was as rotund as the Pharaoh's cattle that Moses had seen as a youth, so fatted with grain that they could no longer stand for their slaughtering. Abutief's wife, he was sure. The next would be the merchant. Moses lifted the sheer net, put his hand over the man's mouth, pressed his dagger to his cheek and whispered, "Not a word, miser, or you are surely dead." In the moonlight, they saw Abutief's eyes pop open and roll with fear.

They half-walked, half-dragged him down the outside stairs and to the door in the wall. Bes-Ahrin, whose sword was at the whimpering merchant's back, whispered portentously in Bedouin as they passed the dead guard, "Poor faithful man. Your death is due to your master's greed." Their captive quaked.

"Water hoarder," hissed Moses, "tell me, is your life worth the three pounds of gold you sought to extort from us?"

"Yes, oh you shall have three pounds of gold in the morning," Abutief sniveled. "I swear. But set me free so I can begin the arrangements, this very night—"

"Sepulchre rat!" Moses interrupted, setting the man to quivering again. "The three pounds of gold that you owe us if we give you your life will be considered paid when we come to the water you would have sold us."

"Oh yes, yes," said Abutief, relieved. "It is eight miles. I will tell you exactly."

"Idiot," said Moses, "do you think I would believe you if even you gave us your wife and children as hostages? You will take us there!"

They jerked him to the horses and walked them to where the hoofbeats would no longer be heard. Then, following the merchant's directions, they rode toward Mount Sinai, skirting the Hebrew encampment and Moses' pickets. Two miles past the tents, Abutief had them turn toward an outcropping of stony hills. For a full fifteen minutes he scrutinized the barren area in the moonlight, unable to find what he sought. They had ceased making their own breeze with their speed and now felt the heavy heat close in on them. After another mile, Abutief pointed to a large rock shaped like a Syrian helmet and surrounded by a scrawny, shadowy growth of desert weeds.

"Behind it, Masters," he said.

There, they saw a still pond. The nettles, so sparse in front of the rock, flourished around the water. Moses dismounted and tasted its sweetness. "Shall we drown him here?" Moses asked his two companions. Abutief began crying for his life.

"He would pollute the pond," said Bes-Ahrin, knowing Moses' threat was only that, but instantly understanding its purpose. "Let me slit his throat in the desert."

Abutief was blubbering. Moses jerked his beard. "I will spare you, but only if you are silent. You see how ready this bloodthirsty dwarf's blade is to drink at your throat? One word about tonight and we will seek you out when you least expect us." They left him without a word at the turnoff to the Hebrew camp. *He could,* Moses thought, *contemplate his future on his walk home.* Moses was satisfied he would seek no revenge.

In the morning, when the malcontents came to his tent, Moses said, "Jehovah has found us water." Still, the Hebrews, even the majority who supported Moses, were unusually restive as they packed up their tents and goods and moved out. The dissension increased as Moses, now on foot like the others, surveyed the desert and then directed them across its dry, hard surface. The light sifting of sand, blown by the hot night breeze, had obliterated the hoofprints of the night before.

Before the rock, Moses summoned the elders and other tribal leaders, including his four detractors. "Hear the word of Jehovah," he said in a voice loud enough to carry over the silence to most of his thousands of followers. "You asked for bread and he gave you manna, for meat and he gave you quail. Now you ask for water."

With Aaron and Joshua beside him, Moses struck the rock with his rod, the same stout instrument he had used to such good effect in Egypt when his people were seeking miracles.

"Jehovah is mighty. His mercy is everlasting," said Moses. Then, turning to the circle around him, he said, "Go behind the rock and see what God has wrought!" He wondered how God would regard his bit of showmanship. With approval, Moses suspected, for it had strengthened his people's faith.

Later, when the Hebrews' thirst was sated, Aaron found Moses alone. "How did you do that?" he asked his brother.

"It is better not to know," Moses said. He was well aware that without the mystery, few if any of the leaders, his own or Korah's, would believe the water was a miracle, which he, in fact, believed it was. For who but Jehovah had helped him devise the plan and allowed him the means of carrying it out? As an unstated warning to his cousin and followers, Moses named the rock Meribah—place of faultfinding. The Hebrews made their camp there that night, planning to rest for a few days.

Chapter Ten
Calf and Commandments

WO MORNINGS LATER, THE PICKETS REPORTED A RAGTAG ARMY approaching from the direction of Rephidim on foot, donkeys, and camels. Two of the sentries had ridden out on horses and been greeted with a dozen poorly aimed arrows. Moses had been wrong. Abutief had been able to enlist an army of revenge, possibly by suggesting to them the plunder in the Hebrews' goods and gold.

Moses' shoulder was still too sore and weak for him to bear a shield, and he was wise enough not to indulge in bravado. He instructed Joshua on how to form the ranks of the partially trained Hebrew troops. With Aaron and Hur, the lean old council leader, he ascended the hill behind the rock. From there he could observe the field of battle and could signal Joshua with his staff. He would raise it horizontally over his head for a charge, lower it for the defense positions, and point it obliquely to left or right to indicate on which flank these orders were to be followed.

In mid-morning, the handful of Hebrew horsemen surrounded a leader of the desert warriors and rushed him back to Joshua for interrogation. The man, once Joshua pricked him with a dagger at his heart, said he was from a nomad encampment southwest of Rephidim. Abutief had rallied a thousand of them, all Amalekites. The rich merchant's promise had been, in addition to their plunder—Joshua smiled—three pounds of gold to be divided among the nomad sheikhs. Joshua immediately sent this information up the hill to Moses.

By noon, through Joshua's own judgment and ingenuity and Moses' strategic instructions, the Hebrews were wearing down the nomads. "Both forces are long on courage, short on military tactics," Moses said to Aaron and Hur. In this field there were more mattocks then spears, more cattle goads than lances.

Throughout the battle, Moses raised and lowered his rod, busy as a high priest at the Festival of Opet, wand in hand, blessing the throngs at Thebes. In the afternoon, the heat was almost intolerable. Moses, spent from his exertions, was wilting. At times, he had Aaron and Hur wield the heavy staff for him. Just before dusk, the defeated nomads finally fled helter-skelter, but the Israelites were too tired to pursue.

The captured Egyptian arms alone decided the outcome. The nomads lost half their number to Joshua's troops, with heavy Hebrew casualties as well. The booty was limited to the nomads' weapons, the few coins the dead and wounded carried in their purses, and a number of desert donkeys. The camel riders had fled with their valuable beasts when the tide turned.

Next day, the Hebrews buried their dead in individual graves, the bodies facing eastward toward Canaan. They rolled the Amalekites into a common grave for the sake of sanitation. That night, the Israelites held a sacrificial feast that lasted until the sun rose beside the dry mounds of their buried soldiers. The battle forced the Hebrews to postpone their decamping for a week until the wounded could travel.

During that time, a picket rode in to report Moses' father-in-law, Jethro, was on the way with Zipporah, Gershom, Eliezer, and a small party of retainers, one of them the hunchback-priest, Praroth. Moses rode out to greet them. His guilt toward Zipporah remained. He knew he had failed her and the children, begrudging them both love and time. He resolved to make it up to them, if he could only find a way.

Gershom was delighted to be with his father. Moses took him on his rounds of the wounded, his inspections of the troop training, and gave him a brief canter on his stallion, Moses riding a mare. He dressed the sturdy boy in his armor, the coat of mail hanging to his shins, the sword dragging as he ran to show it to Zipporah. She laughed, proud of his resemblance to Moses. Eliezer, small for his age, was more timid.

That afternoon, the heat sent even the busiest of the Hebrews into their tents. Zipporah and Moses sat in the shadow of the door flap while the children napped in one of the tent's four separate chambers.

"You have thought about us, Moses?" Zipporah said. "I know you have."

"I want you and the children back with me," he replied, as he had prepared to. "I want to compromise. But I am not sure I can in the ways that you want me to. Think hard. Cannot you take me as I am if I find more time for you and the boys?"

She forced a smile, but spoke firmly, for she, too, had prepared her answers. "More time, yes. That would help. But cannot you pray to your Jehovah that he will let you put us before these people, who often neither love nor respect you?"

Already, he felt anxious, fearing it was not going to work. For Jehovah would always have to come first for him, and that carried with it his duty toward this obstreperous people.

"You are right, Little Bird," he said. "Some of them even hate me. But God tells me to lead them to the land he guaranteed to their—to my—forefathers. I can try to be more of a husband, more of a father. But you can see my flock is more difficult now than when you left. Korah continues to plague me. Dathan and Abiram echo him. And On, a Reubenite—a plucky soldier, but obtuse as a wild pig—has joined them. They feed the people's discontent every chance they get."

He sighed unhappily and took her hand. Familiarly, she tightened her grip on his fingers, but said nothing. Moses continued. "I see myself using actor's tricks to make them believe in Jehovah's miracles." He smiled, almost happy in this familiar talk with someone he trusted. He told her of the merchant Abutief, Meribah, and the water from the rock.

Zipporah enjoyed his story, was even amused, although the dominance of Jehovah in the tale nettled her. She sighed unhappily. His God and his people would always come first. His compromise was not the one she sought. She still held his hand. It had come time to give him his answer. She, who had not even cried in childbirth, teared as she said, "You have answered my questions, Moses. I cannot come back to you."

He looked with pain at her for a full minute, before he said simply, "Please let me try again. I love you, Zipporah."

"I know you do," she replied. "But I cannot."

There stirred in him some of his old want for her. She was still beautiful, although the nomadic life with Jethro's tribe had aged her, as it did all women. But lust came too little and too late to bind them together again. "How do you want to do this? Our sundering," he said dismally.

"The laws of both our peoples are simple, you know that," she said, her eyes dry now. "The husband puts the wife aside. She accepts it and they are both free."

"If there were any fairness, you should be putting me aside, for the fault is mine," he said.

She knew what he said was true. It made her less willing to make it easier for him. "Another woman will come along who will take the few crumbs you can offer."

Moses thought of Sebah. But she, too, was a strong woman. Would she accept only his crumbs? Ah, why think of Sebah? "And you will be free to find another man," he responded.

"Yes," she said.

Has she already such a one in mind? he thought with a twinge. But they were like the regiments of an army who have marched a long time together but separate at the fork in a road to fight different enemies in different lands.

"And the children?" he said. "I will not ask for them both. But Gershom, at least?"

"You say you cannot promise to change for all three of us. Can you promise for him? Can you spend time with him, be toward him more as other fathers are? If you promise me, I know you will do it. But can you promise?"

It was not an oath he could take and then break. He had said earlier that basically he could not change. But on this he must. "Bes-Ahrin and I will be the best of fathers to him."

"I would be proud for him to be like his father," she said now that, in her way, she had won. "But if he does, I hope he finds a more malleable wife."

"I could not have found a better one, Little Bird. It is you who might have found a better husband."

"Ah, let it stand at that. And Gershom, I will want him to come to see me. Frequently."

"That is the easiest part of all this," Moses said.

Now that the decision was made, Moses spoke with Jethro. Clearly Zipporah had already talked with him. When Moses went to his tent, Jethro was morose, but said, "It happens sometimes that two good people make one bad marriage, Moses. And I will be happy to have her among my people again."

"You are kinder than any father, Jethro," said Moses. He paused, thinking of those cool nights beneath the revolving constellations of the desert. "How different my life would have been, how much happier, really, if I had never left you."

Jethro patted Moses' arm. "My god has always been more lenient than yours," he said. "As Hagar was toward Abraham."

Next day, Moses heard, as was his immutable custom, the people's suits against each other. He was irritable and frustrated at the end of a day that he had wanted to spend with his guests. That evening, the last of Jethro's visit, both hospitality and desire dictated that he feast the priest-king.

Over wine—and goats' milk for the abstemious Jethro—and spitted lamb that had been soaked in a marinade of desert herbs, Jethro, Aaron, Joshua, Bes-Ahrin, and Praroth talked of Midian and of the Hebrews' journey. Moses could scarcely keep his mind on the conversation, for Zipporah sat with Miriam and other prominent Hebrew women on rugs at the sides of the tent, both a Hebrew and Midian custom. The end of their marriage hurt his spirit as much as the shoulder wound hurt his flesh.

The men's conversation turned to Egypt, their powerful neighbor, and Praroth told them what he had heard most recently from Ezion-geber. "Ramses has built the most magnificent temple of all at Karnak," said the hunchback. "How he finds time defies imagination, for besides his wars, he has eleven royal princes by a dozen wives." Moses was unable to smile over the unceasing amours of his once friend. For he could think now only of Ramses' murdered son and the other dead Egyptian children.

Jethro said, "Egypt has forgiven him for losing to the Hittites. And he has defeated them since, on the frontiers of Egypt and even in Syria. . . ."

Moses sat silently, the others able to guess that his thoughts were distant ones, and not happy.

As the dinner went on, Jethro turned to Moses' duties as sole judge, which had been on the Midian king's mind. "Moses, you will soon have no time for such suppers as this if you do not delegate authority. Lately, I have conceived a system to handle such disputes. See whether my suggestion has any value for you. Suppose you appointed one honest man, beyond bribery, for each of your thousands, and under him, a man for each hundred, and under them, one for each fifty, and finally one for each ten. Let the lowest of these judges settle what he can, and so on up the ladder until only the most difficult cases reach you."

Moses considered the idea and raised his cup of wine in salute. "Dear Father, for you will always be that to me, I will do it. Would that you could come and take over all the judging of this litigious people." *And their leadership, as well,* he thought but did not say.

Next morning, with Jethro, Aaron, Hur, and Bes-Ahrin as witnesses, Moses and Zipporah recited the few words that divorced them from each other. Outside the tent, Jethro and his party exchanged gifts with Moses, and with Gershom standing proud and tearless beside his father, the two families walked to the dirt road leading to Mount Sinai.

Moses boosted Eliezer onto his camel and Zipporah onto hers. His hand lingered a moment fondly and familiarly on her sandal. "Goodbye, Moses," she said. "Godspeed, until we meet again," he replied. Then they were on their way. From time to time, Moses would see them, and the two sons would visit with their absent parent. But they were, however one chose to look at it, a family forever divided.

At the height of the afternoon heat, after Jethro's departure, Bes-Ahrin came to Moses' tent. Under its flap the two sat and sipped a tea of light grape vinegar and water.

"I questioned Praroth about Barbaht," said Bes-Ahrin.

Moses' tea cup shook with surprise, spilling a few drops on his kilt. "You were quick enough on the heels of my divorce, dwarf," Moses said, more from seemliness than displeasure.

Bes-Ahrin disregarded the feigned reproof. "When again would I have found a chance to ask him? Sebah is not wed. Her father is dead and her first cousin has succeeded."

"Sebah," said Moses, and in the next breath, "Paras, oh good king. He died . . . how?"

"It is said that he was hunting rhinoceros and was trampled. He was too old to hunt pigeons. Surely, it was as he would have wanted it."

It was true. Yet it weighed down the news of Sebah. "I would have liked to have honored him. In another life, I would have done so." And so now, because of death, Sebah would be free to join him. Zipporah no longer wanted him. Would Sebah? "You know nothing more of Sebah?"

"I would have told you," said Bes-Ahrin. He paused, looking for the right words. "Listen to me, Hapi-Set, perhaps in your first years with your wife, the princess faded some in your heart. I was never sure. But I have made a decision." He came to his full three-and-a-half feet as if he were about to make a speech to his troops. "I am going to Barbaht to tell her you are the king of a tribe of Hebrews and have just divorced your wife."

"No, dwarf. You are what, fifty-seven now? If Paras was too old to hunt pigeons, you are too old to hunt larks, much less Sebah. Your bones creak when you walk."

Bes-Ahrin ignored the gibe. "Talk to Joshua, Hapi-Set. Tell him what I plan. Ask him for horses and two of his young officers." He smiled. "Tell him that if I do not go, you might."

"I forbid it. It is too soon. Besides, I need you for your counsel. Who else do I have?"

"You have your God," said Bes-Ahrin, his tone light but not without bite. "Even I sometimes think he is out there someplace. Isn't he enough?"

Moses started to bridle, but then smiled. "Sometimes God is inscrutable, as you are not."

Bes-Ahrin laughed. "Then I tell you that if I am too old to hunt larks, I am also too old to take orders from a man who peed himself from fright when he first saw my face by the Nile. Besides, it is the will of Bes who is not inscrutable."

Moses thought seriously for a long time. "You are a fool," he said. "And I am a fool to let you go."

It had been six months since the Hebrews left Egypt and took the road south in their journey toward Canaan. The delays had rankled Moses: stops to trade for food in villages; to repair carts and wagons; to water herds and flocks; to tend the wounded, the ill, the birthing. Beneath his energy and seeming resolve, beneath his faith in Jehovah, the annoyances and the serious crises sometimes left him feeling hopeless.

Then, finally, they saw Mount Sinai, rising in tall isolation from the hills. They camped three miles from its base. Moses thought of the night he had slept in the desert not far from here, where he had seen the burning bush from which he had been absolutely sure for the first time that God spoke to him.

He had led his people out of Egypt as God had instructed, and as he had agreed to do. He had come as far south as necessary to evade the Egyptians and other strong forces that might impede them. He had seen his brave, half-organized troops defeat, if narrowly, a thousand rapidly assembled nomads. Would that he could now send them against Canaan. But he recalled the Canaanite troops he had opposed as an Egyptian general and how unrelentingly they had defended their land against his best soldiers. Such a military force, he knew, would massacre his present army.

What better place than near Mount Sinai, he thought, *to encamp for a year and hone the Israelites' fighting skills, to thoroughly heal wounds, to prepare the old and the infants for the even longer road to come, and most importantly, to consolidate the fractious Hebrews into a true community of God?*

One evening, after most of the heat had left the day, Moses invited the Council of Elders and his military captains to meet with him outside his tent. There, he put forward his plan to settle in for a year. For hours, the divided leaders argued. Even Joshua and his captains were not entirely behind Moses. They had hoped he would let them do their training along the way. But, at last, they yielded to their leader's experience.

"While we are camped," said Moses, "we must do other things fitting a great nation. Look at the laws of the Egyptians, the Hittites: their laws bind them together. We Hebrews have only a framework of unwritten customs. Jethro's suggestions convinced me that we need rules that will permit us, for all time, to live as one people.

"We need laws to govern relations with the tribes we must conquer when we go into Canaan, laws to punish theft of livestock, grain, even laws for our behavior toward each other. For example, there are evildoers among us who lie with their daughters. We all know that. Yet one judge wants them stoned, another would spare them, another would exile them. We need laws of cleanliness, laws for our worship, and for a system of priests to help enforce the laws."

Moses saw approval on most of the faces before him.

"The Egyptians only half-obeyed their rules," Joshua cautioned. "Maybe we will only obey half of ours."

Moses replied. "You are right, Joshua. We are human. But we need the laws as beacons to keep us on our paths. And we need them now, to end some of our contentiousness. I must have time alone with Jehovah, up on this mountain, to think them out in detail. It was here that I was first certain I was communicating with him."

The group, this time almost without dissent, sanctioned Moses' ideas. Korah, seeing he was outnumbered, held his tongue. Moses' spirits lifted as he sighed with relief, then Aaron and their servants brought out wine and cakes. Later that night, Moses met alone with Aaron and Joshua to discuss how best they could lead Israel while he was gone. More and more, with Bes-Ahrin absent and Aaron unable to rise from his passivity, it was Joshua and his military followers on whom he depended.

When the long day ended, and Moses lay near exhaustion on his low, lonely bed, he smiled with some bitterness. There were those who would be happy to breathe free while he climbed Mount Sinai, to be rid of the exactions of their God-struck leader.

As he drifted toward sleep, Moses thought again of Bes-Ahrin and imagined him riding the hundred miles to the little copper and turquoise port of Bar-Kunr, west of Dophkah on the Red Sea. And then south by boat to Ethiopia, for he would not dare venture into Ramses' Egypt. And on through the mountain passes to Barbaht. And Sebah? How would she deal with this authoritarian middle-aged man when she had last loved a rash young prince? Perhaps no better than Zipporah?

On the overcast morning when Moses walked toward the base of Mount Sinai, all six thousand Hebrews followed him, for they all recognized the magnitude of his task. He had let it be known that his task might take him weeks. By noon, rain had begun to fall, but still the people followed, the adults hunching together over the children. At the narrow rocky path that led up the first of the foothills, Moses knelt in the dirt and silently prayed, and, as a group, the Hebrews fell to their knees.

Prayers done, fearfully, expectantly, they flung their questions at him. "What will these laws say? . . . Will I have to give up all but one of my wives? . . . Will Jehovah make us donate our pittances of gold to others? My family has saved it for generations. . . . What will these laws mean to our everyday life? . . . Can we still eat what we please? . . . You mean, can you drink what you please?" came a rejoinder from the crowd.

Moses patiently answered them, saying generally that he could not anticipate God's will, but that Jehovah had assured him the Hebrews were his Chosen People. As he spoke, a rumble of thunder began in the hills. In minutes, lightning struck at the peak of Sinai and crashed, jagged and frightening, down its sides. For this superstitious people, it was all the evidence they needed that their mighty God was at his work, and the mediator between him and the Hebrews was the tall man still responding to their questions on the wet, rocky slope.

Slippery as was the stone-impeded path upward, heavy as was his pack with its cloak, food, and writing materials, sore as his left shoulder remained, Moses climbed upward with enthusiasm, free of the burden of his people for a while. The path ended, and he crisscrossed the mountain to ascend, avoiding prickly nettles and sharp stones. Like the evening sky, his mind was clearing.

"Thank you, God," he murmured between breaths, knowing that his thanks were meant not just for the endless blue horizon, the hills void of people—for his climbing had taken him to the eastern side of Mount Sinai—but because he was grateful for his overflowing past and present. Gradually he was coming to see that his days in Egypt, its wars, Ramses, Sebah, Punt, Midian, Egypt again, and now Jehovah and the desert were a powerful continuum. This motley but magically seamless garment had cloaked him in knowledge, strength, and purpose. He was serving the Almighty as he was sure he had been born in Amram's and Jochebed's slave hut to do.

Near the peak, he found a rock outcropping that created a space beneath which he would be dry. Between his hands, he spun his firestick against its soft wood receptacle, using it instead of flint and iron because his tinder was damp. Soon he was blowing a fire in twigs he found beneath the rock ledge.

Over the next three days on Mount Sinai, Moses winnowed dozens of general rules down to ten principles, discarding this idea, adapting this, praying, then deciding on yet another that would cover both. When he was done, he was confident that they were what God wanted: His followers must worship only Jehovah, must make no idols, must not defile Jehovah by using his name as a curse or to swear falsely, must keep the Sabbath holy by not working, must honor one's parents, must not commit murder or adultery, must not steal or lie, and must not covet one's neighbor's wife, livestock, house, or anything else.

That night, a bit of bread and cheese in his stomach, snug in his cloak as the fire died, he recited the commandments as he drifted toward sleep. Before he dozed off, he heard the voice of Jehovah saying, "Cut them in stone. I will guide your hand, Moses."

"Stone, Jehovah?" Moses asked drowsily. "Where can I find a stone that I could carve, one I could carry down?"

"Simpleton," God seemed to chide him, "don't you remember on the way up, you passed a patch of slate?"

Moses smiled at the insult. Had he or Jehovah phrased it? "Thank you," he said to be safe, falling into sleep, satisfied with himself and his Lord.

Next morning, Moses walked down the mountain and found two roughly rectangular pieces of slate, each the size of a small domestic stele. He carried them up to his shelter and carefully chipped them into tablet shapes with a sharp quartz stone.

Using his knife, he incised them deeply, abbreviating his rules so they would be easy to memorize. The priests could elaborate on them each Sabbath until they were as familiar to every Hebrew as his own name. On one tablet he chiseled: ONLY ONE GOD, JEHOVAH. NO IDOLS. NO MISUSE OF JEHOVAH'S NAME. KEEP SABBATH HOLY. On the other, he wrote: HONOR PARENTS. NO MURDERING. NO ADULTERY. NO STEALING. NO LYING. NO COVETING NEIGHBOR'S WIFE, PROPERTY.

He put the tablets with the Ten Commandments at the end of his shelter where he could contemplate them, and that same afternoon took out his papyrus and began the far more laborious work of writing the detailed laws for the Hebrews, weighing each to see whether it would stand the test of the unknown future.

The admonitions were specific, such things as making altars only of earth or uncut stone, how to sacrifice sheep or oxen, the fabric for priestly chestpieces (ephods woven of linen threads, some twisted with gold, most dyed blue, purple, and scarlet), permissible incense for the altars (myrrh, sweet cane, cassia, galbanum, frankincense, cinnamon, and so on). The rules prescribed the making of the Ark of the Covenant to hold the laws and the Ten Commandments—for these comprised Jehovah's contract with his Chosen People.

On criminal matters, the punishment for kidnapping or murder or striking one's parent was to be death; if an ox gored and killed a person, the ox would be stoned to death, but the owner would not be punished; a captured thief must make restitution and if he could not, he would be enslaved to the victim.

As to property, a Hebrew slave was only to serve six years before being freed, even if he sold himself; if a landowner was burning off his field and a neighbor's field caught fire, restitution must be paid; if a man dug a well and an ox or donkey fell in, the well digger must pay full damages.

At times, even to Moses, the list seemed endless: Those guilty of consulting a wizard, of adultery, bestiality, homosexuality, and a variety of other sexual acts would be stoned to death; a priest must marry a virgin; foreigners must be treated as fairly as Hebrews; all weights must be accurate; blind people must not be tripped; the corners of fields should not be fully harvested so that the poor might eat.

It was thirty-nine days before Moses was done. On the last night, he climbed to the top of what he now called the Mountain of God—as did the indigenous desert people. He took with him his tablets and his scroll. He would pray as long as he could before sleeping, and in the morning, he would deliver Jehovah's commandments and laws to the Hebrew nation.

At the encampment, all went well for the first three weeks. Aaron and Joshua heard the most difficult cases (more leniently than Moses), continued the training of the army and the collecting of durable stores for the coming march, and ordered the repair of wagons and carts, the making and patching of tents, and the fattening of the cattle. But gradually, the majority of the six thousand, without the regal presence and stricter discipline of Moses, lapsed into self-indulgence.

Joshua foresaw discord and, five weeks after Moses climbed the rainy mountain, went to Aaron's tent. The high priest rose from his evening prayer, and the two looked at Mount Sinai in the dusk. Joshua said, "We have trouble here, Aaron. More, I think, than we can manage ourselves. We need Moses."

"He's been gone too long," Aaron agreed partially, not really wanting to make a decision.

"I'm having a difficult time getting people to help dispose of garbage in the camp, to bring in water, all the little things. The army does its part, but I do not want them to take over the people's duties. Or show an iron hand. It would cause resentments that would not heal easily. I am going up to get Moses. He must be nearly done anyway."

Aaron knew that seeking Moses would not just defy his brother's order that he be left alone, but would be an admission that he and Joshua could not do without him. "If you go," he said, "you do it on your own. Will the army obey me while you are gone? Without you, everything would be on my shoulders."

"Caleb"—a resourceful young officer from the tribe of Judah—will take care of the army," said Joshua. "Deal with them through him. I will be back as soon as I can."

That said, and with as little dislocation as he could, Joshua set off next morning on the narrow path to find Moses.

Two days later, eleven men representing dissatisfied members of all the tribes except the Levites came to Aaron and presented him with the worst dilemma he had ever faced. Behind them was a multitude whose purpose he could not immediately assess. Endabran, a member of the Council of Elders, of the tribe of Gad, was their spokesman. He was a man of some dignity, but one often swayed by the last person to get his ear. Hur, the council leader, was not even present.

"Aaron," said Endabran, trying to sound assertive, for the eyes of his group were fixed on him, "Moses has been gone thirty-eight days. We know Joshua is seeking him. He, too, has not come back. Can we be sure some ravenous mountain lion has not seized Moses, or that Jehovah, who caused the thunder and the lightning at his departure, is not angered and has slain him?" He waited for an answer, looking at his ten representative supporters for concurrence. There were grave nods.

Aaron, surprised by the visit, deliberated before replying. "Moses will return when Jehovah decides it," he said finally. "But tell me, good Endabran, what is the purpose of your delegation?"

"The people," said Endabran as if he had memorized it, "want a sign from Jehovah that Moses is not dead, that he will come back. We have all seen the power of the Egyptian gods to bring victories, particularly their potent bull gods. We know how Jehovah has given us victories over the nomads and over our hardships. We want a god in Jehovah's image, Jehovah as bull, whom we can celebrate and from whom we can ask blessings. Something before us, Aaron. Something we can see and touch."

Aaron was taken aback. "Did Abraham, Isaac, and Jacob worship a bull? Was not their knowledge of God's existence enough to guide them, and is it not enough for us?"

One of the other members of the group, a younger, brasher member of the Council of Elders named Lemrak, of the tribe of Simeon, spoke up. "Aaron, this is no longer the time of Abraham. Just as Endabran says, an unseen Jehovah does not satisfy our people any longer. The bull need not be large, but it must be before our eyes to remind us of the strength of our God. We will give up gold for you, as high priest, to make it for us. Already our potters have fashioned a mold. Melt our gold, make us a god, consecrate it, let us sacrifice to it, and then let us feast in Jehovah's honor. We need a release from this strain of waiting before we go north to fight the Canaanites."

Aaron feared Moses. But he feared more that Moses would find the community in a state of revolt. As a child, many Hebrew children kept crude figurines of Egyptian gods as toys. Aaron had treasured a Thoth, as a painted chalky baboon; an Amun, as a goose (until Miriam lost it outside); a hand-sized Horus in bronze (he had used it to hammer pegs into the dirt). But an internal voice shouted to Aaron, *You never worshipped them!*

"You say the people want this golden thing, this feast. How many of the people want it?" Aaron asked Endabran. "No Levites are here, nor Hur. Nor Korah and his followers"—for they were as strict as Moses in their repudiation of idols—"nor the army." Even Miriam was absent. "Surely others also find this idea repugnant."

Lemrak, a man with a robust, antagonistic face, took over the spokesman's role from Endabran. "Forget those who are not here. Look out there, Aaron. We are far more than half."

The crowd, men and women alike, were ominously silent. Aaron wished Joshua were in camp. He moved uncertainly through the eleven men and stood before the people.

"Is it your will that I make you this little bull, this golden calf, so you can celebrate Jehovah?" His accents spoke disdain for the idea. But above all, he did not want to be the spark that would set this horde afire.

"Yes," the crowd roared back. "A celebration . . . a golden Jehovah . . . wine, food, in Jehovah's name . . . a god we can see . . . and touch . . . a golden bull . . . a calf . . ." came the cries.

Aaron hesitated. He argued with the mob's leaders for a half-hour, seeking every means he could to persuade them to give up the idea, hoping against belief that Jehovah would intervene. But in the end, only the voice of his conscience assailed him. It was not enough. "Then bring me your gold earrings," he said, surrendering, "your bracelets, your beads." The throng fell to cheering. Aaron said to Endabran, "Have your smelters bring me the mold. I do this thing with loathing."

"But you will bless it," broke in Lemrak.

"I will bless it," said Aaron disgustedly.

As he capitulated, rangy young Caleb ran up and, out of breath, demanded from Aaron what was going on. Aaron told him in brief. Caleb blurted, "You cannot do this, Aaron. Moses and Joshua will have you stoned for it." And turning to the delegation, he shouted heatedly, "You will be stoned for this!"

Lemrak confronted the young soldier. "And who will do the stoning, Caleb? The people are with us. Look at them."

Caleb started to upbraid Lemrak, but Aaron, weighing the consequences, turned to the soldier. "Caleb, go to your troops and keep order among them. We will speak later. I will try to save the situation as best I can."

Caleb left and Miriam came up. "You must not do this," she told her younger brother. "It is against everything."

"It is too late," said Aaron.

The misshapen calf, about the size of a fat man's head, was hurriedly cast in three pieces. With a reluctant mumble, Aaron said, "I bless it," and retired to his tent.

While the gold was cooling, Lemrak, surrounded by the jubilant idolaters and fancying himself their great leader, said to the monstrosity, "Oh Jehovah, bless your children of Israel, you are the God who brought us out of Egypt."

Joshua located the stone ledge that had been Moses' shelter, but searched in vain for his leader until nightfall. He slept in the open, and next morning set out again. At last, he crossed paths with Moses, who was descending from the peak.

Moses held the tablets. The scroll was in his pack. Joshua told him of his concerns as they descended. By early evening they were within sight and hearing of the first tents of the encampment. As they approached, they heard cries, and soon saw people moiling about a large stone, some as if wrestling, others animatedly swinging their arms or kicking into the air.

"It's some insane kind of war," said Joshua.

"No," said Moses, "those are not cries of victory. Or defeat. It's singing. And not songs they will be singing long."

Moses began running toward the confused scene, the tablets cradled in his arms. "No, Moses," Joshua called as he ran after him, "the army camp. To find out what is happening."

Moses said nothing, but swerved to the camp without breaking stride. There, Caleb, who had sent reliable spies into the festivities, quickly told Joshua and Moses what had occurred. "So after that, they forced Aaron to bless it—"

"Bless it?" Moses bawled. "Better they had killed him!"

"Let him go on," Joshua cried, "for Jehovah's sake."

Moses held himself in and Caleb continued, ". . . and Aaron went to his tent. When the calf cooled, they built an altar for it, did burnt and peace offerings to it—"

"You could have gone in then, stopped it," Moses broke in sharply. "You have the arms, you have—"

"Moses," Joshua interrupted him, "would you have the army kill a thousand, two thousand people? Besides, Aaron was in charge. Caleb was right."

Moses looked angry enough to strike Joshua, and glowered at him, then breathing hard said, "Yes. But—" He cut himself off, and in a moment, calmer, said, "You are right, Joshua. Forgive me, Caleb. Go on."

". . . and then they began a feast. Everybody brought their best food, their best wine. Particularly their wine. Drunk? I went there. I've never seen so much drunkenness. About half of them left the altar, revolted by the whole thing. But the rest . . . I have an armed company ready in case things really get out of hand, looting and so on."

"Summon them," Moses ordered. He handed his pack to Joshua for safe-keeping, and thrust the tablets under his arm.

Within five minutes, Moses, Joshua, and Caleb were at the head of a hundred and fifty men in battle dress with lances. They marched rapidly across the three hundred yards that separated the army camp from the revelers. Moses was all too ready to believe his eyes. A dozen half-naked men and women were having sex at the very foot of the altar to the Calf-Jehovah, and one couple was made up of two men.

At the sight of Moses, the crowd, even those who had been copulating, grew quiet. The multitude of faces were fixed in fear, surprise, or shame. The silence was broken only by a few gagging sounds of vomiting and a murmured drunken oath or two.

Moses raised his two tablets over his head. He dashed them on the golden calf, knocking it from its altar and into three pieces, and shattering the tablets.

"Kill them!" Moses yelled, pointing at the public fornicators. Joshua, Caleb, and a platoon of soldiers drew their swords and began hacking the screaming men and women on the ground. In a few frenzied moments, every one of them was dead, heads, arms, legs scattered in gory disarray.

Aaron ran up, clumsily stumbling as he came before his younger brother. He looked aghast at the abattoir in front of him. Moses took him by his beard and shook his head up and down. "Fool! Weakling! How in the name of Jehovah did these people force you to bring this sin on them and on yourself?" He let go of his brother's beard so he could answer.

"They came, eleven of them, from all the tribes but the Levites and—"

"Aaron! Aaron! *You* were the leader here!"

"I know, I know. But the people wanted it. There were thousands with them. I thought it would calm things."

"The *people* wanted it? You were *in charge* of the *people!*" shouted Moses, then once again got control of his temper and spoke furiously but levelly to Caleb. "Get the eleven. Instantly. Bring them here. We will put them to the sword, right here on this heap of human offal. No, first force from them the names of those who were their main collaborators, even if it be a thousand. Write them down. Then bring the eleven."

The crowd had been skulking away, although some, unable to break the spell of their fascination, or too drunk to consider their possible fates, lingered with mouths agape.

Moses looked at the broken tablets, the pieces of the idol. To Joshua he said, "Have a captain take the gold to your best armorers. Grind it and have him bring the powder to me as fast as he can. And send soldiers to the Levites, for they were loyal. I want them here, too."

The riot of drunken lasciviousness had turned into the bustle of military order. One after another, the delegation of eleven were brought forward, hands bound before them. Captains turned over to Joshua the scrawled lists of those who had most vociferously supported them, some of them women. A captain arrived with a bowl containing the remains of the calf, more in the size of mustard seeds, due to haste, than in the powder Moses had wanted. The Levites gathered around as they arrived.

Moses had Joshua send out heralds with rams' horns to summon the whole camp, on pain of death. As the Hebrews gathered, many of them on the run, marshalled by soldiers, Moses ordered the eleven to stand in the bloody piles of flesh.

Soon all the people were gathered, silent and fearful beneath the stars and the moon. Moses spoke: "Many, no most, of you have committed adultery both against yourselves and Jehovah. He wants me, I know, to slay all who venerated this vile gold, be it ever so slightly. He wants you among the slain, Aaron, even though you strayed reluctantly.

"I hear his voice in my ear. He says, 'I have seen what a stiff-necked, rebellious people you are. My anger shall be like a blazing fire and I will destroy you all.' But I am begging him not to. I am saying, 'Do you want the Egyptians and the other nations to crow that you tricked us into coming into this desert only so you could utterly wipe us from the face of the earth?' I am asking him to turn from his baneful wrath one more time, to remember his promise to Abraham."

The people stood in silent chagrin. Moses ordered a ewer of water and a large cup. With his hand, he put a substantial measure of gold seeds in the cup, poured in water, and gave it to the captain who had brought the gold. "First, Endabran," he ordered.

The captain, without hesitation, took Endabran by his hair, and pressed the cup to the elder's lips. Endabran gagged, but the soldier persisted until he had swallowed the gold and fell to the ground choking, writhing, and gripping his throat.

The second was Lemrak. "Drink," said the captain. The young Simeonite brought up his hands and knocked away the cup. As the captain bent to pick it up, Moses said coldly, "Stand away, Captain," and drew his sword.

With a two-handed slash, grunting from the bolt of pain in his left shoulder, Moses opened a flaring slash in Lemrak from the base of his neck to deep in his rib cage. The blood geysered as the rebel dropped into the charnel heap.

The other nine drank heartily, earning for themselves a single thrust or two of soldiers' swords to their hammering hearts. When this slaughter was done, Moses turned with a heavy heart to the Levites, who had been summoned by Joshua's men.

"Levites, you have been true to Jehovah. Henceforth, from you will come all the priests of the Hebrews. . . ."

What he knew he must order next came hard to him. In Egypt as a young general, and as the head of the Hebrews, he had not flinched from killing enemy soldiers. Although sorrowfully, he had agreed with Jehovah to the death of the Egyptian children. But here, he was going to slay his own people, the sheep of his shepherding. Even knowing it was Jehovah's will, that without it they could not continue on to Canaan, he was anguished.

He told the Levites, "Take this papyrus and as your first formal priestly duties, go among those in the camp and slay those listed here. There are more than one hundred of them. They have defiled the God you serve. Soldiers will give you the weapons. Do not spare a single one, man or woman. Tomorrow we will meet before a cleansed altar to Jehovah."

Weary, sleepless, still tormented by the deaths of so many fellow Hebrews, Moses nevertheless rose early. He ordered those who had worshipped the golden calf but had not been organizers to drag the remains of their more guilty co-worshippers a day's walk into the desert as feasts for the hyenas and vultures.

That afternoon, Moses instructed Aaron, who in shame could not raise his eyes from the ground, to don priestly clothes. Together they consecrated a new altar, a boulder of quartz at the edge of the camp. There, Moses announced he

HE ISRAELITES HAD BEEN BIVOUACKED NEAR MOUNT SINAI FOR three months when a picket galloped up to Moses' tent and bounded from his horse. "Bes-Ahrin is back!" he shouted even as Moses opened the flap. "And with a black queen!"

Moses, barefooted, ran from the tent, nicked his foot on a stone, and rushed back to put on sandals. The sentry was holding the reins for him as he leaped on the man's sweating horse. "Where?" he demanded.

"There," pointed the man at a hill naked of vegetation where Moses saw puffs of desert dust. He broke into a canter and soon saw on horseback Bes-Ahrin with Sebah and the two soldiers who had brought her over mountains, rivers, and seas. Behind them, he saw three donkeys, one with a rider, the others loaded with what would be Sebah's possessions.

Sebah saw Moses' horse and kicked hers into a gallop, the two steeds meeting in the desert, her sunlit black face shining with sweat, his with a salt-and-carob-colored beard it had not worn when last she saw him.

They reined up, jumped from their horses, and flung themselves into each other's arms. He felt the strength of her tall body, even as she expelled her breath from the vise of his embrace. "At last," was all he could say. "At last, at last." And she gasped, "Hapi-Set, I have come." The name so long unheard from her lips was redolent of kisses and tropical rivers.

Bes-Ahrin, the soldiers, and Sebah's single maidservant discreetly kept their distance until the two lovers rode to them. Moses dismounted again and ran up to the dwarf, pressing himself to the stumpy legs in the shortened stirrup.

"Bes-Ahrin—oh, dwarf—you are my salvation."

He looked up at the little man's face. The beard seemed to have grayed, the skin aged on the perilous trip. But the generous mouth was Bes-like in its godly smile.

Moses had understood the feelings—although he had thought them unfair—of the Hebrews who had been unhappy with his marriage to Zipporah because she was not of their race. He had, after all, married her long before he became their leader. This time, with an even more exotic love, he trod carefully. On the first day after her arrival, he introduced her to the Council of Elders. As she stood beside him in a simple, richly dyed gown of Barbahtian wool, he told them:

"We live with Egyptians, Sea Peoples, even Libyans among us, all who worship gods other than ours. And yet some of these are the bravest warriors in the army of Jehovah. You have fought beside them against the Egyptians at the Sea of Reeds and against the Amalekites outside Rephidim. So it is that I beg you to accept Sebah as my wife. I hope she will turn to our God, the great Jehovah. But I will not force our God on anyone."

Until his marriage, Moses sent Sebah to Miriam, the proper hostess. Sebah happily and generously chose to be married as a Hebrew, although without pledging herself to the faith. Moses could not help comparing the ceremony with his marriage to Zipporah twelve years earlier. He had never fully extinguished his guilt over their divorce. But his love for Zipporah, he knew, had never been as entire as his love for Sebah.

The ritual proceeded by strict rules. Moses left his tent with Aaron, Hur, and Joshua. He wore a multicolored kilt of Lebanese linen. His chest was bare. Despite the deep, livid scar on his left shoulder and the long-healed wound on his right arm, his body remained that of a young man, sleek and muscular. He had not indulged it since his days in Egypt. His belt was of lion skin, from a beast he had killed in Midian years before and reclaimed on a visit to Jethro, Eliezer, and Zipporah. Incised in his silver pectoral were the names of the twelve tribes of Israel, but no depiction of Jehovah, lest it be construed as a graven image.

His way to Miriam's tent was lined with people, all in a happy mood, for the wine was flowing. Although Moses often found it hard to believe, there was, among most of the Hebrews despite their interminable bickering, genuine love for him as well as respect. And in the few days they had known Sebah, they had come to like her in spite of her foreignness, for they had seen her kindness and dignity as she walked among them.

When Moses arrived, Sebah was in her princess's regalia—gold earrings, anklets, and arm bands; a gown of the deep red, yellow, and purple of Ethiopian plant and insect dyes; an ivory comb in her thick hair carved with elephants, water buffalo, and hippopotamuses. Her veil was silk interwoven with gold and studded with pearls and diamonds. It was the gift of her first cousin, the new king, sent along with her for her wedding so that all might see he approved.

She wore a single bracelet, kernels of lapis lazuli in hammered gold settings. It was made by Bes-Ahrin for Moses and he had given it to Sebah, for tradition required the groom to provide the bride with her most valuable jewelry on that day.

Bes-Ahrin stood beside Sebah, his head little higher than her waist, resplendent in his best mail. About his neck on a gold necklace, he wore in defiance of Jehovah a carved agate amulet of Bes set in rare buba antelope ivory.

From his store of gold, he had financed the wedding feast with the merchants of Hazeroth to the north, whose ample springs watered fields of vegetables and fruits. There were fig cakes, raisins, spitted and honeyed locusts and dates. The Hebrews, for only the second time in their lives—the first being the ill-fated episode of the golden calf—drank as much wine as they chose. The festivities would be spoken of wistfully in the hard times to come.

What seemed to Moses the miracle of rediscovering Sebah when he had feared she was forever lost to him rejuvenated in him romantic tendrils that had lain dormant since his days in Barbaht and Cush fifteen years before. And his Nile princess, who had dreamed of him through the long virgin nights of her twenties, came to him with ripened ardor.

His body again felt whole, as it had not been since the early days with Zipporah. From Zipporah he had learned more than lessons of the flesh. In parting from him, she had taught him to listen to his new wife in all things, not the least of them when Sebah urged him to spend time with Gershom, who adored him and was growing into a young warrior.

Sebah had made a proud statement about her royalty with her dress and jewelry at the wedding. Now she packed it away and wore a tasteful brown wool gown. Schooled by her father in everything, from hunting to caring for the ailing, she went about the camp with an aura. She was unafraid to visit the sickest marchers, even the lepers who traveled on the edges of the wayfarers, and mingled with the women of all the tribes, hearing their concerns.

This endeared her to most—and led the men to look at her with the lust that the laws advised so strongly against. But there were some women who, from envy, whispered against her. Among these was Miriam, who, more and more a scold, used her position as Moses' elder sister to lead this pathetic clique.

"She treated me like a servant when she lived in my tent, I, the sister of Moses," Miriam would say in a low voice to her few adherents, though Sebah, in fact, had treated her diffidently. "She counsels Moses about all things that have to do with women. She takes the place of my voice in his ear, although she has never seen a Hebrew woman before she came to us." In fact, Moses had gotten very little wisdom from Miriam. And Miriam, by repeating her lies to Aaron, had convinced him that his counsel, too, was being neglected in favor of Sebah's.

Sebah would have preferred to ignore the acid vapors that emanated from Miriam's followers. Nothing like that had ever happened to her in Barbaht, and she could not imagine it would have any effect on her here. "Poof, it will go away," she said when Moses heard the gossip and asked if she knew of it.

"No, it will fester," said Moses. He had lived with the Hebrews for only two years, but he had thought of them each day of that time, and he understood their genius and their deficiencies.

"Then should I speak with Miriam and Aaron about it? They are my in-laws. Surely it is better to be open about it."

"No, my princess. I will speak to them. Listen to me. Miriam will not come to like you. It is not her way. But when I am done, she will no longer try to make others feel as she does."

Next day, after the usual rounds of meetings with judges, priests, military men, craftsmen, and others, Moses called Aaron and Miriam to his tent. Without preamble, he said, "Miriam, you are my sister. You prevailed on the Princess Mutempsut to let my mother nurse me. You made of me a Hebrew although I did not know it. I have seen your exuberance after the battle of the Sea of Reeds, and how you stirred the women to praise Jehovah. But of late you have stirred discontent against Sebah. What do you have to say about your calumny? Did you think I would not hear of it?"

"She has too much power over you, Moses," Miriam said, hating the whine in her own voice. "Everyone sees it but you."

"You speak of a very small 'everyone,' sister."

"She played the princess when she was my guest."

"She played the deferential sister-in-law-to-be and you envied her good-ness. Am I a fool? Do you think I do not see you as you are? And you, Aaron. I saved you from execution when you made the golden calf. I raised you to high priest. Is this my thanks? That you slander me and my wife? I cherish your teaching skills. I admire the way you have organized the priesthood. Are you a woman's cat's-paw that you let your older sister turn you against those who have done you no harm?"

"I am sorry, Moses," said Aaron. "You have honored me, and I have let my worst ear listen to Miriam."

"I love you, Aaron," said Moses. "You stood beside me when we faced down Ramses. Your life, like mine, was at stake. Think of the Aaron of those days. Think of the Aaron who is our high priest."

Moses looked again at Miriam. Was there no way to drain the poison that had built up in her like a boil? "Miriam, I am sad for you," he said gently. "If Jehovah were not a merciful God, he would make a leper of you so that no one would approach you to hear your cruel words. So, here is my order. Go out among the lepers. Do not get close enough for their infections. Ponder what it means to be one of them, for if you cannot stop spreading malignancy I must with regret banish you, sister or no, as surely as Jehovah in his wisdom drives the lepers from us."

"Moses," interjected Aaron. "She is our sister."

Moses ignored him. "Miriam, return in a week. Be our sister again, a true sister. Or if you cannot, remain silent about Sebah. The people will see your exile for that week and know that if I can drive away my own sister for seven days for bearing false witness, I can send away others for the rest of their lives for defying Jehovah's laws."

There were those in camp much more dangerous than Miriam. Korah, as a Levite, an elder, and of distinguished lineage, had a right to become a priest. And everyone knew he had spurned the golden calf and caused his supporters to do likewise. But behind Moses' back, Korah called him a hypocrite. And, in truth, while Moses honored the dwarfs for their steadfastness as soldiers and protected the cripples, he had in the scrolls barred those with deformities and other abnormalities from the priesthood.

Korah twisted this admonition to his purposes, saying to his supporters, "Moses keeps me from the priesthood. Yet I am no hunchback, and my organs of generation are whole."

When Moses brought it up with Aaron, his brother said, firmly for a change, "Korah is an asp in my armpit. I cannot handle him. He cannot be a priest."

"Can we avoid it?" Moses asked. "He is a Levite. I can think of no way to rid myself of him."

"Bes-Ahrin?" asked Aaron with rare if mordant humor.

Moses smiled unhappily. "Anoint Korah. And watch him."

That evening, in his tent, Moses brought up the matter of Korah and his lieutenants with Bes-Ahrin, though not with assassination in mind. "At present Korah only whispers," said Bes-Ahrin. "He has done nothing overt. Wait until he puts himself in the wrong so seriously that only the meanest of your flock will stand with him. And he will."

Once the priests were instructed, they took the laws to the people, down to the minute details of how to deal with menstruation, their bowel functions, their sores, their food. At the same time, Moses had craftsmen begin constructing the tabernacle, an elaborate, richly decorated tent that was to be a movable temple. In it would be kept the Ark of the Covenant, containing the engraved tablets with the Ten Commandments and the papyrus scroll on which Moses had written the laws.

Administratively, Moses ordered a census and a listing of the leaders of each tribe and each nontribal group such as the Egyptians, Libyans, Sea Peoples, other races, and Bes-Ahrin's "little people." He set up an order of march, a table of command for the army, with Joshua as his chief general, a calendar of festival days, even the locations around the tabernacle where the different tribes would pitch their tents.

In spite of such detailed planning, some of the laws—as Moses had predicted—became a matter of controversy. The priests, relieved of many of the ordinary duties of the camp, immersed themselves in copies of the scrolls rapidly reproduced by the scribes. They argued over every line.

One regulation struck directly at Aaron, as high priest. Two of his sons, Nadab and Abihu, both priests, out of laziness, used a brand from an Egyptian exile's campfire to light the tabernacle censers. This violated a rule that such igniting flames first must be blessed. The sons then placed incense that had been blessed on the "unholy" censer, thus compounding their violation by using "strange fire" in the tabernacle to light sanctified incense.

One passage in the scrolls prescribed death for priests who grossly violated religious rituals and three jealous Levite priests, one of them Korah, raised the possibility that Nadab and Abihu fell under the stricture. Clearly, Korah was using the violations as a means of injuring Aaron, and by extension Moses. The matter went all the way to Moses, who quickly ordered that the tabernacle be cleansed by offering burnt sacrifices there and that Aaron should declare Nadab and Abihu "dead to the priesthood" for four months.

A year after the Hebrews camped at Mount Sinai, Moses felt that they were ready for the long march north. After a few months more of training, he believed, the army would be ready to attack Canaan. The line of wagons, people on foot, and beasts left the Mountain of God and wove again through the hill country of Sinai, this time toward the Wilderness of Paran.

The marchers were soon venting their woes as heartily as ever, and not without reason. The narrow valleys through which they passed had never seen such a throng and their way was often blocked by boulders that had tumbled down. Moses had primitive pulleys made from cart axles and ropes, based on the systems he had used to move statuary limestone in Egypt. Once the boulders were laboriously shifted from the path, the axles had to be restored to the carts. The delays were grueling for everyone.

At other defiles, hard dirt walls had to be shaved with mattocks and shovels to accommodate the vehicles. Cattle and sheep died from thirst, and heat carried off the sickly, mostly infants and the old. One scorching afternoon, a gust blew sparks from a large cart's banked stove fire. It ignited the woven flax of its sun canopy. The wind carried flaming cloth to other canopies. In minutes, the whole end of the caravan billowed smoke. Women screamed and leaped with their children from the wagons, and men beat the flames with cloaks.

Aaron and the priests, ever ready now to see Jehovah's hand in everything, were sure the fire was brought on by the Hebrews' grousing and loudly denounced it. Even Miriam rallied to her two brothers' defense, sounding like the plucky woman who had danced and sung at the Sea of Reeds. Still, it was hours before Moses and the tribal leaders could restore order.

The problems were endless. The foreigners on the march had joined in part so they would be free to worship their gods—Pharaoh Akhenaten and other deities. Some Hebrews wanted Moses to decree that *everyone* must abide by all the rules he had issued. Moses ruled the religious laws were binding only on Hebrews, the rest on everyone. Then, of course, there were squabbles over which were the religious laws.

On a related matter, the Egyptian exiles sent Moses a petition that read, "Esteemed Leader: we long for the good things of our native land—to wit—the meat of fatted cattle, notably the *herysa*, instead of these scrawny animals; our succulent fish, the batensoda; and the giant perch. Take us from this desert without water. Bring us cucumbers, melons, leeks, onions, and garlic. Our souls dry up. Your Jehovah gave us manna and quails before Rephidim, true, but if he cannot bring us these other foods, can you not lead us back to Egypt?"

Moses, chewing a piece of tough beef as he read, suddenly longed for the freedom he had often found in Egypt as a young man, for the feasts he had shared with Ramses, the exquisitely prepared dishes, the draughts of precious wines. Did not these people know that he was human, that he, too, liked the delicious things of life? "Jehovah," he murmured, "why do you afflict me with these people? Hebrew and foreigner alike. Did I father them? Am I their mother, suckling them at my breasts? If you are going to treat me this way, kill me out of hand."

Then, his irritation ventilated, he brooded a few minutes and went out to find Gershom. The boy was near the training area in Joshua's part of the camp, and Moses got him aside for some practice with wooden swords. Both of them enjoyed it. He had not forgotten his promise to Zipporah. His son's cheerful and unquestioning admiration was a welcome reprieve from his adult charges' carping and lamentations.

At Hazeroth, fifty miles north of Mount Sinai, Moses called another rest. The six thousand marchers almost surrounded the little village. On the first day, they bought every bit of food in the market. After a week, they decamped. Ahead they faced two more months of hard traveling across forbidding land before they would reach the port of Ezion-geber.

When Moses and his aides surveyed Ezion-geber, they decided to put down winter roots for six months. The hardships of the road from Mount Sinai had been more than he had expected. They must rest again before the long final march to Kadesh-barnea, at the borders of Canaan. During these months, some of the men worked in the city for merchants, some at the harbor loading ships, some even opened stalls in the market. Others, such as carpenters and metalworkers, plied the trades they had developed in Egypt.

But the respite of good living created a new problem for Moses. A significant minority were now fed up with their onerous roaming and wanted to make their camp at Ezion-geber into a permanent village. They had means now of earning livings as free men—as farmers, dock workers, herdsmen. Moses and his cadre had to keep reminding them they were God's people and that he had prepared for them a land of milk and honey, now within reach.

Moses himself, reborn in his love for Sebah, found new energy to plan that next phase. It was a hundred and fifty rugged miles by road to Kadesh-barnea. From there he would be able to dispatch spies into Canaan and, pending their reports, draft rough plans for his invasion. Meanwhile, he eagerly gathered what information he could in Ezion-geber.

His best source was a midget goldsmith—discovered by Bes-Ahrin—and his normal-sized wife. They welcomed the dwarf and Moses at supper in a richly decorated dining room behind their shop. As they ate the grilled gulf bass, cucumbers, olives, and other bounty, the goldsmith, whose beard reached almost to his knees, said: "I am happy to help you, Bes-Ahrin, and your famous friend, asking only that when you get to Canaan, in matters touching on gold, you remember"—he smiled as he translated his name from Egyptian into Hebrew—"Zuar." Moses laughed, for the word means "very small."

Bes-Ahrin took a large quaff of wine. "Our first question is where the Egyptians hold dominance, and where the Hittite armies do."

Zuar considered the significance of the question. "You would do well to take your time in getting to the borders of Canaan, my lads. Ramses sends new armies there every spring. They drive back the Hittites and Horites. But each winter, the Egyptians are again harassed at every point. I am told from friends who come from Pi-Ramessu as well as from Tarsa and Haran that King Muwatallis and Ramses are seeking some kind of peace, but who knows? Have you time to wait for it?"

Any delay in such a peace would be unhappy news for Moses. The great powers would not welcome more confusion in Canaan at present. But if at peace, the Egyptians and Hittites would be glad to have a single nation— Israel—stabilizing trade, a single leader with whom they could communicate. With the tacit approval of the two regional giants, Moses could try to conquer the divided peoples of Canaan. Such a drive could rally those Hebrews who had never left it. That could mean thousands of new followers, some staying in Canaan as suppliers of food, others joining his army as recruits. "Is there any talk of exactly when this peace might come about?"

"None," said the little man.

Moses looked at Bes-Ahrin. "We need peace there if we are to succeed. But how long will the people camp outside the borders without giving up the whole idea of a Promised Land? Perhaps we should move now, peace or no peace."

Bes-Ahrin smiled tipsily. "A few more years and I will not be around to see this impossible nation of yours in their impossible Promised Land courtesy of your impossible God. . . ."

The midget chuckled. "My god, like Bes-Ahrin's, is a leisurely god, a Midianite version of Baal. He makes no demands on my emotions or intellect, and his priests make only a small annual claim on my pocketbook."

Moses could not help but smile at Bes-Ahrin's sacrilege. He wondered whether Jehovah had a sense of humor. Then he sighed. How abandoned the dwarf's death—for he had not been as hardy since his return from Barbaht— would leave him. Laying his hand on the little man's shoulder, he said, "What is your opinion, good dwarf? Invade now, or wait?"

"My opinion is that we need more information," replied Bes-Ahrin. "Be guided by your spies' reports." And that would come only after the long jour-ney to Kadesh-barnea.

No part of this quest, which was beginning to seem endless, had been easy. No mile had been without controversy. On the wretched hundred and fifty miles to Kadesh-barnea, through hill and desert, across wadis and streams, Moses could feel Israel disintegrating as surely as he had once seen hours of rain gradually drench a muddy bank until it slowly slid into the Nile. The steady rain was Korah, whose hatred for Moses had grown beyond even his own control.

Fifty miles north of Ezion-geber, the marchers, as one, halted. The sun had exhausted people and animals. An ox, six sheep, and four goats had died by the roadside. The herdsmen were seething, because Moses' laws said the beasts could not be eaten. They had died naturally, and thus had not been ritually butchered. The people shared the anger. In Ezion-geber, they had become accustomed to good lamb and beef, and already on the march they were on short rations. And now Moses insisted good meat must rot by the road to be eaten by scavengers.

As Moses, Sebah, her servant, Gershom, and the two soldiers whom Joshua had insisted accompany the family everywhere were pitching their tent, Korah, Dathan, and Abiram approached. Behind them was a crowd of two hundred and fifty, mostly men. Moses was surprised to see a substantial number of priests among them and several members of the Council of Elders. His quick eyes also picked up the absence of On, the giant Reubenite whom he regarded as the most dangerous physically of the four ringleaders—and the most stupid. He had heard that On had broken with the others because they always relegated him to a lesser role in their conclaves.

Moses' two bodyguards and young Gershom, all expressionless, hands on the hilts of their swords, stood beside him. Sebah came up, straight and tall, and moved in beside Moses' right arm. Korah ignored all but Moses, and spoke to him with measured hostility:

"Moses, you provoke us too much. Leaving good meat by the roadside when we are hungry is like the prisoner sentenced to forty lashes who dies on the thirty-ninth. We have studied the laws you said your Jehovah gave you. Some resemble the God of Abraham's. Those we revere. Those that are *your* God's we discard. Who made you a prince over us, anyway? Why should we obey this Jehovah? We have come to tell you that all in the congregation are equal to each other. Henceforth, the will of all must determine what we do. And their will is to abandon this insane, godless journey."

Moses was so irate he dropped to one knee to keep from drawing his sword. Korah had made the ultimate challenge to Jehovah's, and thus Moses', leadership. Through clenched teeth he said, "Korah, you should die for this on the spot, for you have besmirched Jehovah. Is it such a little thing that you and the other priests among you were chosen by God to do service in the tabernacle? Must you now covet Aaron's position as high priest and mine as leader? What has Aaron done that you undermine him with secret talk? Dathan, Abiram, do you feel as Korah does? Let me hear it from your mouths."

Dathan spoke with a brickmaker's bluntness. "I mock you, Moses. You brought us from Egypt, which was already a land of milk and honey." *Alas, Dathan,* thought Moses, *you, like Korah, were once beaten half to death by Ramses' brutes!* Dathan was going on, "Do you plan to kill us in the wilderness?"

Abiram added, "You have not brought us to vineyards and loamy fields. Do you really think you can continue to deceive us? No, Moses, we mock you." Korah gloated and there were chuckles from the crowd, which was growing by the minute.

Moses, almost beside himself, prayed to Jehovah to bring fire down on their heads. Yet, as he had always been on his way to battle, a part of him remained calm, calculating how best to win. How many were with Korah, how many against? He must get an assessment before he challenged these three.

"Come here tomorrow," he said, "all of you, if you believe you are each a leader. We will see who is holy in the eyes of Jehovah and the God of Abraham, who are the same. Come before the tabernacle with your two hundred and fifty censers. I will come with Aaron and my two hundred and fifty, and Jehovah himself will decide who is the surrogate he chooses to lead this people. And bring On, too—if he has not decided at last to scorn you—so we can settle this thing once and for all."

That night, with the Promised Land at stake, Moses met in his tent with Joshua, Bes-Ahrin, Aaron, Caleb, and Hur. From their hurried canvass, about half the people were willing to turn on Moses under Korah's leadership. The rest ranged from those disaffected by the trek to those willing to take up arms for Moses. This latter group was primarily made up of Joshua's four hundred elite troops and another thousand in his militia.

To be sure, the armed men could turn on the followers of Korah and simply massacre them as the soldiers and Levites had killed the hundred and twenty who had led the festival of the golden calf. But killing a thousand, two thousand, of their number was not acceptable to Moses. Brother would kill brother. Father, son. Son, father. Who would forgive that? The journey to Canaan would be wrecked forever.

"We must do away with the four leaders," Joshua said.

"Three, if On does not appear," Bes-Ahrin reminded him.

"And the two hundred and fifty who will find new leaders if we kill these first three or four?" asked Caleb, who was becoming ever more willing to speak out.

"Killing the three is certainly the will of Jehovah, for they have openly insulted him," Moses said, "but killing them is not enough. Jehovah must give us the means to show the people that his hand, not merely ours, wields the sword of retribution."

"Yes," Aaron seconded his brother. "The plagues of Egypt were not just the work of God, but were *perceived* as the work of God by both our people and the Egyptians. And the manna, the quails, the rock that gave water when Moses struck it. All were *seen* as coming from God, working on his own and through us."

"If only this one time," said Moses, "this one vital time, Jehovah would let the earth open up and swallow them, or send sheets of fire to burn them up instantly." *Jehovah,* Moses thought, but did not say, *I am weary. Give me a sign that you will act this one time on your own, as you did in the burning bush and the lightning storm at the foot of Mount Sinai when I left to write your laws.* But Jehovah seemed to answer Moses: "I bring you the opportunity for miracles. And it is my nature to work side by side with you, not alone, to perform them."

"You need a miracle . . ." said Bes-Ahrin without cynicism, then, eerily echoing the words of Jehovah that Moses had just heard, ". . . and must find a way to do one."

Moses' thoughts were galloping over his whole experience, the early studies, the strategies of the wars he had fought on behalf of Egypt, the climate and stars and rivers he had probed in his negotiations for the Exodus.

But it was Sebah, skeptical of all gods—who had been serving tea and cakes to the men—through whom Jehovah seemed to speak now. "The three—or four—of them, this odious Korah and his jackals, can be killed in this way." The others turned to her. "Moses, you said earth should swallow them, or sheets of fire burn them. In my country, warriors hunt animals with spears, but the country people have more regard for their lives. They dig pits, place sharp stakes upright in them and cover them with vegetation. They do it so cleverly that antelopes of all kind, kudu, even elephants fall in.

"If we work all night with mattocks and shovels we can dig such a pit in spite of the dry soil. Moses and Aaron can be the bait, standing before the tabernacle, and when Korah and the other two or three approach with their drawn swords . . ."

The group discussed the proposal. "Risky," said Joshua. "If it fails, all is lost. We could then save Israel only by butchery of half our number. But who among us has a better idea? Sebah has heard Jehovah more clearly than any of us. Let us develop this plan and hope that Jehovah helps us carry it out."

"And the noise of the digging?" asked old Hur.

"My servant girl will play the drum she has brought, loud and soft as we dig," said Sebah. "There are no tents nearby, but some of Korah's people may have very sharp ears. And those who might hear will sneer at her music, saying it is my superstitious Ethiopian attempt to cast spells against Korah."

"But," said Caleb urgently, "there are the two hundred and fifty with their censers. Once this business of the pit is accomplished, could we not just fall on them and kill them?"

Moses uttered a groan. "No, I cannot bear to kill—to murder—them all," he said. "They are mutineers against me, and against Jehovah. But they are also fools, weak, greedy, even as many of us are, blindly following Korah and his promise of better things. No, we will not murder them, for that is what it would be. We must find a way to teach them a lesson, and to hold that lesson up to the people, a lesson without a bloodbath."

Caleb looked astonished at Moses' forbearance, but Joshua, more shrewd now, gave no sign of his emotions even though he, too, saw Moses' restraint as a failure of will. *This is no murder,* he thought. *No more than the slaying of the hundred and twenty who fomented the blasphemy of the golden calf.* Neither Joshua nor Caleb would ever forget this particular moment.

Sebah had also seized on the two generals' moods, and intervened for her husband, defying the role of Hebrew women. "No, no, no, good Caleb, Moses is right. There must be no mass bloodletting. Perhaps a few of the followers of Korah, Dathan, and Abiram must die with them. But even there, it must be done with the same kind of lesson as the pits."

"Moses mentioned sheets of fire," said Bes-Ahrin.

"Fire," said Joshua. "Let us set them on fire."

"Yes, fire, torches," said Caleb.

"Torches," repeated Moses, struck suddenly with the seed of a plan that would avoid a bloodbath, but would have the drama of an act from Jehovah himself, "the torches we bought in Ezion-geber to use if need be for besieging cities in the north. Joshua, after you and Caleb have done away with the ringleaders in the pits, suppose your men surrounded the two hundred and fifty? Then, your soldiers, the most God-fearing, could come up with the torches lit and thrust them into the fire of the dissidents' censers to show that their proffer of incense sacrifice was valueless before Jehovah, was disdained by him.

"Then, let us say your soldiers set the two hundred and fifty afire. Most will put themselves out by rolling on the ground, or by throwing off their clothes. Some few too foolish to save themselves will run, breathe fire, and die. You must have other troops ready with water in containers to put out the fires of those unable to extinguish the flames on their own. All will be scarred, and badly. Jehovah will give me words for the rest of our people so we can go on to Canaan."

The idea satisfied everyone but Joshua and Caleb, whose objections Moses saw in their faces. They, Moses knew, wanted to slaughter the two hundred and fifty and dispatch On at the same time. Moses did not challenge or object to their unspoken dissent. For in Moses' heart, he was not sure but that the jealous, powerful, and just God who had come to him in the burning bush would side with them. Did not the first of his commandments say, "Thou shall have no other gods before me?"

But was the sacrilege so grave for the two hundred and fifty as to warrant death under God's rules? Did not God also order his people not to murder? In this dilemma, Moses, for the first time, did not seem able to get a clear answer from his God. And, moreover, he was sure the others recognized his doubt.

All night long, Sebah's maidservant drummed and chanted. As he dug, Moses heard the rhythmic beat of a tambourine joining the drum. It was Miriam. Though she had been discontented—and sick with a growth—she was helping to save the brother she had once also saved among the bulrushes. Moses was moved.

In the morning, chest vulnerable except for two wide crossed leather bands, Moses stood before the tabernacle beside Aaron, who wore the gaudy ceremonial garments prescribed in Jehovah's scrolls. The entire nation—men, women, and children—waited a hundred yards back from the tabernacle. The drama about to begin would decide Israel's future for all time to come.

All were silent as Korah, also in a multicolored sash and ephod, arrived with Dathan and Abiram, the latter two's swords ready at their waists. They stopped seven cubits in front of Moses. Behind them came their two hundred and fifty allies, the men carrying unlit censers. Some wore the robes of priests, some their dress cloaks. Korah's few women supporters were in their best multicolored gowns with semiprecious bead necklaces and modest armlets. It rent Moses' heart to see so many among them whom he had loved and trusted.

Then, winding their way through the crowd came Aaron's priests, also with their censers. Each group knelt and with fire from their helpers, lit the incense. The smoke and scent rose in the limpid morning air and drifted over the Hebrews around the decorative tent, the whole nation enclosed by the semicircle of the vast and barren hills of Paran.

"Korah," said Moses, his powerful words thrusting through his stutter like a knife through a melon, "if you live to die the common death of all men, then Jehovah never told me at the burning bush to leave Midian and lead my people to a land of milk and honey. But if Jehovah, as I have called on him to do, causes the earth to open its mouth and swallow you and the flames of his wrath to consume your followers, then at last all of you will know the doom that awaits those who provoke God."

The crowd murmured nervously and swayed as those in front passed Moses' dread words to the rear. Korah's men by their censers, though they shifted with fearful eyes, were silent, awaiting Moses' next words.

"You see Aaron and me unarmed except for the living light of Jehovah in our hearts. If, as you say, I have usurped the power of God, come and kill us, Korah, as you have long yearned to do. I will not raise my hand against you. If you will not kill us, go from our midst forever, like beaten mongrels fit only for fleas and ticks."

"He invites his own death. At him!" said Korah. From beneath his robes he drew a glistening sword and the two others also drew. The three stepped out abreast, swords raised. Neither Moses nor Aaron moved to defend themselves.

The two hundred and fifty behind Korah, Dathan, and Abiram left their censers and rose up to join them, but Moses now lifted both arms, and in his loudest voice, shouted, "Stand back! Do you not trust three swords against two men armed only with the justice of Jehovah?" Korah's supporters halted and waited.

With two cautious steps, three, four, Korah and his lieutenants came. On the fifth, Korah and Abiram lurched crazily and fell through the carpet of dirt and twigs. Abiram grabbed upward instinctively, pulling the hapless Dathan in after him. No sooner had they fallen than there were wild screams, and the crowd could see over the lip of the pit their hands flapping upward like flushed birds. The horrible screams continued until Caleb and Joshua, bronze greaves churning, ran to the pit with lances and thrust until, one after another, the screams ended.

Some of the two hundred and fifty rebels sensed disaster and tried to flee, but soldiers moved up in quick time, ringed them, and pushed them back at lancepoint. Instants later, a sterner smoke than incense gushed up over the crowd. More soldiers, all in armor, rushed through the circle of troops and began shoving unlit torches at the unholy burning censers. Once aflame, they jabbed the torches into the ceremonial garments of the would-be priestly leaders.

Again there were screams, the high pitch of the disloyal women spectators shattering through the bellowing of the men. The stink of burning clothes vied with the resinous reek of the torches. All was bedlam. Some bodies whirled like dervishes, others rolled gagging on the ground. Some of the rebel priests flung off their robes and, screaming from their burns, ran naked here and there, trying to get through the surrounding troops. The flaring, tarred flax at the end of the torches stuck to arms and faces, and those so tortured clawed at their bodies as if they would flay themselves.

Aaron put his face in his hands, and Moses, witness to thousands of battle deaths, wrinkled his face in chagrin at the torment of the damned. When he was satisfied that most of Korah's two hundred and fifty had been ignited, he roared at the top of his voice, "Now water," and with bowls and ewers, a third group of soldiers rushed among the burning, dousing them and then letting those who were able to run shrieking to their tents. Those unable to flee were dragged into the crowd, where relatives fearfully carried them away.

Moses did not look at the three dead men in the pit. Instead, he picked up his rod, signaling first to his own loyal censer-bearers who had waited at the side for the tumult to end, then to the multitude, that he wanted to speak. There was hardly a sound beyond the muted weeping of those shaken by fear and pity. The smell of heavy smoke and singed hair and flesh was wafting away. When the crowd was still, Moses began:

"Last night Jehovah spoke to me. He ordered me to kill not just Korah, the two Reubenites, and the two hundred and fifty. He said it would please him if I sought out those others of you who were willing to turn on me. Jehovah and I know who you are, make no mistake. But I begged him for your lives and he relented, saying, 'Then kill the three and scar the two hundred and fifty with fire. Mark the priests among them particularly, so they will be unworthy to serve me in the tabernacle.'

"The wounded will live among us, their scars evidence of what Jehovah decrees for those who oppose him. Eleazer"—Aaron's son and chief assistant—"will gather up the censers of the malefactors. He will have armorers beat them into a sheet. Aaron will bless it and we will cover the altar in the tabernacle with it as a reminder that God will cause the earth to swallow up those who offend him and burn those who follow them."

For Moses to urge the Hebrews never to complain again was like the magicians of Pharaoh ordering the Nile not to rise and turn brown. No more could

Moses—nor did he want to—destroy their contentious spirit. For it was that same spirit that eventually led them into Canaan. It did not surprise Moses that a week after Korah was killed, the people were again cursing. "Where are the figs and pomegranates we were promised?" demanded some. Others griped, "The water tastes of sulphur. In Egypt it was sweet as dew on hyacinths . . . or on lilies. . . ."

A few even dared to say in public, "Oh, why were we not killed by Moses like our dear brothers in battle, or at Mount Sinai, or in the desert?" But there was an important difference in the tone of these mutterings. After the earth opened up, and after the sheets of fire, Moses was sure there would never be another violent rebellion. He could hardly have been more wrong.

As they had at Mount Sinai, Hazeroth, and Ezion-geber, the Israelites set up camp outside Kadesh-barnea. Though larger than Hazeroth, it was also a desert hill town. They pitched their tents in a broad valley sparkling with fragments of flint washed out of the chalky limestone of the surrounding mountains, one of them snowcapped in winter. There was a spring that trickled all year and provided the Hebrews and their herds and flocks with water and even a narrow belt for fast-growing crops.

There were three other towns within ten miles of Kadesh-barnea: Hazar-addar, Hazar-ithnan, and Azmon, the last of which was near a trade route that connected Canaan through the Sinai to Egypt. Thus employment and trading, and equally important for Moses, information, were readily available in Kadesh-barnea.

From caravan leaders and merchants, the Hebrews learned that, just as the Ezion-geber goldsmith had said, Egypt and the Hittite Kingdom were still fighting over Canaan, although there was persistent talk of a treaty. Moses received reports on the strength of the various cities and whether they were dominated by Horites, Amorites, Jebusites, Perizzites, or other Canaanite nations. But the accounts were often contradictory.

He had always planned to send in spies, but until now he had not decided on who they would be. Now he saw that in order to have the support of his people, he would have to send in leaders of each tribe, if not the chief then the second or third in line. Moses made sure that his most trusted lieutenants went out, too, Joshua for the half-tribe of Ephraim and Caleb for the Judahites. Once they were in Canaan, the spies would scatter and assess the cities and towns, their fortifications and military strength, the crops and forests, the wealth of the people. Importantly, they would also seek out the numbers and sympathies of the thousands of Hebrews who had never migrated to Egypt.

Only the Levites, as priests, were exempted from sending a spy. Moses could ill spare Joshua and Caleb, but the army was loyal to him. Should On, his only remaining enemy of substance, seek to rally the Reubenites, the military captains would be as bloodthirsty in revenge as Joshua or Caleb.

The spies left camp after a peace and burnt offering at the tabernacle. They were only sixty miles from the southern borders of Canaan as the eyes see, but twice that through the rugged Wilderness of Zin. The Israelites stood and watched as the spies' donkeys wound through the hill pass and out of sight.

Zetes Two

—ZETES OF MYCENAE, FORMER TRADER IN ARMS AND OTHER goods—have recorded to the best of my ability what I have discovered about Moses, great leader of the Hebrews, up to the time fate joined me to his party at his camp near Kadesh-barnea.

In explaining how I came to be his biographer, I told at the beginning of this scroll of the return of his spies from Canaan, and of how I saved his life and was grievously crippled. I recounted how Moses' generals, Joshua and Caleb, annihilated the nine spies who opposed him and their rebellious leader, On. I told why Moses decided the Hebrews might have to wait ten to twenty years before invading Canaan even though, ironically, Ramses and the Hittites were concluding a peace treaty that would make the conquest easier.

Some have claimed he said forty years more in the desert, but this was not true, for I heard his statement. Even his vow to remain ten to twenty years was mostly a test of the fortitude of his followers. For the actual time proved to be eight years.

During the first two of these eight years, I traveled from Kadesh-barnea to Egypt and back. In Egypt I put forth the story that I was doing a history of the Egyptians for the Greeks. I spoke there with those who had known Moses or had knowledge of him. For the next six months, I traveled the path of the Exodus, talking with those along the way who seemed trustworthy, including merchants and even one nomad veteran of the Amalekite battle outside Rephidim. Near Mount Sinai, I spoke with Moses' father-in-law, Jethro, and his former wife, Zipporah, now remarried, both of whom reminisced about him with affection.

Since then, I have traveled with him, always at his side, often taking part in his counsels with his generals, Joshua and Caleb; his ailing dwarf, Bes-Ahrin; his brother Aaron, also in ill health; Hur, the wise head of the Council of Elders, who died in my final year with Moses; and Moses' wife, Sebah. I spent hours with his sister, Miriam—like Aaron, sickly, yet her memory, even of the deep past, intact—and many others.

I find it interesting that of this group, the dwarf, Moses' wife, and I are, in general, nonbelievers in the God Jehovah. It is a tribute to Moses that he gave no less weight to our advice. I say "in general" because honesty demands I concede that at times all of us have been skeptical of our own skepticism—doubters of our own doubting—in face of the seeming miracles of this Jehovah.

As the reader will soon see, in the most important sense, the story of Moses ended after the rebellion of On described at the beginning of this scroll.

For the leadership of Israel began to pass into the able hands of Joshua and Caleb, and their stories will have to depend on some other scribe.

Following the slaying of On and the dissident spies and despite Moses' speech urging unity among the Hebrews, two thousand and five hundred of his six thousand people abandoned him within a single week.

Out of the deserters, almost five hundred men, defying Moses' and Joshua's orders and what both said was the will of Jehovah, began an invasion of the Promised Land on their own. A few were elite troops wooed by the prospect of battle and plunder. More were militia and untrained volunteers. They were met by a combined force of Amalekites and Canaanites who drove them back to Hormah. Most were killed during their retreat. The rest straggled back to Kadesh-barnea.

The other two thousand deserted Moses for diverse causes. The slaughter of the spies and some of their supporters at Kadesh-barnea was one reason. And some had opposed Moses two months before when he dug a pit and impaled the Levite rebel Korah and his two chief aides like jungle animals, and set fire to more than two hundred of these men's followers. Others were sick, or had new infants, or were tending ailing parents and did not want to travel farther. Still others were simply fed up with their seemingly endless journey.

These two thousand, later joined by the few survivors of the five hundred drubbed at Hormah, left with their possessions for Ezion-geber. They suffered more privations along the route. I am told a man named Magpiash—the name means "killer of moths"—an albino, rose from the rabble and rallied them near their old campsite outside Ezion-geber, and they became a Hebrew colony that functions in reduced circumstances to this day.

The remaining thirty-five hundred stayed at Kadesh-barnea, and there was no further talk now of an invasion. For, because of the loss of the twenty-five hundred, as Moses put it, "We could not defeat a regiment of Philistine geese."

So the Israelites built their encampment into a semipermanent village. Moses, with Joshua always at his right hand, sent out a call to the Hebrews of Canaan, knowing that any who crossed over would be resourceful and dissatisfied enough to eventually make good soldiers or militiamen. Within a month, recruits from Canaan began to dribble in. They had been separated from the people of the Exodus by three hundred years and they spoke, as the marchers saw it, a strange dialect of Hebrew. Joshua instituted training for the men immediately.

During the first year after the internecine battle at Kadesh-barnea, some fifteen hundred men and as many women and children heeded the appeal and came to Kadesh-barnea.

About the time I returned from Egypt and the Sinai, Moses, Joshua, and Caleb—sometimes joined by Bes-Ahrin—began planning their campaign against Canaan. As they drew maps, they called on me for geographical advice. Their first desire was to set up a camp to the west of Jericho, where they could wait and train for the opportune moment. They chose the mountain area around Mount Nebo near the King's Highway between the Hittite Kingdom and Ezion-geber. It would offer high places easy to defend should they be attacked.

The shortest route there would be first east through the Kingdom of Edom and then due north toward Canaan. But Edom's monarch was hostile and eccentric. So Moses, accompanied by a troop of elite guardsmen, rode by horseback to Teman, the royal residence, on a scalding summer day. He took me along as his translator in case the king refused to speak anything but Hittite, the language of his protector. Ever solicitous of me, Moses stopped several times along the way for me to rest my aching, stiff leg.

The king refused to let us even into the foyer of his throne room, but sent his servile vizier outside to us. "Tell your sagacious king, astute vizier," said Moses, "that Moses, leader of Israel, reminds him that the Edomites and we are both children of Abraham, and thus cousins. You know the tragedies that have befallen us. Let us pass. We will not trample your fields or vineyards, but will keep to the highway."

The vizier started into the palace, but the embossed bronze doors burst open and the king, a fat man with brown hair falling down to his shoulders, rushed out with two soldiers. I was sure he had been listening behind the doors, for his face was flushed. "You shall not pass! Try to and I will put your men, women, and children to the sword."

Moses had made up his mind to be judicious, so, although the Israelite guardsmen could have easily minced the king and his guards, he said, "Sapient ruler, we will not drink from your wells and will even pay for the water we and our animals drink from your streams."

The mad king, for we thought him to be, pulled out his sword and both Moses and I drew back as our soldiers reached for their weapons. But the monarch only dashed his sword to the ground and said, "That is my answer!"

When we returned, Joshua and Caleb began drafting a plan to put the whole country to the sword. But significantly, Moses did not say, "Jehovah will guide our hands against these stiff-necked people." Instead, he decided Israel was not strong enough to fight them, particularly after his spies reported the king was moving chariots and infantry to his borders facing the Hebrews. "We will march around them," Moses said firmly. "It is out of our way, but we cannot fight yet." Joshua and Caleb yielded.

The Israelites waited another year, a total of three, at Kadesh-barnea, getting troops and logistics in order. One night, a few weeks before they were to decamp, Moses and Aaron were called by a servant to Miriam's tent. Aaron arrived panting and stumbling, for he had weakened physically ever since the conflict with On. Miriam was dying, her chest in mortal pain. Two days later, she was dead. The whole nation mourned her, for although at times she had carped and schemed, she was the sister of their leader and, at her best, had been spirited and courageous. In a cave in one of the encircling hills, Moses and his comrades and captains built a ledge where her body was laid.

Inside, they left the tambourine she had played for the dancing and singing after the victory at the Sea of Reeds. Moses, his voice breaking, recited over her part of her song: "Sing to Jehovah. Glory streams from him." Beside her body he put her jewelry, perfume flask, best dishes and cups, and her favorite chair. Then, the men closed the cave with a boulder.

Moses and Aaron observed the traditional rituals. They tore their clothes, shaved their beards, smeared ashes on their faces, and for a week stayed in their tents, eating as little as they could, drinking nothing but water. Moses spoke only with his wife and Bes-Ahrin. For Moses, some of the mourning was to accommodate custom. But for Aaron it was as if he and Miriam had been twinned by her dying, and he felt closer to her in death than he had been since his days as a boy with Amram and Jochebed.

Soon, Aaron's steps grew even slower, and his breathing faster, as we broke camp and started on the long road to Mount Nebo. We marched south to avoid the forces of Edom, then headed north again. Faced, however, with an arid section of the Wilderness of Zin, we risked crossing into Edom to the mining town of Punan for supplies of water and food. As the Edomite troops began to approach, we quickly withdrew toward Obath.

It was just outside the Edom border, at a mountain called Hor, that Aaron, barely whispering now, for his heart was giving out, said to Moses, "Take me to the mountain, brother, I want to die where I can look north toward the Promised Land and praise Jehovah for the distant sight of it." Aaron's wife dressed him in his embroidered shirt, his ephod with its resplendently colorful threads, and onyx shoulder fasteners.

Moses and Eleazer, Aaron's son, helped the dying man up the mountain. At a lookout, with the Hebrews gathered far below, Aaron raised his two hands in a final blessing of his people. Moses and Eleazer then put their arms around Aaron and they walked to the top of the mountain. There, Aaron looked out and saw Beer-sheba visible through the haze. He said he was satisfied and signaled that he wanted to lie down.

"Take my garments from me, Moses," he whispered, fumbling at his linen sash and looking at them with flat eyes. "Give them to Eleazer. Let me lie in my tunic, and when I sleep, Eleazer, let your first duty as chief priest be to give me your blessing. I love you both," he murmured, "second only to our God." He closed his eyes. Moses and Eleazer, clad in his father's gowns, waited. Moses put his hand gently to the pulse in Aaron's throat. It faltered erratically and then ceased.

That night, before going into mourning again, Moses called to his tent Joshua, Caleb, Hur, and Bes-Ahrin. Sebah served them wine and cakes, and then joined them. Moses spoke in tones that carried a burden beyond his years.

"I must be frank. Even before my brother and sister died, I was giving much thought to my leadership. I lost almost half our number by my actions, or lack of them, at Kadesh-barnea. And even before that, I often asked Jehovah whether it might not be better for him to take his cup away from my lips and let me and Sebah go back to Barbaht. But he told me no."

It did not escape Moses—or Sebah—that Joshua glanced quickly at Caleb, for the two soldiers were so close that they seemed to communicate wordlessly and without a change of expression. Moses went on: "Now, thanks to the wisdom of our God, and to Joshua and you others, and yes, to my own work, the rivalries that threatened to destroy us are behind us. But I am fifty years old and the burdens I have carried make me feel a hundred. Do you realize that in Egypt, where as a youth I studied such things, the average time from when a baby leaves its mother's womb until death is only thirty-six years?

"My old shoulder injury was hurt again in the episode of the spies. I can no longer hold my shield. I have spoken my heart again to Jehovah, and he is pleased that I have brought his people to the foothills of the Promised Land. But he, as I, believes Israel needs a new leader, one who should fight the preliminary battles so that the people will know that he can succeed in Canaan itself."

Sebah, his redoubtable princess, had tears in her eyes. Moses, hardly able to speak himself, went on, "Jehovah feels it wisest for me not to enter our land of milk and honey. For one thing, that will make it impossible for this unmanageable people to appeal Joshua's decisions to me." Moses reached over and put his hand on the back of Joshua's hand, and now Bes-Ahrin's old eyes also filled with tears. "Joshua must have, as I had, the chance to reap his own victories, and suffer his own defeats. He will have Caleb, and both will have Jehovah by their sides."

Joshua gripped Moses' hand. The tears came freely from everyone's eyes, including my own. For we all saw that Moses' lions and lionesses had all been played, to use a metaphor from a children's game in Egypt. Two new players, Joshua and Caleb, now sat at the game table. Perhaps, in a way, they had been there ever since they took matters in their own hands and slew the spies and their supporters at Kadesh-barnea.

Moses asked those in the tent to keep his confidences until Joshua began his march on Canaan. But we all knew that the events of the coming days would inform the people that they had a new leader as surely as any speech by Moses. Indeed, Moses' week of mourning was the bridge for Joshua's crossover to power.

The scrolls of Moses' Egyptian scribes, as I ascertained from reading them, tell, I am aware, a somewhat different story. But I am less critical of them than I was, for even the best historians see events through smoked glass full of air bubbles.

As Joshua began to exert control over Israel, Moses took on the role of ultimate judge, the final appeal in his judicial system. He still settled matters of the priesthood when Eleazer could not. But, in fact, he became, in my view, and in the view of his people, the adjutant of Jehovah—interpreting him, advising his people, but no longer himself carrying out Jehovah's dictates. That duty fell to Joshua.

Fatigued, dyspeptic as always, but a nation at last in every sense of the word—save for landowning—the children of Jehovah marched on toward Mount Nebo. At the northernmost corner of Edom, they turned east by way of a brook called Zered, which defined the no-man's-land between Edom and the kingdom of Moab. They found a well called Beer, widened it with shovels, and broke through a natural underground rock conduit that released spring water to them. There they camped a week before continuing east, then turned sharply north around the kingdom of Moab, whose king, Balak, also had denied them passage.

The Hebrews forded the river Arnon and arrived at Dibon-gad only nine-teen miles south of Mount Nebo, which, at twenty-six hundred feet, rose high above the treeless hills. Moses, Joshua, Caleb—indeed, all of us—felt Israel was ready for battle. Joshua and Caleb had trained the militia to where they oper-ated almost like elite troops. The Hebrews enlisted from Canaan were proving to be avid soldiers. We could now send two thousand formidable men into the field with lances, spears, swords, slings, bows, flails, and throwing sticks.

This fighting force at Dibon-gad was on the borders of the Amorite Kingdom ruled by another unpredictable despot, this one named Sihon. Joshua, Caleb, and Moses all went to him to appeal for safe passage. The vain old man received them at his unfinished palace in Heshbon in cloth of gold garments, flanked by generals in polished bronze armor, their pectorals gleaming with tiny silver representations of Baal, the principal Canaanite god. Joshua, clad in a simple kilt of orange, blue, and red, asked politely for permission to pass through his land and take up temporary residence near Mount Nebo.

"And settle a nest of scorpions in our temples?" demanded the king, his caved-in lips twitching in anger. His generals quickly seconded him.

"We are not scorpions," said Joshua. "Nor would we befoul your temples. That is not our way. We seek only a land promised to our fathers centuries ago by our God, Jehovah."

"Does your God tell you to be out of my sight in five minutes and out of my country before nightfall? If he does not, he is no god compared to the exalt-ed Baal."

This was too much for the Hebrews. Without a salute or word, they left the raw sandstone palace, walked between rows of Sihon's slouching lancemen, many of then clearly overweight, and rode off without a glance backward.

Haughty Sihon immediately began to mass his troops for an attack on the camp at Dibon-gad. It was to take place in four days, but the Hebrew spies alerted Joshua almost as soon as the Amorite march south began. Joshua had learned strategy well from the master. He did not want to wait for the arrival of the Amorites' hundred flamboyantly armored regulars and the raggle-taggle band of two thousand spearmen and other soldiers. After a quick conference with Moses, Joshua marched north all night.

Sihon's troops were only fifteen miles outside Heshbon, thinking the Hebrews were waiting for them a day's march to the south, as they straggled through the village of Lemba. They forded a stream there, full of laughter and idle chatter. Their pickets would not even be sent out until afternoon.

Just across the stream, behind an uneven rampart covered with weeds to hide its newness, Caleb's bowmen were waiting. They cut down the first ranks of the Amorites, and those just behind the fallen splashed back into the stream. Joshua's men, who were crouching upstream in a wadi, swept down beside the stream with their lances, spears, and slings.

The Amorites fled, throwing down their shields as they staggered out of the stream. Joshua's spearmen hurled their weapons. And as they did, his slingmen, using flint balls the size of apricots, felled many of those who escaped the spears. Some of the poorly trained Amorites tried to cross the stream yet a second time and were killed by a second volley of arrows. The remainder, as they scrambled back toward Lemba, were exterminated to the man by the Hebrew lancers and swordsmen.

Moses, once battle had begun, longed to be part of it. He paced a hundred yards back from Caleb's bowmen, his sword in his still powerful right hand, a small shield made of plaited osiers on his left forearm where once he had worn a massive shield of bronze. The fighting was all over in less than an hour and the Hebrews quickly searched the bodies for booty. Soldiers dragged the still-refulgent body of the old king to where Moses stood.

A slingman's missile had struck Sihon beneath his ear, so fiercely thrown it had dented his narrow head. Baal, as desert lion, embossed in gold on his pectoral, had not protected him. "Strip him and take his armor to Joshua," Moses said to a soldier. Jehovah and Joshua had given Israel its first major victory over another nation.

Moses, alone now, surveyed the heaps of dead. *So many,* he thought, *farmers, vineyard workers, stonecutters, all men like me, or boys, no older than Gershom.* Many had been slain from behind as they fled. Moses did not blame Joshua. For had he not ordered the same thing against the nomads outside Rephidim and countless more times when he fought beside Ramses for Egypt? Standing among the corpses, he asked Jehovah, "Is it murder to slaughter defeated troops?"

"No," he heard.

There was now no army to oppose the Hebrews in all of the former kingdom of Sihon. After the battle at Lemba, Joshua marched with ease into Heshbon, to which the Israelites moved their camp. They took over the homes of the dead and used the palace as a storehouse. From Heshbon they invested Jazer, though a militia of townspeople made it a costly victory for a company of the Hebrews' new recruits. With Sihon's former domain conquered, Joshua turned to the north, where a hundred miles away, King Og of Bashan, fearing he might be next and seeking to preempt a Hebrew strike, marched south.

As with the Amorites, the intelligence organization that Moses had set up, based on his Egyptian military days, expertly reported the movement of Og's forces. The Hebrews again moved up to surprise them. Joshua and Caleb marched boldly and openly along the northern extension of the King's Highway. Og, sure that he could meet this force head-on and glad to be able to use his chariots, rumbled cumbersomely down the highway.

On the night before the battle, Joshua, with four hundred picked troops, split at Ramoth-gilead from the main army under Caleb. Using torches, Joshua marched ten miles at night across the desert to Idrei, a town at the source of a tributary of the Jordan River. Og's pickets discerned the lights—as Joshua intended—and from the number of torches took it to be the main force. Overly anxious, Og sent the bulk of his troops toward Idrei. At daybreak, Caleb and the main army attacked the astonished remainder of the Bashanites on the King's Highway, broke a charge of the chariots with arrows and slings, and fell upon the outnumbered survivors.

Then, with all speed, Caleb moved up behind King Og as he approached Idrei. Like the jaws of a crocodile, the two Hebrew generals snapped up Og's army, which was disorganized from the march across the desert. Caleb himself slew Og—who was every bit the giant he was said to be, for Caleb measured him and he was seven feet tall. In the battle, the king's three sons—none as tall as he—were all dispatched by Hebrew lancers.

Reports of the successes of the Israelites spread throughout Canaan. More and more Hebrews left their villages and farms to join their long-lost brothers. These new enlistees and the people of the Exodus began to colonize the former kingdom of Sihon and Bashan as far north as Idrei. Israel now reigned over a land seventy miles long and thirty miles wide, its western border the Jordan, its eastern Ammon, its southern Moab, and its northern a line from Edrei to the Jordan.

The only threat still on the Jordan's west bank was from King Balak, who had denied Israel passage four years earlier. This time, fearing if he did not move now he would also be devoured by the Hebrews, he employed a wizard from Pethor on the Euphrates. The story is an odd one. The king asked this wizard, Balaam by name, to curse the Hebrews. Supposedly, the wizard got in an argument with his talking donkey on the way to Moab. The long and the short of it—for I never believed a word of the tale—is that the wizard refused to curse the Hebrews.

Joshua, as Balak had feared, invaded and conquered Moab, defeating a thousand seasoned northern Midianites hired as mercenaries. Moses hoped none of those Midianites he had known and loved in the far south had ventured north to seek their fortunes among the Janissaries.

With Balak conquered, and Canaan substantially at peace, it was clearly time for Joshua to begin the conquest of the Promised Land. Every Israelite leader was aware that blood would flow in rivulets beside the milk and the honey. Before this happened, Moses spoke his thoughts. On the way back to Heshbon, he said mildly to Joshua, "I wonder whether we need to kill every soldier we take captive when we win these victories? In Egypt we generally preferred to enslave them. Sometimes we trained them. The Libyans, for one, when you were sure they were loyal to the Pharaohs, made exceptional troops. None braver."

Joshua had long since developed Moses' habit of thinking out serious problems before answering. He conferred with Caleb. They deferred talking about any change in these practices until they were back in Heshbon. Two evenings after their return, Joshua and Caleb came to Moses in his tent. Bes-Ahrin, now hardly able to walk on his wobbly legs, and Sebah sat with them. The five of them drank wine and ate fig cakes.

Joshua opened the serious part of the conversation, a little defensively: "Caleb and I are opposed to having slaves in our camp. Slaves mean unhappiness, as who knows better than those of us who were in Goshen? And why enlist them? True, the Egyptians we brought with us make loyal soldiers, but there is something in having every warrior feel he is personally in the hands of Jehovah as he fights."

Moses looked at Sebah and Bes-Ahrin and breathed deeply. "I have worried about our commandment not to murder. And now, I am afraid I understand it to be that if there is any way not to kill, we should not do it."

Joshua was upset, for he hated any disagreement with Moses. He knew that not he, nor Caleb, nor any Hebrew had, or perhaps would ever have, the unique wisdom and stature that Moses had brought to the Exodus. Nor would they have the personal rapport with God. Nevertheless, Joshua had always been a man of zealous convictions. "Moses," he said, "we have come to the borders of the land promised by Jehovah to our fathers. I do not like to kill either, but 'Thou shalt not murder' is only the sixth commandment. The first three tell us to obey Jehovah. And those we kill are men who have challenged Jehovah."

Moses considered Joshua's words. Were they as valid as his own? "Long ago," he said, "I learned that there is not just one way of interpreting laws and rules. I believe there is only one Jehovah, as you do. But I also believe there are many ways of understanding his will. He at times wanted me to be more fierce than I wanted to be toward our own people. And I know he will want you to be unflinching, for he realizes you will beseige and burn the cities that oppose you, and women, and children, and the elderly will die along with the warriors."

Joshua looked tormented. "Moses, if you with your great genius could not be sure that you interpreted the will of Jehovah correctly, how can I, a slave, a simple worker, follow his commandments and the laws he has passed to us through you?"

Moses looked at him affectionately. "You cannot be sure. You can only do your best. And there you will have Jehovah at your side." He sighed, realizing it was too late for him to preach compassion. It was a virtue, if it were a virtue, that he had not often practiced. There was, however, one other thing. "Joshua, I must ask you a favor. Take Gershom with you to Canaan. He is a child of Midian, yes, but much more a warrior of the Hebrews. Do not prefer him, but watch over him."

Joshua nodded in assent, and Moses went on: "Tomorrow I will tell our people that I will not go with them into Canaan. I will stay behind awhile with Sebah and Bes-Ahrin and some few servants. Later, we may fare on to Barbaht, where I was happy when I was young, if Ramses will not hinder me. Or good Zetes will find us some peaceful island off Mycenae, for he thinks now of going back to his father's people."

Joshua and Caleb did not argue with his decision, although a part of them did not want this father, who had first been strict and wise and who was now only wise, to ever leave them.

In the morning, Moses summoned the people for the last time as their leader. There in the hot sun, on the steps of the unfinished palace of the late King Sihon, he said, "It was thirteen years ago that I came to you from Midian and told you that Jehovah had asked me to take you out of Egypt and into the land promised to Abraham, Isaac, and Jacob. Then you were six thousand. Now the Lord has made you a multitude as numerous as the stars. Jehovah has put that land before you, and my heart is sore that I cannot lead you into it. But the Lord has said that my task is done, and to let Joshua take it up, with the strong arms of Caleb and the leaders of the tribes that you picked and that Jehovah has ratified.

"Jehovah," Moses went on, "has been my shepherd. And he has promised to be yours and the shepherd of your seed for all time to come. Although you doubted him, he took you against kings whose palaces reached to heaven, and gave you victory over them. When you starved in the desert, he gave you manna and quail and when you thirsted, he gave you water from a rock. He bore you across rushing rivers on his back as a man does his son until you have now come to this place."

Moses then recapitulated the history of how the Hebrews had come from Egypt to the borders of Canaan and he recited the most important laws he had brought down from Mount Sinai. He had been studying the geography of Canaan and had, after conferring with Joshua, detailed what territories each tribe should occupy. "When you obey the Lord's laws and commandments, his face will shine over you. When you disobey them, he will afflict you as he did when you corrupted yourselves before the golden calf, and as he scattered and destroyed the Amorites, the Moabites, the Bashanites when they came against you with sword and graven images. If you fail to hearken to him, he will put an iron yoke around your neck, and bring you together again only after many centuries, and then only if you repent and come humbly to him."

Altogether, he spoke for an hour, eloquently in spite of his stammer. His voice at the end was hoarse but still powerful. Some of the people were asleep on their feet, others had crept away to their tents, but most still stood raptly.

Even in the weeks before Joshua began his invasion of Canaan, he had problems with his flock, and Moses let him deal with them. Some of the Hebrews, particularly young men from Canaan who had not been long under Joshua's discipline, began whoring with the profligate young women of Moab. And some of the older people from Canaan, women as well as men, worshipped Baal in the form of a golden bull, who, after all, had been the god of their neighbors down through the centuries.

Joshua's vengeance was swift. He asked Moses and the chief judges of the Hebrews to stand by him as he ordered Caleb and Phinehas, the grandson of Aaron, to kill every one of the miscreants. Phinehas, on surprising a young Hebrew soldier from Canaan in the embrace of a Moabite whore, ran through with his lance both the soldier and the woman beneath him.

Joshua proved his sternness again when a second Midianite force attacked an Israelite garrison on the borders of Moab. They inflicted severe casualties. Joshua ordered an immediate counterattack.

Moses, learning of it, was determined to fight one more battle for Israel. His reasons were several. His friendship for Jethro and Zipporah, though members of a Midianite tribe far to the south, was well known and he did not want Israel to imagine his loyalties were ever the least bit divided. Then, I think, he wanted to prove himself one last time in battle. And, finally, now that his main work was done, I sincerely believe he wanted to give Jehovah a chance to take him up, if that was Jehovah's will.

In any case, telling only his objecting wife and dwarf, he donned his armor and took up his pathetically small braided osier shield. Before dawn, when Joshua's avenging force was marching, Moses joined it as a common soldier.

His figure, a head above his comrades, was immediately recognized by the troops in the sector he joined, and he led the charge against the desert warriors. The younger Hebrews tried to protect him, but the leonine courage that had surged through him at Semna thirty-eight years earlier when he was not yet seventeen again engulfed him. He broke through his protectors, and shouting hoarsely first toppled a Midianite captain's war camel with a cleaving slash to the poor beast's neck, then skewered its rider. He fought on, hardly knowing what he was doing, until the battle was over.

When he returned to Sebah, covered with the blood of others and no small number of bruises and scratches, she fell on him, kissing his lips and crying, "Fool! Fool! Fool!"

On the day of the invasion of Canaan, Moses, Sebah, I, and the little band of retainers who had remained behind with him climbed the rocky slopes of Mount Pisgah, near Mount Nebo. Moses' servants laboriously bore Bes-Ahrin on a litter, glad that he was no heavier. Sebah and Moses had taken to caring for the dwarf as if he were their child. They even humored him by grinding up pigs' teeth and mixing it with wine and honey, a time-honored Egyptian cure for coughs.

We could see the route from Heshbon all the way into the Promised Land. The tabernacle and tents had all been packed away in the wagons and carts. The spies had returned breathlessly with the final reports, and the ram's horns now sounded throughout the encampment, summoning the various units into line. We saw clearly in the lead Joshua and Caleb and the captains of the archers and slingmen on horseback. Then came the spearmen, and behind them the lancers and swordsmen who, once the enemy had been terrified by the flying spears, stones, and arrows, would race past their comrades to begin the killing, just as Moses had taught. Among the marchers we could discern the foreign troops who had left Egypt with Moses, and the Legion of Little People, Bes-Ahrin's followers, as eager as the full-sized for the land that now seemed equally promised to them.

Moses looked proudly at company after company of eager troops. He had built the army, using the same formations he had learned and used so well as an Egyptian commander against Hittites, Libyans, Nubians—among them, the troops of Sebah's father—and the numerous other enemies of the Pharaohs.

After the armed forces came the supply troops, their ox-drawn carts filled with arrows, flint rocks for the slings, spears, spare lances and swords, bindings and ointments for wounds, hemp rope to bind prisoners, although few would be taken, bridles, and reins—all the accouterments of war.

Then there were the Levites—the priests—who did not ordinarily go into battle, but who were ready if the tide turned against Israel to take up the suppliers' extra arms and fight to the death. At their head was the cart bearing Joseph's mummy, now in a handsomely crafted cedar box, over which lay a woven cloak of many colors, which figured in the story of his life.

Behind the warriors and priests came columns that, it seemed, would never end: the people themselves, the old, the very young, the women, pregnant ones in vehicles with the disabled, and the mad, some with guards, for unlike other lands, the Hebrews did not put their insane out in the desert to die.

How could Moses not be uplifted by this sight? When he was in his midtwenties, he had stood only a pace behind the ruler-to-be of the most powerful, the richest, the most far-flung empire in history. From that height, he fell like a cheap plaster scarab to the desert land of Midian, a shepherd. And now he saw beneath him a nation that, under the aegis of his God, he had created—its army, its judiciary, its social customs, its sure place among the mighty peoples of the world.

The sun struck with dull glints the thousand bronze spear points; the hundred thousand bronze disks on the Hebrews' mail; the variety of polished helmets, some with plumes; the blue, gold, and scarlet of the priests' raiments. All of them moved slowly from this narrow conquered land into what all these people believed would be a paradise on earth.

Zetes Three

YEAR HAS PASSED SINCE JOSHUA INVADED CANAAN. HE HAS ESTABLISHED a strong encampment near the ruins of Jericho, laid waste two hundred years ago. But there remains the greater part of the Promised Land to be conquered. Strong forces are arrayed against him. And there will, no doubt, be battles, skirmishes, and stalemates for years before he and Caleb can extend their rule to all of Canaan.

I have stayed with Moses here in Heshbon with the Jewish settlers. He is in his fifty-fifth year and plans to leave before he is too old to do so. Last week, Bes-Ahrin died. He was almost seventy—a wonder, for dwarfs generally die much younger. He left directions with Moses about how to contact the few younger members of his little band who are loyal to him in Heliopolis. They will dig up Bes-Ahrin's gold and find a way to get it to Moses and Sebah in Barbaht, where they plan to go.

The dwarf's last words, uttered with a smile at Moses, became him: "I go to join my princess. I will tell her she should have left you in the bulrushes. For the gods of Egypt decreed you would never amount to much, old comrade."

Only a final comment is necessary to make my history of Moses, as leader, complete. As I have mentioned before, Moses ordered me to look at the work of his Egyptian scribes, and the Hebrews whom they trained to continue it. In fact, there are similarities in their story and mine. And inordinate dissimilarities: they ignore, for example, Moses' life from the time he was found in the bulrushes up until the time when, as a young man, the Egyptians discovered he was a Hebrew.

Their exaggerations about Moses and his predecessors are sometimes as fantastical as the writings on the stelae of the Pharaohs, impossible tales of men turning into falcons and ibises and even beasts that themselves do not exist. And why not? They learned at the feet of their Egyptian teachers.

Their recordings—like works that have come down to us on scraps of papyrus from a thousand years ago—will be changed in the millenniums to come, as will mine. The reasons will be political; or recopiers will let their own views control what they think should be copied; or scrolls will be lost and new scribes will depend on legend, word of mouth; or new copiers will simply be incompetent. It is the way of history.

I have told how I confronted Moses with the Egyptian scribes' excesses, and how he chose not to correct most of them because they might constitute useful myths to maintain Israel as a nation. He had said he would try to amend the worst distortions. For example, he never recalled Jehovah saying that if a woman helps her husband fight off an assailant by grabbing the man's testicles, then her hand must be cut off. But Moses was always busy and put off deleting dubious statements until it was too late. And now priests, scrolls, and all have marched off to Canaan. I intend to do what I can to preserve my own history.

I will return to my father in Mycenae, not to usurp dear Tsu-ting or whomever Father has working in my place, but to use my skills to earn money for what I shall make my project during the foreseeable future. My plan is to have scribes make ten copies of my scrolls. I will store them in long pottery jars, some copies in a single one, some in as many as four, which might be more convenient to hide.

I will secrete these urns in places that time is unlikely to disturb. I think of tombs in Egypt and the Hittite Kingdom and other lands that probably will endure, of caves in Ethiopia, of burial cavities beneath the temples of Greece and in Crete. The cost will not be daunting. Some will be opened as time unfolds, some will be copied, and perhaps also changed, some will be lost, destroyed by fire or flood. But somewhere down the ages, there will be men who will compare my work with other histories of this great man. Then Truth, if it exists in that far age, will be the arbiter.

Moses and Sebah will mourn Bes-Ahrin before they leave for Barbaht. On the way south, they will visit the aged priest-king Jethro's encampment near Mount Sinai so that Moses can bid goodbye to him, to Zipporah, and to his son, Eliezer, who we hear may want to rejoin his brother and fight beside the Hebrews.

In a perfect world, Moses would also visit Pi-Ramessu to pay his respects to the unmarked grave of his parents. And he would go to Thebes and the Princess Mutempsut's tomb in the Valley of the Queens. Near the tomb, he would inter Bes-Ahrin. But this cannot be. He will bury the dwarf here beneath a handsome limestone stele, one recounting some of his brave deeds.

Moses believes Ramses will accept his presence in Barbaht because it is so distant from Pi-Ramessu. He has spoken, not entirely in jest, of a possible second reason, one he, Sebah, and I find ironic. The Pharaoh's representatives, he reasoned, will surely have told him that the nation of Israel is a warlike force to be reckoned with in Canaan. And would Ramses, whose mind Moses knows so well, want to offend a potential ally against the Hittites? Moses has sometimes even mused that when both he and Ramses are older, they might somehow see each other again. Would that I could be there to record the meeting.

Bibliographical Notes and Acknowledgments

I could not have written this book without Pierre Montet's *Everyday Life in Egypt* (Philadelphia: University of Pennsylvania Press, 1981) and E. W. Heaton's *Everyday Life in Old Testament Times* (New York: Charles Scribner's Sons, 1956). They are a blessing to the layman and the amateur scholar alike. For their detailed suggestions on the manuscript, I am most grateful to Jennifer Houser Wegner, Egyptian Section, University of Pennsylvania Museum of Archaeology and Anthropology, and to Shelly Kale, Santa Monica, California.

Among other sources consulted were Cyril Aldred, *The Egyptians* (New York: Thames and Hudson, 1987); Sholem Asch, *Moses* (New York: G. P. Putnam's Sons, 1951); Howard Blum, *The Gold of Exodus* (New York: Simon & Schuster, 1998); James Henry Breasted, Carl F. Huth, and Samuel Bannister Harding, *European History Atlas* (Chicago: Denoyer-Geppert, 1947); Gaalyah Cornfeld, *Archaeology of the Bible: Book by Book* (New York: Harper & Row, 1976); Henri Daniel-Rops, *Daily Life in the Time of Jesus* (Ann Arbor: Servant Books, 1980); John W. Flight and Sophia L. Fahs, *Moses* (Boston: Beacon Press, 1942); Gary Greenburg, *The Moses Mystery* (Secaucus: Birch Lane Press, 1996); Bernard Grun, *The Timetables of History* (New York: Simon & Schuster/ Touchstone, 1991); William W. Hallo and William Kelly Simpson, *The Ancient Near East* (New York: Harcourt Brace Jovanovich, Inc., 1971); Miriam Lichtheim, *Ancient Egyptian Literature,* Vol II: *The New Kingdom* (Berkeley: University of California Press, 1976); Seton Lloyd, *The Art of the Ancient Near East* (New York: Praeger, 1961); David M. Rohl, *Pharaohs and Kings: A Biblical Quest* (New York: Crown Publishers, 1995); John Romer, *People of the Nile* (New York: Crown Publishers, 1982) and *Ancient Lives* (New York: Holt, Rinehart and Winston, 1984); George Steindorff and Keith C. Seele, *When Egypt Ruled the East* (Chicago: University of Chicago Press, 1942); Merrill C. Tenney, *Pictorial Bible Dictionary* (Grand Rapids: Zondervan Publishing, 1963); Albert A. Trever, *History of Ancient Civilization,* Vol. I (New York: Harcourt, Brace, 1936); Charles Turnbull, *Trouble with God* (Old Lyme: Longview Press, 1995); Ivan Van Sertima, *Egypt Revisited* (New Brunswick [USA]: Transaction Publishers, 1989); George Ernest Wright and Floyd Vivian Filson, *The Westminster Historical Atlas to the Bible* (Philadelphia: Westminster Press, 1946); and the various versions of the Bible, particularly the Jerusalem Bible (New York: Doubleday, 1968), the Anchor Bible (New York: Doubleday, 1962 et seq.), the Interpreter's Bible (New York: Abington-Cokesbury Press, 1952 et seq.).

I have also benefitted from the resources of the Metropolitan Museum of Art, New York; the Deutsches Museum, Antikensammlungen und Glyptothek, and Staatliche Sammlung Agyptischer Kunst, Munich; the Louvre, Egyptian Antiquities, Paris; the Field Museum and University of Chicago Museum, Chicago; the National Museum of African Art, Washington, D.C.; the Montgomery County (Md.) Libraries; and the Eder Library, Saint Colomba's Episcopal Church, Washington, D.C.

Among the many people who gave me advice and information, I am particularly grateful to Gus W. Van Beek, Ph.D., and David R. Hunt, Ph.D., Smithsonian Institution; David Hendin; Michael Viner; Steven Wondu; Paul Craig; Judy Hilsinger; Stanley and Phyllis Whitten; Sophy Burnham; and Roderick MacLeish.

About the Author

Leslie H. Whitten, Jr. is a novelist, poet, and translator and was a prize-winning investigative reporter. Among his published work are nine novels, a biography, translations of the French poet Charles Baudelaire, a children's book, and a book of his poetry. His biblical novel, *The Lost Disciple: The Book of Demas,* was highly praised in *The Washington Post, The Chicago Tribune,* and *Publishers Weekly,* among others.

As a journalist with *The Washington Post* and other newspapers, he covered presidential politics, political scandals, and numerous national events. He has reported from the Middle East, Europe, and Asia on a variety of topics, from the Indochina war to natural disasters. Despite being jailed by the F.B.I., he refused to reveal his sources for his work on Native Americans; he later received the American Civil Liberties Union Edgerton award and was made a Blood Brother of the Iroquois.

He has been a visiting professor and speaker at universities, the Naval War College, and the F.B.I. academy and has appeared on *Today* and other nationally televised shows. He is a magna-cum-laude graduate and recipient of a Doctorate of Humane Letters from Lehigh University. An avid skier, golfer, and cyclist, he also works with the terminally ill as a home-care hospice volunteer. He and his wife live in Maryland.